# YES, I DO

# YES, I DO

GWYNNE
FORSTER

ARABESQUE®

ISBN-13: 978-0-373-83186-9

YES, I DO
© 2010 by Harlequin Enterprises S.A.

The publisher acknowledges the copyright holder
of the individual works as follows:

NOW AND FOREVER
Copyright © 2010 by Gwendolyn Johnson Acsadi

LOVE FOR A LIFETIME
First published by BET Books in *Wedding Bells*
Copyright © 1999 by Gwendolyn Johnson Acsadi

A PERFECT MATCH
First published by Pinnacle Books in *I Do!*
Copyright © 1998 by Gwendolyn Johnson Acsadi

Recycling programs
for this product may
not exist in your area.

www.kimanipress.com

**Printed in U.S.A.**

# CONTENTS

Dear Reader,

I write romances because I enjoy the beauty and harmony of the most precious and intimate aspects of human relations—the arrival of a woman and a man at a place in which they pledge themselves to each other. I have received many letters from readers asking whether the heroine and hero in my romances got married. Although I may not include a wedding in my novels, when lovers resolve their issues and declare eternal love, implicit in that bond is marriage. In this anthology I do not leave that to the reader's imagination.

The lovers in "Now and Forever" do not travel an easy path, since they meet as competitors. But our hero is a man who knows what he wants, and when he sees it, he will stop at nothing to get it. These two set a torch to everything they touch, especially each other.

Love comes in many ways and circumstances, sometimes with ease but more often not. In "Love for a Lifetime," both the heroine and the hero are coming out of divorce. They meet by chance, far from home. Both need validation of their worthiness, but are too wary to expect that from a stranger, in spite of their fierce mutual attraction and intense longing.

The leading characters in "A Perfect Match" appear in every respect to be mismatched. Their relationship is a perpetual tug-of-war, but fate has their number.

I sincerely hope you enjoy this anthology, which reveals the different ways in which love can develop, grow and reach fulfillment.

Drop me a note at GwynneF@aol.com and please visit my Web site, www.gwynneforster.com.

Sincerely yours,

*Gwynne Forster*

## Acknowledgments

To my editor, Evette Porter, who has made writing romance novels and novellas a delightful and rewarding experience.

# NOW AND FOREVER

# Chapter 1

Deanna Lawford approached the counter in the home-accessories section of McCall's department store. She pointed to the lavender-and-pink-colored candles nestled in a nook behind the counter and asked the clerk, "Are those for sale?"

The woman looked over her shoulder at Deanna. "They're part of our store display. How about these?" She pointed to a group of purple and peach candles that varied in height from two to twelve inches and in width from one-half to four inches. "They're similar height and width," the sales clerk said.

"Sorry, but they don't match my color scheme. The other ones are exactly what I need, and I've been looking for over a month. Thanks, anyway."

The clerk shrugged apologetically and turned her attention to the next customer. Deanna knew that if she couldn't find what she wanted in that department of McCall's, she might as well stop looking. With an air of resignation, she turned to leave.

"Sell her those candles," said a deep voice as Deanna was about to leave. "Never mind, you're busy now. I'll do it."

Deanna spun around, arrested as much by the voice as by the prospect of getting the candles. The smile that greeted her seemed almost bright enough to light the candles.

He put one of each color on the counter. "Anything else, miss? Is it miss?"

Her smile must have frozen on her face. At twenty-nine, she had long ago stopped becoming infatuated by men with nothing more than a handsome face and a come-hither smile. That is, until now.

He stopped smiling. She looked around, thinking he must have been looking at someone else, but he'd focused his gaze on her. Embarrassed, she fumbled in her purse for her list, though she knew precisely how many of each color and size she wanted. But she had to distract herself. If she didn't know better, she'd swear he'd hypnotized her.

He placed both hands on the counter. They were polished, well-manicured hands with long tapered fingers—powerful hands. "Do you want them?"

Grateful that she could look at something other than him, she unfolded her list and pretended to read it. "I... uh...I want all of them, please."

"All of... There are sixteen candles up there. Are you an interior decorator?" She was, but she wanted the candles for her bedroom. "They don't seem appropriate for the dining room," he said. "But—"

"They aren't for the dining room."

"Then I assume they're for a lavender and pink bedroom." She nodded. "Very feminine. Have a seat over there in the lounge while I have these cleaned up for you. They're dusty."

She hadn't planned on the waiting and she didn't have the time to spare. But getting precisely what she wanted was worth having to change her plans. She looked up as a woman wearing a black-and-white uniform approached.

"You have to wait ten or fifteen minutes, miss. So I've been asked to bring this to you." She placed a cup of coffee and a plate of cookies on the small table beside Deanna, handed her a copy of *The Woodmore Times* and left. Deanna drank the coffee, but ignored the cookies, because she'd planned on getting a quick lunch in McCall's dining room before heading for her appointment. The man brought the candles to her wrapped and sealed with the department store's logo in a convenient McCall's shopping bag.

"Are you about to have lunch?" he asked her.

She stood up and tried to steel herself against the charm that went with the voice. She was five foot eight, so he had to be at least six foot three or four to tower over her as much as he did.

"I'm just going to have a quick bite," she told him.

"What a pity. Thursday's lunch menu is always excellent. Will you join me?"

She was about to ask him if he always ate at McCall's with its pricey lunches, then decided, after she looked long and hard at his suit, that he could well afford it. He certainly wasn't a clerk, she decided.

"Well, if you don't eat with me, I'll have to eat alone, and you'll have missed the opportunity to do a good deed."

"Don't tell me you don't have a lunch date!"

His eyebrows went up sharply. "No, I don't. And that's the weakest line on record. Come on, join me, and tell me where you got that notion." He opened a door. "After you."

Curiosity killed the cat, she reminded herself. Nevertheless, she walked through the door. "Well, all right, but it'll be a quick lunch."

A waiter greeted them. "Your table is ready, Mr. McCall," he said. She quickly realized that she was not in the department store dining room that served the public, but in a posh setting that had to be the executive dining room of McCall's.

She waited until they were seated and asked him, "Who are you? The waiter addressed you as Mr. McCall."

He seemed nonplussed. "I'm Justin McCall. Thanks for sharing your lunch hour with me."

"I doubt that you'd be eating alone, Mr. McCall. You can dine with almost anyone in Woodmore, male or female."

"That's part of the problem," he said under his breath, although she heard him despite his attempt at whispering. "In your case, it's my own choice," he said.

"This is a beautiful room, and I'm enjoying myself, but I have an appointment, so if you don't mind, I'll eat and not talk."

"I do mind, but only because I like your voice. I've heard that some women place lighted candles around their bedrooms and bathrooms, but isn't that a fire hazard, especially if you fall asleep while the candles are burning?"

"Mine sit on a metal tray. I love the ambience they create."

"I can imagine." He leaned back in his Louis VX-style, upholstered chair and looked at her. "I want to see you again. And if you knew how enchanted I am with you, you'd agree."

Deanna had always thought of herself as a working-class woman who had struggled financially to get through the Fashion Institute of Technology in New York with a degree in interior decorating and design. She did not intend to spend her life genuflecting to the McCall family and their wealth. She might as well be honest with him now, she said to herself, although something in her wanted to accept his invitation.

"I'm sorry, Mr. McCall," she heard herself say. "You're very kind, but I'm not interested. How much are the candles?"

Like a flash of lightning, his entire demeanor changed. He sat forward, looking her in the eye and said, "My clerk told you that the candles were not for sale, and they are still not for sale. Enjoy them."

"Thank you for lunch and for the candles. They are precisely what I needed. Goodbye."

# Chapter 2

Deanna hurried back to Burton's Department Store, and was about to lock the candles in her desk drawer when it occurred to her to look in the shopping bag. "Whoever heard of anybody wrapping candles in star-spangled gold aluminum paper and tying the package with a gold-colored satin bow?" she asked aloud. Then she saw the small envelope and the handwritten note inside.

*Pleasing you gave me great pleasure, and I hope to have the opportunity to do that again and again.*
*Sincerely,*
*Justin McCall*

Taken aback, she sat down and rubbed her forehead. Maybe she hadn't been wise to reject him in that way. After all, he had been gracious and kind. The telephone rang, and she shrugged. Woodmore was a relatively small town, and if Justin McCall was serious, he'd find a way to make his point. Still, an involvement with him didn't make sense, she thought, as she answered the phone.

"Decorating department, Deanna Lawford speaking."

"Miss Lawford, Mr. McCall asked me to tell you that you dropped your wallet beside your chair as you were about to leave the dining room. If you'll tell me where you are in Burton's, we'll have someone bring it to you."

"I didn't know I'd lost it. Thank you for calling, and please thank Mr. McCall for his graciousness. I'm in the decorating department on the seventh floor."

She hung up and looked in her purse, knowing she wouldn't find her wallet there. *Why would I let that man get to me so that I dropped my wallet with my credit cards, driver's license and cash in it? I don't need to be around him. I've never met anyone with such magnetism.*

Half an hour later, her assistant knocked on her door. "Someone's here from McCall's to see you, Deanna. He has a package, but he wouldn't give it to me."

"Thanks, Dee. Have him come in."

"I'm sorry, ma'am," the messenger said, "but Mr. McCall told me to give this to you and nobody else, and he told me not to accept a tip," he added when she handed him a bill.

"Please thank him for me."

"I will. Y'all have a good day."

He left, and she put the wallet in her pocketbook, locked her desk drawer and glanced at her watch. In five minutes she had to present her plan for the mountain retreat to one of Burton's most valued customers, and she didn't even like designing for remote settings. The rustic lifestyle was not her taste. After convincing the couple that bold reds and brilliant blues didn't complement a log-cabin mountain house, they agreed to soft, nature-inspired colors. But as she settled down to enjoying her work, thoughts of Justin McCall and his note came back to her repeatedly.

"I love the woven bamboo blinds," the woman said.

*Get your act together,* Deanna said to herself when she realized that she hadn't been listening to her clients. "Of course, we'll go over this again before I make any purchases.

I have to sketch all this out and see how it looks. I should get back to you in a couple of weeks."

The couple left apparently happy, and she was glad she could rely on her long habit of taking notes during her consultations with clients. The woven bamboo blinds were for the family room only. She let out a long breath. One more reason why any involvement with a man might be a distraction in achieving her goal.

Justin shook his head from side to side in dismay as Deanna walked away from the table. A woman had a right, even an obligation, to discourage a man if she didn't want his attentions. But if the man behaved as a gentleman, she was obliged to be gracious and to leave him with his dignity intact.

"Your usual cappuccino, sir?" a waiter asked him.

He nodded in an absentminded way. "Yes, thanks, Norton." He shouldn't have let it get to him, but he did, and it hurt. He sipped the coffee, hardly tasting it. She'd stood there so disappointed and looking so vulnerable and unhappy, her big brown eyes near tears, and he'd felt as if he'd give her anything she wanted. She didn't plead or beg, but accepted the clerk's verdict. He drained the cup, signed the check and started back to his office.

"What's this? Someone dropped a wallet here?" he said to no one in particular, picked it up and pulled out a card. "Deanna Lawford, Director, Interior Decorating, Burton's Department Store." Hmm. He returned to his office and asked his secretary to send in Jethro, one of the messengers. He put the wallet in an envelope and, after giving the man strict instructions as to where to take it, he said, "Deliver this to her and hand it to her yourself, and do not accept a tip."

"Yes, sir. Anything else, sir?"

"It has her wallet and credit cards, so be careful."

"Of course, sir."

After Jethro left, Justin stood, slapped his right fist into

the palm of his left hand, walked a few paces to the window
and looked down on Fifth Street. "Wonder if she'll thank me
for finding her wallet and sending it to her. He didn't believe
she had bad manners, and the fact that she didn't see him as
such a prize catch amused him. Suddenly, laughter rolled out
of him. He'd met a woman who he was attracted to and who
intrigued him, and she'd let him know unequivocally that he
did not have the music to make her dance.

"It's good for whatever's been ailing me," he said aloud.
"Now, maybe I'll get down to work and stop thinking about
her."

"Mr. Robert McCall on one, sir," Melanie said through the
intercom.

"How are you, Granddad," he said to the person closest to
him and who he had adored since he was a small child.

"I'm as good as anybody my age could expect to be. Maybe
better. Have you given up the idea of putting second and third
tier designer products in the store, I tell you, it'll kill our
image. People shop at McCall's because they want to feel
superior. They'll spend the money because they know that
seventy-five percent of Woodmore, most of Danvers and half
of Winston-Salem don't even consider entering McCall's.
You're making a mistake."

"I'm not planning to stock anything of poor quality in the
store. My concern is that Burton's does not serve the middle
class well. It marks up everything and because the people
don't have other options, they have to accept it. I don't like
going against you, Granddad, but try to see it my way. We
carry the top American, French and Italian designers, as well
as the finest in home furnishings, all for the rich, that they
can't get anywhere else near here."

"What will you do if they stop shopping at McCall's?"

"They won't."

"Well, you go ahead, but remember, once you start down
this road, you can almost never turn back. Don't they teach
that to you Harvard MBA guys?"

"I learned well what *you* taught me, Granddad, long before I got to Harvard." He hated going against the old man, but his gut feeling said otherwise. "I'll let you know what I decide."

The following morning, he found her letter in his incoming mail-box and, for reasons unclear even to him, he put it in his desk drawer, went to the staff cafeteria for coffee—he did not allow secretaries and assistants to carry coffee or food for their bosses—went back to his office, closed the door and prepared to read Deanna's note thanking him for returning her wallet. He hoped she would at least make it worth the time it took to read it.

He read: "Dear Mr. McCall, I appreciate your returning my wallet. If you hadn't found it, I would have been in big trouble. I was not even aware that I'd lost it. Thank you so much. Deanna Lawford."

He read it again, put it into his desk drawer and muttered, "She could at least have called." Then, he laughed. "Nothing will please me except her acknowledgment that I'm not such a bad guy and that a respectable woman would want to have dinner with me."

He buzzed his secretary. "Melanie, would you get my tickets and put what I need for that conference in a folder on my desk? During the flight, I can prepare for my lecture week after next. I want to leave the office at four this afternoon."

"Yes, sir. Everything's ready, sir. Do you need batteries for your recorder? If so, I can get them at lunch time."

"Why not send a messenger for them, I need four AA batteries."

At six-fifteen, he boarded a flight to New York. When he took a seat in the first-class section, the flight attendant was immediately at his elbow, and he almost wished he was traveling coach.

Since his teenage years, women had looked at him and

seen not a person, but money. So he'd avoided involvements with them. He sipped the wine placed in front of him and thought of Deanna, a woman who seemed not to care about his background and wealth and who told him flatly that she wasn't interested in him. "What a mess," he said to himself. "Arlene's after me, I'm trying to get to know Deanna, and heaven only knows what Deanna wants. Whoever he is, he can expect a run for his money, because that woman hasn't heard the last of me."

In New York, he met with several top designers of men's clothing and settled on a fragrance that would carry McCall's name and logo. "I'd like to name it Deanna," he told the perfumer, knowing that could cause problems. Maybe next time. Ordinarily, he left decisions like that to his department heads after consulting with him. But he didn't like some of the menswear in his store, and he meant to change it.

"I like the single color for men," he told one designer. "For example, gray suit, shirt and a tie in a different shade of gray." Satisfied that, in his region, he could lead a trend in single color and that he'd be able to offer a top quality perfume, he headed back to Woodmore.

"That perfume idea is wonderful," his grandfather told him. "I don't know why we didn't think of it before. I'm proud of you, son."

At home that night, he ate the dinner that his housekeeper prepared, read *The Woodmore Times* and watched the political pundits on MSNBC TV. He got up from the television to get a bottle of beer and stopped. His gaze took in the fruits of his labors, elegant surroundings, every perfect thing.

"And it's so damned quiet here," he said aloud. "Not a single sound unless I make it, turn on the TV or radio or drop something. What the hell kind of life is this? Priceless Persian carpets, cathedral ceilings, the finest furniture and accessories do not a happy home make." He leaned against the dining room table, reached for the telephone and replaced it in its cradle. He knew plenty of women, but he couldn't call one of them without mortgaging his freedom. He blew out a long breath. Not one of them had ever had a paying job, nor did they volunteer at anything supportive of human life and well-being. The problem right then was that he couldn't call Deanna. He had to know why she behaved toward him as she did.

Maybe the problem was that his ego had taken a punch, but he could handle it. With a shrug, he put on a CD of Alexander Borodin's Polovtzian Dances, leaned back in his favorite chair with his eyes closed and let stress melt away from him. She would do that for him, too. He knew it in his gut. He'd never been wrong about his reaction to women, and he was going for it.

Two weeks later, Deanna stepped out of New Orleans' Louis Armstrong International Airport and into the steamiest air she had ever tried to breathe. Nothing and no one had prepared her for the blast of damp, torrid weather. She dropped her carry-on, pulled off her linen jacket and signaled for a taxi.

"That taxi gon' cost you an arm and a leg, lady," a man said. "You better wait for the shuttle. It'll take you right straight to the hotel, and it won't cost half as much."

"Thanks," she said, "but I want to get out of this heat and into something that's air-conditioned."

The man beckoned for a cab. "Don't pay him a penny more than thirty bucks."

"Hilton River Walk Hotel," she told the driver, "and please turn up the cool air."

"Yes, ma'am. I sure will, but you might as well get used to the heat. Heat's good. All you gotta do is move slow and take ya time."

After the pleasant, twenty-minute ride, she stepped out of the taxi and, while following the porter to the registration desk, she nearly stumbled. Justin McCall walked toward her, beaming, with his charismatic smile illuminating his face. But almost as soon as the smile began, he erased it, deliberately, too, she thought. But he had communicated to her his pleasure at seeing her, and he couldn't take it back. He nodded a greeting, walked on past her, and although she knew she deserved it, it troubled her nonetheless. She presumed that, like her, he would be attending the convention of home furnishings designers.

She checked into her room and looked out of her window to see what kind of view she had. The Mississippi River stretched out in front of her, and the first paddle wheel boat she'd ever seen greeted the hotel with a blast of its horn. She hung up her clothes, pressed the linen jacket, took a shower and crawled into bed, exhausted from the long flight.

At about three o'clock, she dressed and went down to one of the restaurants in search of food. To her chagrin, Justin was one of only two people there. She pretended not to see him, and not because she wouldn't like his company, but because she did not want to appear to invite his attention. However, she was repaid for her pretense by nearly missing the chair on which she attempted to sit. She couldn't help glancing toward Justin to see if he had witnessed her embarrassment. He had, and he showed his delight in a wide and wicked grin.

She would have loved to throttle him. Mildly irritated, she focused on the copy of *The Times-Picayune* that she'd brought with her. She hated eating alone in restaurants unless she had something to read while waiting to be served. However, she needn't have concerned herself about that. A glimpse of his beige-colored trousers beside the table at which she sat alerted her to his presence.

"Hello, Ms. Lawford. Do you mind if I join you?"

If she said yes, would he return to his own table? She doubted it, and thought it best not to test him. Besides, she would appear foolish even to herself. "Please have a seat," she said, deciding not to tell him she didn't mind, although she didn't. "It surprised me to see you when I arrived."

"I imagine so. I don't ordinarily attend these conventions,

but in this economic climate, things are changing, and if I want to know precisely what's going on, I have to go to the source. Since I assume you operate on the same principle, I certainly am not surprised to see you here." He sipped the coffee that he brought from his table. "I hope you had a comfortable flight."

"I did. It was a six-thirty flight, so you may imagine that I slept for most of it." She did not want to sit there trying to eat while making small talk. Besides, when he looked at her in that way of his, she didn't know whether to shrivel or bloom. Either he was hell-bent on reminding her every minute of her femininity, or she was in danger of allowing his masculine aura—powerful that it was—to stupefy her.

"It's rather late for lunch," she said, ill at ease because of the awkward silence.

He leaned back, ignored her comment and cut to the chase. "I'm having a difficult time digesting your curt reply to my telling you I'd like to see you again." She couldn't hold back a gasp, and he held up his hand to ward off her reaction. "Hear me out. You'd said you were "miss," so I had assumed that you were not currently married. You knew from the start that I was interested in you, so you couldn't have been caught off guard. You had a right to say no, but my behavior required you to be at least gracious, and you were not. I'd like to know why."

After forcing herself to look into his riveting gaze, she tried to smile to lighten the mood. She knew she'd failed at that when he began opening and closing his right fist in a show of impatience. "I don't want a relationship."

But he wouldn't let her off with that. "Relationship? I had dinner in mind or something like that, so that we could talk and I could get to know you. Look, Deanna... Do you mind if I call you Deanna? My name is Justin." A half smile played around his lips.

"I don't mind at all." What she did mind was the way he seemed to pull her into his orbit.

"Look. I'm straight with women. In fact, I'm straight with people. I don't play games with women. I want to get to know you because you interest me. You still haven't told me why you rejected me as if you thought I was a player."

"A what? What's a player?"

An expression of disbelief settled on his face. "It's a man who exploits women."

She felt her eyes widen. "How could I think that about you? I wouldn't know a player if I saw one."

"But you'd know it soon enough if you gave him an opportunity. Are you familiar with New Orleans?" Here it comes, she thought when she shook her head.

She told the truth because he could easily tell if she lied. "This is my first trip here."

"Want a personal tour with me?"

She stalled for time, though she knew that seeing New Orleans with Justin McCall would be a delightful experience. "So, you've been here before."

"You bet. I love jazz, and this is the jazz capital of the world. Are you going to answer my question? I'll be glad to give you a bio and some references if they'll help you change your mind."

She imagined that her eyes sparkled at the thought of visiting the jazz clubs and sampling New Orleans' famous food with Justin. But the opportunity to needle him gave her nearly as much pleasure. "Oh, I'd love to see your bio. I'll bet it's fascinating. And don't give me your daddy for a reference. I want a recommendation from at least three of your lady friends." When he gaped, seemingly speechless, laughter poured out of her.

"I don't play games, either," she said, "though I'm not above getting a laugh at another's expense and pulling a few pranks."

"So I see. By the way, my granddad raised me. He's the one you'd get a reference from."

It didn't escape her that he wasn't forthcoming about why

his father didn't raise him. Well, her closet wasn't broom clean either. "You're a gracious man, Justin," she said, deciding to be serious. "However, although I'm not married, I do have a good reason to avoid a relationship with you." He sat forward, and she could almost see his antenna alert itself. "I'm head interior decorator for Burton's Department Store, your chief competition, and I do not want to clutter my life with problems."

"What? He set the coffee cup down with such force that she thought he'd broken it. "But I asked you if you were an interior decorator, and you obviously didn't tell me the truth."

"Wait a minute. I did not answer your question directly. I evaded it and got you off that subject by answering that the candles were for my bedroom. Remember?"

He nodded as he seemed to recall the conversation. "The more we talk, the more intriguing you are." He reached across the table and took her hand. "Have dinner with me tonight."

Let him think he had to persuade her. She wanted to have dinner with him, if only to know what it would be like to have a date like Justin McCall. She wasn't using good judgment, but she'd worry about that another day.

She looked down at the long and tapered brown fingers that held her hand, and managed not to suck in her breath. "What time would you like us to meet?"

He stroked the back of her hand with his index finger, and a grin altered the contours of his face. "How about five-thirty? The earlier we meet, the longer we can make the evening. In about an hour we can see the river and the Arts District. Too bad that on this short visit we can't go down to the levee and see how it's shored up against flooding. Ever since I read Mark Twain's stories as a child, the Mississippi has fascinated me."

And the more he talked, the more he fascinated her. She'd begun to suspect that they had many common interests, beginning with jazz and the culture that nurtured slavery.

"All right. I'll meet you in the reception hall at five-thirty, and I will not be fashionably late."

"Thank you. I appreciate promptness."

"I'd better get back to my room, Justin. I brought along some work."

He stood. "So did I. Have a productive hour or so. I'll be waiting for you down here at five-thirty."

Was she going to be sorry? She had a feeling that this was the beginning of something important. A man with Justin McCall's background and self-assurance did not stop until he reached his goal. She signed her check and went back to her room. What would her boss say to her having a close friendship with the man for whom he reserved his most vitriolic attacks? She was not going to worry about it. She didn't have any trade secrets to give away, she was grown and she didn't have to ask anybody who she could date.

"I hope I'm not walking into a hornet's nest," she said as she sat down to her laptop computer and began drawing sketches for a contemporary-style living room in a rustic mountain cabin. Whoever heard of such a thing?

Justin decided that on a sizzling afternoon, the best place to pick up trade hints and tips would be around the swimming pool, so he changed into swim briefs, put on the terry cloth bathrobe he found in his closet and went to the pool.

"White is it for this winter," a self-assured blonde told her companion. "But some people will resist, so I'm protecting my behind with cocoa, which goes well with white."

He moved away. Women in Woodmore would have his head if he offered them a choice of only two colors, especially tan and white, no matter the season. In any case, he liked to see women in warm colors. After joining two men who seemed interested only in the attributes of females decked out in bikinis, he swam two laps, went back to his room and stretched out on the bed.

He had decided that if Deanna dusted him off again, he'd

leave her alone. To his amazement, she displayed genuine humor and the warmth that he had sensed in her. He wasn't going to allow himself to expect anything from her other than a pleasant evening. But he wished he'd stop looking forward to the evening with such impatience. He was a cautious man, wasn't he? Oh, what the heck!! He got up, showered and looked around for something appropriate to wear.

He wanted to give her some flowers, but how could he when he was meeting her in the lobby? When he realized that the florist hadn't closed, he bought half a dozen American Beauty roses and handed them to her when she arrived.

"I would have preferred to give them to you at your door."

"They are beautiful, and I love flowers. Will you wait a minute while I take these to my room?"

"Of course." She'd done precisely what he'd hoped she would do.

"I've made reservations at Nola, one of Emeril Lagasse's restaurants. I like the food as well as the ambience, and I hope you will, too."

"I'm sure I will. Thank you for choosing it. He's a wonderful chef."

They walked outside and a doorman signaled for a taxi. They arrived at the big row house that had once housed a wealthy family. The neighborhood had an air of elegance. A climb up a high flight of stairs brought them to their table in a beautiful room where crystal chandeliers provided the light and the table setting might have been in a well-appointed private home.

"Justin, this is beautiful, and cozy, too. Thank you for bringing me here."

"My pleasure." What a melodious voice he had!

"Do you sing, Justin?"

"Actually, I don't, except around the house sometimes, entertaining myself."

"But you can sing if you want to. Right?"

"Yeah. Why are you so sure of it?"

"Your speaking voice suggests it."

"Which means you sing. Am I right?"

He held her chair while she sat down. "I've sung in choirs most of my life. I'm not doing it now, because I don't go to church. I got into the habit of sleeping late on Sunday mornings, but guilt and I don't live well together."

"Same here, and my granddad rebukes me for that every Sunday that he can reach me. What would you like to drink?"

"I prefer white wine to hard liquor."

He signaled for the sommelier. "White wine for my guest and a vodka comet for me, please."

"Yes, sir."

"I want to know all about you, Deanna. Where did you grow up? Do you have a family, and if so, where do they live? I'm overflowing with questions. Thank you for wearing this beautiful dress. It's so lovely on you, but I'm sure you would make any dress look beautiful."

"I think you're exaggerating, but it sounds nice. Thank you. I grew up in Winston-Salem and attended universities in Washington, D. C., and FIT in New York. Both my parents are dead now. I don't have any siblings. Although, in his second marriage, my father adopted a very nice girl. She and I have a close relationship. Now please answer the same questions you asked me."

"I grew up in Woodmore and Danvers. Substitute Boston for New York and omit your adopted stepsister, and we've had similar lives. You asked for my bio, and I left it in your box at the registration desk."

"Gosh, I'd forgotten that."

He forced a long sigh. "How little they care, and how quickly they forget."

"You ought to be paddled for that," she said. "It wasn't even a fair piece of acting."

"Was, too."

She leaned forward. "You've got a wicked streak, and you were so serious in the Hilton restaurant that I wouldn't have guessed."

"I don't know about wicked, but I can hold my own with any nonsense you care to dish out."

"Hmm. So you think so," she said. "What a delightful thought."

She didn't know it, but she was getting to him. Each of her signals told him that she would be a warm and wonderful companion. But she was right about the problems she might encounter if she became involved with him. Laurence Burton was not a charitable man. He probably should end it before the evening was over, but he didn't want to do that. He couldn't, and it wasn't because of the challenge she represented. The more he saw of her, the more certain he was that he wanted to know her.

After a delicious meal served with first-quality wines, topped off with key lime pie—the best he'd had since his last visit—and espresso, he was in a mellow mood. "Let's drop in at the Palm Court Jazz Café. They play some serious jazz there. What do you say?" he asked her.

"Sounds wonderful," she said and grasped his hand as easily as if she'd done it a hundred times. She seemed a little startled at his touch, but the lady wore class like a king wears his crown.

"Then we'll go," he said, feeling more lighthearted than he remembered. He hailed a taxi and, after they got in, he made a point of leaving some space between them. Unfortunately, she had released his hand when she got into the taxi, and she didn't reach for it again.

The taxi stopped on the corner, and the driver informed them that cars couldn't enter that street. "Palm Court's half a block in, cap'm," the driver told them. "And it's really jumping tonight. The big boys are there."

She didn't take his hand, so he took hers and waited for her to withdraw it, but she didn't. "My gosh, Justin, this place rocks," she said as they wove their way through the crowd. "Will you look at that? The man has the inside of his body painted on his flesh-colored jumpsuit. That's…"

"Garish," he finished for her. "If you walked these streets on Halloween, you'd be half-scared for a year. It's amazing what people can think of."

Inside the Palm Court Jazz Café, he ordered drinks and held her hand while Jimmy Bowdin and his band paid respects to traditional New Orleans jazz. He wasn't crazy. She could only spend nearly ten minutes looking beyond him and anywhere but his face because of an uncomfortable awareness of him. He didn't doubt that she liked jazz and enjoyed Bowdin's music, but she couldn't make him believe she was so enraptured with the music that she forgot his presence. He let her pretend for another minute.

"Dance with me. With music like this, there's no point in trying to sit still."

Without a word, she stood, took the few steps to the dance area and turned into his arms with the grace of a woman who had done that every day of her life. He would have expected anything but that, since minutes earlier she'd pretended not to be sexually aware of him. He resisted pulling her close and showing her that he could rattle her as easily as she'd just done to him. The piece ended, and Bowdin began an old-fashioned gut-bucket blues tune guaranteed to titillate. He took her back to their table.

"You're a very good dancer, Deanna."

"Thanks, but you make dancing wonderful. You do it with such ease. I love music, and my whole self responds to it." Her nervousness made her talkative. Fine with him. She didn't want to admit that he attracted her, but the evidence was there, and he intended to cultivate it.

"Thank you for the compliment. It's after midnight, and I have a lecture at nine so, as much as I'm enjoying this evening with you, I'd better take you back to the hotel. I think best when I'm well-rested."

"I'm ready when you are, Justin. The evening has been so…so wonderful that I had no idea of the time."

The minute they stepped on the elevator, she seemed uncomfortable, avoided eye contact and stopped talking. When they reached her room, he'd swear that her hand shook when she fished in her purse for the door key. He took it, opened the door and handed her the key.

"Thanks for a wonderful evening. Will you go with me on the Natchez tomorrow night for a jazz dinner cruise? I've never been on a paddle wheeler. They're probably the oldest type of commercial boat used down here."

"Of course. Isn't the paddle wheeler the type of boat that Robert Fulton invented? I know he didn't build the first steamboat."

"Right. His was the paddle wheeler. The Natchez is said to be the best of its type, but who knows. Will you come with me?"

"I'd like to," she said, and he appreciated her lack of coyness. She wanted to go and she said so. He stood there gazing down at her, telling himself to say good-night and leave her. But she was like a magnet, a lovely, tantalizing magnet, and he—

She reached up, kissed his cheek, pushed open the door and left him standing there. *Don't knock on that door, man. Use your head!* He made himself hurry down the hall, get on the elevator and go to his room. *Whew!*

# Chapter 3

The ringing of the phone in her room within minutes after she closed the door did not surprise Deanna. She had already pegged Justin McCall as a man of action, one who left nothing to chance, but she refrained from addressing him by name when she answered.

"Hello."

"This is Justin. It took all the common sense I could muster to resist knocking on your door. I felt like banging on it. Woman, you shook me up. You could at least have warned me."

Better not bite this one, she thought. "Hi, Justin. I'm not sure I follow you. What, uh…what do you mean?"

"If you knew what I know, you'd be thankful for the four floors between us. You kissed me a fraction of an inch from my mouth."

"Oh, come now. That was as innocent as a kiss from one kindergartner to another."

"Really?" he said, his tone just short of sarcastic. "But it was a woman who kissed me, and it felt like a woman's kiss. I'm glad to know that you approve of that kind of innocence."

"But, Justin, it wasn't a big deal. You were so nice, so gracious all evening, that I couldn't resist it."

"Then why didn't you do what you really wanted to do?"

"That would have taken a lot more nerve and a lot more courage," she said, annoyed that he insisted on pushing her into a corner. "Besides, I didn't know what kind of response I'd get. When you push me hard as you're doing now, Justin, you usually get more than you're asking for. Thanks for a delightful evening."

"You're hanging up on me?" he asked in something akin to a growl.

"Not yet," she said, holding back a laugh. "I'm waiting for you to do it. See you at five tomorrow afternoon."

"Right... And don't forget your boxing gloves."

She was certain that her laughter registered with him before he hung up. She had to watch her step with that man. If she had seemed shy or coy about that simple kiss on his cheek, he would have taken advantage and created a scene more intimate than suited her. *I'll bet he's fun to be with, once he trusts you.*

She got down to the restaurant early the next morning, got her coffee, fresh fruit cup and waffles with bacon and syrup and found a table in a remote corner. After reading the headlines on the *USA TODAY* front page, she drained her coffee cup and rushed to Justin's seminar on contemporary design, consumer comfort and consumer taste. Perhaps she should have told him that she planned to attend his seminar, but she hadn't remembered and anyway, it shouldn't matter to him that she was there.

Justin flashed side by side several series of photographs of modern living room and family room accessories in an expensively furnished home. "I don't have to tell you," he said, "that in homes where a family can afford whatever it likes, the more comfortable—and often the more attractive—furniture is not in the living room but in the family room. It is difficult to be comfortable in truly modern chairs with sofas so low that sitting and standing create a problem and in chairs without backs or with short seats. I appeal to designers to create with the average human body in mind. Buyers, please leave the ridiculous stuff in the warehouses."

He had expected resistance to his ideas, so the applause both surprised and pleased him. He glimpsed to his left and saw Deanna. Why hadn't she told him that she planned to attend his lecture? Mystery, thy name is woman! She looked ravishing in a pink-looking tank top, big silver loops in her ears and her thick hair warming her shoulders. He told his hormones to take a nap and shook off the momentary disruption. Not that there was anything momentary about his attraction to Deanna Lawford; she was the kind of woman that he wouldn't give up on until he had explored her thoroughly, no matter how long that took. He pushed aside the thought and focused on his lecture.

But she was there, and he couldn't ignore her. He glanced back at her, and a frown altered the contours of his face. He didn't like it. How could she have the crassness to take notes on his lecture so as to use his ideas for the benefit of his competitor? Annoyance fired him up, but he controlled his mind and his attitude and completed his lecture to a rousing ovation.

From his peripheral vision, he saw her approach. "You were wonderful, Justin. Very forceful. And I'm sure the designers will be taking account of what you said. Congratulations."

"I'm not sure that I should thank you. I don't mind telling you that I'd rather not coach my competition in the means of catching up with me and surpassing me." The sarcasm that tinged his words sounded unwarranted, even to him, and he could see that she was taken aback.

She thrust the notepad toward him. "Here. It's all yours.

I assure you that I don't need it. I took the notes purely out of habit. Give me a pad and a pen, and I automatically start writing. I've made notes on the contours of many a monkey." She turned and walked off, leaving him with the notes.

He had asked for that. Apparently, she had a boiling point as low as his, and she wasn't in a habit of biting her tongue, either. He suspected that she had a keen intellect and that knowing her would be challenging as well as interesting.

Shortly before noon, on her way back to her room, Deanna stopped at the reception desk, and a clerk took two envelopes from Deanna's box and handed them to her. She opened first the one which bore McCall Department Store's return address, and read:

*My name is Justin Robert McCall. I was born in Danvers, to Eleanor and Robert McCall, Jr. I am thirty-four, hold two university degrees, never married and have no children that I know of. I live alone in a two-story brown brick house at 37 Butler Street in Woodmore. I am an only child, father deceased, mother who knows where and raised by my grandfather, Robert McCall, Sr. I'd rather not get references from any women I've known, because none of them wanted to let me go. They may not be fair. My granddad will give you a reference, but he thinks I'm perfect, so what good would it do? Yours faithfully and humbly, Justin.*

After reading the note several times, she thought of sending him a set of questions to supply the information that he had deliberately omitted. But she told herself that it was in fun and turned her attention to the second envelope, which bore the hotel's return address. During Justin's talk, she wrote comments on his ideas and suggestions. When she opened the letter, she saw her notes and Justin's comments on what she had written there. She sat in the lobby, wrote her comments on each of his comments, put the papers back into the envelope, addressed it to Justin and gave it to the desk clerk.

She worked in her room that afternoon and around four

o'clock answered the phone and heard Justin's voice. "Hello, Deanna. This is Justin. Will you please accept my apologies for my manners this morning? I'm not pleased with myself about that. I do not doubt your integrity or your skill, and if you will forgive me, I promise to prove to you that I am worth your trust and respect."

She thought for a minute. "Your temper isn't much more controllable than mine, though I at least didn't lash back at you."

"You didn't?" His voice held the tone of one awed. "I thought you were pretty sharp. Are you going to forgive me?"

"Yeah. But don't test me too often."

"You are still having dinner with me this evening?"

"Sounds like a nice idea, but it won't prove that I've forgiven you. After all, I have to eat, and I don't like dining alone in restaurants."

"Then consider it a part of my penitence."

She couldn't help laughing. "Remind me again, what time we are meeting and where?"

"I can stop by to pick you up, but you'll say no to that, so why not meet at the registration desk as we did yesterday. We can take the Natchez for a dinner cruise."

"I only brought one evening dress."

"And I only brought one formal suit. It won't kill you to wear the same dress this evening. Will it?"

"I guess not, but if I were at home, I definitely wouldn't do it."

"But you will go with me?"

"Okay. See you at five." Why didn't she tell him no? What would she do if she met one of Burton's buyers while out on the town with Justin? She lifted her shoulder in a shrug and went to the closet to check her dress. *Que será, será.* She pressed the dress as best she could, showered, set her hair with the help of the hair dryer and crawled into bed to rest and watch television. She awakened at four-thirty, jumped up, brushed her teeth and raced around the room hardly aware of what she did.

The telephone rang. "Ms. Lawford, some flowers here for you. Shall I send them up?"

"Yes, please." She took a dollar bill from her pocketbook and minutes later tipped the deliveryman, put the bouquet of roses on the dresser and began a frenzied effort to dress and get down to the registration desk by five o'clock. As she started out the door, she remembered to look at the card that accompanied the flowers.

"Dear Deanna," she read, "Thank you for honoring me with your company this evening. And thank you especially for overlooking my remark this morning. Yours, Justin."

Deanna had seen traits in Justin that she admired and among them, his kindness and considerateness were more important to her than his lapse that morning. She hurried to the elevator, got on and, to her delight, he stood facing it when she got off. He reached for her hand, and when she took his, his face bloomed into a smile.

"If you hadn't forgiven me," he said, "you wouldn't have bothered to look so beautiful."

She laughed because she felt good, and it occurred to her that being with Justin made her happy. *Watch it, girl,* her common sense reminded her. *This guy sits on top of the McCall millions.* "How can I forget it?" she mumbled.

"How can you forget what?"

She evaded his question, took his hand and walked with him across the lobby to the door, where he asked for a taxi. "I'm just hoping I don't meet one of Mr. Burton's buyers while I'm out with you."

"If you do and there's an opportunity, be sure and introduce us, because all of them know me. If you attempt to make an introduction, no one can accuse you of trying to hide anything."

"Thanks," she said, making up her mind to enjoy the evening no matter who she met or where she met them.

When she thought of those old steamboats, she associated them with the slavery era, and she had expected them to be as ancient as they seemed on the exterior. Her surprises included the rich carpeting, elegant lighting, seating and other elegant interior fittings that she and Justin discovered as they strolled through the boat. After a sumptuous dinner, he took her upstairs to dance, and she admitted to herself that the prospect of dancing with him again had motivated her to accept his invitation to join him for the evening.

In his arms, she hardly even heard the music as he glided them to the beat of lovers' songs from the sixties and seventies. At last, the jazz band replaced the intermission band on stage and to her chagrin, Justin wanted to merely sit and listen. But she remembered his sensual, rhythmic rocking and loose way of dancing. "Can we dance to this one?" she asks him when the band commenced to play "I'll Never Be The Same." He caught her mood, and his body began to answer the invitations of her movements until she realized that the two of them were speaking in the frankest terms without saying a word.

When he took her to her room hours later, she made a joke of her behavior the previous evening. She didn't want him to expect more than he would get, and certainly not all that their dancing suggested.

"Your cheek is safe from me this evening. Honest!" she said.

He stared down at her. "Whoever told you that I wanted to be safe?" He half smiled, apparently to sweeten the now-acrid air.

"My plane's at ten-ten tomorrow morning, and I have to leave the hotel by seven-thirty," she said, "so I'll see you in Woodmore." She extended her hand, and he took it, shook her hand, waited until he heard the lock turn on her door and walked off thinking that if there were three and a half billion females in the world, he'd bet that there were also three and a half billion *different kinds* of females in the world.

\* \* \*

Justin telephoned the airport and checked the flight schedules. Then he packed, scheduled a six o'clock wake-up call, ordered breakfast for six-thirty and went to bed. He had plans for Deanna Lawford, and until she told him for the second time that she had no interest in him, he meant to occupy as much of her time as she would allow. At twenty minutes past seven the next morning, having determined that Deanna had not checked out, he waited for her at the porter's desk.

"I didn't get a thing to eat," she said when she saw him, "not even a swallow of coffee."

"Have you checked out?"

"I did the express checkout in my room."

"But you need a bill, don't you? Get the bill while I get you a container of coffee and a croissant." *She hasn't even asked me why I'm down here.* He got the coffee and croissant, handed it to her and took her elbow. "I have a limousine waiting for us." The porter stored their bags in the trunk of the car, and they headed for the Louis Armstrong International Airport.

"What time does your flight leave, Justin?"

"Ten after ten." She took a long sip of coffee and closed her eyes as she savored it. What a sensual woman. He told himself to think of something other than the way her lips glistened, and the pressure of her nipples against her sweater.

"Thanks for the food, Justin. This is wonderful." She licked her top lip, and he looked away.

"I'm glad I thought of it."

At the check-in counter, he asked to see her ticket and changed his seat so that they sat together. Fortunately, she also had a first-class ticket, and he didn't have to change it. He handed it back to her. "The flight's on time, so let's head for the security check."

"Are you and I on the same flight, Justin?"

He grinned down at her. "Looks like it. I didn't think you

were going to ask. I changed my seat so that we're sitting together. I hope you don't mind."

"I don't, but I'm not much company on planes. Whenever possible, I sleep."

"I make a very nice pillow. So why not?" he asked, more prophetically than he could have realized. In the cabin, while he stored their carry-on luggage overhead, she took the window seat. After takeoff, the stewardess gave them a choice of orange juice or champagne. They accepted the juice. But almost at once, it sloshed on the armrest.

"We're in for some turbulence," the captain said. "We'll be flying above the storm, but we'll get the effect of it for a good bit of the trip. Stay in your seats, and keep your seat belts fastened."

The plane took a sudden dip, and he saw that her hands shook. "Are you all right?" he asked her.

"I d...don't know," she said, and when it seemed that her teeth chattered, he removed the armrest between them and pulled her into his arms. To his amazement, she needed no prompting, but snuggled up to him with her head against his chest and her right arm across his body. With each dip of the plane, her hand tightened on his body. He hurt for her.

"It's okay, Deanna. I know it's rough, but I've been in much worse turbulence. The captain isn't worried."

"This is your captain speaking. As soon as this turbulence eases up, we'll serve. All drinks are on me this time, so don't hesitate to calm your nerves with a few fingers of vodka or bourbon. We've got another 100 miles of turbulence, but the worst is behind us."

"I th...thought he was going to tell us the t...turbulence was over," she said. "Aren't you scared?"

"I'm not in the mood to dance, but I'm not petrified, either. If you fly as often as I do, you get this from time to time, although this is a bit severe. To be honest, I'm rather happy."

"I'd l…like to know what the d..devil you've g…got to be h…happy about."

"I try to find the good in every situation. There is no way you'd be in my arms if this plane was flying smoothly."

"Well, I'm g…glad you're happy."

"Come on. It's not so bad. It just happened a little sooner than it would ordinarily have."

"A gentleman w…wouldn't remind me."

About the time he realized that the turbulence had ceased, the captain announced that service would begin. "I'm going to drink all of the liquor on that cart," she said.

"Somehow, I doubt that." He looked down at her snug in his arms and the plane flying as smoothly as an eagle. Damned if he'd call her attention to it.

The stewardess interrupted his heaven. "What would you like, miss?"

Still holding on to him, Deanna sat up. "Some strong black coffee. I don't dare eat a thing."

"What about some fruit?" Justin asked her. He wondered why her hands suddenly held such interest for her. Then he realized that having enjoyed nearly an hour in his arms embarrassed her. *Too bad,* he said to himself, *but I certainly am not complaining.*

*You liked it here, you got used to it and you'll be back for more.*

The limousine that he regularly reserved for special trips waited for him when they emerged from the luggage claim section. "I'll drop you home," he said, not giving her a chance to refuse.

"Straight home, sir?" the driver asked him when they had seated themselves in the car.

"Take Ms. Lawford home first. Give him your address, Deanna." She did. "I could walk to your place," he said when she gave an address on Mountain Lane. "I'm on Butler Street, a block from Pine Park."

She settled back into the soft leather seat. "Really? I walk in that park some Sunday mornings in midsummer."

"So do I. It's strange that we never met there. At six o'clock on a June morning when the air is fresh, the wind is soft and the chirping of birds is the only audible sound...that's balm for the soul."

She turned to see his face more fully. "Justin, you're a romantic. We've never met in the park because you're back in bed before I get out there. I wouldn't run there alone when the rest of Woodmore is asleep."

"Suppose we run together?"

"Okay, but wait till autumn. It's too hot now."

The car pulled to a stop in front of her door. "Wait here, driver. I'll see Ms. Lawford to her door. I'll take it," he said of Deanna's luggage when the driver removed it from the trunk.

"Thank you, Justin. You made the return trip home very comfortable and trouble-free. Sorry if I was poor company on the plane, but getting on a plane is a big deal for me, and the slightest irregularity sends me into a tizzy."

He held out his hand for her door key. "I'm sorry if you were ill at ease, but I enjoyed every second that I held you in my arms." He dropped her bags on the floor inside the foyer. "It whetted my appetite, and I need more," he said, easing his arms around her and gazing down into her face. He saw nothing negative in her soft brown eyes, only expectancy.

"Kiss me. Put your arms around me and kiss me, sweetheart." As the last word left his lips, he bent his head and she came up to meet him with lips parted to receive his tongue. Desire slammed into him, and tremors shook him as she sucked him into her. Closer. He pulled her closer, and her arms tightened around him. He broke the kiss and stared down at her. She licked her lips, and he went into her again, probing and searching, lapping up the sweetness in her. When he felt the craving for sex with her begin to arouse him, he set her away from him and let the wall take his weight.

"Something's happening with us, Deanna. Will you give me your home phone number and your cell number? I need to…will you let us see each other as often as possible? I mean, on a regular basis?"

"I don't know, Justin. I'd like for us to see each other, but in this town everybody knows when you change eyeglasses, and I have to think about my position at Burton's."

"Burton's needs you more than you need that store, but I respect your feelings about this. I hate not having things aboveboard. Sneaking around to be with you is not going to sit well with me. I want to see you, and I want everybody to know that I value you and your company. You're not ashamed to be seen with *me,* are you?"

Her soft gaze became a glare, "How did you fix your mouth to say that? You can't be serious."

He hugged her. "No, it wasn't a serious question. I asked that because I wanted to know where I stand with you."

She squinted at him. "And you think you know now?"

"Well, one more kiss and I'll know."

A grin spread over her face. "You're a slick one. Kiss me. That driver must think we're in here making out."

"That driver must know I'm a better man than that. I'll call you tonight." Her kiss, long and sweet, didn't satisfy him, but his time would come.

*What was she thinking?* "That's the trouble," she said aloud. "I wasn't thinking. What woman could think when that guy opens his arms and parts his lips? Thank goodness I don't have that much willpower." But did she want to see him, to be with him on a regular basis? *Stupid question!* She'd wanted that from the moment she first saw him. But, with only two department stores in Woodmore, until she was able to strike out on her own, she needed that job at Burton's.

She didn't feel like working, but she wanted to hand in her report Monday when she got to work. She didn't have to do it on her first day back at the office after a field trip, as her boss called attendance at conventions and business conferences, but she wanted to complete the report while all was fresh in her mind. She decided not to include Justin's talk.

But that would be dishonest. His getting angry about her making notes during his lecture was not a reason to omit it in her report. She compromised by including a summary to the effect that McCall's recommended furnishings emphasized comfort rather than design. After completing the report and printing it out, she considered cleaning her refrigerator, but listening to the music of Louis Armstrong, Sidney Bechet, Duke Ellington and Billie Holiday seemed a much better idea and didn't require the expenditure of much energy.

Soon, the sound of Louis Armstrong's "A Kiss To Build A Dream On" filled her living room. She turned it up higher, and was soon dancing, giving herself over to the music, back in New Orleans and back in Justin's arms.

She went to the kitchen for a glass of cranberry juice—her favorite drink—and heard the phone ringing. "Hello," she said in a rather short fashion because she didn't want to be disturbed.

"Hello. This is Justin. I rang a dozen times. Where were you?"

"Right here, but I'd turned the music up so loud that I couldn't hear anything else."

"I hear it. Isn't that Armstrong's 'Hello Dolly'?"

"It is that. I was in the mood for some jazz."

"I'd ask if I could come over and listen with you, but you've been away from home for four days and you have to work tomorrow."

She laughed at the excuse he gave her. "That's true, Justin. Tell me. What would you do if I said you're right, but I'm not in the mood to be sensible?"

"I'd be over there as fast as I could put on my shoes and get into my car. Is that what you're saying?"

"No, it isn't, but I wanted to know where you're coming from."

"Make it easy, sweetheart. Ask me what you want to know. I'll always give it to you straight. I called because I miss you. These last three days with you were…I don't want to lose them. What are you eating for dinner? You didn't eat lunch. Remember?"

"Funny, but I'm not thinking about food. I just want to listen to music. Hold it while I put on Billie Holiday."

"Gosh, I wish I was there with you."

She was crazy, but she wanted to be with him as much as he wanted to be with her. "Then…put on your shoes."

"You mean it?"

"A bird doesn't fly on one wing, Justin. Jeans and sneakers are fine. That's what you'll see when you get here." She hung up and looked toward the ceiling. "Lord, help me to keep it between the lines. I could lose everything in the space of two short hours."


Justin debated stopping by a gourmet take-out shop and getting their dinner, but discarded the idea; a phone call from her house would do just as well. He went to his pantry, got two bottles of white and one bottle of red wine, put them in a shopping bag, got into his car and drove to her house. Midway there, it occurred to him that it was the perfect distance for a bicycle ride. She opened the door with an expectant expression on her face that tempted him to look behind him. Instead, he leaned forward and brushed her lips with a quick kiss, but it lasted long enough to heat him up.

"That was quick," she said.

He didn't attempt to stifle his grin. "Which? The kiss or my trip here?"

Both of her eyebrows shot up. "I was talking about your trip here."

He handed her the wine. "I can phone out for some food later. You have to eat."

He decided to try and ease the tension. He wanted her, but if he rushed her, he'd lose a lot more than he gained. Deanna's attitudes toward her job and him were almost as rigidly rooted as the foundation of a skyscraper. "What do you say?"

She looked at him for a long time, and he realized that she was making a decision about him and her. "Should you be feeding me in my house?"

"Yes. I definitely should be." He laughed to take the punch out of his words, for he had said it much more forcibly than he'd intended.

"Let's listen to Billie Holiday first," he said. "I don't have many of her records."

"I have every recording she ever made," Deanna said, and put three Holiday CDs on the CD player.

Justin pushed a leather pouf beside an armchair. "Sit with your back to this," he said, and when she did, he stretched out on the floor, put his head in her lap and closed his eyes. While Billie sang "Easy Living," he let himself dream. After a while, when Billie switched to "Back In Your Own Back Yard," soft fingers stroked his cheek, then began playing with strands of his hair, as if she were absentmindedly stroking and caressing. He expected that any minute she would lean over and kiss his forehead. Her hand moved down to his chest, then began to pat his belly to the tune of "Sunny Side Of The Street." He hoped she retained the presence of mind to avoid his erogenous areas.

He wanted to turn on his side facing her, wrap his arms around her, nudge her sweater out of the way and kiss the flesh of her bare belly, but if he did that, he'd want to go further, and that would shatter the contentment flowing between them. If he had to walk on a tight string, he'd do it. The more he had of her, the more he needed.

When her belly made a telltale noise, he sat up. "I want lobster, tiny potatoes sautéed in butter and minced parsley, asparagus, green salad with blue cheese dressing, lemon meringue pie and, let's see, maybe a quenelle with…no, I'd rather have New England clam chowder for an opener."

She stared at him. "It sounds wonderful, but where will

you get it? I don't know a restaurant open on Sunday evening that serves that."

"Gourmet Corner's open. I'll call Kix, place the order and send a limousine for it. Meanwhile, we'll set the table here, and I'll send the serving dishes and utensils back to Kix tomorrow. What would you like?"

"You make it seem so simple. I'll have what you're having, except that I want a plain oil and vinegar dressing on my salad. While you order, I'll find some snacks. I'm starving."

"You have every right to be."

He dialed Gourmet Corner. "This is Justin McCall. May I speak with Kix Shepherd?" He ordered the food, called the limousine company and went to the kitchen to find Deanna. "Fifty minutes to an hour from now, I'll be eating clam chowder. The food's good at Pinky's, but when I want something wonderful, it's Gourmet Corner for me."

"I've never been there, but I've heard that it's first class."

"We'll go there one evening soon. Not on Mondays, though, because Kix is off on Mondays. He's the owner and chef. He has a couple of good sous-chefs, but they're not at his level."

He opened a bottle of white wine, got two stem glasses and went back to the living room. She followed him with hot pigs in a blanket, cheese squares and crackers. He sat on the pouf beside the chair that she occupied.

"Deanna, being here with you is so restful and peaceful that I may not want to leave. What I've seen of your home is conducive to rest and relaxing, with soft and warm colors and furniture meant for living."

"Yeah," she said with a grin. "And I did this before I heard your lecture on the subject."

"Do you think we could be closer? Seriously, I mean." He held up his right hand to stop her answer. "That was not a fair question. I think we can, and I hope you feel that way. I'm going to do what I can to make my company so enjoyable to you that you won't want to be away from me a single minute. Will you mind?"

"Will I mind if I want to be with you every minute? If it gets that bad, I don't suppose it will matter whether I mind."

*Better not touch that one,* he said to himself. To her, he said, "The food will be here soon, so maybe we'd better set the table. Where can I wash my hands?" He washed up and noted that she placed linen placemats and napkins on the table along with the stem glasses, and breathed a sigh of relief. He doubted that he disliked anything in a house more than he detested paper napkins.

The food arrived, and he took it to the kitchen, opened the parcel and called her. "Look at this, will you. Kix always sends my orders in nice serving dishes because he knows I'll either send or take them back. He served the chowder. "You like it?"

"It's wonderful, Justin. Nice and hot."

After they finished the meal, he told her to wait in the living room while he washed the serving pieces and put her dishes in the dishwasher. It was his treat, and he didn't want her to do the cleaning up. When he got back to her, she sat in the big chair with her eyes closed, patting her foot to Benny Goodman's "Pickin' Apples."

He stood behind the chair, leaned forward and kissed her lips. "I'd better go now, Deanna. This has been one of the most delightful evenings in my memory. Walk me to the door." She sprang out of her chair.

"I'm glad you came, Justin. I enjoyed being with you. And thanks for that delightful dinner."

When she opened her arms and looked up to him, his heart began to pound. He wrapped her close to him and parted his lips above her for the kiss she offered. It seemed so long before she touched his mouth, and when she did, his nerves began to riot in his body. She took him in, savored him and then released him.

'You're so nice, Justin. Good night."

# Chapter 4

Justin awakened the following Monday morning at five o'clock, put on his running togs and headed for Pine Park. He'd give himself a month and no longer in which to make up his mind about Deanna, because she was not a woman that a man strung along. Nor did he believe she'd allow it. He increased his pace and ran until nearly exhausted before flinging himself on a park bench. Several starlings played around his feet, and he wished he had food for them. What did he want from Deanna other than the obvious? She reached him where he had never allowed himself to be touched, and she did it consistently. She made no demands on him, and he didn't understand that. She lived comfortably, but she clearly was not wealthy, yet she asked for nothing, though she must know that he was worth millions. And another puzzling thing: she had discouraged his attention, though she was attracted to him the minute she saw him, just as he was attracted to her.

He jogged back home, showered and dressed for work. As he prepared to leave, he thought of Deanna's warm and cozy home, gazed around him at the wealth and stark beauty and released a mild expletive. There was nothing wrong with his house; he was the problem.

Curious about Deanna's work at Burton's Department Store, Justin decided to go there on a Saturday morning when Deanna would be off and the store would be crowded, in which case there was less likelihood that he would be recognized. He went first to contemporary living and dining rooms, checking both the designs and materials she used as well as the way in which she arranged them. Impressed with Deanna's taste, he checked all of her sample rooms, including kitchens and baths.

"She has taste and style," he wrote on his notepad and added, "For each kind of room, she has a signature motif. If she decorated it, you know you're looking at a Lawford job. Classy." That evening when he called her, he told her of his estimation of her work and congratulated her.

"I'm hoping to build a following at Burton's so I can venture on my own. I know it will be difficult, and I'm fully prepared for that."

"You'll do well. I've checked decorators' work in New York, Washington and practically every major city I visit. You can hold your own with the best of them."

"I owe you a hug for that."

"I could use a hug, too. There's an old movie at the Rialto that I'd love to see with you, but I know you aren't going out with me as long as you're at Burton's. What about driving over to Danvers and getting a cone of ice cream at the ice cream factory? I need a kiss."

"Okay. I love ice cream."

"You love ice cream? Woman, the point here is for you to kiss me."

"That, too," she said, enjoying teasing him. "I'll be ready when you get here."

"I'm on my way."

She dashed up the stairs, flung off her T-shirt and shorts, slipped on a white embroidered peasant blouse and street-length red and white peasant skirt and some big silver hoop earrings, combed out her hair, grabbed a pair of espadrilles and raced down the stairs. She finished tying the last shoe as the doorbell rang.

"Hi," she said to him, so casually that she almost fooled herself.

His grin eclipsed his face. "You're not fooling me. You almost broke your neck getting dressed before I got here. I love it! I'm not waiting until we drive to Danvers and back. I want my kiss now."

She stroked his left cheek with her right hand. "No point in being strident about it. All you have to do is take it."

She didn't know when or how her feet left the floor, but he was holding her chest to chest and belly to belly. His tongue plowed into her mouth, and she sucked it in greedily, loving it and feasting on it. Suddenly, he penned her between himself and the wall, and smothered her face with kisses as his hands roamed over her body, her hips, back, shoulders, neck and—

"Oh, Lord," she moaned, and his hand stroked her breast. "Oh, Justin. Justin." He pulled the ample globe from the bodice of her blouse and bent his head. Nearly out of her mind with desire for him, she held it and he sucked its nipple into his mouth. She let out a scream and undulated helplessly against him. It was too much. Nothing and no man had ever made her feel like that.

"Stop," she said softly. "Please stop. I can't bear it."

"Are you angry with me?"

"No. No. I was a willing participant. I never felt anything like it. Nothing. No one. I…I don't think I have the strength to stand on my own two feet. We'd better go get that ice cream."

He didn't move. "I told you that something important was going on between us, and I think we ought to try and sort it out."

She eased down until her feet touched the floor, and he

straightened her blouse. "How can we work out anything as long as I'm at Burton's? You're special to me, but I have to keep my integrity. That's also important to me."

"I'm not going to stay away from you, Deanna. I can't, and I don't want to. I need to be with you. You give me something that no other person, thing or situation does, and I need it."

"Let's go get the ice cream." She looked in the foyer mirror to check her blouse. "Do you really like this outfit? It's Hungarian. I bought it at a fair in New Jersey."

"I love it. It's so feminine. Let's go before I cross the line. I came pretty close to it a minute ago, and I don't want to do that."

"Never mind. I won't let you."

His laugh was short and almost cynical. "Yes, I know. Like you were helping me a minute ago. You were as lost as I was. But at least you're not a phony." She let that pass.

"This is the best ice cream I ever ate," she said as they left the ice cream parlor, and she would have licked her lips if he hadn't been gazing at her mouth.

"You do something to me." His fleeting kiss barely touched her mouth before he draped an arm over her shoulder and walked with her on the flat stone path toward the back of the restaurant. "Let's check out the moon over that creek. This is a fantastic night."

Deanna tried to assess his mood. She wouldn't call it possessive, but it seemed to her that he was giving himself some previously unused licenses. Did she mind? She told herself to wait and see how far he took it and what guarantees accompanied the privileges he assumed. Standing with him in the moonlight with their bodies reflected in the still water of the creek, she turned to him and put an arm around his waist.

"It's so beautiful, Justin. I'd hate to stand here alone on a night like this."

"I was thinking the same thing. I'm alone almost all the time, even when I'm working, because almost nobody treats me as an equal. I don't ask for it; I inherited it, and I am not complaining, but when I'm with you, the world just seems different. I think I'll get half a gallon of that peach and put it in my freezer."

"But you didn't eat the peach."

He hugged her to him so tightly that she wondered if something bothered him. "I didn't eat peach, but you did." He left the meaning of that comment to her interpretation.


Deanna's opportunity to establish her own business came sooner than she had thought it would. She accompanied one of Burton's wealthiest and most long-standing clients through the three "family" rooms that she had decorated and furnished. She wondered at the man's interest in them, since they were intended to meet the needs of middle-class individuals.

"I've been looking at your work for some time," he told her. "My cook's retiring, and my wife and I are settling her in a two-bedroom house over in Danvers. She's been with us forty-five years, so we're taking care of her. Another thing. My niece wants her new twenty-three-room house on the Albemarle Sound decorated and furnished. I've told her about you, and she's ready to make a deal with you. Of course, I'd like you to take care of my cook's house over in Danvers. At her age, furnishing it would be beyond her."

Deanna did her best to appear as if such deals were commonplace for her and thanked him. "I'll do my best, sir."

After meeting Netta Cross, the man's niece, Deanna decided that, although she wasn't crazy about the woman, she couldn't refuse her huge offer. She reminded herself of Justin's comment that most of the rich don't appreciate a thing unless it's very expensive. She signed the two contracts, and marbles rattled in her stomach as she became Deanna Lawford & Associates, Inc., Interior Decorators.

With shaky fingers, she dialed Justin's cell phone number. "Hello."

The sound of his low and mellifluous voice added to her turmoil. She told him what she'd done and waited for words of caution and criticism. "Congratulations, Deanna. I'm happy and excited for you. You've got precisely what it takes. Netta Cross always used my store, but you would do a much better job for her than my guys have done. We need to celebrate. Let's have dinner and then go to the Watering Hole where everybody will see us."

Hmm. So he really had been bothered about their seeing each other clandestinely. "Wonderful. I'll look forward to it. By the way, you mean your store decorated for both Ms. Cross and Mr. Motley?"

"Well, yeah. Where else would they go? How about I pick you up at seven and we eat at Gourmet Corner?"

"That would be super. See you at seven." She hung up slowly. Did he want her to believe he was happy for her, when she'd just taken two big jobs from his store? He may think he meant it, but she didn't believe it. She'd better watch herself.

"What's the problem, Deanna?" Justin asked her when she opened the door for him that evening. "We do have a date, don't we?"

She hadn't counted on such perceptiveness from Justin, and she knew she had better level with him. She stroked his cheek with the back of her hand. "You're right, something is bothering me, and it's probably just me. I can't understand how you can be happy about my going out on my own when I'm taking away two of your clients."

When he shoved his hands into his pockets and slouched against the wall, she wished she hadn't brought up the subject. Had she forgotten that Justin did not permit his fields to go untended?

"So, you think I'm capable of duplicitous behavior! Well, I am not. Cross and Motley like your work, so they would have found a way to get you to do the jobs whether on your own, at Burton's store or another place. Neither of them cares two hoots about loyalty to McCall's or any other place or person. And they won't have any loyalty to you."

"I have a lot to learn, so I hope I don't exasperate you, at least not regularly."

That remark brought a smile from him, and he gathered her to him in a fierce hug. "If someone drives a wedge between you and me, Deanna, I won't be that person."

"I don't want to be the one to do that, either, Justin, but I know I'm not perfect."

He raised an eyebrow at that. "Touché!"

He'd dressed carefully for their date, because he wanted Deanna to know that he took pride in his relationship with her and wanted everyone to know that they were a couple. He'd hesitated while tying his tie. They hadn't settled that matter, but they would before he slept. He wanted to know where he stood with her and what he meant to her. He only had to touch her and she glowed like a hot coal. Was it because of him, or would she fire up like that for any man? He didn't believe that and he wanted her to verify it. And another thing: if she got into financial trouble with her business, he'd be the last person to know it, and that irritated him. Still, he preferred that to dates who asked him for a twenty dollar bill for the lavatory attendant, when he knew the poor woman got fifty cents, or a dollar at best.

"That's the best crown roast of pork I've ever tasted," Deanna said to Kix when he came to their table. "It must be gratifying to be able to cook like that."

"I've had years of practice," the owner and head chef of Gourmet Corner told her, "and I began by studying at the Cordon Bleu School in Paris. Like anything else, you need a thorough knowledge of your craft."

"Deanna is an interior decorator," Justin said, his voice colored with pride.

Kix looked from one to the other. "When I redo this place, which one of you do I call? Do you work together?"

"She has her own company," Justin said quickly, "and she's definitely superior to the guys who work for me. So don't hesitate to call her."

Kix appraised Justin with respect. "Way to go, man. Cassie and I have always said that you're one of the few true gentlemen we know."

"Thanks, Kix," Justin said without the semblance of a smile. "Every recommendation helps." He looked at Deanna. "Why not give him your card?"

"Give me a handful of them, and I'll put them in the lounge." She gave the cards to Kix and thanked him. "And thanks for the wonderful meal," she added.

Justin drove to the Watering Hole, where he knew he'd probably see half of the people he knew by first name. But he didn't plan to be there long, for he had other, more important things on his agenda. He ordered a bottle of Moët and Chandon champagne, toasted Deanna and greeted the dozen or so people who passed close enough to their table to confirm that he was indeed with Deanna Lawford.

"We've aroused their curiosities and given them enough fodder for a month of steady gossip, so I'd like to leave now, if you don't mind." Her facial expression was that of one totally bemused, so he stood, leaned over and kissed her. When she gasped at his brazenness, he laughed aloud. He'd caused at least one female in there to come near fainting, and he didn't mind one bit. Hopefully, she realized from his having kissed his date in public that she should stop pestering him with phone calls and invitations that he never accepted.

He held Deanna's hand as they left Woodmore's most famous gathering place. And to assure her that he was in a good mood, he launched into "Blueberry Hill," Louis Armstrong's hit. "I knew it. I told you that you could sing," she said.

"I already knew it," he said, feeling good and doing his best to bring her into his element.

He parked in front of her house, and walked with her to

her door where he held out his hand for her key. He unlocked the door, opened it and looked down at her. "I want to come in with you."

"I rather sensed that," she said and walked in leaving him to follow.

After locking the door, she turned on the foyer and living room lights. "Have a seat. We should have brought the remainder of that champagne with us. I have the bottle of white wine that we didn't drink when you were here before. Would you like some?"

He had to do something to put her at ease. "I'd rather listen to some music."

She walked over to him and, standing before him, she braced her hands on his shoulders, kissed his forehead and asked him, "What's the matter? Is everything all right with you?"

"No," he blurted out. "I want the right to tell people that you're my girl and to introduce you that way. If you think I'm not good enough to introduce to your family and friends, tell me, and I'll take a hike."

She sat on his knee. "What on earth's the matter with you, and what are you talking about?"

"I'm talking about I want to know where I stand with you. I haven't been near another woman since I saw you trying to buy those candles in my store. I want to know if you and I can make a go of this. Do you have another guy? If I didn't call you or ask to see you, you'd let more than a week go by without seeing or hearing from me. You've done it. Don't you care about me?"

"Yes, I care a lot about you, and if you'd told me this before, we might not be having this conversation right now. You know that as long as I was at Burton's, I didn't feel free to get…oh, you know what I mean."

He pulled her closer and cradled her in his arms. "You don't work for Burton's now, so is there a reason why you won't be my girl, I'm not seeing anybody, and I don't want any other man's hands on you. I've never been more serious, Deanna. Talk to me."

"There's no one else, Justin, and…yes, we can date on a regular basis."

"Look, baby. That's fine, but…oh, hell." He sucked her bottom lip into his mouth, stroked her from her shoulders to her knees, caressed her buttocks and trailed his tongue from her neck to her cleavage. "This is what I want," he said, feeling as if he'd drool if he couldn't get her nipple into his mouth.

"Give it to me."

She lifted her left breast from the confines of her dress. He licked the nipple and then sucked it into his mouth. Tremors shook her. *I'm not leaving here tonight until she's mine.* He let the fingers of his right hand play with her knee, threatening to go higher, but seeming not to dare. Her moans excited him, and he snaked his hand up her thigh, but hesitated, fearing the result if he claimed the prize. When he suckled more vigorously, her body moved from side to side and her moans began to sound like pleas. Suddenly, she raised her right knee in what was clearly an invitation.

He covered her breast and stood, all the while cradling her in his arms. "Where is your bedroom?"

Upstairs on the right. Within minutes, he had her in bed and her skirt and blouse on the floor beside it. "Are you protected?"

"No. I haven't needed to be."

"It's all right. I'll take care of it." He put the condom beneath the pillow, got in beside her, put his arms around her and, looking down into her face, he asked, "Is there anything I should know? No matter what it is, tell me." He didn't want to make a mistake with her, because he sensed that if he did, he might regret it for the remainder of his life.

She reached up and kissed him. "I haven't had a lot of experience with this, and I haven't been successful at it."

"Trust me, and we'll make each other happy."

"I'd trust you with my life."

"You upset me even in my dreams, and when you look at me like that... Deanna, sweetheart, I need you to love me. This is it for me."

She gazed up into his face and his expression of love and adoration nearly took her breath. "You're everything to me."

"Shhh. I want you to love me. I'll teach you to care for me."

"I already care for you."

"I want you to love me. I need it."

His lips adored her eyes, cheeks, ears, the hollow of her neck and when she parted her lips, he let her have his tongue. But only for a few seconds. He sucked one nipple into his mouth and toyed with the other one until she began to writhe beneath him, undulating and begging for penetration.

"Why won't you get in me?" She reached down to take him but he wouldn't allow it.

"You're not ready, and if I went in now, I could hurt you. I'm a big man." He kissed a line down to her navel while his hand teased the inside of her thigh just close enough to her vulva to heighten her desire.

"Can't you...? Honey, I'm burning up. I'm not used to this."

He opened her legs, hooked her knees over his shoulders and kissed her. Screams poured out of her as his tongue found the right spot and he worked at her until she shouted, "Get in me. Something's happening."

Heat seared the bottom of her feet, her legs and thighs trembled and she thought she would die. He rose above her and she looked into his face as he smiled. "Take me in, baby. Take me in your hands and let me in."

She didn't let herself wonder how she would accommodate him because he was big, but he slipped in with little difficulty, and began to rock.

"Are you comfortable?"

"Yes. Yes." His rapid and powerful strokes drove her nearly senseless, taking her to the brink, bringing her back and when she thought she would lose the sensation that surged in her, he said, "All right. Be still now." Then he rocked her until the pumping and swelling began, the contractions in her womb and in her vagina shook her until she screamed aloud as she erupted into orgasm and gripped his penis with such strength that he trembled uncontrollably, tightened his buttocks and splintered in her arms.

"You're mine, Deanna. You will always be mine." The words tumbled out of him, neither arrogantly nor possessively, but as the plea of a man humbled by love. "You're precious to me," he whispered. "Give me a chance to teach you to love me." He braced himself on his elbows and smiled down at her. "How do you feel?"

"I don't know. I've never had an experience like this."

"Do you feel satisfied? I know you had an orgasm, and a powerful one, too, but do you feel sated?"

"I feel wonderful. Can I have…I mean, can we do that again?"

"That's what I like to hear, baby. Whenever you want me, find a way to let me know. I want you to need me and love me." He got her nipple between his lips, eased his hand down her body and let his talented fingers work their magic. She realized that he'd learned what it took to reach his goal, for within minutes he had her ready to climb the wall.

"I'm ready. Stop torturing me and get in me."

He tested her for readiness, and within seconds he began storming inside of her, claiming her, sure of his goal. She wanted to make it last, but he drove relentlessly until both of them erupted in orgasm. Totally spent. After a while, he separated them, rolled off her, wrapped her in his arms and slept.

Justin awakened the next morning groggy and not quite aware of his surroundings. He didn't know when he'd last gotten home at four in the morning, and he rarely went to bed so late that he slept for only a couple of hours. He tried to fix his mind on the wonder of his experience with Deanna the previous night, but was deprived of that joy when his phone rang.

"Don't tell me you're still asleep, son. You feel all right?"

"I'm fine, Granddad." He pulled himself up and sat on the edge of the bed. "How are *you?*"

"As sound as the US mint. Now I want to have a word with you before you start making changes in McCall's. Butcher told me you're planning to put third-line designer products in the store, and that's not wise. Our clients won't like that." After an hour, during which he hadn't had a drop of coffee, he said goodbye, although they hadn't settled the matter.

For the first time in his life, he was at odds with his grandfather who he had idolized almost since birth, and he didn't like it. But with only two department stores in Woodmore, the middle class needed more options and, with its monopoly, Burton's overcharged them. He could offer higher quality at a lower cost to those customers.

The disagreement with his grandfather depressed him. Deanna was his one source of joy, and he couldn't stay away from her. He didn't want to. His attempts to reorganize the store failed to satisfy him, and he suggested to Deanna that perhaps going against his grandfather's wishes had not been a good idea.

Lying on Deanna's living room floor with his head in her lap—his favorite way of relaxing—he told her that he might have erred. "Granddad's marketing instincts have made McCall's what it is. Maybe I shouldn't have gone against his wishes."

"Would you like me to take a look at the new arrangement and the decorators' work?"

He turned on his side, wrapped his arms around her and kissed her belly. "I can't tell you how much I'd appreciate that."

The next morning, she walked through the store from the second to the top level making notes and jotting down ideas. That afternoon in her study at home, she sketched out some changes, and telephoned Justin that she had some ideas for him.

"May I come over right now?" he asked her.

"Sure, but I don't wear shoes when I'm working at home."

"Wonderful," he said. "I've wanted to get a good look at your toes."

She decided to risk a provocative question. "Any special reason?"

"Mind your manners, woman. See you in a few minutes." His laughter warmed her, and she'd found that nothing pleased her more than making him happy.

*What a man he is!* she said to herself as she hurried to make a pitcher of lemonade. *I may be headed for trouble, but I am definitely going to enjoy the ride. Wait until he discovers that my biggest client, Netta Cross, has the hots for him.* She'd learned that Netta had a big mouth, and everything the woman knew or imagined spilled out of it. The doorbell rang, and she raced to it.

He picked her up, swung her around and kissed her. She grabbed his hand and led him to her study.

"Hey," he said and stopped as they passed her bedroom. "So, that's what you wanted to do with those candles. Hmm. Interesting. I spent most of a night in there, and I didn't see a flicker, much less a candle."

"You came here to look at my sketches. They're in my study," she said, dragging him by the hand. "We're not going in there."

"You wound me. I only wanted to see what magic you

made with those candles. What did you think of the way we rearranged the store?"

"I have a few suggestions that I think you'll like. Check that out while I get us a glass of lemonade." She handed him the sketches and went downstairs to the kitchen.

"This is great," he said when she returned. "This way, most of the second lines will be on the seventh floor, and the remainder on a different side of the same floor as our regular lines."

"Yes, and all will be displayed in the attractive and elegant McCall settings."

"I won't try to thank you for this, but you know what it means to me that you're willing to help me. I want to go back and get started on this. Kiss me."

When she opened her arms to him, he rushed into them and held her. "For the first time in my memory, I don't feel lonely. My house still feels like an overfurnished mausoleum, but I no longer feel as if I don't belong to anyone. My grandfather has been wonderful to me, but he's from an age when there was rarely camaraderie between parents and children." Her fingers stroked his cheek, and she kissed his chin, adoring him and unashamed of it.

"I'll call you," he said as he left.

Having already decided that she didn't like her wealthy client, Netta Cross, she had to force patience with the woman.

"I want you to buy all of my furnishings at McCall's, and you're to let me see them before you purchase them. I'm talking everything. Do you happen to know what time Justin McCall is in the store? Well, you can find out," she went on, not waiting for an answer. "Make my appointments to check the purchases at a time when he's in the store." She waved her left index finger. "And don't forget to do that."

Deanna took her copy of their contract out of her briefcase and read that portion of it that specified the conditions under which the decorator was to purchase furnishings.

"I consult Ms. Cross only if I have doubts," she read, "and so far I don't have any doubts. I buy wholesale, and I'm having many things made to order. The more you interfere, the longer it will take me. I don't work with the kind of control you seem to want to impose."

"Please! I don't know a damned thing about decorating a house, which is why my place in Danvers is such a hodgepodge of this and that. But if you don't choose the furnishings at McCall's, I can't think of any other way I can get to see Justin McCall. Our families have been as tight as concrete all my life, but he's so detached. Like I'm not the only woman in this town who wants him, but my spies say he walks alone. And I don't believe he's gay, either." She stopped pacing the floor. "But I'd take him even if I knew he was. He's gorgeous."

*Thank goodness she talks so much that she doesn't know I haven't said one word.* "I always complete the downstairs before I start on the upper floors, Ms. Cross." Satisfied that she could proceed with her biggest account without interference, she went home and began sketching ideas. Netta's passion for Justin hardly crossed her mind. She could imagine Justin with other women, but Netta Cross was not one of them. Besides, he had an appetite for her, and she meant to make certain that his hunger increased.

Two mornings later, Justin walked into his office at McCall's minutes before his grandfather knocked on the door. "Come in. If you want an appointment, see my secretary in—" He looked up. "Granddad!" He rushed to his grandfather and embraced him. "It's great to see you. Sit down. Would you like some breakfast?"

"You're looking well yourself, son. In fact, you're looking exceptionally well, but we'll get into that later. I see that you went ahead and changed things here, but I tell you it looks great. Spectacular, I'd say." He crossed his knees and leaned back in the chair. "It's going to make a difference. I've been through every floor from here on down."

"I'm glad you're pleased, Granddad. I didn't want to go against you, but I knew this was right on principle. We just completed it last night."

"Who's plan is it? Yours or Duke's? I can't see Horton doing anything of this level."

"Deanna Lawford did it. Duke and I tried it and made a complete mess of things. Deanna asked me if I minded if she looked at it, and a few hours after she saw what we did, she designed what you see."

"Hmm. Who's Deanna?"

"She was Burton's decorator. Now she's got her own business. She's first class."

"I'll say she is. How about some fishing over on the sound this weekend? I haven't taken the boat out but once this summer, and it's getting close to Labor Day."

"I'd love to, but I…made other plans."

A smile creased the old man's weathered face. "Hmm. So now you've got secrets from your old granddad, huh? Well! I can't tell you how glad I am to see it. I expect you'll let me meet her one of these days?"

"Why are you so sure there's a woman involved?"

"First time I ever knew you to pass up a chance to take that boat out for a fishing jaunt. Nothing stays the same, son. The worst thing you can do is hold on to the past when it's time for a change. You just proved that with what you've done here in McCall's."

He phoned the dining room and asked a waiter to bring coffee, one with cup and saucer and the other in a mug. The coffee arrived with toasted bagels as he knew it would. He sipped the coffee, spread raspberry jam on his bagel and looked at his beloved grandfather.

"Yes, there is someone. We're getting closer." He told Robert McCall as much about the friendship as he wanted to know. "Now that she no longer works for Burton's, we have a chance."

"Seems to me she has integrity."

"Oh, she has that, and she's tender and…and loving. She's independent and strong-willed, too. I don't know. There's something about her."

"Yeah," Robert said. "And pretty damned clever, too. You left out that part. For the past five years, I've envied Burton's showrooms." He sipped the coffee and apparently enjoyed the toasted bagel and jam. "Success is being able to pick up the phone and tell somebody to bring you a cup of coffee. I'll get Jim to go fishing with me. We can take his boat. I'll be going."

After he left, Justin sent an ad to *The Woodmore Times* announcing the changes in McCall's along with a sale guaranteeing that his usual customers would put aside their antipathy to the idea. Robert McCall was a crafty man. As deeply as Justin felt for Deanna, their meeting would have to wait. When a man took his girl to meet his grandfather, marriage was the reason. He wasn't there yet, and whether he'd get there was still in question.

# Chapter 5

That weekend, shoppers clad in sneakers, T-shirts—many with baby carriages—crowded McCall's department store. The majority headed for the seventh floor, but many did not. Justin walked through the store marveling at what he saw: his regular customers shopped in their usual designer boutiques and seemed to pay no attention to the large crowd or to shopping among people they didn't usually meet.

"We've made some changes," he said to a long-time customer, "but you'll find Dior in the usual place."

"Yes, I did, and I got some great T-shirts on the seventh floor that were exactly what I need for gardening. They didn't cost much, so I bought them in different colors."

He walked on, satisfied that he'd done the right thing. Monday morning, he telephoned his grandfather and reported the heaviest one-day sale that McCall's had ever recorded.

"That crowd astonished me. Lines in the restaurant and at cashier stations on the first and seventh floors. I wish you could have seen it. How were the fish?"

"It rained over there, so the fish were really jumping.

Looks like the changes you made were overdue. That's great news."

"Yes, but the place would have been a disaster if Deanna hadn't reorganized it for me."

"I expect you're right. I want to meet that young lady. Invite her to lunch tomorrow. I ought to at least thank her."

"I'll ask her, Granddad, but she may have a lunchtime appointment. I'll let you know."

"McCall men have always known how to make women want to please them."

"Well, I'll be… Who would have thought it? I don't play games with Deanna. She's too important to me."

"Then she'll do as you ask because you're probably equally important to her. I'll see you at lunch tomorrow."

Justin hung up thinking that Robert McCall must have been quite a man in his youth. He telephoned Deanna.

"Hi. I was right to change the store, and your ideas proved to be just what we needed. McCall's had a rollicking success this past weekend. We've never had weekend sales like that. My grandfather wants to meet you and thank you. At least, I assume that's why he wants to meet you. He's a wonderful man, but I admit he can be cagey."

"When and what time?"

"He suggested tomorrow at noon."

"How old is he? In his eighties?"

"Eighty-seven."

"Then what he actually said was closer to, 'You bring her to meet me tomorrow at lunch.' Right? A man of his age and accomplishments is more likely to dictate than to ask."

He rested his head on the heel of his right hand and whooped. "Baby, you've nailed it. Will you come to the restaurant at twelve-thirty? Or I could be at your place at twelve and bring you to McCall's. I'd prefer that."

"I'll be at the home of a client, so I'll take a taxi and knock on your office door at around twelve twenty-five."

"Thanks. How about meeting me for a drink around five-thirty today?"

"Justin, you've seen me every day for the past two weeks."

"You don't want to see me?"

"I do, but I gotta clean my refrigerator *some* time." He told her he'd help her. "I'll bet you've never cleaned a refrigerator in your life."

"Well, I won't lie; I don't do it every day, but I have definitely done it."

"Okay. I'll let you help me. Where shall we meet and what time?"

Did he detect reluctance? "Well, if you'd rather not—"

"Hold it. If I'd rather not, you'd be the first to know. I'm longing to see you."

"I wish I could hug you. See you later."


That morning, Deanna debated the efficacy of looking feminine or businesslike for her meeting with the renowned Robert McCall. *I am who I am,* she said to herself and opted for a look somewhere in between. As a result, when she knocked on Justin's office door wearing a three-quarter sleeve, dusty-rose linen suit with the skirt skimming her knee and revealing a pair of prize-winning legs, his sharp whistle split the air. She had added to the effect by combing her hair down.

"Man, is Granddad going to get an eyeful," he said and wrapped her in his arms. "You're just in time. He's probably sitting at his favorite table in his private dining room."

They walked a few paces down the hall to the elevator and rode two flights up. "This isn't the dining room you took me to," she said. "How many do you have?"

"That was the executive dining room. This is Granddad's private dining room. He loves this place. See the balcony over there? That's his flower garden. Come on in. He a stickler for time."

The old man stood as they approached. If she had envisaged him as bent and toddling on a cane, she couldn't have been further off the mark. Robert McCall stood nearly as tall as his grandson, slim and immaculately dressed. "This is a genuine pleasure, Miss Lawford. I'd begun to think that Justin didn't plan to introduce us, so I told him to bring you to me. Thank you for coming."

She'd been right about one thing: the old man went after what he wanted, and he expected to get it. "Thank you for inviting me, sir. I'm bowled over. You're iconic in these parts and a real legend. This is such a pleasure."

Robert accepted the compliments as his due, called the waiter and they ordered their meal. "You did a great job with this store, Miss Lawford. It's already paying off. I was against the entire idea, but that just proves that I should stay out of it now, and let Justin handle it. He's CEO, and that's his job. Fortunately, he ignored me. Right now, I want you to consider working for McCall's."

She couldn't stifle the gasp. Why hadn't she realized that getting her to work for McCall's was the old man's reason for wanting to see her? She pushed back the furor that threatened to ruin the luncheon and glanced at Justin, who sat forward with his gaze penned to his grandfather.

"This was not my idea, Deanna," he said without glancing her way.

"I've just opened my own business, sir. I've already learned that the years I spent at Burton's raised Burton's status, but not mine. Unless I get very hungry, I don't plan to work for anyone but myself."

"Humph. You're obviously first class, so I can't blame you for wanting credit for what you do. Not to speak of the rewards in income. But you haven't heard the last of me. If the two of you worked together, no competition within a few hundred miles could match you, and you'd be happy doing it."

What on earth was he saying? A glance at Justin told her that he thought the old man had stepped over his bounds. She smiled her best smile and said, "I can't tell you how much I appreciate your opinion of my work, but I think we'd better leave things as they are."

"Yes," Justin said, standing. "Deanna has an appointment at two-thirty, and I promised to see that she's there on time. I'll call you this evening, Granddad." He didn't seem like the type of grandfather you should hug, so she walked around the table and kissed his cheek. "Thank you for a very tasty lunch. I'm glad we met."

"From what I'd been told, I expected a lot, Deanna. But you are much more."

She looked at Justin, but he didn't smile, and she realized that his grandfather might have displeased him. As he drove her back to her client's house, he said, "I'm sorry. I know he's cagey, but I never dreamed he'd ask you to work for McCall's. You didn't equivocate, and I admire you for that."

She patted his hand. "Don't worry, honey, I understand that he reaches far in order to get what's nearby. Reminds me of a Browning poem: "'A man's reach should exceed his grasp—'"

He completed it. "'Or what's a heaven for?'"

They arrived at the house in Danvers precisely at two-thirty. She told Justin that a couple had bought the house for their retiring cook and engaged her to decorate and furnish it. "I have to be sure not to include anything that could prove hazardous to a senior, no small area rugs, tile floors, low seating, that sort of thing. I love my client. She's sweet and motherly, and she seems to like my taste."

He pulled the strand of her hair that hung beside her ear. "That's because you've bothered to understand her and to learn what she likes and dislikes."

"I try." She had a sudden urge to move into his arms and let him hold her, but she couldn't do so unprofessional a thing while at work.

"I like what you're doing here," he said. "Maybe if my

house was less of a showplace and more of a warm and inviting home, I'd spend more time there."

Better not comment on that, she thought. "Thanks for the ride, hon. I'll see you later. Where are we meeting for the drink?"

"How about Pinky's? The Watering Hole will be crowded at that time."

"Okay. See you at Pinky's at five-thirty." She kissed him quickly and moved, for if she hadn't, he'd have started a fire.

She closed the door behind him, thinking that she was not going to decorate his house unless she was living in it. She almost fell up the stairs. Had she just decided that she wanted to marry Justin McCall? I must be out of my mind. He'll marry a woman who is as rich as he is, and I'd better..." She sat down midway up the stairs. It was too late. Much too late. She wanted him as much as she wanted to breathe.

Struggling under the impact of her moment of self-awareness, Deanna pulled herself up and lugged the sample rolls of wallpaper to the first bathroom. *This is the guest bathroom,* she said to herself. *It will have silver shells for wallpaper, all silver accessories and a brick-red carpet on the floor.* She made notes, then headed for the second bathroom for which she chose purple irises on a pale green background as wallpaper and purple accessories including the carpet. The woman had said that she loved purple and never got enough of it. Deanna planned to repeat the motif in the woman's bedroom.

She looked at her watch, dashed down the stairs, freshened up, phoned for a taxi and prayed that it would come immediately. She needed forty minutes. Justin waited for her at the bar in Pinky's Restaurant. He greeted her with a kiss on the mouth, and she managed not to let a single one of the patrons catch her eye. Woodmore would buzz with that gossip for days, and she knew that Justin did it intentionally. If he was making a statement, she wished he tell her what it was.

"Let's get a seat at that table over there," he said, pointing to a corner.

"If I continue to hang out with you, Justin, I'll learn to drink."

"You think so? I don't drink much."

"I know that, but I didn't drink at all, and I've learned to enjoy various kinds of white liquor as long as it's diluted with tonic and lime."

A grin played around his lips. "I'm scared to ask you what else you've learned to enjoy."

"That, too," she said and poured half of a vodka Collins down her throat. She wondered if the drink loosened her tongue when she said. "I don't like working for Netta Cross."

He sat forward as he had a habit of doing when someone suddenly raised a serious question, and an expression of concern settled on his face. "What's the problem?"

"She's got about as much depth as a teaspoon, and she wanted me to buy products at your store and let her examine them before I made a purchase. Further—now get this—she wanted me to insure that when she went to the store, you would be there."

*"What?"*

"You heard me. And she had the nerve to tell me that she wants you bad enough to have you even if you're gay. I didn't punch her. I didn't even say a word, though I damned sure don't know why."

"Get outta here! I'm not even sure what she looks like, but I know enough about her to know she's poison, and I learned it sitting at the bar in the Watering Hole. Did she pay you up front?"

"Half of it. According to our contract, the manufacturer sends her a bill for products, but he pays me my cut. That way, I don't have to hassle with her about the money."

"You're smart. By the time we have a second drink, we'll be hungry enough to eat dinner."

"You get a second. I'll nurse this one." She wanted to find

out if that night with him was what it seemed to be, and she wanted to be completely sober so as to enjoy every second of it.

As if he'd read her mind, he said, "One drink is just about enough considering what I have in mind for later. Besides, we'll have wine with our meal. My housekeeper complains that I'm never at home these days, and that she hasn't cooked dinner for me in two weeks. If I don't keep her happy, she might leave me. So, suppose you have dinner with me at my house tomorrow night. Okay?"

Was that ever a surprise. "I'd love it. I want to see how you live."

"I don't live there, Deanna. I stay there. I'm alive when I'm with you."

Half an hour after he walked into her house with her that evening, he lay buried deep inside of her, loving her senseless. She surrendered completely, and for hours after he left her, she remained there feeling as if she'd just mortgaged her soul. There had to be some changes.

Justin waited until the next morning to telephone his grandfather. Old age carried with it certain licenses, but there were limits.

"I'm surprised you didn't call last night," the old man said when he heard Justin's voice. "You're hot under the collar because I suggested that you and Deanna should get married and pool your businesses. I'll say it again, because I know I'm right. Besides, she's a lovely woman, soft, feminine and beautiful with a sharp mind. Did she give you a hard time?"

"She didn't mention it to me and I didn't bring it up to her. She isn't the type to fall for that, Granddad."

"Listen, you marry that girl. You're crazy about her, and she looked at you as if she'd seen you change the direction of the wind. She's the right one for you. My Adele used to look at me that way. Yeah. She could look at me like that, and I'd feel ten feet tall and bulletproof. Yep. Deanna's the one for you."

"How could you figure that out after being with her an hour and a half during which time you did most of the talking, Granddad?"

"I've lived a lot of years, son, forty-three of them with a happy woman. You've given Deanna Lawford a lot of pleasure and she shows it when she looks at you. Don't bother to answer."

What could he say, except that he prayed that Robert McCall knew what he was talking about? He believed he'd made her happy in bed, but what man knows that for certain?

"You know that you were meddling, Granddad, and you know I don't like that. I hope you realize that by doing that, you may have caused Deanna to raise some barriers that I wouldn't be able to surmount if I wanted to."

"Pshaw! If she lives for any length of time, she'll have McCall on her headstone when she's buried. If you can't manage it, I'll be glad to tell you how."

He couldn't help laughing then. His grandfather had enough polish for half a dozen men and no lack of women friends, but he also had a level head and guarded his money wisely.

"You claim that a man with money should stay single if he wants to keep it, but you seem to think I can have the money and the woman."

"That's because you had the sense to fall for one who doesn't care about your money. If she did, she would have knocked herself out pleasing me instead of telling me point blank an unequivocal no. She's not after your money. She plans to make her own."

"I know that."

"Well, you're thirty-four, and it's time you got married. You should be thinking about giving me some great-grandchildren while I'm still alive to see them. I won't live forever, you know."

"Loneliness in that big mausoleum I call home will prompt

me to get married before you do, Granddad. The moment I
realize it's what I want to do, you'll be the second to know.
I'll see you Tuesday as usual."

He hung up and called Deanna. He would have called her
first, but he knew she slept later than his grandfather. "How
are you, love?"

"Sleepy. I'm supposed to go over to the sound today, and I
dread it. The house is looking fantastic, but she may be there,
and she gets on my very last nerve."

"Can't you tune her out?"

"She's walking behind me with every step I take. It makes
me nervous, and I'm afraid I'll make some mistakes. I'm
thinking of taking Cain along with me, although there isn't
much for him to do there at this stage. But he's young and
good-looking, and he's great at buttering female egos. He can
do that while I work."

"Go ahead. It may work. Remember, you're having dinner
at my home today. I'll be at your place at six-thirty. It'll be a
long day, baby. I feel as if I've been away from you for weeks.
Crazy, isn't it, but you're growing on me like moss on a great
oak. Kiss me, and let me get dressed. Lizzie probably has my
breakfast ready. I can smell the coffee."

"Who is Lizzie?"

"My housekeeper. I'll tell her you asked," he added with a
laugh. "Stay sweet for me."

"And you stay sweet for me."


Deanna had not imagined what Justin's house would be like.
Indeed, she had rarely ventured into the area in which he lived,
although she knew that the wealthier citizens of Woodmore
lived either close to Pine Tree Park or Wade Lake. They
approached the imposing structure shortly before twilight,
in the cool and brisk air of the first day of September, which
heralded a chilly autumn. The surrounding trees seemed a
part of the house, proud and stately, as if they had been built

along with it. He drove around the house to the garage, which sat well back from the street, almost behind the house.

When she asked him about it, he explained, "I had never liked the idea of a garage hooked on to the front of a house, so I built it this way, and I like it. This walkway shields me from the elements," he said of the covered, glass-paneled tunnel that connected the garage to the house.

They entered a hallway and, once inside, he closed the door, bent down, kissed her and said, "Welcome to my home."

She wouldn't call it a mausoleum as he had, but it certainly lacked warmth. "I furnished this rather like the house in which I grew up, since it remains one of the few houses with which I'm familiar." Rich Persian carpets adorned the dining and living room floors. She sat in the tufted velvet sofa, which had matching chairs, and looked around. Yes, she would be lonely there. Very lonely.

A tall woman of around sixty came into the living room with hot hors d'oeuvres and greeted them. "Good evening, y'all. I thought you'd gotten lost."

"We're ten minutes late, Lizzie." He stood. "Ms. Lawford, this is Mrs. Palmer."

"I'm glad to meet you, Ms. Palmer," Deanna said, and added. "I assume your first name is Lizzie, since Justin told me that a person by that name takes care of him."

"I'm glad to say that it is, because I can guess how much trouble he'd be in if I said my name was Claire or something like that. It's a pleasure to meet you, Ms. Lawford." She looked at Justin. "Would you like some ice?"

"Thank you. That would be nice." He went to a large wall unit and opened a door that revealed a variety of liquors and liqueurs. "Gin and tonic?" Deanna nodded. "I'll have the same."

Lizzie brought the ice, and he mixed the drinks. "This is the first time I've used this bar in months. I don't drink alone. I'll have a beer or some wine with my meals, but that about does it."

She wanted to ask him if he was lonely at home, but he might give that the wrong meaning. So she asked him, "Where do you spend most of your time when you're home?"

"As I think of it, I mainly sleep here. Otherwise, I eat breakfast in the kitchen and work in my study. I have a movie theater downstairs, but I've used it once, because Granddad wanted to see 'The Russians Are Coming, The Russians Are Coming.' I guess I prefer being around people."

She sampled a tiny empanada. "If the dinner is going to be anywhere near this good, I'd better not eat any more of these."

"I'll tell her to wrap some for you to take home. A person could get addicted to those things. While we're waiting for dinner, let me show you the back garden. It's faded now compared to what it was in June and July, but it's still lovely."

He took her hand, walked down the hall in which they came and out to the garden on the left side of the garage. Through the tall trees beyond, she could see red, yellow and gold streaks decorating the sky in homage to the sun that had already set.

"It's so beautiful here, Justin, and so quiet. All I hear is the rustling of the trees. Is it always like this?"

"Yes. I'm at the end of this cul-de-sac, so unless someone is coming to see me, no one comes this far down, and there are no dogs in this area."

"Do you tend the garden yourself? It's beautiful, and I especially like those French marigolds and the calendula. I love autumn colors."

"So do I," he said, as darkness encroached and fireflies emerged. His arm slid around her waist. "The more I'm with you, the more I want to be with you." He gazed into her eyes, but she couldn't divine his feelings. "Let's go inside," he said as if he'd experienced a change of mood or had exposed too much of his inner self. But she didn't care. She was getting to him, and since she had decided that she wanted him, his being confused did not bother her.

They sat down to an elegant meal of salmon en croute, saddle of veal, tiny roasted potatoes, broccoli rabe, green salad and for dessert, vanilla ice cream with raspberry sauce and whipped cream. They sipped espresso later in the living room.

Suddenly, as if on an impulse, he leaned to her and said, "I could really enjoy my home if you were in it."

She nearly spilled the coffee, but she was glad she had the presence of mind merely to smile, put the coffee cup aside and snuggle closer to him. If he wanted a response from her, he had to ask the right question. Later, when he took her home, his long, drugging kiss rocked her, and she had to fight to keep her wits.

"Thank you for taking me home with you. I loved being in your private world. It was a very special evening for me, Justin. And I mean that. If Mrs. Palmer hadn't left, I would have given her my thanks. Please thank her for me". She stood on tiptoe, parted her lips and received his kiss. His possessiveness stunned her, and it cost her a lot of willpower to behave as if he wasn't acting out of character. She understood that he wanted more, but was not ready to ask for it. Fine with her; she was a patient woman.

Several days later, Deanna looked at the invitation in her hand. Ms. Netta Cross requested the pleasure of her company at a housewarming, etc. Of course, the woman wanted to show off her house and her decorator. *I couldn't say no if I wanted to, and I plan to fill my handbag with business cards. If this doesn't get me a few contracts, nothing will. I'm doing well, but if this works out, I can hire an assistant decorator. Ms. Cross is using me, so I'm sure she won't mind if I do the same.*

Justin's call saying that he had a similar invitation from Netta Cross surprised her, and she told him as much.

"I suggest we go together," he said, "and in that way she'll understand that she doesn't and will not interest me."

"I have a feeling that the woman's brain doesn't operate like that of a normal person, but I'll be delighted to go with you."

The mid-September Saturday afternoon of Netta's housewarming party arrived. Knowing the house and Netta, and in view of the 82-degree weather, Deanna arrived wearing a rose-colored, mid-calf chiffon dress, matching hat and white gloves.

When Netta opened the door, a gasp escaped her. However, she quickly recovered her aplomb, looked from Deanna to Justin. "How nice. Where did you two bump into each other? Come on in." She took Justin's arm. "It's so good of you to come. Deanna's an excellent decorator. Of course, she used my ideas."

Justin removed Netta's hand from his arm. "Thank you for the invitation, Ms. Cross. We need to get this one thing straight. I did not bump into Deanna. I've been courting her for the last six months, and I've just begun to make some headway with her."

"You're lying," she shrieked and turned to Justin. "She told you a lot of things about me and what I said about you." Several people gathered near. "How could you?" she said to Deanna.

"You felt free to talk to the hired help about your personal business, and I listened. I had no choice. And you did not give me a single idea for the decoration of this house."

"You're lying," she screamed. "You told him what I said; otherwise he wouldn't look at you. Come on, Justin. I want you to meet my other guests."

"I don't know when I've been so shocked," he said. "You insult my date and expect me to walk off with you and leave her standing here? Deanna Lawford is my reason for living."

Netta stamped her feet, whirled and strode through

the crowd that had gathered to witness the scene. He took Deanna's arm. "I'd give anything if I could have spared you this—"

"Humiliation," she said. "Let's go. At least she's paid all of her bills, and I no longer have any reason to contact her."

"You look beautiful, and that was enough to upset that woman." He took out his cell phone and called for a cab. "I learned a lot during that fracas." A taxi arrived immediately, and they headed back to the airport. "Now, to get an early flight," he said in a casual tone, but she knew him well enough now to know that the incident at Netta's house had distressed him. "Wait here while I see what we can get," he told her in the airport.

She thought she would burst from having to control her anger. "I'll fix that woman. She'll have to eat her lies, because I'm going to put an ad in *The Woodmore Times* stating that I decorated her house along with the others I've done."

Justin walked back to her. "We have an hour and a half wait. I thought it would be worse." He patted her knee. "Don't let it bother you. There's a reason why she's building a house like that for herself when she already has a big one."

*How does he know she has another house and that it's a big one, and why was she so proprietary with him?* She told herself not to think such things. But what *was* she to think? He said he didn't want her with another man, but he didn't commit to her. She was taking nothing for granted. She loved him, but he hadn't told how he felt about her, so she had to keep how she felt to herself. But when he'd made love to her the previous night, she'd wanted to yell at the top of her lungs how much she loved him. *Never will I be captive to my feelings,* she said to herself and prayed she could keep that vow.

"You're withdrawn, Deanna, and if you'll tell me what I did to bring this about, I'll try to set things straight."

"That woman behaved as if she'd been your constant companion for years. I was mortified."

"You can't be serious. Are you suggesting that there is

or ever has been anything whatever between me and Netta Cross?"

*Watch it, girl.* "No. I am not suggesting that. I'm just…just miserable is all."

"Deanna, if she hadn't opened her door, I wouldn't have known who she was. In fact, I didn't address her until I was certain as to who she was. Can you imagine me spending any time in the company of such a shrew? Give me credit for better taste."

"I'm not accusing you, Justin. I'm… Oh, I don't know. I wish I'd never seen her."

At the flight call, he handed her her ticket, put an arm around her waist and headed for the gate. They seated themselves, and she rested her head on his shoulder, relishing the comfort of his nearness.

"That's right, you're not comfortable flying." He got up, walked toward the back of the plane and returned. "I thought I'd get you a blanket. It's very chilly in here. He removed his jacket and put it around her shoulders."

"Won't you be cold?"

"I don't mind for myself, but I don't want you to be uncomfortable."

She removed the jacket and snuggled into his arms. "I don't want you to be cold, Justin."

He put the jacket around her shoulders and brought her back into his arms. "I want you to be comfortable. I need to take care of you, and if that means I'm cold, I don't mind it."

She kissed his chin. "I need to look after you, too." What she didn't say that came to her mind was that instead, Lizzie Palmer had the job of looking after him. His arms tightened around her, and she told herself that he said positive things about their relationship first to Netta and now to her, and that he was not a man to take a serious step unless he weighed every angle. *Besides, he's only known you six months.*

When they reached the exit in the Woodmore airport, rain came down in torrents. "Wait here while I get the car."

"But it isn't far," she said. "I'll go with you, and you won't have to circle the airport to get back here and circle it again to get out."

"What did I tell you right after we boarded the plane? If I didn't want you to get cold, why would I let you get drenched in order to save me ten minutes?" He grasped both of her shoulders. "It's time you and I got on the same page."

Where was this headed, she wondered, but she wouldn't question him about it. He'd said he learned a lot during their five-minute visit to Netta Cross's house. She wished he'd let her in on it. She handed him her umbrella.

"I stand corrected, sir." She added the *sir* to lessen the gravity of the moment.

The rain had tapered off by the time they reached her house. "Look at that," he said. "Too bad. I love the crepe myrtles, and when the flowers begin to drop, I know cold weather is on the way. Do you like them? I'm planning to put some around the front of my house and at the edge of the woods."

"Yes. I love them, and I set out a pair in my front garden, but I put them out too early and they died."

"You can enjoy mine," he said without looking at her.

"Would you like to come in?"

"Yes, but only for a short while. I want to discuss something with you."

"In that case, why don't I make us a crab salad, slice a tomato, toast some bread and open a bottle of beer? We can have some blueberry blintzes for dessert. I'll heat them in the microwave oven."

"If you can do all that while wearing that lovely dress, I'd say it's a good idea."

She removed her hat and gloves, combed her hair, added more crabmeat to the salad she made the night before. She remembered the leftover peas and added those along with chopped scallion, peeled and sliced a couple of tomatoes, put the crab salad on red leaf lettuce along with the tomatoes. She glanced up and saw Justin leaning against the doorjamb.

"Your movements are so gracious. Let's eat in here. I'll set the table."

They'd nearly finished eating, and hadn't discussed anything in particular, so she decided to cut to the chase. "What did you want us to discuss? It's driving me nuts waiting."

He leaned back and looked at her. "Do you trust me enough to spend a weekend at my place on Nags Head with me? Just the two of us?" He seemed to hold his breath.

"Of course I do. I didn't know you had a place other than your house on Butler Street. Sounds like a lovely idea. When did you have in mind?"

"This coming weekend."

"Oh. Okay. I suppose it will be cooler there?"

"Yes. And I have a boat over there. So prepare for that. I'll look forward to our being there. We'll have a wonderful time."

"I can hardly wait."

# Chapter 6

Deanna hadn't spoken with her stepsister in almost six months, not since Jenny, as Jennyse was called, went on a religious retreat to the Ivory Coast in West Africa. They had corresponded by mail, but she hadn't expected Jenny back until mid-October.

"Jenny, darling, this is such a wonderful surprise. Is everything all right? Let's meet for coffee or something and talk."

"I've got so much to tell you. What about Friday evening? It'll take me a couple of days to open up my place, buy some food and get settled. It's as if I've forgotten how to negotiate life in a developed country. Oh, Deanna, I met a man, and he's wonderful."

"Whoa! Is he African, a preacher, an American or what?"

"This gorgeous brother was born in St. Louis, Missouri, and if I'm still crazy about him three months from now, I'll be headed for St. Louis. He is definitely not a preacher."

"I wish we could meet Friday evening, but I'm…uh, going away for the weekend."

"Tell me more, sis. You going solo? Lord, I sure hope not."

"I'll be over on the Outer Banks with Justin McCall."

"*The* McCall? You're not serious. What's going on since I left here?"

"Simple. I fell in love with him."

In her mind's eye, she saw Jenny's hands lock on her hip bones as she gazed toward the heavens. "Girl, you get outta here! You're going to spend a weekend with him? Does he know that premarital hanky-panky is against your morals?"

"Yeah. I've impressed that upon him each time he's made love with me."

She imagined that Jenny's neighbors heard her whoop. "I wasn't gone but six months, and look what we have. What else is new?"

"I've formed my own company, and I'm doing good, as they say."

"Congratulations, I always thought you were too good for Burton's. That store didn't even promote you. Let's get together Monday evening…unless you'll be too tired."

"Mind how you speak to your elder. Let's meet at Pinky's for dinner..say six-thirty."

"I'll be there. Make the most of your weekend. Love ya."

"Love you, too, sis."

Deanna hung up, thumbed through her mail, saw a letter from a hotel chain and tossed it aside along with other advertisements. She'd glance at them later. Occasionally, such letters announced a private sale, which she preferred to big public sales. She laid out the clothes she'd take with her to Nags Head on the Outer Banks, finished her sketches for Lougenia's living and dining rooms and placed the orders with her suppliers. Deanna knew the woman would enjoy her retirement in that beautiful home the Motleys bought for her, because Deanna had furnished it with every convenience available for an older person.

Friday morning finally arrived, and Deanna awoke at the crack of dawn. She had been able to sleep only intermittently. Justin had said that he'd be at her place at nine o'clock. What was she to do with herself for the next three hours? A shower took ten minutes, and fifteen minutes later, she was ready to leave the house.

*Slow down, girl. You may be heading for a disappointment.* "I don't believe that," she said aloud, brought her weekend bag down the stairs and put it in the foyer. "I could make some biscuits. No, I'd better make popovers. There isn't much of a chance that I could ruin those." She started to mix the batter and stopped. "Maybe I should just fix us some breakfast."

She telephoned him. "Tell Mrs. Palmer to skip the breakfast. I'll feed you this morning." She wondered what he found so amusing that he laughed until he could barely catch his breath.

"Listen, honey. I was counting on that. I gave Lizzie the rest of the weekend off. If you don't feel like cooking, we can stop at the IHOP or some place like that."

"Hmm. Whenever you make plans for me, hon, it's best to let me in on them. I didn't think about breakfast until a minute ago. Try to get here before nine."

"As anxious as I am to start this day, you don't have to ask twice. Give me thirty minutes."

She put some fresh sage sausage in the frying pan, turned the waffle iron on and put the water on to boil. "If he doesn't like fresh pineapple, he can have grapefruit juice. That's all I have." She set the kitchen table, mixed the waffle batter and looked at the clock. Three minutes to go. She started the coffee to dripping, poured batter into the waffle iron and headed for the front door. He rang as she reached for the doorknob.

"We've got this thing synchronized to perfection," he said, lifting her and swinging her around.

She kissed him on the mouth and pulled away. "Wash your

hands and let's eat. If we start the heavy stuff, who knows when we'll leave here."

"Gotcha," he said and headed for the powder room.

"This is wonderful," he said of the food. "And this coffee is great."

"I use the best dark-roast Columbia coffee that I can get. Anybody can measure water and ground coffee."

He savored a sip. "That's what you think. I once had a cook whose coffee was so thin you could read a newspaper beneath a glass full of it."

"Methinks you're fibbing."

"Not by much." He put the dishes in the dishwasher, washed the frying pan and turned out the kitchen lights. "Let's go, baby. We've got a three-and-a-half hour drive ahead of us, provided I don't run into heavy traffic. Say, bring some of your jazz CDs."

"I'm way ahead of you," she said and closed and locked the door. As they walked to his car, she said a silent prayer. When she returned to her house, she'd either be way up or way down.

He made the trip in three hours and seventeen minutes. "That's because we didn't stop," he said, "and you must be exhausted."

She assured him that she wasn't, got out of the car and looked around. "Gosh, you can see water everywhere."

"From every window in the house. That's my granddad's place on that corner, and of the property in between our houses, mine stops where that tennis court begins."

"Does he still play tennis?"

"You bet. Every day he's here. My boat's docked on the other side. Let's go inside."

She walked through the rooms, airy and spacious, but she knew that her favorite place there would probably be the sun-filled plant solarium, a large room off the dining room. "This is exquisite," she told him when he joined her. "How do you take care of it when you're in Woodmore most of the time?"

"This was the breakfast room, but I prefer to eat in the kitchen or, if I have guests, in the dining room. I love plants and flowers, so I turned this room into a solarium and put in a watering system for when I'm away. Come, and I'll show you your room. I thought we'd have a cookout for dinner and take the boat out tomorrow morning. We can have turkey sandwiches and leek soup for lunch, or if you don't want—"

She stopped him. "I eat everything except brains and chitterlings, so I'll enjoy whatever else you've got. Please don't think I have to eat gourmet food. I like it when I get it, but I definitely was not raised on it. Collards and black-eyed peas can make me very happy."

"I'll tell Lizzie that, but she won't cook it."

"Then, I'll cook you some," she said, "but I'll need a couple of smoked pig knuckles."

"You're in business. I'll dock the boat at Kitty Hawk tomorrow, and we'll get some. I love simple food." His gaze locked on her, and she saw the heat begin to rise.

"Show me the rest of the house," she said quickly, because she didn't want their weekend to begin with lovemaking.

"Later. Right now, I'd better feed you."

"You didn't make this soup," she said. "Not that you couldn't. It's wonderful."

"Lizzie made it. I'll clean the kitchen while you unpack." A gasp escaped her when she walked into her room. White walls, furniture, curtains and carpet, interrupted only by the lavender spread of silk taffeta. The window, as wide as the large room, revealed the Atlantic Ocean with its dancing waves as far as she could see.

She whirled around, saw him slouched against the doorjamb looking at her. And ran to him. "Hold me, Justin. Just hold me. This is…it's so beautiful, so special that it's overwhelming."

"Do you like it?"

"Yes. It's…idyllic." He held her tighter. "It's wonderful, but I don't see how you can bear to be here alone."

"That's why I'm so seldom here unless Granddad's at his place. I never realized what it meant to be alone until I met you. I liked my company, and I enjoyed listening to music, reading and working, and that was enough. Yes, there was someone, but she wanted me to dance to her tune without regard for what I wanted and needed, so after a time, I said goodbye. When I saw you, something happened to me." He kissed her forehead. "At that moment, you were so unhappy, and you needed me in a way that no one else had. When you looked at me, I knew you felt what I felt, and I had no intention of letting you get away from me. You tried, but even if I hadn't seen you at that convention, I knew where to find you, and I meant to see if the feeling was real."

"I did like you on sight, Justin, but I thought you were a player with women swarming all over you, so I decided you were not for me. I watched you at the convention, and you didn't seem that way at all." She rubbed his nose. "But you have a way with words, and you have a short fuse, too."

"Maybe, but I'm always able to control my temper, so I'm never tempted to embarrass myself."

She kissed his jaw and then rested her head against his shoulder. "That's my standard, too, and I may live up to it if I don't meet too many like Netta Cross."

"She has no place in our life, Deanna. I need to get the marine forecast, so I'll know which side of the house to put the outdoor grill. It's sometimes very windy."

He had to get away from her in that setting. It hadn't occurred to him that being alone with her in his house meant having to protect her from his ravenous libido. He went to his room, grabbed a pair of bathing trunks and headed for the sound; the Atlantic would be too cold for swimming, especially so late in the day. Thinking that she might want to swim, he went back to Deanna's room and knocked on the door.

"I'm going for a swim in the sound," he told her. "The water will be rather chilly, so I suggest you swim midday. But if you want to swim now, I'll wait for you."

"Go ahead. I'll wait till tomorrow. Please don't stay too long."

The hell with it. He strode into the room, lifted her and locked her to his body. "Kiss me. Make me know that you care for me."

She sucked his tongue into her mouth, savored it and suddenly locked her legs around his hips. He bulged against her.

"That wasn't my intention, baby, but I wanted you so badly. Look, I'll be back in a few minutes." He raced down the stairs and out the side door to the sound. To his disgust, the cold water did nothing for the wild desire that had come upon him. "Dammit, I'll deal with it," he said to himself and released another expletive as he headed back to the house.

After a shower and a change of clothing, he felt better and was able to laugh at himself. "If I were a teenager, my nonsense would be more acceptable." He checked the marine forecast and set up the grill on the side of the house facing the Atlantic.

"We'll be able to see the sunset," he told her when she joined him. "It's strange how I manage to ignore all the wonders of this environment. I haven't watched the sunset here but once since I had the place built. I saw it from my bedroom window. It was awesome."

"If you ever retire, would you retire here or in Woodmore?"

He stopped brushing oil on the grill. "I haven't given that serious thought. I think I'd retire wherever the woman who loved me and who I loved wanted to live. As long as she was happy, I know I would be."

He tried to read her facial expression, but couldn't. "If you had the choice, what would you do?"

"I imagine it's very cold here in winter, so I'd probably live here from early spring till autumn and stay somewhere else in winter. At Thanksgiving and Christmas, I love the crisp weather and especially the snow."

He got two brown rattan chairs from the garage, set them near the aluminum grill facing the ocean and the rapidly approaching sunset and beckoned her to sit down. He put a low bench near the chairs, got two glasses of white Burgundy wine and handed one to her. He crossed his knees and leaned back in the chair, and when her fingers curled around the fingers of his left hand, he closed his eyes and let peace flow over him.

*This is right. For the first time in my life, I know I'm in a state of grace. This is it, and I want it for all time. I don't miss anyone or anything. She's all I want and all I need. I could lose McCall's, and I'd fret about it for a time, then buckle down and build it up again. But if I lost her, I'd be eternally devastated, and nothing, including McCall's, would mean anything to me.*

"Look!" she said. "Just look at that."

The sun had become a huge red disk that seemed to hang by an invisible thread that gently lowered it into the swirling Atlantic. For a minute, it hung seemingly perilously at the edge of the horizon and then dropped into the ocean, leaving behind streaks of red, orange, gray, blue and yellow on the most beautiful sky he'd ever seen.

"It's breathtaking," she whispered.

He reached over, picked her up and sat her in his lap. "Yes. Maybe it's like this tonight because we're together. I can't believe I never take the time to watch it."

"Maybe you needed company."

"No doubt about it," he said, and she didn't know how right she was. "I'm going to put the meat and potatoes on to roast. It only takes the vegetables a few minutes."

"What can I do to help?"

"I don't want you to do anything. Just be here with me."

As they ate, she watched the moon emerge as if it had been buried in the bowels of the ocean. As it cast its long ray of light, she could see the waves undulating beneath it like a woman beneath her lover. She heard herself utter the unimaginable: "Those waves are making mad love to the moon."

"Yeah. Undulating is the word for it. I never thought about it before, but I can imagine what some poets have done with this scene. It's pretty cool. Do you want to go in?"

"Okay," she said. "Let's put the chairs and the grill away, I'll get out some of the CDs I brought along and we can listen to some music."

After that sunset, she was not in the mood for any wild music, so she chose some CDs of old Teddy Wilson, Benny Goodman and Duke Ellington recordings and headed back downstairs. She wanted to spend the night in his bed, but she was playing for high stakes. Should she postpone that for Saturday night? She knew he was like a firecracker, and she was pretty close to exploding herself, but...

"I'm on my way," she said when he called her.

He played Teddy Wilson, walked over to her and said, "I want to dance with you." She didn't look into his eyes, for she knew what hers would tell him. He didn't stop until the last piece finished. She looked at him, and the hunger in his eyes shook her until she reached out to him in order to steady herself.

*He only wants what I want,* she said to herself, took his hand, made her way up the stairs and led him to her room door. "Do you want to come in?"

"Are you sure? Do you want me?"

"You know I do."

He picked her up, kicked the door shut behind them and, with the moon for their only light, he stripped away their clothes. As they stood together holding each other, nude, he said, "I have more worldly possessions than any man needs, but if you won't share my life, it will be meaningless."

She needed to hear it in plain, first-grade English. "I am sharing your life."

"But not to the extent that I want you to and that I need."

She moved slightly, and the hairs on his chest tickled her nipple and she rubbed it. "Let me do that," he said, widening his stance, lifting her to him and sucking the nipple into his mouth. She stroked and squeezed him, and he suckled her while moving against her until screams erupted from her throat.

He'd done all kinds of things to her, but he'd never positioned her on the edge of the bed and made love to her while standing above her. Minutes after they both exploded in orgasm, he lay on his back, raised his knees, positioned her above him and taught her how to guarantee her satisfaction.

"I love you, Deanna. You're my life. Tell me you love me," he said, when she was nearing completion. "I need you to love me. Do you? Do you love me?"

She tried to hold back, but when she exploded all around him, she shouted his name. "Yes, I love you. I loved you from the start."

"Sweetheart, I love you so much," he said and gave himself to her as she knew he'd never done before.

"I'm yours," he said quietly and matter-of-factly. "And I will always be. Will you marry me and be the mother of our children?"

She hugged him. "What will I say when our daughter asks me where I was when you asked me to marry you?"

"You can tell her Nags Head. You don't have to tell her what you were doing."

"But suppose she asks what I was doing."

"Tell her we were addressing some important issues." He moved her from him, knelt at the side of the bed and asked her again. "Will you be my wife?"

"It will be the greatest honor of my life, Justin. Yes."

A grin lit up his face. "There was a time when I thought the word yes wasn't in your vocabulary. I'll spend the rest of my life doing my best to make you happy and to take good care of you and our children."

"I'm only good for three, Justin."

"Three what?"

"Children. Three's enough."

"Fine with me. I just want a family." He got back into the bed, gathered her into his arms and loved her until they were spent and their bodies lie useless and entwined like a heap of used and discarded furniture.

She awakened the next morning to the smell of coffee when he put a breakfast tray on the night table beside her bed. He leaned over and kissed her.

"Good morning, love. Did you sleep well?"

"Best sleep I ever had. You're spoiling me, and I love it."

"It's my pleasure. Your rings are in a safe deposit box in Danvers. I'll get them Monday."

"Gosh. I hadn't remembered. That's right, I'm supposed to stick my left hand out for everyone to see. I have a dinner date with my stepsister Monday evening. She's just back from six months in the Ivory Coast where she fell in love, and we have a million things to talk about."

"Can we meet Tuesday at lunchtime? I want to seal our commitment as soon as possible."

"Of course, but as far as I'm concerned, it is sealed."

After the happiest three days of her life, Justin kissed her goodbye in the foyer of her house at around seven that Sunday evening. The house looked the same as she'd left it, but it didn't *seem* real. It would take her a while to get used to the fact that she was engaged to marry Justin McCall.

Justin walked into his big, sprawling house, turned on the foyer lights, dropped his weekend bag and his euphoria seeped out of him like liquid through a sieve. He didn't see how he could bear being away from her, being lonely in that big house after having been with her twenty-four hours a day. She filled his life so completely and so perfectly.

"What the hell. I've been alone for most of my thirty-four years, but now that I know that a life with her awaits me, I can tough it out for a couple more months. At least I know she's mine and that she loves me."

Deanna arose early the next morning anxious to greet the day. She didn't walk, but tripped around her house with the spring of new life and new hope permeating her being. She answered the phone at eight o'clock, knowing she'd hear Justin's voice. And after a breakfast of coffee, toast and juice, she sat down to go through her mail. She picked up the letter from Dupree Hotels, was about to throw it into the wastebasket, changed her mind and opened it.

A gasp escaped her, and she nearly lost her breath. It was not an advertisement, but an offer for a contract to decorate the new, high-rise hotel being built in downtown Woodmore, a hotel that would aim for a four- to five-star rating. She shouted and whooped. A phone call to Justin went unanswered. So she telephoned the builders of the Dupree Hotel, said she was interested and a few minutes later was on her way to Fifth Street and Court House Square to meet the builders.

"We want this hotel to be the best in Woodmore," the builder told her, "and we want its interior design to guarantee that it stays that way. That means its furnishings will be elegant and subdued."

She looked the man in the eye. "That costs money."

"And we're willing to spend it. We have one caveat: You must buy everything wholesale. I can give you the names of some linen suppliers, but you don't have to use them. We know your work, and we're willing to give you a contract."

She glanced over the contract that he handed her. "You have twelve floors and a penthouse of guest rooms. I suggest three different patterns for the twelve floors and a different

one for the penthouse. The three patterns would alternate. If
you like that idea, I'll let my lawyer go over this contract and
I'll bring it back tomorrow morning."

"Wonderful, Ms. Lawford. What about tomorrow morning
at nine right here?"

She agreed, thanked them and left. Not in her wildest
dreams had she contemplated such good fortune. After her
lawyer corrected two strategic points, she signed the contract.
Where was Justin, and why didn't he answer his cell phone?
She was boiling over with joy, wanted to share her good
fortune with him, and he was nowhere to be found.

"Mr. McCall is in Danvers today," his secretary told her.

"He doesn't answer his cell phone, so—"

"I suppose he doesn't want to be disturbed. Is there a
message?"

"No," Deanna said, imagining the delight of wringing the
woman's neck.

She met Jennyse, her stepsister, for dinner and enjoyed a
loving embrace with her. "Jenny, a million things happened to
me since we spoke Thursday. Justin asked me to marry him,
and I get my ring at lunch tomorrow. And would you believe
I'm going to decorate that new Dupree Hotel?"

"Slow down, girl. *You're engaged to Justin McCall?*"

"He's wonderful, and oh, Jenny, I'm nuts about him."

"I said I was going to give up all forms of alcohol but,
girl, this calls for champagne." She signaled for the waiter.
"Now tell me about this hotel contract. Did you show it to a
lawyer?"

Deanna nodded. "Oh, Lord, I just remembered something.
This could cause a problem. If I hadn't started my company,
McCall's would have gotten this contract."

The waiter opened the champagne and filled their glasses.
"Here's to you, sis," Jennyse said.

"And here's to you and happiness with your new love, sis,"
Deanna replied.

"I wouldn't worry about McCall's," Jennyse told her. "If the guy loves you and you're marrying him, it's all in the family."

Jennyse could not have been further from the truth. "Great," Justin said Tuesday morning, when she spoke with him on the phone. "That's a huge job. I hate to lose it, but since you'll be buying the furnishings through McCall's, we won't be out too much."

She could feel icy prickles on her back, arms and legs. This was not going to be pleasant. No point in procrastinating. She took a deep breath. "Justin, my contract requires that I buy everything wholesale."

"*What? What did you say?* You take a job that would normally go to McCall's and then you sign a contract that says you will not buy even a string from me. How could you do such a thing? You're undermining my—"

She didn't want to hear another word. "Justin, we'd better hang up before we say some hurtful things. I don't accept your castigating me as if you didn't know how decorators work. Let's talk another time."

"Another time? You tell me you love me, and then you—"

"Don't say it. Just hang up. We'll talk when you cool off. That is, if you ever do."

She hung up without waiting to hear more. He knew well that no decorator worth his or her earnings would buy from a department store or any other retail operation. After pacing the floor for fifteen minutes, she picked up a porcelain vase and tossed it across the room, striking the corner of her dresser and breaking the vase into smithereens.

"Damned if I'll cry."

Maybe she'd never wear the ring that was purchased for Justin's grandmother and which she wore. And maybe she wouldn't live as long as Justin's grandmother lived. Such was life. It wouldn't kill her. One thing was certain: when she finished with Woodmore's Dupree Hotel, not even the great Oriental Hotel in Bangkok, Thailand would outshine it. Sleep was a long time coming.

In his office later that day, Justin answered the telephone. "Yes!" If he sounded angry, he didn't care, because he *was* angry.

"Who got the better of you? That's no way to greet customers. I assume you'll be over for dinner tonight as usual. Cook said to tell you she's having roast pork and that jalapeño corn bread you like."

"Really? Ask her to cook some collards southern-style."

"I'll do that, and you get whatever's ailing you straightened out."

Fat chance. If she'd signed the contract, it was a done deal. He opened his desk drawer, picked up the red velvet box, opened it and gazed at the fiery two and three-quarter carat diamond ring flanked by two one-carat diamonds. His grandfather gave him the engagement ring and the matching wedding band when his grandmother died, and he had never seen a woman other than Deanna to whom he wanted to give it. He locked his desk drawer and dropped the key into the vest pocket of his jacket. Maybe it wasn't meant to be. But it hurt. He felt as if he'd die.

Justin didn't want to go to his grandfather's home for dinner that evening, but it was Tuesday, and from the time he left home to live on his own, he'd had dinner every Tuesday night with his granddad. He didn't want to talk about Deanna, but the old man was like a riveter; he kept digging until he got to his target.

He arrived promptly at seven that evening with a bottle of Courvoisier VSOP Napoleon cognac for his granddad and a bunch of yellow roses for Wilma, who his grandfather called Cook.

"Good!" Robert McCall said when he saw the cognac. "Nothing's better than a good brandy after a fine meal. We'll have some." His grandfather didn't discuss anything of serious importance while eating, so Justin knew he'd have to wait until after the meal to hear what his grandfather would have to say about McCall's losing the hotel contract.

Justin kissed Wilma's forehead as they left the dining room. "That meal really hit the spot." He followed his grandfather into the living room, waited for him to sit down and leaned forward. "Granddad, this past weekend, I asked Deanna to marry me, and yesterday, I got Gramma's ring out of the vault to give to her."

"Well, now that really calls for a toast. She's a fine woman, and I liked her the minute I saw her. Is she planning to give me any great-grandchildren?"

"Don't move so fast, Granddad. That's not the end of the story." Robert's face had a sudden look of alarm. "She told me Tuesday morning that she signed a contract to decorate and furnish the Dupree Hotel that they've started building on Fifth Street. It's a contract that would normally have gone to McCall's and she knows it, but she actually contracted to buy everything for that hotel from wholesalers and not one scrap from McCall's. We're out of more than a million dollars."

Robert leaned back and savored his cognac. "And that's got you mad enough to eat nails. I hope you didn't say anything to her that you'll have to eat."

"I'd barely started, and she hung up on me."

"I don't blame her. Son, you've been in this business long enough to know that every decorator buys from wholesalers, unless that's impossible. How's she going to make any money if she buys from a retailer? You've already added thirty percent, and that's the thirty percent that she'd get." Robert swirled the cognac around in the snifter, inhaled the fumes and smiled his satisfaction. Then he savored another sip. "If McCall's had the job, we would have purchased everything wholesale or used something that we had already purchased wholesale. Ease up. You've got some work to do, son, because she expected support, and look what she got."

"That's your view, Granddad, but she could at least have discussed it with me before she signed that contract or figured out a way for us to work together."

"You hate to lose, son, and that's a good thing, because it makes you work hard. But don't be stubborn about this when you know you're wrong. If you don't shape up, you'll lose that woman, because neither you nor any other man is going to walk over her. Love doesn't cover everything. Mark my word!"

Upon returning home, Justin lifted the receiver of his house phone to call Deanna, remembered his irritation, savored it a bit and hung up. He wasn't going to lie. She'd hung one on him, and no man wanted his woman to beat him out of a prize. She should know that.

Deanna made up her mind that if Justin didn't call her, they had spoken for the last time. She hadn't dreamed that he'd regard her as his competition to the extent that he'd try to control her and lose his temper when that didn't work. Well, maybe that was overstating it. He hadn't tried to control her, but he wasn't proud of her and he expected her to do something stupid like furnishing that big modern hotel out of his store and giving McCall's the profits while she got peanuts. In love, she was; an idiot, she was not!

Ten days passed, she didn't hear from him, and she wondered if she was therefore free to marry somebody else. Was she? He hadn't given her a ring, either. While wondering as to the efficacy of asking Justin that question, her telephone rang.

Although trembling, she was able to keep her voice steady. "Hello."

"Miss Lawford, this is Robert McCall. Would you do an old man the honor of coming to my home for dinner Tuesday evening at seven? Not everyone in the McCall family is foolish, my dear."

Taken aback, she hesitated for a second, for she hardly

knew how to answer him. "You're very kind," she managed when his words finally penetrated. "Yes, I would love to come if you'll give me directions."

"That won't be necessary. My car and chauffeur will be at your place at six-fifteen. Thank you so much. I'll be looking forward to seeing you."

"Do you have my address, sir?"

"Oh yes. It's on the card you gave me. Goodbye."

She sat still, trying to imagine what he wanted. Obviously, Justin had told him about her contract with the hotel. If he wanted her to work for McCall's that was out, but she didn't mind his asking while she enjoyed a good meal. She looked through her closet, saw nothing that she wanted to wear and headed for the shops. She found an avocado-colored silk crepe, sleeveless with a fairly deep cowl neckline, flared from the hips and with a fitted waistline. Not too much in the presence of a senior citizen, but feminine enough for a date. When the big, custom-built Lincoln Town Car arrived at her house, it gave her a good feeling to have the respect of one of Woodmore's icons.

# Chapter 7

The old man greeted her warmly, and walked with her into his living room. Her eyes widened when she saw a handsome brother stand and wait for an introduction.

"Miss Deanna Lawford, this is John Macon."

She accepted the introduction, retrieved her hand from the handshake and sat down. What was Robert McCall up to? She'd be wise not to drink more than one glass of wine, for it was immediately obvious that John Macon liked what he saw and wasn't timid about going for it. She answered his questions while not allowing herself to appear interested.

"There's the bell," Robert said, and when he didn't get up, she knew that the other guest was not a woman. 'Hi, Granddad. Sorry I'm l…

"Deanna! I didn't know you'd be here."

"Hello," she said, having heard *him* before he saw *her*. "I didn't know you'd be here either."

Robert ignored them. "Deanna, John owns a printing and publishing company. One of the newest movers and shakers in the Danvers Chamber of Commerce."

"I hear you're a top-flight decorator," John said. "I'd like you to list with our chamber of commerce. To my knowledge, we don't have a top-flight decorator."

"Certainly not like Deanna," Robert said. "She just signed a contract to decorate and furnish the new Dupree Hotel."

"You don't say." John cast a quick glance in Justin's direction, shrugged off whatever he saw and sat forward in his chair. "I'd be glad to introduce you to some opportunities."

"That's so kind of you," she said, "but right now, I have as much as I can handle. I'll bear that in mind."

"It'll take you a year to finish that hotel," Justin said, his voice devoid of warmth or friendliness, "so it seems to me that should be enough for now."

"It doesn't hurt to plan ahead," John said.

"Any successful businessman knows that," Justin retorted. "I plan three seasons ahead."

"Really?" Deanna asked. "Most stores are only two seasons ahead at best. I can see the virtue of your tactic."

Deanna eyed Robert McCall with the vision of sudden understanding and took pleasure in joining his game. The cook served a memorable meal, and John Macon seemed to have decided to give Justin a run for his money and openly courted her.

Robert served after-dinner drinks, looked at Justin and said, "Not much makes me happier that a warm circle of friends and spirited conversation. I don't know when I've had such a delightful evening."

"Yes, I can imagine," Justin said without the semblance of a smile.

Deanna stood, walked over to Robert McCall and took his hand. "Thank you so much for inviting me to dinner. It was wonderful. I enjoyed every minute of my visit. I hope you'll have dinner at my home. I'm not a bad cook." She leaned forward and kissed his cheek. "I'd like to leave now."

She felt the pressure on her arm, but didn't turn around.

She'd know his touch if she was blindfolded, but she didn't say a word.

"I'll take you home," Justin said. She glanced at John Macon at about the moment he surrendered to Justin's advantage.

"Your grandfather's chauffeur brought me, and he was supposed to take me home," she said to Justin. "You may imagine that I am not one bit pleased with you, and if I'd known you'd be there, I may not have come."

"I don't doubt that for a minute. You didn't need to be that nice to John Whatever-His-Name, either."

"He was gracious to me and exceedingly charming," she said, getting some of her own. "Your grandfather wouldn't have any other kind of guest."

"It is not my intention to spend another second talking about him."

"You're the one who mentioned the man."

Justin parked the car in front of her house, cut the engine and got out, but she didn't wait for him to open her door. "For the past ten days, I've been opening and closing doors by myself and with considerable success."

He grasped her arm and walked with her to her door. "May I have your key, please?" She gave it to him. He opened the door, held it for her and followed her inside without asking her permission.

"Well?" she said, provoking him and not caring if she did.

He took her hand, walked with her into the living room and switched on a floor lamp. "An engaged woman is supposed to have an engagement ring. Would you please sit down, Deanna?"

"Why?"

"Please."

She sat down, and he knelt at her knee. "You're more important to me than McCall's or any other person or thing on this earth. I know I hurt you, and I'm sorry. If I acknowledge the truth, I was sorry the minute I hung up, and this is not the first time I've suffered because of my stubbornness. Can you forgive me? I love you, and I've lived in hell these days. I promise never again to be that selfish. I'm proud of you, and I want you to succeed. Can you forgive me and love me?"

She gazed down at him, at the sorrow etched in his face and the sad shadows in his eyes and wanted more than anything to hold him against her breasts and comfort him.

"I hurt, too, Justin. Terribly, because I needed your support. But I love you, and I'm willing to forget it because you've promised that it won't happen again."

"It won't. McCall's will close its decorating department, and I'm offering you space on the executive floor to conduct your business. It will not be a part of McCall's, but will have your company name and logo on the door and in all advertisements and you can pay rent for the space. I guarantee you'll never be out of work. What do you say?"

"It's a deal."

"Now that we have that out of the way, will you marry me?"

"I haven't changed my mind. I want to be your wife and the mother of your children."

He took her left hand and slipped his grandmother's engagement ring on her finger. "My three children, remember? Oh, sweetheart. I love you now, and I know I will love you forever."

"I've loved you more each day that I've known you— through the pleasure and the pain, and I know that I will always love you," she said, looking at the ring and gasping. "This is an heirloom!"

"Granddad gave it to my grandmother, and when she died, he gave it to me. It's yours now."

"I'll cherish it."

He picked her up and carried her to bed. An hour later, he gazed down at her. "I think you were hungry."

"I wasn't. I was starved, and I could use some more."

His grin lit up his face. "A man likes to know that his

woman wants him and enjoys him." Then he shifted his hips and took her on a fast and rollicking trip to an explosive climax.

One month later, gowned in her mother's white satin and lace wedding dress, Deanna walked alone up the white calla-lily bedecked aisle of Woodmore's First Presbyterian Church behind Jennyse Lawford, her maid of honor. On the aisle end of each pew hung a bunch of white calla lilies tied with silver ribbon, a match for the silver slippers on her feet. With his grandfather at his side, Justin McCall waited for his bride and a few minutes later, The Reverend Mildred Holmes pronounced them man and wife.

"You may kiss the bride."

"This is not the place for French kisses," Deanna whispered to Justin after he stole a fast one.

As befitted a bridal reception, the entire first floor of McCall's department store glittered in silver and white. Silver bells dangled from the ceiling amidst clusters of silver stars and crescent moons, and globes of silver light gave the vast room an air of romance. An orchestra of women and men dressed in silver and white played the romantic tunes that Deanna and Justin had loved during their courtship. The store's employees and numerous town citizens welcomed the newlyweds at the reception and dance, at which champagne flowed and every kind of delectable party food was served in abundance. Minutes after the cutting of the cake and Robert McCall's sentimental toast, Deanna and Justin sneaked out, changed their clothes in a nearby hotel and headed for Interlaken, Switzerland and the luscious valley of the Swiss Alps.

* * * * *

# LOVE FOR A LIFETIME

Ginger Hinds stepped out on the balcony of her hotel room in Harare, Zimbabwe, gazed up at the red, blue, and purple streaked sky and took a deep, restorative breath. *Free at last!* Four years of marriage behind her, and she didn't know a thing about life. But, beginning today, she planned to make up for lost time. She smiled at the birds—at least two dozen of them in every color—resting on the edge of her balcony, unafraid of her. *That's for me,* she told herself. *Free as a bird.* She raised her arms toward the heavens and let the breeze swirl around her body. For the next two weeks, she was going to live. She ducked back inside, got dressed, and made her way to the dining room to see what the Zimbabweans served for breakfast.

Waiting for the elevator, she wondered how she'd let things get out of hand. For four years, she'd withstood Harold Lawson's constant harassment and nagging. If a man wanted his wife to be a carefree playgirl and to tag along when and wherever he chose to go without regard to her own interests, he shouldn't have married an attorney with a host of clients and fixed court dates. She had thought him obsessed with her until she figured out that he was attempting to control her with his nightly passion. He hadn't realized, and she hadn't had the guts to tell him, that he'd wasted a lot of time. She had compromised until she risked losing her identity—and she'd lost more than a few clients.

When he wanted them to spend the summer hiking through the Tennessee Smokies and then start a family, and she'd refused because they had neither substantial funds nor a house, he'd told her he wanted out. She'd quickly recovered from the blow to her ego and let him have his wish. Her sister, Linda, had encouraged her to clean the slate and start over. Three months later, here she was where nobody knew her, where she was on her own, and New York was over two thousand miles away.

She slid her tray along the shining chrome and inspected the steam table. Sawdust-like sausages, violated eggs that someone had labeled "scrambled," crisp, greasy bacon, porridge, hard rolls, orange juice, and the most exquisite fruits she'd ever seen. Might as well live dangerously. She filled her plate with eggs, bacon, fruit, and rolls and found a corner table. A waiter brought coffee and the local paper.

"Good morning."

Ginger glanced up from the paper and quickly looked up again. The fork she'd held in her hand clattered against her plate as she stared into his gray mesmeric eyes. Tall, handsome, and a clean-shaven, golden beige complexion. Butterflies danced in her belly, and she tried to break the gaze, but he held her transfixed. She had the presence of mind to bite her bottom lip or it would surely have dropped and left her gaping at him. She picked up the paper that had fallen to a spot beside her plate and dropped it again when she realized she was about to fan herself with it. A smile lit his unbelievable eyes, and her heart seemed to roll in her chest.

"We seem to be the only Americans in this place. Do you mind if I join you?"

"What? Oh. Uh…no. I don't mind."

He took his food off the tray, put his plate, knife, fork, spoon, and napkin in their proper places, and took the tray back to the counter. "Thanks," he said when he returned. "My name is Jason. Who're you?"

Considering her unsettling experience just looking at him, she hadn't intended to shake hands, but he gave her no choice. "I'm Ginger," she told him and submitted to the electrifying current that coursed up her bare arm when he took her hand.

"Glad to meet you, Ginger," he said, and she noticed that his deep baritone carried a Southern lilt. "What brings you almost to the end of Africa?"

He could smile all he wanted to. She wasn't going to tell this good-looking stranger her business. "I needed a change, something drastically different. What about you?"

He took a sip of coffee and leaned back in the chair, and it struck her that this man knew and liked who he was. "That about says it for me, too. I got here last night, so I haven't seen a thing. Been here long?"

She told him that she'd also arrived the night before.

"What do you say we spend the day together?" he asked. "It's no fun sightseeing alone. How about it?" He frowned. "Unless you're with someone."

If he wanted to know whether she had a man with her, he'd have to ask. She was about to decline, when she remembered her vow to live life to the hilt for the next two weeks, to let the sun shine on her, the water flow over her, and the breeze blow around her. To be a whole woman. "I'd love company," she said, knowing she sounded less than convincing.

As if unaware of her seeming reluctance, he stacked their dishes on her tray and rose. "Meet me at the desk in half an hour?"

She nodded and sat riveted in her chair as he sauntered off. Her intuition told her that she was in for a rollicking ride, but after four years of standing still, so be it.

* * *

Jason Calhoun stood at the reception desk waiting for Ginger. When she'd looked up from her newspaper, he'd had a wallop to the gut. He'd lived for thirty-four years, been married, in love and out of it, and for the first time in his life he knew what it was to have a woman dull his senses with a single glance. Her eyes had telegraphed a need that started a twinge in his belly, that had melted something inside of him."

"Ah. Here you are." She hadn't kept him waiting, and he liked that.

They settled on a tour and headed for the bus. Jason hadn't expected to be so at ease with her, not after the eviscerating experience he'd had when she'd looked up at him. "I assume you like animals," he said, looking for a conversation opener.

"Animals? I like puppies. But I can't stand anything that crawls. Even the picture of a snake scares me."

"Good," he teased. "When one swings out of the bush, you'll grab hold of me."

From the look on her face, she wasn't joking. He changed the subject. "Did you leave a husband at home? Or a fiancé?"

"Jason, if I had either of those, you wouldn't be holding my hand, and you *are* holding my hand."

He released it. "Aren't you going to ask about my marital status?" As she stepped on the bus, he put a finger to her elbow, then followed her to the seat she chose.

She looked up at him. "I figure the less I know about you the better off I'll be."

"What do you mean by that?"

"We're strangers, Jason. Let's enjoy each other's company today, and no more personal questions. That way, we'll be as free as the birds."

He came close to asking what she was running from, and bit it back. "What are you scared of, Ginger? You're a grown woman. How old are you? Twenty-seven? Twenty-eight? What happened to us back there at that breakfast table when we met—and something *did* happen—won't erase itself no matter how much we deny it. We clicked, and I don't plan to pretend otherwise." She raised an eyebrow, and he added, "Pretense is a waste of time."

"Suit yourself," she said, trying to shake off the effect of his words. "I'm going to enjoy myself, and I doubt that'll be possible if I have to worry about what could be or might have been between you and me. No point in our getting enmeshed in a libidinous snare when we know we'll say goodbye tomorrow."

"So you admit the possibility?"

"Why should I deny it? You're a smart man. Let's just have fun. And, to answer your other question, I'll be thirty my next birthday."

He mulled over her words, so different from what he would have expected of most women he'd known, women who didn't put a distance between him and them, who didn't want to be independent, but who lassoed and clung. He did what came naturally to him—extended his right hand to her and waited.

"All right, Ginger. Let's agree that this day is ours, that we'll enjoy every second of it…together. You game? One day…for a lifetime."

Her gaze shifted from his hand to his face. He didn't know what she saw there, but he'd never seen a more serious expression on anyone. She might well have been judging, measuring him by what she found in his eyes.

Stunned at her suddenly tense, prayerful expression, her unmistakable appeal to his decency, he squeezed her fingers. "Ginger, I'm an honorable man. No one has ever doubted that."

Her eyes widened, as though he'd surprised her by reading her so well and, at last, her damp fingers clasped his palm. Reluctantly. As tentatively as a baby taking its first step. "All right," she said. "No promises. No confessions, and—"

"And no regrets," he finished. "Just one day together."

He thought she flushed with embarrassment, but why would she? He hadn't suggested anything unseemly. "Ever been here or anywhere else in Africa before?" he asked for want of something more interesting to say. After all, he couldn't talk about them without getting personal. She'd vetoed that.

"I was in Kenya once, but I didn't see much of it because the rain never let up, and there wasn't much joy in walking around in a downpour. I did get to a place where some gnarled, old men sat carving clusters of people on a single piece of ebony wood. I bought one carving for ten dollars. Can you imagine the talent and work that went into it?"

"Yes, I can. Let's check out the museum when we get back to Harare. Look, I want to go to Victoria Falls tomorrow. Can't you stay one more day and take the trip with me?" Why was he pursuing a relationship with this woman when he knew they would go their separate ways tomorrow or the next day? She didn't move her hand from his but leaned against the window, turned sideways, and looked at him. She had the most penetrating gaze, and such lovely, light brown eyes punctuated her dark face. Everything about her beckoned to him.

He liked the way she looked at a man, too. Straight in the eye. No coquettish nonsense. "I've heard that the Falls are unforgettable. We'll see."

He should have relaxed into contentment, but instead he got an unfamiliar jolt of ill-defined anxiety, and he didn't like it. But if she decided to go, he'd welcome her company.

By noon, she'd had enough of lions, cheetahs, and alligators. Even her lunch included alligator croquettes. She ate it with relish and wouldn't have guessed what it was if the waiter hadn't been so proud of the great delicacy he had placed before them. She resisted telling him that she'd rather he'd told her it was ground turkey breast. They finished the meal, walked to the door of the rustic but attractively decorated lodge, and looked out at the darkened sky, almost black at one o'clock in the afternoon. A great roar rattled her eardrums, and she felt his hands on her, lifting her.

Holding her tightly to his chest, he sprinted off the porch. "We'd better make a run for the bus. These storms can last for days."

Her arms found their way to his neck and locked themselves there. Strangely, she had the urge to rest her face in the curve of his neck and no doubt would have, if he hadn't said, "Open the door. Quick!" as they reached the tour bus.

Thanking God for presence of mind, she managed to slide the door open, and he jumped inside with her. "You can put me down now," she told him as he continued carrying her until he reached their seats.

He settled her on her feet. "Yeah. Looks like the other tourists got stuck in the lodge." He sat beside her, and her shoulders tensed as his left arm curled around her and she could feel the heat of his fingers through her blouse.

"I thought that noise was thunder."

"It was the rain announcing its arrival. Might as well relax, Ginger. We could be here for hours. The driver is in the lodge, or at least I hope he is. This rain brings out all kinds of crawling things. *Look over there going up that—*"

"Will you please change the subject. I told you I was afraid of—"

His hand tightened on her shoulder. "Gee, that's right. I forgot."

What she'd intended as a quick glance settled on his face just before he laughed, and without thinking about it, she let her elbow give his chest a lesson. He laughed harder.

"What's so funny? Are you sadistic or something?"

His shoulders shook as he tried but failed to control his mirth. "Me? No. It's just that...you were actually scared. How on earth could anything out there get in this bus? Besides, I'm sitting here with my arm around your shoulder, and you actually thought I'd let that thing get to you. What kind of guys have you been hanging out with?"

"I haven't been hanging out with any guys, and would you please give me back my shoulder?"

"Sure, so long as I can keep your hand. You wouldn't begrudge me the comfort of your hand, would you? I could be scared of...of...let me see...I could be scared of...of all this rain."

"If you ask me, you're a smart aleck."

He let out a long breath, and she wondered about that until he followed it up with quiet, deliberate words. "Better for me to tease you than to do what I'd like."

Her senses whirled dizzily, exciting her. Exhilarating her. Recklessly, she dared him to say it. "I had the impression that you're man enough to do whatever you want."

His rapt stare, powerfully and wildly masculine in its challenge, rocked her. "And you were never more right," he said as his right index finger tipped her chin.

This thing was moving at the speed of sound, and she should move away, put out her hand, anything to stop him, but her traitorous mouth went to meet his lips, and both his hands locked behind her head as he warmed her from her head to the bottoms of her feet. She had never trembled for a man, but the tremors rolled through her, and her heart bounced out of control in her chest.

He stopped kissing her and, still cradling her head with his hands, stared into her eyes. "If I ever get into serious trouble, it will probably be due to my failure to pass up an exciting challenge. Daring me can be the same as begging me, Ginger."

*I don't know this man,* she reminded herself, regrouping as best she could. "Now that you've gotten it out of your system," she told him, "you don't have to think about it anymore. Wonder what time that museum closes?"

This time, his laugh held no mirth. "You're kidding. The way you responded to me? Woman, all that did was whet my appetite."

She withdrew the hand that he'd reclaimed. "Your imagination is out of control."

A wide grin revealed snow-white teeth and sparkles in his gray eyes. "Really? Well, I won't dispute your word, but I'm willing to test it, see if I'm losing my perceptive skills. What about you?" His arms maneuvered around her shoulders again, and he leaned toward her.

"All right. All right. So I knew you were here," she admitted, shielding her emotions with the remark. "That kiss only proves I'm not dead."

His laughter curled around her like a protective blanket comforting her on a cool evening. As quickly as the laughter came, he sobered. "I could like you. Really like you, Ginger."

She could only shrug, because she already knew she wouldn't soon forget him. "I've decided it must be a case of forbidden fruit." She slapped her hand over her mouth, her nerves a riot at the thought that she might have reminded him of what that fruit did for Eve.

The rain slackened, and the driver and five other tourists boarded the bus. "I'm going to have to head back to Harare," the driver told them. "If the rain continues, the roads will be muddy, and we could get stranded out here. No refunds, though."

Ginger listened for grumbles, but didn't hear any. She wasn't sorry to get away from Jason and to work at getting her head straightened out. She hadn't thought of herself as being vulnerable, but Jason had lowered her defenses from the minute she'd looked up and seen him holding that tray of fruit, porridge, and two cups of coffee.

"Have dinner with me?" he asked as they entered the hotel lobby.

She shook her head. "Thanks, but I'll have a bite in my room. After that huge lunch, I don't want much dinner."

He rubbed his right index finger across his chin and looked into the distance as though alone with his thoughts. Then he set his gaze on her, and the muscles in her stomach tightened as his grin crawled over his face.

"It's been great, girl of my dreams. Have a good life."

"I...thanks. You, too." She scampered away from him, wanting to get a last look, but not daring to tempt herself.

She rested, wrote some letters and ordered dinner in her room. She'd seen half a dozen women in the hotel who appeared to be unattached, and she didn't doubt that some of them would be glad for his company. What woman wouldn't want the company of such a handsome, intelligent man? She answered the door, and a porter handed her a bouquet of calla lilies to which an attached note read, *Thank you for a day that I shall never forget. J.*

How could he know that she loved calla lilies? She broke off a petal, put it in one of the little plastic Ziploc bags that she always carried in her luggage and pressed it flat. It might be all she'd ever have of him. She would keep it forever, though she'd be better off if he hadn't sent them. Just one more reason why she could never forget him.

She was tempted to ignore the telephone, but after it rang a full two minutes she lifted the receiver. "Hello."

"You knew it was I, Ginger. Let's not say goodbye yet. I still want to see Victoria Falls. The flight leaves at noon, and we'd get back just after nightfall. What about it? It's something special that we'll have to remember."

The brochure lay open on the desk before her. She looked at the picture of the Falls and thought how much more wonderful they must be in reality. Her gaze drifted to the bouquet of calla lilies, thoughts of what they would always represent swirled in her mind, and something deep inside of her wouldn't let her say no.

"All right. But no sweet stuff, Jason."

"A woman doesn't have to tell me no," he growled. "She only has to shake her head once. Get it? If I get sweet, you'll have to suggest it. You going?"

"Okay. And don't be so self-righteous. The saints are all in heaven."

"Whatever. Meet you at breakfast? Say, around nine?"

"I'm eating early. I want to go to the soapstone museum. See you on the plane. And, Jason, thank you for the beautiful flowers. I love them."

"My pleasure."

She hung up and considered kicking herself for agreeing to join him on that trip; she wanted to see the Falls, but she knew she wanted to see him more.

The soapstone museum proved to be an outdoor factory and a tiny room in which the carvings were displayed in glass cases. All were for sale. She bought two small heads, one of an old woman and the other of a man with eighty years of toil and grief etched in his face. She paid the few dollars without bargaining, ashamed to have them for such a pittance. When she turned to leave, she faced Jason, who held his own purchases—an ebony free-form that would have been at home in New York's Museum of Modern Art, a statue of mother and child, and one of an old man bowed beneath the weight of the heavy bag on his shoulder.

He pointed to the latter. "This is for my father," he said, affection abloom on his face as he caressed the figure.

*He loves his father,* she thought. A second sense, or maybe it was a premonition, warned her: fate was shadowing her. She forced a smile, and told him he had good taste, but she could have said that in that short sentence he'd said a lot about himself and his background. They ate a lunch of roast chicken sandwiches, French fries, and iced tea at a nearby hotel and waited for the limousine to take them to the airport. Sunset found them at the Zambezi River looking at the Falls.

"Want to take the cruise up the river?" he asked, the urgency in his voice pulling at the woman in her and pushing aside her common sense.

She remembered her trip on Maid of the Mist at Niagara Falls and nodded. "I...I'd love it."

Her response seemed to energize him, for his wonderful face lit up with the sparkles in his eyes, and he threw an arm around her, lifted her from her feet, and spun her around. "I can hardly wait. Let's go get our slickers."

They rented hats, boots, coats, and pants of heavy, yellow plastic and joined the cruise.

"From what I can see," he teased, "we're the only couple here that isn't honeymooning."

She glared at him and pointed to one couple. "They're kissing because the gal is scared, and he doesn't want her screaming."

Jason doubled up with laughter, put his arms around her wet slicker, and hugged her. Well, the whole thing was crazy. She hugged him back.

The Sundowner cruiser took them along the spray at the entrance to the great gorge and into the ever changing rainbows that flexed their awesome beauty against the rays of the setting sun. He didn't expect ever to see a sight that compared to it. He looked down at the woman whom he had folded to himself and whose hands gripped his biceps, hoping for the look of recognition that would tell him he'd found a kindred soul. He didn't want to speak and spoil the moment, so he tipped her chin up with his right index finger and gasped when he saw the tears that cascaded down her cheeks. He wanted to kiss them away, but he only held her close to him. Who knew what memories, if any, the sight before them had triggered in her? The short cruise ended before they reached the river's bend, and they watched the sunset. It didn't surprise him that no words passed between them. What could anyone say in the presence of such beauty?

He thought he understood her silence as the Fokker 12 flew them back to Harare. Once more, he didn't want to say goodbye, and they would both depart the next day. At the elevator, he took her hand. "Have dinner with me this last night. I'm just not ready to say goodbye."

He held his breath as he waited for her answer. "Yes." The word came out slowly, as if she were giving birth to something. "That would be nice. What time?"

He let himself breathe. "Seven?"

She nodded, and he let go of her hand. "See you right here at seven."

Ginger dressed carefully, knowing that she played with fire, because Jason could be the tornado that wrecked her life. Butterflies flitted around in her belly, and perspiration made ringlets of the hair at her temples. *If you go down there, you'll regret it,* her mind warned. But she ignored all caution, slipped a dusty rose, sleeveless, chiffon minidress over her dark brown skin, bare but for a bra and bikini panties, dabbed some Opium perfume where it counted most, brushed her hair around her shoulders, and left the room.

Good Lord, what a man! Elegant in a white linen suit, white shirt, and red tie, he filled her vision as she stepped from the elevator, his face wreathed in a welcoming smile. If he had opened his arms, she wouldn't have hesitated until he'd wrapped her securely in them.

*You're beautiful,* he told her in unuttered words that seemed to come off the wings of his breath, but spoke loudly in his smile and demeanor. "I wish the place was crowded," he said, "and hundreds of people could see what a lucky man I am."

He had ordered jacaranda blooms, the national flower, for their table. "What would you like?" he asked after she'd read the menu.

*A healthy helping of this wonderful man sitting across the table from me.* "Roast duck, and whatever goes with it," she said, knowing that he'd taken her appetite.

She made herself eat it and noticed that he appeared to force down the veal scallopini. The rapport they'd had in the afternoon had deserted them. They looked at the few other tourists in the dining room, sipped their wine, and made insignificant small talk.

At last, she had to stop pretending; "This is…I enjoyed the meal, Jason, and you're wonderful company. I'd better say goodbye."

She attempted to push back her chair and stand, and he rushed to assist her. Impulsively, she kissed his cheek and headed for the elevator as fast as she could without actually running, but it was his hand that pushed the button, his hand that grasped hers and led her from the elevator. At his room door, he took the key from his pocket, held it in his hand, and gazed into her eyes in a wordless entreaty for permission to open it.

"This doesn't make sense, Jason."

"I know. Nothing has made sense from the minute I laid eyes on you. Will you come in here with me?"

She nodded, and he opened the door. Before it closed, he had her in his arms, where she wanted to be. At last, she could feel his fingers on her bare flesh, caressing, teasing until bolt after bolt of hot want tore through her. Why didn't he kiss her?

"I don't play at this, Ginger, and I don't make love lightly. I'm already fifty percent gone. Will you kiss me?"

"I don't think I understand what you mean."

"Then kiss me. Put your arms around me and kiss me."

The trembling of her lips betrayed her as she reached up to him, fastened her hands at the back of his head, and parted her lips. The force of it shook her, pummeled her loins like pellets of hot steel rocketing from a smelter's fire. His tongue grazed her lips, and she took him into her mouth and knew the heat of his passion as he loved her until her strength ebbed, and she let him take her weight. His fingers went to the zipper at the back of her dress, and she froze. In four years of marriage, she hadn't once wanted her husband as she wanted this man. She'd slipped up somewhere. She was a rational woman, and women who used their minds didn't let themselves go wild with a stranger, one they'd never see again. The Ginger Hinds she knew wouldn't make love with a man she hadn't known for two whole days, no matter how much she wanted him. She couldn't change into another person just because she was in Zimbabwe and not at home on New York City's Roosevelt Island.

As though he sensed her misgivings, he put an arm around her shoulder and drew her close. "You've changed your mind?"

Was he going to be angry and unruly? No matter, she couldn't do it. "About what I want? No, Jason. I want to be with you, but I can't move so far out of character. All my life I've toed the line, lived a conservative life. I wanted nothing more than a piece of the American dream, and I worked hard for it, but it burst all around me. I came here to begin a change. I realize now that I set out to do something reckless, wild, unlike myself, and I can't go through with it. I know I've disappointed you, and I'm sorry. You made a dent in me, and I didn't know how to handle it. Will you forgive me?"

He rubbed the back of his neck and took in a long breath. "I don't hold it against you."

"I'd better leave."

His smile held no humor, and his gray eyes didn't twinkle. "You won't forget me, Ginger. Not in this life."

He walked to the door, opened it, and brushed her cheek with the tips of his fingers. "No. You won't forget me."

"I don't expect I will, and don't you be surprised if I show up in your thoughts sometimes. All the best, Jason."

"The same to you, sweetheart. Get home safely."

The door closed, and the most intriguing and wonderful man she'd ever met was out of her life. The next morning, she took Swissair 1102 to Lagos, Nigeria, en route home. She wasn't bubbling over with happiness, but she wasn't ashamed of herself, either.

Jason Calhoun closed the door of his hotel room and considered packing his bag and going home. Ginger—maybe that wasn't even her name—had made the right decision, but for the rest of his life he'd wonder what he'd missed. He could get a woman any time he wanted one, but he didn't care for casual sex, and he hadn't wanted that from Ginger. He had needed to explore something in himself that hadn't been there before he met her, to blend his soul with hers, for he suspected that, with her, he would have known at last who he was. He'd heard that newly divorced individuals had to deal with vulnerability. Maybe that explained his awful need for Ginger. He'd been restless since his divorce, but he hadn't thought himself particularly vulnerable. He unlocked the bar that stood beside the dresser in his room, opened a bottle of ginger ale, and got rid of the dryness in his throat. Six billion people inhabited planet earth, and one of them had a piece of him—maybe the most important piece—and he'd never get it back.

Ginger walked into her eleventh floor apartment on Roosevelt Island, closed the door, and looked around. Same place, she thought; just a different woman. In the short span of six weeks, she'd gotten a divorce from one man and came dangerously close to falling for another one. She kicked off her shoes, walked barefoot to her bedroom and called Clarice.

"Hey, girlfriend, how'd it go?" Clarice asked.

"Full of adventure. You should have come with me."

"You don't mean that. If I'd been with you, you wouldn't be moaning about the gray-eyed man."

Clarice's psychic ability made Ginger uncomfortable, but she tolerated it because she valued Clarice's friendship. "Girl, I don't want to hear one word about your visions of that man. You got lucky with the color of his eyes. Now, let's drop it. Do I have any mail?"

"Yeah. You want me to bring it to you?"

"No. Thanks for keeping it for me. I need to get a nap so I'll feel like working. I've got a court date day after tomorrow."

"I'll ring your bell and hang it on the doorknob."

Ginger didn't object, because Clarice lived in an apartment several doors down the hall from her.

She told herself that she hadn't met a man named Jason, that he was a part of a surrealistic dream. A minute later she swore at herself for demanding his agreement that they not exchange any information about themselves, including last names. Was he married? Did he have any children? Where did he live, and what did he do for a living?

The doorbell rang and she waited ten minutes before opening it and getting the bag of mail. She loved Clarice, but right then she didn't want to see her or anyone else. Except Jason. Thumbing through her mail, her gaze caught the schizophrenic handwriting of Steven Roberts, her client and the first party to a divorce. The trouble with Steven was his lack of familiarity with his own mind. She read his letter, rolled her eyes in disgust, and dialed his number.

"Mr. Roberts, this is Ginger Hinds," she said after hearing his clipped hello. "I'm afraid it's too late for you to drop your suit, because Mrs. Roberts has entered a countersuit. I received the notice in my mail today. She's asking for half of your property and one-third of all you earn in the future, plus full payment of two hundred and eighty-two thousand dollars in loans that she made to you. Your case will be considerably weaker if you drop your demands."

She could imagine that his eyes widened, as they did when he received a surprise. "Well, she sure is a bag of laughs," Steven said. "Last time she tickled my funny bone like this, she didn't want quite that much—just a little old house on Cape Hatteras where the dozen and a half hurricanes that stop by there every year could blow my three hundred thousand dollar house smack out into the Atlantic Ocean. She needs to get her head screwed on right."

"Now, Mr. Roberts, let's just work on the things we can control," she said. "And please don't talk like that when we're in court. It won't do your case one bit of good."

"But you listen to me, Miss Hinds. I have never borrowed one cent from my wife."

They'd been over that before. She took a deep breath and counted to ten. "Can you prove that?"

"'Course not. When you're in love, you don't keep records on things like that."

"Evidently, she did. Let's concentrate on your charges. You say she's only interested in sensual gratification, won't work with you to build a home, acts like a teenager, wants to party all the time, and refuses to speak to you if you don't join her, while you want to strengthen your relationship with her, save, and build a future. Right?"

"Right. And I want irreconcilable differences thrown in there."

She stifled a laugh. Nobody who'd been through one would think divorce amusing. "That much is obvious, Mr. Roberts. This is the second time you've indicated a change of heart about this divorce. If it happens again, get another attorney. Some counseling wouldn't hurt."

"Look, maybe I've been too hard on her. She's got a right to enjoy life. Maybe if her mother had stayed out of it…damn. I must be crazy. I just had a weak moment there thinking about how it was, how perfect it used to be. I never thought it would come to this. See you in court."

*Tell me about it.* She hung up and checked her court hearings. Nancy Holloway was suing her stock broker for fraud, and she figured they had an eighty percent chance of winning. Not so with Jake Henderson, a sculptor, who was suing his landlord for having shut off all services in the hopes of forcing him out of his rent-controlled apartment.

She called her sister, Linda, to let her know she was back at home, showered, put on some work clothes and headed for her garden. She always had to explain to people that there were two hundred and fifty individually owned outdoor gardens on Roosevelt Island—her little village in the middle of the East River, twenty minutes from Times Square—along with a rose garden that was the pride of the community. Her garden was clear of weeds, which she guessed was Clarice's handiwork. With nothing better to do in the blistering heat, she walked back to Andy's Place, the Island hangout for company, food, drinks, coffee, or whatever, and waited to see who'd come in. Minutes later, she was rewarded with Clarice's company.

"Hey, girl, what kind of weather is this for April? I thought I'd die out there yesterday getting the grass out of your garden. Sure could use some of Andy's good old iced tea."

Ginger hugged her friend. "You can get the folks out of the south, but everybody knows where they come from. Don't tell me your strange mind told you I was here."

Clarice beckoned the waiter, ordered iced tea for herself and ginger ale for Ginger. "Nobody has to ask you what you want to drink, Ginger. You take your name seriously. Now, about those gray eyes. Where'd you leave him?"

Ginger pushed back the irritation she always felt when Clarice discussed things she wasn't supposed to know. "He's in Harare."

Clarice let her have a look of disdain. "Is that so? You and your principles. I got principles, too, Honey, but they wouldn't let me walk away from *that* man. What are you going to do?"

Ginger looked long and hard at Clarice. If the woman was such a great psychic, shouldn't she know what was going to happen? She shrugged. "What's past is prologue."

Clarice's giggle stunned Ginger, because her friend prided herself on her refinement. "From the sound of that, I'd say you're capable of *seeing* a few things yourself?"

Nervous at the turn of the conversation, Ginger gulped down her drink. "I'd better run. How're things over at the United Nations? Maybe you can tell the Secretary-General whether our country is ever going to pay the UN all that money we owe it." She slid out of the booth, picked up her garden gloves and trowel, and looked down at her friend.

"Please don't pester me about Jason, Clarice. It's over, and I want to forget."

"Whatever you say. Just don't say I didn't—"

"Clarice, *please!*" She waved at her friend and walked out into the heat. So much for her attempts to push Jason out of her thoughts.

Jason paid the taxi driver, picked up his bags, and started into the building at Fifth Avenue and 110th Street, the lower edge of Harlem, where he lived in a two bedroom duplex condominium. He walked with legs that fought with his mind, seemingly wanting to go elsewhere, nodded to the concierge, and strode rapidly toward the elevator.

"I have a bundle of mail here for you, Mr. Calhoun," the concierge called after him. "Ring me when you're ready for it, and I'll bring it up."

Jason thanked him but didn't pause, because he didn't want conversation or anyone's company. Except Ginger's. Unable to stop thinking of her, he cursed himself for not at least having gotten her last name. *No promises, no confessions, and no regrets.* They had agreed to remain strangers. And in spite of the soul-searing intimacy they'd shared, they knew nothing of one another. Nothing, that is, except that their need for each other had almost overpowered them. He opened the windows to rid the apartment of stuffiness, then quickly closed them as the oppressive heat assaulted his body. He turned on the air-conditioning units, emptied his suitcase, and dumped the clothing into the hamper. After stripping down to his shorts, he got a Coke from the refrigerator, propped himself up on his bed, and telephoned his father in Dallas.

"I didn't expect you back so soon, son," his father said after they'd greeted each other. "How'd it go?"

"All right, I guess."

He had to be careful, because his dad had a sixth sense about him, and keeping secrets from him was hard work.

"Didn't you like Mother Africa?"

He kept his voice even. "Yes. What I saw of it."

"Something or somebody got between you and it. Right?"

Jason enjoyed the last swig of his Coke, set the bottle on the floor beside the bed, and answered, "You could say that."

"It's not a good idea to get involved when you're on the rebound. I know you think you're master of all you survey, but don't forget that Napoleon met his Waterloo."

"Right. Come up July fourth and go fishing with me in the Adirondacks."

He heard the low growl of a laugh that, for as long as he could remember, had given him a sense of peace and security. "All right. I'll butt out. Glad you're back safe."

He hung up, went to his computer, and began a search for travel agents who booked tours to Zimbabwe. By midnight, he had collected the names and phone numbers of one hundred and forty-seven such agents, and he gave up the search when he realized that there could be a thousand more. Maybe he ought to hire a private investigator—but who could he tell the man to look for? Churning heat violated his belly, and sweat dripped down his bare chest as the scent of her perfume came back to him, a ghost bent on torture. They'd been magic together, flint and dry grass, and he refused to accept that he'd never see her again.

Ginger hadn't seen groups of youth congregating in the streets of Harare. When she'd asked one of the hotel clerks what the young people did for entertainment, she'd learned that the people looked primarily to their families for that, as well as for social life and economic support and that they rarely made close ties with individuals who were not members—first of their family, and second of their tribe. That information had been the germ of an idea for a mother-daughter club on her beloved Roosevelt Island, and she decided to start the club with Saturday morning movies for mothers and their adolescent daughters. Fired up with the idea and its potential, she telephoned Clarice.

"Think I can pull it off?"

"You can try, Ginger, but if these mothers had enough control over their daughters to bring them to a Saturday morning movie, would the girls be hanging out in the street at midnight in the first place?"

She'd thought about that. "Girls will go to free movies. I'm going to start with something like *Sleepless in Seattle,* and maybe I can get some of the older boys who have good manners and values to speak to them once in a while. What do you think?"

"The boys will certainly bring them out, but if you want a crowd, get that gray-eyed hunk you walked out on in Harare. Now, they'd stand in line to listen to him."

She subdued her rising hackles, took a deep breath, and warned Clarice, "Listen, girl, if we're going to be friends, you have to stop prying into my life with your…your so-called psychic gifts. Only God knows my future, and you stop painting your crazy pictures of things you can't possibly know."

"Want me to describe him?"

Ginger stared at the receiver. When Clarice got started with her soothsaying, she gave her the willies. "No, I don't."

"Okay by me, girlfriend, but I wouldn't have turned *my* back on a six-foot, two-inch guy with a washboard belly, a complexion the color of fresh pecans, long-lashed gray eyes, silky black hair, and a smile to die for."

Thank goodness Clarice couldn't see her surprised face. "Maybe he was rough around the edges."

"Honey, if that man got any smoother and any sharper, you could use him to chisel stone."

Pictures of him flashed through her mind, and her blood sped through her veins, dizzying her. She had to sit down on the edge of her bed, but she wouldn't give Clarice the benefit of triumph. "Go feed the pigeons."

Clarice's merriment greeted her ears like the mockery of a conqueror, as though she knew Ginger was doomed to remember Jason forever. "I've already fed them. See you down at Andy's Place about four o'clock?"

Ginger agreed and hung up. She didn't usually work on Saturday afternoon, but she had to make up for the two weeks in Africa, not to speak of the time she'd wasted daydreaming about Jason since she'd returned home. Unable to concentrate on the case she was preparing, she decided to take some clothes downstairs to the dry cleaner. She dipped her hands in the pockets of the linen jacket she'd worn on the trip with Jason to Victoria Falls, and her fingers brushed a piece of folded paper. Part of a menu.

She unfolded it and read: *Thousands of miles may separate us when you read this, but our souls will never be apart.*

"I will not shed a tear over him. Not one," she said and wiped drops of moisture from her cheeks. The man hadn't been made who could cause her to shrivel up in mourning like a dried-up, inedible prune. She brushed more moisture from her face. "Drat you, Jason who-ever-you-are, I could love you to the recesses of my womb," she whispered, "and I could hate you, too. You have no right to torment me this way."

Jason fared no better than Ginger. In the month since his return home, he'd managed to get one case postponed and had gotten a mistrial in another by proving jury tampering. He had a divorce case pending, but couldn't develop an enthusiasm for it, because the suit reminded him too much of his own divorce. That Saturday afternoon, disconcerted by his inability to do any serious work, he put on a pair of white Bermuda shorts, a yellow, knit T-shirt and sneakers and took the Lexington IRT subway down to SOHO, where his younger brother, Eric, a sculptor, lived.

He walked around an unfinished form that stood in the middle of Eric's living room. "What's that supposed to be, Eric, a modern Aphrodite?"

"No idea. She just tumbled out of my head. I was working on her a couple of days ago, looked up at her, and couldn't believe my eyes."

Jason paced around the figure again and again. "Did you ever meet a woman named Ginger?"

Eric looked up from the spatula he was cleaning. "Ginger who?"

Jason shook his head. "I couldn't even guess, but this figure you've done here reminds me of her. Something about the set of the shoulders and that 'I'll cry tomorrow' smile. It's eerie, man."

He must have sounded foolish, because Eric stopped cleaning his tool and stared at him. "And you don't even know her last name?"

"You insinuating something?"

"Uh uh. No indeed. I'm saying you wanted her, you still want her, and you don't know who or where she is. Where'd you meet her?"

Jason walked to the other end of the room and back. "In Harare. If I knew where she was, I'd be there right now. And that's all I want to say about it."

Eric's hand rested on his brother's shoulder, and he spoke in a voice heavy with concern. "I'm sorry, Jason. Man, I really am sorry."

Jason shrugged. "I've been through floods, hurricanes, the rigors of a law degree, and a nasty divorce. This won't kill me, either."

Eric resumed cleaning his tools. "Maybe not, but it hurts you like hell."

"Tell me about it. How about putting that thing away and we go down to Dock's sidewalk café and get something cool to drink?"

Eric's raised eyebrow was proof of his disinterest. "It's too hot. I've never known it to be this hot in April."

"Me, neither. Put on something cool and let's go."

It seemed as though Ginger took possession of his thoughts

whenever he was indoors. He could only surmise that she left him free of her memory when he went outside, because nothing could compare with the beauty they witnessed together at Victoria Falls and in the environs of Harare. He stuck his hands in the pockets of his shorts and trailed Eric out of the apartment. When had he known such emptiness that he wanted company, crowds of people around him, so that he wouldn't think? He loved Eric's company, but didn't want to talk with him, only to sit with him in a crowd with such a din that it made conversation impossible. *Ginger! In the name of heaven, where are you?*

G.A. Hinds, as Ginger was known to her clients and in court circles, stepped into the judge's chamber and froze, rooted in her tracks as though struck by lightning. *It couldn't be!* She forced herself to take one step closer, willing him to turn around so that she could see his face.

"Good morning, Ms. Hinds," Judge Williams said—and then *he* turned to face her.

"*You!*" she shrieked. "It can't be. It... My God, it's *you!*"

As if coming out of a thick fog, he stared, shaking his head as though mute, his feet taking him slowly to her. When barely a yard separated them he grabbed her, lifted her from her feet, spun her around, and squeezed her to him. "*Ginger. Ginger. Ginger!* I can't believe it. I'd given up all hope of ever seeing you again. I—"

"Uh hmm." Judge Williams cleared her throat. "I hope this isn't what it looks like. Attorney Calhoun, I assume you didn't know your client's husband was being represented by Attorney Hinds. This is unusual, but if you aren't married or lovers, I suppose we can continue." She looked at Ginger. "Well?"

Ginger didn't know how she found her voice. "We've never been lovers, Your Honor."

"Mr. Calhoun, do you agree?"

His eyes sparkled with merriment, and he rubbed his chin contemplatively, like a wise man seeking the truth. He told her, "Yes, ma'am, Your Honor. I certainly do."

Ginger saw no reason why Her Honor should smirk. "Good," Judge Agatha Williams said, adjusting her wig. "You may unhand her now, Mr. Calhoun. And if I ask you two that question at any time before this case is closed, your answers had better be the same as now."

"Yes, ma'am," they replied in unison as Jason released Ginger.

Judge Williams cleared her throat, louder than Ginger thought necessary, shuffled some of the papers on her desk, and resumed her official demeanor." "Ms. Hinds, your client is bringing the suit, so I want to hear his charge first."

"Basically," Ginger began, "my client's wife is immature, interested only in sensual gratification, parties and fun and—because he works hard trying to make a good life for them—she accuses him of putting his career before her."

"And he does, Your Honor," Jason broke in, presenting the wife's countersuit. "He's a workaholic, saves money because he hates to spend it, and pays her absolutely no attention."

"That's not true," Ginger declared. "A person has a right to expect complete cooperation, to have a true partnership with his spouse, not a firefly who wants to run out every evening at sundown."

"And my client has a right to expect some joy in her life with her husband, not to shrivel up with a dull spud who comes home at eight or nine o'clock every night, wolfs down whatever she's cooked, and passes out in front of the TV."

Judge Williams banged her gavel. "I see I don't have to worry about the two of you shacking up any time soon. I had agreed to hear this case with the principals absent, but I've changed my mind. Case recessed for today. Bring those two adolescents in here Monday morning at ten sharp. And go your separate ways."

* * *

Jason stood on the top step of the Municipal Building at 60 Lafayette Street in lower Manhattan and made an effort to settle his nerves. In the course of half an hour, he'd had as many shocks as a man ought to have in his lifetime. He'd found her. She proved to be an accomplished woman, and he liked that. But she was his adversary in court and, worse still, she might beat him. He took comfort in the way she'd behaved when her gaze lit on him; she had surely missed him every bit as much as he'd missed her.

He looked back toward the door, hoping to see Ginger stroll through it. After the way in which they'd greeted each other, she couldn't expect him to walk out of there and leave her, no matter what Judge Williams said. And if the judge had meant they shouldn't see each other, she needed to learn something about the behavior of men and women when a sizzling chemistry hooked them together.

After what seemed like half an hour, she walked out of the building, and he rushed to her; he couldn't have restrained himself if his life had depended on it. He had to touch her, to assure himself that she was really Ginger. "What took you so long?" he asked her.

The warm and welcoming lights in her wonderful brown eyes made a mockery of her effort to maintain a cool, professional façade. "Hi, Jason. I figured you'd get tired of waiting and leave. I'm not in the habit of ignoring a judge's orders."

He took her hand and walked with her toward the steps, still wondering whether he could be dreaming. "Ginger, that judge is not stupid. She said what was required of her, but she'd think us both insane if we obeyed."

Her fingers tightened around his, but her words denied her gesture of affection. "I don't disobey judges, and that's that. I'm glad to see you, though. I really am, Jason."

The tone of finality in her voice gave him a feeling of anxiety, and he stared in shocked disbelief as she dropped his hand, ran down the remaining steps, jumped into a cab, and rode away. He went back to the clerk's office.

"Hi, Ann. Could you give me the phone number of the lawyer for my client's husband?"

"Your reasons, Mr. Calhoun?"

"I'm going to try for a deal." She didn't ask what kind of deal, and he didn't see a need to tell.

"Sure." She flipped through her files, wrote two numbers on a scratch pad, and handed them to him.

He thanked Ann, and headed for the street. "Ginger, Girl," he said to himself, "you won't get away from me this time," and strolled down the steps whistling Marty Stuart's number one hit, "Till I Found You." He spotted a florist, went in, and asked for a Manhattan telephone directory. An address for her matched the phone number that Ann gave him, so he ordered a bouquet of calla lilies and had them delivered to her.

Ginger told herself she'd done the professional thing, but she'd used as much fortitude as any woman ever had when she walked away from Jason Calhoun. Calhoun. She liked his name. She hadn't guessed he'd be an attorney, though she had realized he was a man of some accomplishment. She didn't let herself imagine what could come next. Maybe he had a wife. The taxi driver pulled up to West View, the building in which she lived, and she paid and got out.

Who was that man? she wondered. Every time she saw him he had a thick, hardcover book in his hand. Something about his demeanor, his clothing, and his carriage suggested academic life. Always a book, even while he ate his meals, which he took at Andy's Place. She supposed he was retired. Oddly, he seemed as curious about her as she was about him, but neither had bridged the gap and spoken. She thought that strange, because Roosevelt Islanders spoke to each other whether they'd been introduced or not. She made up her mind to put an end to it first chance she got.

\* \* \*

With the afternoon free of court duties, she changed into casual dress and went to Andy's Place for lunch. One of the local clergymen walked in and was soon joined by the mystery man with his book. Seeing an opportunity for an introduction, she left her table, walked over, and greeted the minister.

"Hello, Ginger," the Reverend Armstrong said. "You know Amos Logan, don't you?"

"I've been wondering who you were. I'm Ginger Hinds," she said to Amos, who rose to his feet and extended his hand.

"Same here, Miss Hinds. How do you do? I figured you were either in banking, education or law. How far off was I?"

"Law."

"Why don't you join us old folk?" Reverend Armstrong asked. "Amos retired last year from his cushy job as a law school dean."

Amos raised both eyebrows. "About as cushy as running a church." He regarded Ginger with the penetrating stare of a judge. "What kind of law do you practice?"

"Criminal, but right now I have a divorce case, my first, and I'm not sure I'll take another one."

"Why?" Amos wanted to know.

"Because my client can't make up his mind. He's called me twice to indicate he may be making a mistake, but he has no choice now, because his wife has entered a countersuit."

"Smart woman," Amos said.

The Reverend Armstrong pulled air through his teeth and strummed his fingers on the table. "If they'd only go for counseling and work out their problems."

Amos shrugged. "A lot of them do...just before they file for divorce."

She ordered bean soup and a green salad and finished it quickly. Amos had come too close to her life, to the crumbling of her own marriage, and she wouldn't put it past the good Reverend to pounce on it in the presence of this stranger.

She gulped down the last of her ginger ale and stood. "See you Sunday, Reverend Armstrong. I'm glad to know who you are, Mr. Logan."

Amos wiped his mouth with one of Andy's paper napkins and stood. "Call me Amos. Perhaps we can have a cup of coffee together sometime. Not many people around here want to talk law."

"I'd love it," she said, and headed back to her apartment. Amos Logan was an interesting man.

She stopped by the mailbox, collected her mail, and hastened to the air-conditioned haven of her apartment. Who ever heard of ninety-one degrees in April? That and the equally high humidity had sapped her energy in the short walk from Andy's Place to the building in which she lived. The first letter confirmed her sister Linda's wedding date in late May, a month away, and she hadn't shopped for the dress she'd wear as maid of honor. She looked at the long list of things that Linda couldn't find in the small town of Easton and wanted her to purchase in New York, and made some notes as to where she might find them. Anything except settling down to her work, because the minute she tried it, the face of Jason Calhoun mocked her from the pages before her.

The sound of the doorman's buzzer irritated her, because she didn't want company. "Delivery, Ms. Hinds."

"Thanks, Allan. Please send him up."

Minutes later, she stood in the doorway of her apartment and stared at the bouquet of one dozen calla lilies in her arm, winded as if she had run for miles. She closed the door, found the note, and read, *Fate has caught us in her net. What shall we do about it? As for me, I'm overjoyed. Jason.*

She kissed the flowers, placed them in a vase, and sat staring at them. She had found him, and he was more than she had thought existed. And he wanted *her!* She hugged herself and danced around and around until she collapsed on the sofa, giddy with joy. She didn't want to work or do anything but think of him.

Suddenly, she sobered and, annoyed at her frivolity, got up and went to her desk. "I'm not going to let him control me this way," she admonished herself, opened her file on Roberts versus Roberts and got down to work. Until Steven's wife contested the divorce, she hadn't worried about the reasons Steven was giving for wanting one. An uncontested divorce posed no problem. But in her view, her client's grounds were no better than his wife's charges and, from the judge's order that the contestants be present at the trial, she suspected that Agatha Williams meant to raise some tough questions. Well, she could only represent her client as best she could with the flimsy reasons he'd given her. She worked until dinnertime, called the Chinese take-out shop, and ordered her dinner. Minutes after she'd finished it and destroyed the evidence, her phone rang.

"Hello, Ginger. This is Jason."

At the sound of his voice, a sharp, unfamiliar sensation shot through her, but she spoke with a calm voice. "Hello, Jason. I don't remember giving you my address or my home phone number."

Laughter tinged his words. "Of course you don't. I have my sources. If you had remembered giving either one to me, I'd start worrying about your truthfulness."

"Jason, we're not supposed to be consorting socially. You know that."

"What do you think we can do through these telephone wires? I spent weeks cursing myself for letting you get away without a clue as to who you were or where to find you. God let you back into my life and, unless there is a compelling reason for me to do otherwise, I am not, I repeat *not*, letting you get away from me again."

She grabbed her chest to still her heart's pounding, but she was doggoned if she'd let him know how he excited her. Coolly, she told him, "We don't know each other well enough for you to say things like that."

"Speak for yourself, Ginger. I let you walk away because

you wanted to go, and because I'd never had a one-night affair with anyone and agreed that it wasn't wise. But after you'd checked out of the hotel the next morning, I saw the hole you'd left me in, and I knew that if we had made love you wouldn't have been a one-time fling. In those two days, you got so deep in me, sweetheart, that you'll be with me forever. I don't know what it means, but I want to—"

"Jason, please don't. You can't say things like this to me. We're adversaries, and the judge said—"

She heard him pull air through his front teeth. "Hang that woman. Alma Roberts and Steven Roberts are adversaries. You and I are not, and don't you forget that."

A flush of blood warmed her face. "What are you talking about? You practically bit off my head in that judge's chamber this morning."

"You were taking your frustrations out on my client, and I wasn't going to stand for it."

She looked toward the ceiling and rolled her eyes. Another self-satisfied male chauvinist. "Jason, a wife isn't somebody you stash away at home to eat chocolates and watch the soaps. Women have brains, and they can use them for something other than sterilizing baby bottles."

She figured from his long silence that she'd hit a tender spot, and she was certain when he said, "Women who think like you are the reason for half of society's problems. A man has no rights in a marriage, as far as you're concerned. You never heard of fifty-fifty. A woman can work if she wants to, but nobody should force her to do it. Women who stay at home, though, are less likely to get a divorce than those who work outside."

She pulled her hair away from her face and got comfortable. "Spoken like a true Republican, a species for which I have no use. And don't forget—Alma Roberts stayed at home and didn't work."

"You probably love Republicans about as much as I love Democrats, especially the so-called liberals." When she didn't respond to that sally, he asked, "Ginger, what in the devil are we fighting about?"

"You're asking me? It all started because you went after me in court this morning with all your guns blasting."

"Come on, Ginger. That's between Calhoun and Hinds. It's got nothing to do with Jason and Ginger."

Images of his gray eyes lit with merriment, of the way his smile sort of hung on the right side of his mouth, danced before her eyes, and she slapped her forehead to dispel them.

"What was that I heard?" he asked.

"Don't change the subject," she said, increasingly wary of the force of her feelings for him. "I'm not a schizophrenic with two personalities and two minds, so don't expect me to split myself into DayGinger and NightGinger. No socializing until this case is over."

"When it's over, lady," he growled, "I'm going to delight in reminding you of the way it feels to slump against me in submission when my tongue is deep in your mouth loving you and teaching you who you are. Have you forgotten how close we became?"

When awareness slammed into her, she would have enjoyed throttling him for tampering with her brain and shaking up her sense of self. "For that, you would need my cooperation, mister," she shot at him.

"And I'll make sure I get it," he drawled.

"I'm going to hang up, Jason."

"Ginger." His voice was no longer assertive with self-confidence, but carried an urgency, a need that found its destination in her heart. "Ginger, I am serious. I called to ask if we can be friends. It got personal today, but I want us to be as we were in Zimbabwe. I need that woman in my life. I've never known anyone like her. For two days, she lit up my horizon, brightened my world. While I roamed those hills, preserves, parks and streams with her, the world strutted brand new all around me, every place I looked. You and I were ourselves, then, not the products of our training, not public personas acting out the roles that society and the people we know have set for us. I want you back with me, Ginger."

Stunned, she parted her lips but no words came out of them.

"I mean every word I'm saying," he went on. "I missed you more than I can describe, and I can't believe that feelings this strong, this deep, are one-sided. Will you walk away again from what we found in Harare? Or maybe I'm wrong. Can't you tell me you reciprocate what I feel?"

She had forgotten how direct he could be. "Jason, surely you know that you touched me. I didn't forget you. I didn't even try. But I have to do my best for my client, and that won't happen if I'm moonlighting with you. So let's be glad we found each other and let the future take care of itself—after this case is over."

"Well, thanks for that much, Ginger. I'd better tell you, though, that I don't leave my life to Miss Future's whims. I do whatever I can to shape it the way I want it, and I want to get to know you well enough to find out where you fit in my future. You ought to want the same."

"I do, Jason, but right now I want you to give me some room. You needn't worry. You won't be out of my mind. Can I count on that?"

"You can always count on me, Ginger. No matter what. I'll be there for you." His tone turned sheepish. "You wouldn't give a guy a goodnight kiss would you?"

The thought of kissing him sent her emotions into high gear. She didn't recognize the sultry voice that said, "I'm parting my lips."

His silence shouted to her through the wires. "Jason?"

"I...I'm loving you. Goodnight, Ginger."

"Jason! Thanks for the beautiful calla lilies."

"My pleasure. Goodnight, sweetheart."

He hung up, leaving her to stare at the receiver. After a few minutes, she shrugged. No point in wondering why he'd done that, because she doubted he'd tell. She wanted to be with him, to know again the strength of his arms around her, to loll in his sweetness. She rubbed the goose pimples on her forearms as thoughts of how she'd felt believing she'd never see him again crowded all else from her mind. She reached for the telephone, remembered that she didn't have his phone number, and laughed. Thank God she didn't have to decide whether to be stupid or heated to the boiling point. But one day soon she'd have to choose whether to call him when she needed him, because he would surely give her his telephone number. Of that, she was certain; Jason Calhoun had served notice that he didn't wait for things to happen to him. He acted.

What a woman! He walked out on his balcony that covered part of the roof of the building in which he lived, and looked out over Central Park. Sprawled out on a chaise lounge, he reached into the bar that stood beside it and got a bottle of iced tea. At sixteen stories above the street, the traffic below was barely a hum and, though he wouldn't have minded hearing the nightly jazz that floated up from the club around the corner on Fifth Avenue, he preferred the more serene atmosphere of 110th Street. He mused over his good fortune in finding Ginger. He understood himself and his needs, and he knew right down to his gut that Ginger Hinds was the woman for him. He hadn't meant their first kiss that day in the tour bus to be serious, but she had responded to him honestly, giving all of herself. He didn't even want to think about that night in his hotel room. For a while, he looked at the lights that made New York famous and conjured up pictures of himself showing Ginger what lay behind so many of them. He wanted to show her the world. Several hours later, raindrops awakened him, and he went inside, dried off, and climbed into bed.

Jason rose early the next morning, went down to the exercise gym and did thirty push-ups and half an hour on the treadmill. After swimming a few laps, he went back to his apartment, dressed, and took the elevator down to Hilda's coffee shop on the ground floor of the building.

"Your usual, Mr. Calhoun?" the waitress asked.

He nodded, and within minutes she returned with cheese grits, buttermilk biscuits, fried country ham, red-eye gravy, scrambled eggs and coffee.

"I tell you, you Southern fellows do love this ham, grits, and biscuits, and I'm sure glad you do."

"Yeah," he responded, sampling a biscuit, "when I get homesick for some real food, I make a beeline for this place." He tasted the ham and grits. "Midge, this stuff is good."

Her smile struck him as being a little too sweet, and he stopped eating and stared at her. "Well, I'll be damned," he said to himself, when her olive-toned face turned crimson. Best to pretend he hadn't seen it, because he was doggoned if he was going to give up the best breakfast in New York City. He laid beside his plate a tip that was much too large, went back home, left a message on his secretary's answering machine, and called Ginger at her office. When he got the answering service, he called her at home.

"Hello, Ginger, this is Jason."

"Jason? But I thought you promised me last night that—"

"This is strictly business. I'll be out of town till Sunday night, and I wanted to make sure you didn't want a conference with me or our clients before we see Judge Williams Monday morning."

She resisted asking him what good he thought that would do, and asked whether his client was going to withdraw her countersuit and stop wasting their time. He countered with the remark that her client was a cheapskate for refusing his wife a small monthly allowance.

"Now, you wait a minute," she fumed. "A woman who refused to work and help her husband build a life for them, who wanted to go out to dinner every night to expensive restaurants because she hated the sight of the kitchen, now wants a pile of alimony so she can sit on her lazy behind for the rest of her life? Give me a break, buddy. A man with modern ideals wouldn't represent such a parasite."

"And a lawyer with humane consideration for her fellow human beings wouldn't— Ginger, for heaven's sake, what are we doing here? This is ridiculous!" He took a deep breath, hating the feeling of defeat. "Ginger, I didn't have that case on my mind. I really called to wish you a happy weekend and to tell you that I'll be down in Dallas with my dad. See you Monday morning."

"Oh, Jason. I'm…sorry I flew off the handle, but you made me so mad with—"

"Don't say it. We're both sensitive about this case, and I wish I knew why. See you."

Jason telephoned American Airlines and reserved a seat on the twelve-forty flight from LaGuardia to Dallas International, packed a few personal items, and left for the airport. In Dallas, he rented a Ford Taurus and headed for the brick Tudor thirty miles from Dallas that he'd bought for his father the year before. He couldn't have said why he wanted a couple of days with his father, but when he saw Aaron Calhoun he was immediately enveloped in that peace his father always exuded.

"What brings you here, son?"

"Everything. Nothing. I have to get away from New York City every so often so I can stay human, and I hadn't seen you for a while."

Aaron took him at his word, as he always had, and didn't probe. "Fish been jumping that high." He held a hand five feet above the floor. "We can still get a mess of catfish 'fore sunset."

Jason grinned as pleasure stole over him. "You cleaning 'em?"

Aaron's left eyebrow shot up. "Don't I always? Want a bite before we head for the lake?" The local people called it a lake, but it was actually the wide, bowl-shaped area of the river.

"Thanks. I ate on the plane. Let's go. I haven't fished in months."

They walked to the river, put their gear in order, and cast their lines. "Eric said you'd found a girl and lost her," Aaron began, while they watched their little red and white floaters bobble with the rush of the river.

"That's right, but I found her again. I still can't believe I've seen her and talked with her. When I saw her in New York for the first time and realized I'd found her, we were in the judge's chamber. Ginger's a lawyer, opposing me in a case. You wouldn't believe how totally unprofessional I acted."

"I can imagine what a shock it was." Aaron grabbed his line. "Oh, oh. There goes my fish."

"Would you believe that judge told us not to see each other socially until the case is settled?"

Aaron stopped lighting his pipe and looked at the son who, even as a child, disliked taking orders from anyone, including his father. "And you're doing it?"

Jason had to laugh at the look of incredulity on his father's face. "I don't have a choice. Ginger believes in obeying authority."

Aaron Calhoun threw back his head and enjoyed a guffaw. "Well, I'll be doggoned. You love her?"

Jason ran his left hand over his silken curls, a move certain to alert his father to his bemusement. "I don't know, Dad. I haven't seen much of her."

"Pshaw. Sometimes, it only takes that first glance, one minute, and you're in for life."

"That didn't happen with Louise and me."

Aaron took a few puffs on his pipe and furrowed his brow. "You can say that again. You two backed into it, and it should never have happened. You were about as well-suited as a donkey and a thoroughbred racehorse."

"I don't think much of that analogy, and I hate hearing you say, 'I told you so.'"

"And I didn't say it, either. Soon as you can manage it, I want to meet your Ginger."

He wished she was his Ginger. "If she's the one, I'll bring her down here."

"Whether she is or not, I want to meet the woman who shook you up like this. Never thought I'd see the day it happened to you. Louise didn't know who you were, but this one's got your number."

"You've got a fish, Dad," Jason said, glad not to have to comment on his father's arrow-straight observations.

Aaron pulled in a big catfish, looked at his elder son, and grinned. "We can go now."

"Wait a minute. Not until I get—" The line jerked in his hand and, when he began to reel it in, the big fish fought him, jumping high out of the water, until Jason managed to get him in the net.

Jason looked down at the fish, still wiggling and trying to jump. "We don't need both of them," he told his father. "I'm throwing him back in."

Aaron got up from the rock on which he'd been sitting and dusted off the back of his trousers. "When your mother was living, we used to say you must be the strongest softhearted man on this planet. Go ahead and throw him back."

"You wouldn't make some hush puppies to go with this fish, would you?" Jason asked him.

"That and some stewed down collards, too. Doesn't take much to make you happy, son, but what it does take isn't one bit ordinary."

Jason slung an arm around his father's shoulders as they began the half-mile walk back to the house. Peace. He hoped he'd someday give at least that much to his sons. A stream of fear streaked down his back. What if Ginger wouldn't consider having children? He'd seen many women lawyers in court, but not one of them looked as if she might be pregnant. No, it didn't take a lot to make him happy, but children were a must.

* * *

Ginger dressed with extra care that Monday morning. She had to look smart, businesslike, and feminine, too. She had Jason on her mind, but she also wanted that judge to take her seriously, so she settled for an electric blue linen suit and knotted her hair at her nape. Hot as it was, it didn't much matter how she wore it, but at least her neck would get a little air. As she'd expected, Jason arrived dressed to kill in what had to be a Brooks Brothers suit and a red tie guaranteed to keep the judge's eyes glued to him. She smirked at the sight of Alma Roberts in a clinging, red miniskirt dress and long, dangling earrings—a walking confirmation of her client's accusations.

"You may begin, Ms. Hinds," Judge Williams announced at precisely ten o'clock.

She looked toward Jason and wasn't surprised to find his gaze fixed on her. Her respect for him climbed a notch when she noticed nothing personal in the way in which he observed her.

"Good morning, Your Honor. Mr. Calhoun." Thank goodness she hadn't forgotten that; Jason had a way of disarming her without trying. "Your Honor, my client, Steven Roberts, is seeking a divorce from Alma Roberts, his wife of seven years, on the following grounds." She repeated the statement she'd made at the preliminary hearing.

Jason greeted the judge and Ginger and followed with his client's countersuit. "If it pleases the court, my client rejects Steven Roberts' charges as nonsense and wants them thrown out. A wife has a right to expect affection and companionship from her husband, but all she's gotten from this man is a constant diet of her own company. All by herself, Your Honor."

"Your Honor, my client has had to work so that this…his wife could live comfortably and he could still provide for their old age. Did she help him? No, ma'am. She spent what he earned trying to be a teenager. Pop records, clubs, parties, shopping sprees, and lunch two or three times a week with the girls, while he wanted to build a home and a future for them."

Jason dropped his court manners and pounded his right fist into his palm. "A man has no right to expect his wife to work," Jason growled, "not even if he has to hack two jobs. A guy is supposed to pamper his woman. Besides, how's she going to have children and raise a family if she has to punch a time clock every morning?"

"Mr. Calhoun," the judge said in a tone just short of sarcastic, "are you saying a woman's place is in the home?"

Jason stuck his hands in his pockets, paced, and then turned to the judge with a half-smile at the corner of his mouth and his smooth demeanor intact. "Your Honor does me a disservice."

"Glad to hear it," Agatha Williams replied. "For a minute there, I was afraid you hadn't made it into the twentieth century."

"Wasted worry, Your Honor," he shot back. "At times I get the feeling there aren't many of us in it. If I may proceed? My client deserves restitution."

Ginger couldn't believe he'd risk flippancy with that straightlaced judge. She looked at the woman on the bench. Doggoned if he wasn't getting away with it. Maybe she wasn't the only female with whom that red tie and those gray eyes paid off.

She glanced at her notes. "Restitution?" She stuck a hand on her left hip and glared at Jason. "Your Honor, a person can only take so much. You work yourself to death giving one hundred percent, and find out you're the only one giving. You're struggling to build a home and a future, and all that wonderful person you married is interested in is having a good time. My client deserves a partner who shares his goals."

Jason propped both hands on the bar and gave the impression of someone whose patience was fast eroding. After a second, he leaned toward the judge, his voice low and soothing like cool water lapping softly over and around you on a hot summer day. Ginger braced herself for a smooth job of conning.

"Your Honor," he began, his face glazed with childlike innocence, "shouldn't a young woman have the company of an energetic man rather than a burned-out Joe who straggles home late every night and conks out on the sofa in front of the TV?"

Ginger had to marvel as a smile brought sparkles to his eyes. "You'll agree, I'm sure," he continued, "that a woman should be able to enjoy her man when she's young, and not have to wait until she's over the hill."

Who did he think he was? As if driven by a nest of hornets, Ginger bounded to within two feet of Jason. "Why don't you men stop letting your libidos take the place of your common sense? A levelheaded man doesn't try to have his cake and eat it, too. He plans for his family, makes certain that his wife and children will have a good life, and *then* he has a good time. Deliver me from the guy who wants his wife to start having a family the day they get married."

She ignored the storm brewing in his eyes and the sparks that seemed to fly from them as he glared at her, his expression thunderous. "I suppose your client gets his ideas about family life from his mother. That's usually what undermines a marriage, isn't it? A spouse who hasn't gotten three feet from the womb? A smart attorney would have advised Steven Roberts to seek counseling."

She stepped closer to him, the presence of the judge and the divorcing couple forgotten. "I *did* advise it. And, anyway, what business is it of yours what I do or don't say to my client? You obviously approve of your client's adolescent frivolity. She's too immature for marriage, a crybaby who doesn't appreciate a solid, hardworking man. I would never have expected that of you."

*Bang! Bang! Bang!* "Mr. Calhoun. Ms. Hinds. Those statements do not appear in the briefs you gave me, and I can only conclude that the two of you are either stretching the truth or you've gotten personal. I think you've gotten personal, and I won't have any more of it."

Ginger didn't hear the judge's words and, from the expression on Jason's face as he stared at her, she suspected that he hadn't heard them, either.

Steven Roberts stood. "Your Honor, could I please say a word?"

Ginger whirled around, and a gasp escaped her. She hadn't seen Steven move across the room and sit beside his wife. "You're supposed to consult with your attorney first," she told him.

"Let me hear what he has to say," Judge Williams interjected, "because up to now I don't see any grounds for divorce. Marriage isn't a game for the entertainment of adolescents, Mrs. Roberts."

"Your Honor," Steven pleaded. "We just decided we don't want a divorce. After we heard Ms. Hinds and Mr. Calhoun going at it, what we thought was so important just kinda sounded childish."

Ginger restrained her impulse to shake her fist at him. Hadn't she told him that half a dozen times?

"I'm glad to hear it, Mr. Roberts," Judge Williams said, "because childish is precisely what it is. And Mrs. Roberts, take my advice and grow up. Case dismissed."

Ginger stuffed her papers into her briefcase, locked it, and turned to leave the judge's chamber. "Thank you, Judge Williams," she said in the mandatory gesture of politeness, nodded in Jason's direction, and headed for the door.

"Just a minute, Ms. Hinds," Agatha Williams called after her, "I want to speak with the two of you. If you're having a problem, straighten it out. Better still, avoid cases in which you're working against each other. And do something about this thing between you that's so hot you forgot yourselves and behaved unprofessionally." She grinned at Ginger. "Surely you can handle it, Ms. Hinds."

"I'm not so sure," Ginger replied and left Jason and the judge gaping as she walked away.

She took a taxi to her office on Broadway just below Houston and walked into the refreshing softness of blue walls, tall ficus trees, desert cacti, and warm mahogany furnishings that always seemed so inviting. Whenever she raised her gaze from the papers on her desk, she looked directly into the vision of artist Edward Mitchell Bannister, of whose calming seascape she never tired. Feminine, yet professional. Elegant, like the Turkish carpet beneath her feet. She sat down, wrote a summary of the trial's conclusion, and buzzed her secretary.

"I didn't know you'd come in, Ms. Hinds," her secretary said. "Mr. Calhoun called. He said it was urgent. May I ring him?"

A shiver jetted up her spine. If only she knew what to expect of him. "Yes. Then I want you to take some notes on Roberts versus Roberts."

"Yes, ma'am."

Minutes later, his voice soothed her ears like a liquid prelude from a master flutist. "Ginger, this is personal, so if your secretary is on the line, ask her to—"

"No one's on but me. What is it?"

"Look. We sat alone on that tour bus looking at rain as thick as ocean water pouring all around us, and with lightning streaking around in it like naked dancers frolicking through time. We sat there dazed by it, and it made you shiver, pulled at your insides until you turned to me with your lips parted and ready for my mouth. Now, you act as though it never happened. What about Victoria Falls in that little boat in the middle of the Zambezi River, when we stood at the stern with our arms around each other and watched a sunset that made you cry? You held me then, Ginger. And I mean you held me so close to you that everything you felt—your longing, your desire for me, and your fear of it—seeped down into me, trashing my will to avoid getting involved with you."

She couldn't find words to respond, though he waited.

Then he let out a long breath. "*Woman, what is it with you? I am the same man you wanted to make love with that night in Harare. You were honest, then. Talk to me.*"

She clutched the phone until her knuckles stretched the skin on her right hand. He didn't have to remind her of what she would never forget. She searched for a safe, impersonal answer, couldn't find one, and settled for the truth.

"You want to know what's going on with me, Jason? Well, I'll tell you. I'm scared, Jason, and I have been from the moment we met. I kissed you less than six hours after I first saw you, and I still marvel that I had the sense and strength to leave you that night, because it wasn't my conscious self that did it. The woman who walked away from you was the woman I am the other three hundred and fifty-one days in the year taking over. Do you think I ever did anything like that before? You bet I'm uneasy around a man who gets between me and my common sense just by showing up and smiling."

"Ginger. Ginger. Honey, did it occur to you that we might be each other's salvation? Destiny? If you've never responded to a man as you did to me, shouldn't you go for it, see what it holds for you? Do you think *I'm* in the habit of taking strange women to bed? No way! After two days of the happenings between us, you were no longer a stranger, but someone I needed. And, mind you, I didn't say *want*."

Goose pimples popped out on her arms and her pulse jumped into a wild gallop. How could he say he needed her? In four years of marriage, Harold hadn't used the word. "These are strong statements, Jason. Be careful what you say."

"I always choose my words carefully, Ginger. We have a second chance now, and you know who I am. The case is closed, and I want to see you. Can I bring this champagne or not?"

The thought of being alone with him again burned her brain with anticipation. Unwanted. Yet, uncontrollable. She didn't want a repeat of her life with Harold, and if this man was wrong for her and she let him into her life, she'd pay a heavy price. She remembered her feeling of desperation when it seemed certain that she'd never see him again.

"Jason. I'll have to think about whether we should continue what we started—"

She'd bet those gray eyes shot fire as he said, "Sorry. I'm not giving you that luxury. You promised."

She wanted desperately to be with him, but she didn't think she could handle him. Her experience was limited to her ex-husband, and he hadn't needed handling. After having spent time with Jason, she suspected that the chemistry between Harold and her had been as weak as steam in a tunnel of trapped air. Well, if she spent the remainder of her life protecting herself, she might as well shrivel up right then.

"I promised we'd have champagne," she said in a voice that bore an unfamiliar weakness. "So come over about six-thirty, and we can drink it sitting at the riverbank."

"Watching the sunset again? Sure you want to hazard that?"

"Watching the boats. Six-thirty."

Jason waited for the city bus at the corner of 110th Street and Fifth Avenue, in front of the building in which he lived. He loved Harlem, but preferred to live close to it rather than in it. Every few minutes he glanced at his left wrist. Time seemed to be playing a game with him, crawling along with all the deliberate speed of a snail. He put his watch to his ear and satisfied himself that it hadn't stopped. He walked to the corner, turned, and walked to the other end of the short block, didn't see a bus, and walked back to the bus stop. He'd gladly hail a taxi, but if he stood there until Christmas he probably wouldn't see one. He didn't want to admit that the prospect of seeing Ginger in her home, of being alone with her again, had his blood flying through his veins. The bus arrived, and he took it as far as Seventy-ninth Street, got off, and hailed a cab. Fifteen minutes later, his right index finger pressed her doorbell.

The door opened, he looked at Ginger and lost his breath. With her hair down below her shoulders, her softened, guileless appearance pulled at the man in him, and he had to check his spiralling desire.

"Hello, Ginger."

"Hi. Uh...come on in while I get the glasses and some snacks."

He eyed her closely. A bag of raw nerves or his name wasn't Jason Calhoun. "I can wait out here, if you'd rather."

Her eyes widened and then blinked rapidly. "Oh. It's okay. Come on in."

He figured he'd scored some points by offering to wait in the hall. At least, he hoped so. He handed her a dozen calla lilies, and joy suffused him when she made no attempt to hide her pleasure in receiving them.

"Calla lilies have been my absolute favorite for years. Thank you. They're so beautiful."

"My pleasure. Beautiful lilies for a beautiful lady."

He followed her into the living room, anxious for any clues to her personality. Curtainless windows and track lights beside them told him nothing. He took in the burnt orange chairs and antique, gold-colored sofa that sat on a soft, beige-patterned Tabriz Persian carpet. Tall, live plants stood near the windows, and a James H. Johnson reproduction dominated one beige-colored wall. Her good taste didn't surprise him. He'd expected it. His gaze swept over her books. History, biography, politics. A rack beside the piano held—*a piano.* He stepped closer to see what she played. Handel's *Largo,* Duke Ellington's sacred music, and Bix Beiderbeckes's haunting "In a Mist," a jazz classic from the nineteen twenties. He shook his head. Where was she in that mélange of interests? He shrugged off the question. With such catholic tastes, at least she wouldn't be narrow-minded.

Her footsteps announced her arrival. "I see you play the piano."

She glanced toward the door. "Yes, but I don't often have time these days."

Maybe if she played, he'd find her through her music. "Play something for me."

"I, uh... She looked at the bag he'd rested on the coffee table. "What about the champagne?"

He picked up the bag, stepped closer, and handed it to her. "Put it in the refrigerator. I want to hear you play."

He could see that he made her ill at ease, and he didn't like it. Might as well get it out in the open. "Ginger, relax and get used to me."

Her smooth dark skin took on a reddish cast from a rush of blood to her cheeks. He'd give a lot to know what went on in her mind, but he didn't want to play games, so he didn't query.

"Why do you think I'm not relaxed?"

He believed in straight talk. "If a bird chirped behind you right now, you'd jump. You're scared to death that I'll shake your sugar tree."

*"Jason!"*

"Don't act so surprised. You know the truth when you hear it. Play something, will you?"

"Anything special?"

He shook his head. "I only want to hear you play."

A soft, barely audible whistle slipped through his lips as he watched her slow, lazy glide across the room to the piano and the easy grace with which she slid onto the bench. Her fingers moved over the keys with practiced skill as she coaxed from them Duke Ellington's haunting "Mood Indigo." She threw back her head, closed her eyes, and teased the music until it surrounded him, flowing to him from every corner and nook of the room. He thought he'd lost her to the music until she opened her eyes, fixed them on his, and let their soft, brown beauty tell him that he was the most special of men.

KIMANI
ROMANCE

# An Important Message from the Publisher

Dear Reader,

Because you've chosen to read one of our fine novels, I'd like to say "thank you"! And, as a special way to say thank you, I'm offering to send you two more Kimani™ Romance novels and two surprise gifts— absolutely FREE! These books will keep it real with true-to-life African American characters that turn up the heat and sizzle with passion.

Please enjoy the free books and gifts with our compliments...

*Glenda Howard*
For Kimani Press

*Peel off Seal and*

*Place Inside...*

We'd like to send you two free books to introduce you to Kimani™ Romance books. These novels feature strong, sexy women, and African-American heroes that are charming, loving and true. Our authors fill each page with exceptional dialogue, exciting plot twists, and enough sizzling romance to keep you riveted until the very end!

*KIMANI ROMANCE...LOVE'S ULTIMATE DESTINATION*

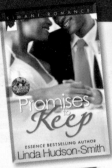

Your two books have a combined cover price of $13.98, but are yours **FREE!**

We'll even send you two wonderful surprise gifts. You can't lose!

# THE EDITOR'S "THANK YOU" FREE GIFTS INCLUDE:

Two Kimani™ Romance Novels
Two exciting surprise gifts

**YES!** I have placed my Editor's "thank you" Free Gifts seal in the space provided at right. Please send me 2 FREE books, and my 2 FREE Mystery Gifts. I understand that I am under no obligation to purchase anything further, as explained on the back of this card.

PLACE
FREE GIFTS
SEAL
HERE

About how many NEW paperback fiction books
have you purchased in the past 3 months?

❏ 0-2          ❏ 3-6          ❏ 7 or more

E7XY          E5MH          E5MT

**168/368 XDL**

Please Print

FIRST NAME

LAST NAME

ADDRESS

APT.#                    CITY

STATE/PROV.             ZIP/POSTAL CODE

## Thank You!

◀ Detach card and mail today. No stamp needed.

▲ If offer card is missing write to: The Reader Service, P.O. Box 1867, Buffalo, NY 14240-1867 or visit www.ReaderService.com ▲

**BUSINESS REPLY MAIL**
FIRST-CLASS MAIL    PERMIT NO. 717    BUFFALO, NY

POSTAGE WILL BE PAID BY ADDRESSEE

**THE READER SERVICE**
PO BOX 1867
BUFFALO NY 14240-9952

NO POSTAGE
NECESSARY
IF MAILED
IN THE
UNITED STATES

With her soul still open to him, her soft, mezzo-soprano gave life to the words of Ellington's great song, one that he'd loved since listening to his parents' records when he was a child. With every breath she took and every note that flowed from her lungs, he lost a little more of himself.

At last no sound could be heard in the room, and she stared down at her hands lying in her lap. "Did you like it?"

He longed to touch her, but controlled the urge for fear of destroying the moment. "The last time anything moved me so deeply, I was holding you while we gazed at the sunset and your tears dripped over my hand. You sing and play beautifully. Everything about you is beautiful."

She diverted her gaze and lowered her head. "I'm glad you like it so much. I...I don't know what to say."

He figured he'd better get them out of there before he did something stupid and got on the wrong side of her. "This seems like the perfect time for champagne. Ready to go?"

When she stood immediately, he got the impression that she wanted to get out of there as badly as he did and, he suspected, for the same reason.

She returned from the kitchen with the champagne and a small wicker basket. "Ready when you are."

She seemed nonplussed, but he told himself to stop second-guessing her. She'd said she was scared, and that made sense, because anybody who was headed for what he knew they faced would be foolish to barge into it fearlessly. Giving yourself to another person wasn't all that the muses claimed; it could ruin your life.

Ginger laid a red-and-white checkered cloth on the concrete seating ledge beside the East River facing Manhattan and opened the basket.

"What's in there?" Jason asked as he eased the champagne from the confines of its bottle.

"Some sandwiches."

He poured the bubbly wine into the long-stemmed glasses

she'd brought, linked their right elbows and looked into her eyes. Her pulse raced crazily, and her senses whirled with the giddiness of a moth dancing around a flame. She fought the old, habitual caution that threatened to drag her back down to reality, back to the staid, conservative Ginger—the Ginger who didn't take chances. This man meant business. If only she could ignore his mesmeric gray eyes, his tempting lips, and his air of power and authority, and concentrate on who and what he seemed to be—the real man.

"Here's to the woman who, with a single glance, rocked my world."

She raised her glass, smiled at him, and let the cool liquid caress her throat while he stared at her, stripping her bare with the naked desire in his eyes.

"Don't I get a toast?" he asked.

She clicked her glass to his own. "A man such as you will always get his share in life and so much more."

His face clouded, though not, she knew, with bemusement, but impatience. "Try not to talk over my head, Ginger. All I'm seeking right now is some assurance that you'll give us a chance. Nothing more. That doesn't mean commitment, just openness. How about that toast, so I can enjoy my drink?"

She tipped the glass toward him. "Here's to the man with whom I have dreamed."

She didn't think she'd ever seen a man change so quickly. The heated desire of minutes earlier dissolved into a kind of warm sweetness, and something else that she was scared to name.

That smile. Lights danced in his eyes and his face bore such a gentleness, a softness that she wanted to hug him to her breasts. "Sail with me, Ginger, and I'll make silver sails for you. If you'd rather we flew, I'll give you golden wings, and if you'll walk with me, I'll put the spring of joy and life into your steps. Come with me, and your eyes will see only things of beauty, your ears will hear heavenly music, and you'll dine on food prepared for the gods. What do you say?"

Her breath had lodged in her throat, and she had to gasp for air, but his magnificent gray eyes refused to release her from his spell. He unlinked their arms and smoothed her cheek with his fingers, something he'd done twice in Harare, as though his fingers communicated what words could not. She wanted to drown in him.

"Well?"

"I'm speechless, Jason. You offer me a world I never heard of. One day at a time?"

"All right. You said you weren't married, living with a man or engaged. I don't have any of those ties, either. You know I'm an honorable, law-abiding man, so I can't understand your reluctance to let us get closer. I understood why you walked away in Zimbabwe. You didn't know anything about me. But now you do."

Male logic. He couldn't see a reason, so there wasn't one. "Jason, would you walk into a roaring fire without an asbestos suit, or jump into the Atlantic Ocean knowing you couldn't swim? You swept me off my feet in Harare, and I don't like not being able to control my behavior. We're a couple thousand miles from there, and...and—"

"And you still want me? Do you think you didn't sweep me off *my* feet? Honey, this is a mutual thing. You turned me around every bit as much as I unsettled you. Maybe more, from the looks of things. If we're honest with each other, we don't have anything to fear." A full smile bloomed on his face. "Problem solved. What kind of sandwiches you got in there?"

She uncovered the food. "Ham, smoked salmon, and cheese. Some grapes in here, too."

His grin couldn't have been broader if she'd said she had a basket of diamonds. *I could love this man,* she admitted to herself when he lifted the bottle, winked at her, and said, "A loaf of bread, a jug of wine, and thou beside me singing in the wilderness."

A barge floated by with the aid of her favorite tugboat. "I

named that tug Midnight," she told him, "because it moves by my bedroom window all times of night. I welcome it when I can't sleep." What she didn't tell him was that those sleepless nights had begun after her return from Zimbabwe. Lovers barely into their teens strolled by holding hands, and a man and woman stopped a few feet from them and kissed with such passion that she had to close her eyes. She opened them to find Jason's gaze locked on her and didn't have to wonder as to his thoughts. They had once kissed each other like that. They finished the sandwiches and champagne, and Jason put the glasses, napkins, and tablecloth in the basket.

"Where's that garden you told me about?"

"Not far. Want to walk down there?"

She delighted in showing him her handiwork. Although it was still April, scallions, turnips, spinach, and lettuce grew six or more inches above the soil, and blooming jonquils, crocuses, and evening primrose beautified the small plot. He rested his arm around her shoulders and, as though programmed to do so, she moved closer to him. When his arm tightened around her, she snuggled nearer still, and savored once more the perfect peace that she'd known only with him.

"Don't move," he warned, his voice hoarse with passion. "It won't take more than a deep breath for me to wrap myself around you and get lost in you right here and now."

Her skin tingled, but she refused to be caught up in the web that he spun. She'd walked blindly into a life of unhappiness with Harold, but not again. Still, she knew that Jason was different, that he offered her more. So much more.

"You're moving too fast, Jason."

He squeezed her shoulders. "But you're moving with me, sweetheart. It's a tidal wave, and nothing we do is going to stop it."

He asked her not to move, but shivers shook her and she settled against him.

The wind picked up velocity, and a whiff of perfume from the purple crocuses teased her nostrils. "This wind's bringing a storm," she told him, "and it's getting darker. I think we'd better get out of here."

"Yeah. Let's run for it," he said, picked up the basket and grabbed her arm as the first big raindrops spattered them.

"There's the minibus. Come on," she urged.

They boarded the red Island Transport bus as torrents of rain fell around them.

"What does this remind you of?" Jason asked her.

She put two quarters, one for each of them, in the fare box and pulled her damp shirt away from her body. "You didn't let me get wet in Zimbabwe. You're slipping."

He shrugged. "We're on your territory now, sweetheart, so *you* should have protected *me*."

They got off at the second stop and dashed into West View, the building in which she lived.

She couldn't speak, because conflicting emotions clogged her thoughts as her desire to be one with him wrestled with her fear of losing her very soul.

She pressed the elevator button and turned to him. "I'm crazy, Jason. Everything about you appeals to me, but right now I feel like putting a couple of miles between us."

A half-smile curled around his lips. "Okay to feel like it, so long as you don't do it."

At her apartment door she noticed that he stepped back, leaving the decision to her. Marbles rattled around in her belly when she turned and looked into his turbulent eyes.

"Come on in."

"You sure?"

"No, I'm not sure," she said, able to laugh at her own foolishness, "but come on in, anyway. You can put that basket in the kitchen while I get out of this wet shirt. Be right back."

He wasn't wet, but he didn't sit down. He had to get control of the longing for her that had begun to drive him like a locomotive sucking the wind in its headlong plunge out of control. The sensation of being propelled to her by some supernatural force had begun that morning in Harare at breakfast and hadn't slackened; if anything, it had intensified. He had dissected it, analyzed it and prayed about it, but he still needed her.

"Why didn't you sit down?" she called out in a tone of gaiety that he knew was forced.

Well, he wasn't going to string it out. Quick steps took him to her, and she stared up at him with want blazing in her eyes. Hot energy shot to his belly, and he pulled her into his arms. Her breasts nestled snugly against his chest, and when their hard tips rubbed against him, he lifted her from the floor, parted her lips with his tongue, and knew heaven at last. When she took him into her warm, sweet mouth, desire vibrated through him like atomic waves. She asked for more of him, and he gave, visiting every nook and crevice of her mouth, sampling the sweetness he found there. He thought he'd explode as the fullness of his manhood nestled against her belly. What sense he could muster told him he'd better ease up, but she wouldn't release him and clutched him to her as she groaned in pleasure. He wanted to burst within her, but if he did, he'd regret it. They both would. What they needed wasn't a quick fix standing in the middle of a room, but a place and time to savor, to revel in each other's bodies.

With one hand, he loosened her grip on him. "Ginger, sweetheart, if we can lose ourselves in each other as we just did, nature is telling us something. I'm not going to see any other woman. Will you cut any romantic ties you have, and let's see if we can make it together? We haven't spoken about our lives, things we experienced that might affect us now, but it's time we did that. I'm in deep here and so are you. Right?"

She nodded. "All right. I won't see any one else until we know where we're going."

He hugged her to his heart. "You want me to leave?"

"I don't think we ought to make love right now, if that's

what you're asking. Oh, I know I would have, but I believe
we can have more if we do as you suggested."

"I know we can. See you tomorrow evening?"

"I'd like that, but I have to prepare for a case, and I don't
know anything about the business involved. I need to do some
research at the Schomburg Library, and it doesn't open till
noon. We can talk when I get home, though."

"Okay. I'll call you about nine-thirty. Right now, I'm out
of here before things start to heat up again. Kiss me?"

His heart turned over when she raised her mouth to his,
and he knew he'd never be able to live without her. Her lips
brushed his, then parted for his tongue, but he resisted her
invitation. No point in steaming himself up again.

"Goodnight, sweetheart."

"'Night." She opened the door, and as he walked through
it she reached up and kissed his cheek. "Till tomorrow."

He had to control the temptation to follow her back into
that apartment.


Ginger grabbed the nearest chair and barely missed sitting
on the floor. No use lying to herself; he made her come alive,
and she couldn't wait to know the ultimate about him—how
he'd make her feel and whether what churned inside of her
was strong enough to last a lifetime. But maybe he wouldn't
want that. With his steel-like willpower, he could dance on
the edge and walk away without a backward glance. Well, she
wasn't bad at that herself. She jumped up, crossed her arms
and stroked her shoulders. Laughter poured out of her, and she
whirled around and around. *Work,* her conscience reminded
her, but who could think of work when the taste of him still
lingered in her mouth?

At seven the next morning, she took a brisk walk along
the river, after which she went to Andy's Place for breakfast.
Amos Logan sat at his usual table in the corner reading *The
New York Times.*

"You want to read, or may I join you?" she asked him.

He put the paper aside. "I can read any time. How'd that case go?"

She gave the waiter her order of half a cantaloupe, toast, eggs, and coffee. "The opposing attorney and I got into a hassle over the charges, and that apparently inspired the couple to make up. At their request, the judge dismissed the case."

"You got into an argument with the attorney of your client's wife? In front of the judge?"

She took a few sips of coffee. "Yes, and yes. Judge Williams called us on it, too."

"Agatha Williams?" Ginger nodded. "Can't say I'm surprised. I taught her. She's just the type. Agatha can split any kind of hair. What did you argue about?"

She told him, and had to experience the discomfort of a knowing look from a man of the world.

"Ginger, if I may call you that. Sounds personal to me."

"It *was* personal. The problem is that I don't know in what respect."

"You'll find out," he said and beckoned the waiter for more coffee. "I expect he'll let you know pretty soon, if he hasn't already done so. Keep me posted."

They talked of the local political scene, of the candidates running for different posts and what they thought of them. "A lackluster bunch," he pronounced.

"I'd better be going," she said as Clarice walked in dressed in white slacks and a yellow T-shirt that proclaimed, "Pray for Spring. Summer is killing me," and brought a gale of laughter from Amos.

"You two know each other?" Ginger asked.

They didn't, so she invited Clarice to join them and soon made her way back to her apartment to dress for work.

Her afternoon and evening at the Schomburg netted her the information she needed on the nightclubs in Harlem and on The Cat's Pajamas in particular, and she left there shortly after eight o'clock to begin preparing her case against the city, which had begun closure proceedings against the club. The club's owner had a right to bar from entrance anyone who had ever been evicted from the premises legally for drunkenness, use of drugs, or similar undesirable behavior. If the owner rejected the offender's apology, that was his right. Too many Harlem establishments had been closed for a first violation of a city ordinance, and the owner of The Cat's Pajamas wanted to avoid that penalty. She stopped by Andy's Place, got a hamburger and soup, and took it home with her.

Exhausted but fulfilled after a productive day, Ginger finished her supper, took a shower, and prepared for bed. With an eye on the clock and nine-thirty—when Jason had said he'd call—she found Donna Hill's book, *Pieces of Dreams,* and got set to find out what happened to Maxine, the girl Quinn Parker had left behind. Trouble was, she hated to put the book down once she'd started it, and Jason would call at any minute.

By ten minutes to ten, she had stopped wanting to hear his voice and had developed an urge to tell him what he could do with his silver sails and golden wings.

When the phone rang at seven minutes after ten, she was tempted not to answer it, but decided to hear him out.

"I thought you'd decided not to answer," he said after a greeting that she was certain would have been more affable if she'd picked up on the first two or three rings. "I called as soon as I could. After dinner downtown, I took a taxi home and would have been here in plenty of time, but the taxi driver elected to drive through the park and went right into a police check. So there I sat for forty minutes, while the police investigated the driver's green card and driver's license, and the cab's inspection certificate. And trust me, they took their time doing it."

In her impatience for his call, she hadn't considered that he'd have good reason not to keep his word. "I admit I was annoyed, and I know I should have waited for your reasons. I'm sorry."

"If your dander got up because you couldn't wait to hear my voice, I won't find it hard to forgive you."

"And if I tell you that's not why I got annoyed—"

"Then you'd be lying, honey. His low, sultry laugh warmed her soul. "We promised honesty, remember?"

"You're pretty sure of yourself, mister."

"I've learned it never hurts to give that impression."

"What about that honesty you were talking about a second ago?"

A teasing laughter colored his voice. "That was seconds ago. I'm sure you're familiar with the saying, 'Never look back, something may be gaining on you'? Say, I love the woods in spring. You've got the rest of the week to get that brief together. How about going hiking with me in the Catskills Saturday morning? Some of those trails are magnificent. We could go fishing, too, if you'd like."

She loved the outdoors, though hiking wasn't high on her list of fun things. Neither was fishing. But if that's what he enjoyed, she'd learn to love it if it would enrich their time together.

"I've always been able to take both or leave them, but I might enjoy hiking and fishing with you. All right, I'll go."

"Great. All you need is a pair of sturdy shoes and a sweater."

She couldn't resist the jab. "Good heaven, Jason, that's what you wear in the woods—shoes and a sweater?"

"Your imagination is telling tales on you. If that's what you want to see, we don't have to go to the Catskills."

A picture of Jason in shoes and sweater flashed through her mind, and her amusement at it manifested itself in a hearty laugh. "Hmm," was all she said.

"What's so funny?"

"My imagination is both mental and visual."

She supposed that he'd settled back for a good set-to when he said, "Like what you saw?"

Catering to the wickedness that always hovered near the surface, she shot back, "Well, I suppose I've seen worse."

"You bet you have. Give me a kiss, huh?"

She made the sound, and added, "Sweet dreams."

Letting her know that he was as devilish as she, he said, "Oh, I'll dream. Be sure of that, because I'll doze off with a picture of the two of us gamboling through the woods in our shoes and sweaters." He hung up before she could tell him what she thought of his observation.

Ginger got up early Saturday morning, fried some chicken drumsticks Southern-style, made buttermilk biscuits, and put the food in a thermal bag. She put a box of ginger snaps and some bananas and apples in her wicker basket along with linens and cutlery. If she were going to walk herself to death in Jason's fairy tale woods, at least she'd be able to eat when she got hungry. She dressed in a cotton shirt, jeans, and low-heeled leather boots, and dropped a sweater on the wicker basket.

At seven sharp, the doorman announced Jason's arrival.

"Hmm," he said, after a quick kiss on her mouth, "do I by some rare piece of luck smell buttermilk biscuits?"

She nodded and picked up the basket, ready to leave.

A look of incredulity masked his face. "Wait a minute. You just made buttermilk biscuits?"

*What was so unusual about that?* she wondered, but she answered, "Yes," and pointed to the thermal bag. "I put some in here. Come on. It's after seven."

He cocked an eye and stared at her. "If you just made them, that means they're still hot. You'd need a towtruck to get me out of here before I sample some of those things."

So much for getting to the Catskill Mountains by eleven o'clock. "All right. All right. Just have a seat. She pointed to a dining room chair, but he followed her into the kitchen, sat on a stool, and watched her. She put four biscuits in the toaster.

"Any butter and jam? Just give it to me right here," he said when she started toward the dining room. "I grew up eating in the kitchen."

She poured a mug of coffee for him and learned that he drank it straight. Minutes later, he stood, patted his stomach, and extolled her virtues as a biscuit maker. "A woman who can make biscuits that taste like that," he marveled, shaking his head. "Ginger, you have so many talents. You're a fine attorney, a pianist with a wonderful voice, a gardener, and now, a biscuit maker. Before I start to feel inept, tell me about some of your shortcomings."

"Don't worry, I've got my share of them. For one thing, I'm notoriously lousy at judging men."

"At judging..." As though frozen, he stopped unlocking the door of the Buick he'd rented and stared at her. "What do you mean by that?"

He had to know sometime, and the sooner she could test his reaction the better. "Just what I said. And that's one reason— maybe the main one—why I'm so indecisive about you. With my record, I've gotten cautious." She wished he wouldn't look at her as though he could see through her.

"We need to save that for serious conversation, for that time when we get down to the business of sharing everything about ourselves." He threw the keys up, caught them, and looked into the distance. "Ginger, I don't believe in saying important things in a casual manner, playing down their significance. Besides, when I'm driving, I don't like to concentrate on anything else."

She wished she hadn't let those words slip off her tongue, for she hadn't meant to diminish the importance of Harold's request for a divorce. She had poured one hundred percent of herself into the marriage, while he'd merely watched her do it. She'd been devastated. In her reckoning, it was she for whom the marriage had not been fulfilling and when, without warning, he'd said he wanted his freedom, the wounds that his demand inflicted on her pride had scarred her deeply.

Jason took the New York State Thruway to Elmsford and crossed the Tappan Zee Bridge without slowing down.

"I knew this was too good to be true," Ginger said when he came to a complete stop on Route Eighty-seven behind what seemed like miles of stalled traffic.

He shook his head. "Beats me. At this rate, it'll be dark before we get to Stone Hollow. You dead set on it?"

Was she breaking her neck for the opportunity to expose herself to ticks and poison ivy? She let a look of concern cover her face. "I would have enjoyed it. Yes. But I'd be content if we just found a place to have a little picnic."

He pinched her nose in what she recognized as a gesture of approval and affection. "Great. If I drive along that zebra for about a quarter mile, I can get off this highway. There's a nice park and lake not far from here. We can go there. What do you say?"

"Sounds good to me. All we wanted was an outing together, and we'll have that."

He moved onto the white-striped lane and was soon able to turn into Route Nine W. He stopped, turned, and faced her. "Are you always this agreeable?"

"To anything reasonable that doesn't inconvenience me, why not?"

He moved onto the road and headed for the park. "That has not been my experience with most people, and certainly not with the women I've known. The lake's about a mile from here. I think I'll pull over there and get some soft drinks. Come in with me and have a stretch."

They entered the shabby building and rang the bell.

A woman stopped mopping the floor, wiped her hands on the sides of her skirt, and looked them over. "We don't have no rooms right now. Come back in a couple of hours."

Ginger knew she gaped at the woman, but Jason stuck his balled up fists to the sides of his hips and glared. "Run that past me again."

And run it past him, she did, adding, "It'll cost you seven-fifty an hour."

He ran his fingers through his silky curls in an air of frustration. "But that sign says... All we want is a Coke and a bottle of ginger ale. What kind of place *is* this?"

The woman went back to her mopping. "Rooms by the hour. The drinks are next door." She nodded to her left. "Be sure and tell 'em Effie sent ya."

Jason took Ginger's hand and stepped outside. "I'm sorry about that. Wait here. No misunderstandings like that one. I'll get the drinks."

"For goodness' sake, don't mention Effie," she called after him.

He walked back to her. "You think I'm crazy?" A grin played around his lips as he flashed a set of white teeth, and mischief sparkled in his eyes. She knew she could expect some of his special brand of deviltry, and he didn't let her down. "Of course, when I turned Effie down, I was only speaking for myself. If you want to go back in a couple of hours, I'm not totally opposed, though I'd prefer something elegant, more worthy of you."

She punched her finger in his middle. "In your dreams, Buster."

She loved his laughter, and he gave her a good sample of it before going to get the drinks. As he walked away, she asked herself if she cared for him but refused to hear her heart's answer. They ate lunch by the lake, with their bare toes cushioned in the grass.

"Time flies when I'm with you," he told her. "We've been here three hours."

She sat on the grass with her back resting against an old tree, and he lay supine on a blanket with his head in her lap. "I could spend forever right here with you."

His hair held a peculiar fascination for her, and she yielded to temptation and stroked it with the palm of her right hand. "Worse things could happen," she admitted. "What would we do? Forage for berries and nuts?" She let her thumb caress his lower lip. "What would happen when it got cold? Oh, *I* know. We could scoot back to New York and hibernate."

Suddenly his hand gripped her wrist, and she realized she'd been stroking his neck. He sat upright. "Do you know you've been making love to me for the last twenty minutes?"

"I…no, I wasn't."

"Deny it all you want." That grin again. "If you're that skilled at it when you're not thinking about it, I can't wait to have your undivided attention."

"Jason, you're starting to get a one-track mind."

"Don't blame me, sweetheart. It's your influence. I think we'd better start back.

"How about stopping by my place while I change? Then I'll return the car, get a cab, and take you home. You change, and we can have dinner and take in some jazz down at The Village Vanguard. Would you like that?"

*You're going to his place. If it gets out of hand, are you prepared to make love with him?* She was, she admitted to herself, though it didn't matter. If she said she wanted to leave, she knew he would take her home at once. Nonetheless, the little mental exercise had been useful: she'd made an important decision.

"You're pretty quiet, lady."

"I was thinking. Sounds good, but why not drop off the car before we stop by your place?"

He shot an inquiring glance in her direction, so she hastened to explain. "That way, you won't have to look for a parking space."

After an Italian meal in a mom-and-pop restaurant on Thompson Street, they wound their way to the city's hottest jazz spot. From the minute they entered, Ginger wished she hadn't been so agreeable. A waitress barely out of her teens sauntered over to their table, her face an open invitation.

"Hi, Jason," she cooed. "Haven't seen you for a while."

For a second, she thought he'd stand up and kiss the little flirt. "I was here, but you weren't. How's everything?"

"You know my situation, Jason. Seeing you is the only good thing that's happened to me this week."

Ginger thought she'd burst. He could at least introduce them or, at worst, glance at her to let her know he remembered her presence. The waitress took their orders and left, and she took great pains not to look at the man who, only hours earlier, she had admitted to herself that she loved. To exacerbate her displeasure, he seemed oblivious to her quiet manner.

If it weren't enough that she had to tolerate the waitress, the comedian who performed during the band's intermission delivered the final insult.

"My wife doesn't understand me," he proclaimed. Then he looked at Ginger. "You'd understand me, wouldn't you, baby? Soft, pretty thing like you." He looked at the audience, then back at her sitting beside Jason in front of the stage. "Man, look at those warm, brown eyes. Ain't no black chicks supposed to walk around with eyes like that. A lot of our women have big black eyes, but this beauty here—"

Jason grabbed the mike from him. "You say one more word to or about this woman, and you'll wake up a lot smaller than you are now. Got it?"

The comedian looked up at Jason. "I was just teasing, man. Can I have my mike back? Thanks. I have to tell you, though, if she's yours, you can afford to be cool. She's choice."

Jason glared at the little man. "I thought I told you—"

"Okay. I heard you. No offense meant."

Jason sat down, and she could see the furor boiling up in him. "Would you like to leave?"

So he had a short fuse. She'd have to remember that. Certain that he felt as badly about the incident as she did, she covered his hand with hers and told him, "It never happened. What I want to know is who that child is who waited on us and called you by your first name?"

He leaned back and raised both eyebrows as though he

hadn't understood her. "Mindy? She's the wife of one of my clients. She left him and calls herself teaching him a lesson which, I'm sorry to say, he isn't getting. Don't tell me you thought I was foolish enough to bring you to a place where you'd run into..." He stared at her. "Ginger, if you don't learn to trust me, we aren't going anywhere together."

She stared right back at him. "If you had introduced us, maybe I wouldn't have thought anything of it."

"I would have, if I'd known what to call her. She isn't using her husband's name now, and I don't know her maiden name. I certainly wasn't going to introduce the two of you as Mindy and Ginger. Okay?"

His light touch warmed her arm. "If we put ourselves to it, we can fight nonstop, but these misunderstandings will cease when we become closer and we're not so uncertain about each other."

He squeezed her fingers with affection, and she couldn't help leaning from her chair and letting her shoulder brush his. "You're positive that we'll be closer?"

"I am. It's something that I can't afford to doubt, sweetheart. Yes, I am absolutely positive." He moved his chair until it touched hers, and she had again that peculiar sensation of peace when his arm stole around her shoulder. They sat that way through the show.

"I don't think I'd better go in tonight," Jason said at her door.

As far as she was concerned, he'd wasted his breath. "I'm not kissing you in front of my neighbors should any of them walk by, and I'm not letting you go without giving me my kiss."

She'd known that her words would amuse him, but her heart still took a dive when the lights danced in his eyes and his face bloomed into a smile just before he laughed. He held his head with both hands and told her, "If I don't hold it, there's no telling how big it'll get with you saying things like that."

She walked into the foyer, dropped the wicker basket on the floor, and turned to him. "I waited all day for this, Jason."

Gone was his laughter, his lighthearted demeanor, as his face took on the somber cast of a serious man. He took a step to her. "Come to me, sweetheart."

She'd been anticipating the explosive passion that he'd unleashed Tuesday, the first time she'd been in his arms since they'd found each other. But he brought her to him with a gentleness, a tenderness that seeped into her soul the way a long, breaking sunrise robs you of all but your deep spiritual self. He looked into her eyes, and she searched them for whatever truth he offered her. Her heart quickened at the adoration, the sweetness that she saw there—an openness that said, *Trust me and I will be all good things to you.*

"Jason, don't…please don't mislead me."

He continued to look at her, his eyes telling her that he adored her. "Whatever you see, Ginger," he said at last, "comes from inside of me." He pulled her closer, as if he wanted to lock them together, and lowered his head.

Surely he felt her tremors when his lips finally touched hers in a shadow of a kiss. Feather-light, it was, until she held his head to intensify the pressure. He capitulated, but only for a second, and placed soft kisses on her mouth until she thought she'd scream for more.

"We can't go to the brink as we did last time, honey. We're not ready for more, and if we get that far again, I'll have a hard time stopping."

She let him take her weight when he squeezed her to him and brushed her lips with his kiss. His hand was already on the doorknob. With a wink, he left.

She stuck her hands on her hips and, for want of a human target, glared at the door. "Tell me about the next time," she said. "I guarantee you, you won't stop."

She put away the wicker basket and threw the linen into a hamper while her mind went to work. After Harold obtained the divorce, she'd sworn off men. When she first met Jason, he intimated something about the virtue of being alone. Now they'd both backtracked, and she didn't see herself changing course unless forced.

Jason walked to the bus stop, leaned against it, and waited. Somewhere in the last five weeks, his vow to avoid involvement with women had gone down the drain, and he didn't regret it. Unless Ginger showed him something that he hadn't imagined or anticipated, he was in deep with her for the indefinite future. He knew she cared for him. But did she love him? If he'd learned anything that long day, it was that she meant more to him than any woman ever had. He thanked God that they'd found each other again. It couldn't have been luck or coincidence, and he didn't intend to treat it as such.

When he got home, he stopped by the mail room and found a letter in his box. Mr. and Mrs. Roberts requested the honor of his presence at the renewal of their vows. Would Mr. Calhoun please stand with them. He couldn't help laughing. That case had been both a miracle and a nuisance.

He stepped into his apartment and telephoned Ginger. "Sweetheart, would you believe this? The Roberts are actually getting back together, and they want me to stand with them when they renew their vows. Did you get an announcement?"

"I haven't been to my mailbox. I'll check it."

"If you got one, call me." He made the sound of a kiss and hung up.

Sure enough, she had received a similar announcement and request, but Roberts had added that Judge Williams would preside over their ceremony. She told Jason she wasn't sure she liked that, but he thought it amusing and said he could hardly wait until the four of them strolled into the judge's chambers for the ceremony.

Marriage filled Ginger's thoughts in the days to come. As she awaited the impending marriage between her sister, Linda, and Lloyd Jenkins, she had begun to wonder if she would ever know true love. Everlasting love. She set aside a weekend in which to do Linda's shopping. On the following Monday she put on her electric-blue linen suit and joined the Roberts and Jason in Judge Williams' chambers.

"Well, well," the judge observed. "If this doesn't beat all." She put on her glasses and looked from Ginger to Jason. "I suppose I can count on you two not to go at each other's throats?"

Ginger noted that Jason seemed taken aback, but since the occasion had no legal implications, she decided to get some of her own.

"Yes, Your Honor," she replied, "but that's all you can count on our not doing."

Agatha Williams removed her glasses and stared at Ginger, and Jason cleared his throat several times, obviously in the hope of quieting her. She ignored them both.

"A lot of water's flowed under the bridge since we last saw you," she told the judge.

"I can imagine," Judge Williams replied. "That water was rushing pretty fast while you were arguing this case. Now, if we may begin…"

As the judge read the ceremony, Ginger looked up to find Jason's eyes on her, and their gazes clung. His lips formed words that she couldn't hear, and his eyes pierced the distance between them, drawing her into the orbit of his being.

The words, *Till death do us part* reverberated in her head, and her right hand reached involuntarily toward him. His smiling eyes promised her the world, and she knew without doubt that she wanted his universe, to have her being in Jason Calhoun. If only he wanted the same.

Jason invited the Robertses to lunch with Ginger and him, but the couple barely had time to make the plane that would take them on the start of their second honeymoon.

"Think they'll make it?" Ginger asked Jason.

"I'd bet on it. You don't go to that much trouble a second time unless you're certain."

At that, her antennae zipped up, and she wondered what he'd left unsaid, but she didn't voice her thoughts. She couldn't, because she had her own dark chasm to cross. During lunch she told him she'd planned to rent a car in order to take to Easton, Maryland the things she'd purchased for her sister. He offered to drive her, and when he wouldn't be dissuaded, it occurred to her that he might relish the opportunity to meet her only close relative.

"She's getting married, and I'm standing up with her." She had almost said *matron of honor,* but it wasn't the time to go into all that, though she suspected they'd soon have to tell each other of their pasts.

"When's the ceremony?"

"Saturday night. That's why I have to leave here Friday morning."

His glance held no annoyance, but his voice did the job for him. "Good thing you told me, so I can pack something other than jeans and sneakers."

"Sorry. I'm not thinking straight, but I'm glad you're going with me."

They held hands as they left the restaurant. "I'm not going to see much of you this week, honey," he told her. "Taking Friday off means cramming five days' work into four days and nights. Okay?"

"All right. It's the same with me, and I also have to get my dress fitted."

Still holding her hand, he pressed a quick kiss to her mouth. "We'll talk. Prepare to leave home at seven-thirty Friday morning." Another kiss fell soft on her lips. "And stay out of mischief."

Jason parked the rented Ford Taurus in front of Glenwood Street's only yellow brick house at ten forty-three that morning. He didn't usually speed, but there had been no traffic, and he'd had the wind at his back, so to speak. He busied himself collecting parcels from the car trunk, all the while wondering why he didn't follow Ginger into the house and meet her sister.

A man paused in passing and stopped. "Man, you need any help with those things?"

He swung around defensively, remembered that he was not in New York, but a small Maryland town, and accepted the offer. Together, they lugged Ginger's packages to Linda's front door.

The stranger spoke as he rang the bell. "You down for the wedding?"

"Yes." Why did he feel as though he had to pick his way through a briar patch? "I drove Linda's sister."

The man's face brightened as footsteps could be heard approaching the door. "Well, glad to meet you. I'm Lloyd, Linda's fiancé." He extended his hand. "I live right across the street, so be sure and come over anytime."

"Hi, sugah," a tall, good-looking woman very much like Ginger crooned when she opened the door and saw Lloyd. "I thought Jason—" Her gaze landed on him, and she flung her arms around his neck. "Jason! I'll never believe she really found you. I'm so happy to meet you. I tell you, the Lord was with her. Lloyd, honey, you and Jason bring those things on in."

He soon learned that Linda organized people. Three women sat on the back porch peeling potatoes, wrapping cutlery in linen napkins, and making party favors, and in the garden a man painted silver stars and crescents to form mobiles. Linda evidently didn't believe in letting a person feel useless. She walked into the dining room where he stood talking with Ginger.

"Ginger, honey, could you take Lloyd—he's gone home across the street—and run down to Dillard's and get me two rolls of silver ribbon about four inches wide? They have it.

And Jason, honey, you come in the living room and help me practice my song."

He blinked. "Your song?"

"Yes. I'm singing. Why should I let some other woman sing to my man at my wedding when I can do it, huh?" She had his hand, leading him to the living room. He didn't say, *Whew,* but he thought it. A real steamroller. She played and sang "For You Alone," and her voice brought back to him the moments when he'd been lost in the web Ginger had spun around him as she sang "Mood Indigo."

He applauded her. "You and Ginger have beautiful voices, and very similar, too."

She thanked him. "Just think. After tomorrow, I won't be in this big house all by myself. We're going to live here and rent out Lloyd's house."

He had wondered why she lived alone in such a big house, and voiced his thoughts.

"It's our family home. Our parents died, Ginger went to New York, and I was left." She got up and walked to the window, let out a deep breath, and spoke with her back to him. "I'm a very lucky woman, Jason. Lloyd and I were engaged once before, and a couple of weeks before we were to marry we had an awful spat. It was my fault. I'd always been insecure, and I saw this beautiful woman crawling all over him at our annual NAACP dance. I went nuts. He didn't push her away, so I decided there was something between them. I guess he'd gotten tired of my foolishness, because he walked out of there and left me. When I called him, he said he didn't want to spend the rest of his life accounting for every blink of his eyelids. I begged forgiveness and he gave it, but two days later the same woman came into church and sat beside him. He moved over to make a place for her. I couldn't keep my mouth shut about it, so I strutted out of that big, crowded church.

"As you may imagine, I didn't crawl back, and he didn't ask. Several days later, I heard he'd left town. That ended it, but for the next three years, I was perpetually depressed. I loved him so much that not an hour passed that I didn't long for him. One day I decided to find him. I wrote a letter telling him what I felt and what I knew I'd lost, and asked his forgiveness. Then I hired a private investigator and gave him the letter to give to Lloyd. The PI found him in Denver, and Lloyd called me. I asked if I could go out there to see him. He met me at the airport, and nothing that happens to me in the future will ever supersede in my heart that moment of reconciliation there in his arms in the Denver airport. That was about eight months ago. He moved back here and bought that house, got a job teaching at the University of Maryland in Princess Ann—about thirty miles from here—and we've never looked back."

She turned and faced him. "I grew up, Jason, and I now know what's important between a man and a woman."

"What?"

"Love, trust, and fidelity. I learned the hard way what it means not to trust."

Analyzing events and situations was his business, and he thought about all she'd told him without any provocation on his part. "You arranged this opportunity for us to be alone. Why?"

Her light brown eyes, so like Ginger's, appraised him carefully. "My sister was practically a basket case when she got back here from Zimbabwe. She'd found more with you in two days than she'd had in her entire life, and she'd let it slip through her fingers. I hurt for her. As with Lloyd and me, a second chance is not to be taken lightly. The angels aren't happy when you throw their gifts back at them."

He wouldn't argue with that. "What do you do, Linda?"

"I teach math at the University of Maryland."

He nodded absentmindedly. "Two talented, accomplished sisters."

Linda had a right to be concerned for her sibling, but pressure of any kind had never sat well with him and, though she did it subtly, she was nevertheless leaning on him. Not that he blamed Ginger; it wasn't her idea that he drive her down there. As the day wore on, he saw similarities to the life he'd known in Dallas: privacy was nonexistent. One neighbor after another greeted him and gave him and Ginger their blessings, assuming that they also planned to marry. Linda hadn't arranged a bridal supper, but a party at her home for neighbors and friends, and he soon had a surfeit of the neighborly well wishes.

He sat on the bride's side of the church the next evening and looked back as Ginger, breathtakingly beautiful in a mauve pink silk evening gown, preceded her sister to the altar. His head did battle with his heart as he watched the proceedings, wanting to the pit of his soul to take that man's place and stand there with Ginger beside him, but at the same time struggling against the irritating thought that the whole town was trying to shove him into it.

At the end of the ceremony, he kissed Linda and was about to shake Lloyd's hand, but he recoiled when Linda's new husband addressed him as brother-in-law.

A glance at Ginger told him she'd seen the action and understood his reason.

As they left the church, she said, "Jason, I appreciate your driving me down here and helping us, but I have the feeling that you're fed up, that you'd rather be somewhere else. I can rent a car and drive back, so you can go on home. This long-suffering of yours is unnecessary. I'll be in touch."

He grabbed her shoulders, but he hadn't meant to do it so fiercely. "You listen to me, woman. I brought you down here, and I am taking you back home. You're not dismissing me as if I were your third grade pupil. I'd think you'd also have gotten tired of these people telling us what a great couple we make, what beautiful children we'll have, and how lucky we are to have each other, and hoping you'll come back home so you can be married before the altar at which you were christened.

All that, and not a soul told them we were getting married Damned straight I'm fed up."

He had to hand it to her. The woman was as cool as spring water. With her regal head high, she didn't miss a step as they walked toward the cars that waited for the bridal party.

"Fed up is written all over you, Jason. If you want to leave you have my blessing."

"When I leave, you're going with me."

"I won't fight with you in public."

He took her arm as they reached the car that had been assigned to them. "Ginger, we are *not* fighting. I'm going to turn in early, so I'll be out of the way, and I'd like to leave around noon tomorrow, as planned. All right?"

When she nodded, he relaxed, leaned over, and kissed her on the mouth. "The bride is beautiful, but she can't hold a light to my Ginger." The smile on her face warmed his heart. He needed her badly. Right then. *Some day soon,* he promised himself, reached for her hand, and counted his blessings.

In spite of the warmth they'd experienced in the car as they left the wedding, they began the drive back to New York with relations between them strained. She knew it was useless to broach anything of importance to Jason while he drove. Several miles before they reached the Delaware Memorial Bridge, the dark clouds exploded into a heavy downpour forcing Jason to drive into the rest stop.

As streaks of lightning flashed in the sky, Ginger drew herself up and pushed back her lifelong fear of thunderstorms. Not for anything would she let him see her afraid and needing him. "Why do you think the rain has showered us almost every time we've been alone together? Do you think it's trying to tell us something? It's like an omen, hooking us together."

He leaned back in the seat and closed his eyes. "Hardly I suspect it's something about lightning that turns you into sweet putty." His half-smile seemed forced. "Ginger, we have to settle some things. I had promised myself I was going to treat women as if they carried the plague. And then you came into my life. When you met me, I was looking for equilibrium. Peace. Trying to straighten out my life. I was married for almost six years. I wanted a family, a real home that felt like one. I didn't want a place where people dropped in for cocktails, and I didn't want to go out to dinner or a club or a movie every night. I could have handled some of that, if my wife hadn't sought counsel from her mother about everything in our lives. I put my foot down finally, and she went home to mama. There was a lot more, but a man doesn't tell tales about his marriage, not even after it's gone sour. Her mother told her to bow out, and she did. I did not give up that relationship easily, but I managed to do it, and I'm glad.

"You're nothing like her, Ginger. You go after what you want. I like that. You and I will always be able to meet on some common ground, to have an understanding, because you speak your mind and stand up for what you believe rather than sulk passively in a corner. I believe that if we give ourselves a chance, we can make a life together." He opened his eyes, stretched his right arm out on the back of the seat, and turned to her. "What haven't you told me that you think I should know?"

She took a ginger snap out of the wicker basket and chewed without tasting what she ate. He'd chosen an odd time for them to bare their souls to each other—sitting in a strange place in a rented car while rain drenched it and lightning danced all around it, but she was glad he'd opened the door.

"As you spoke, Jason, I marveled at the similarity of our lives. I, too, was trying to find myself when we met in Harare, but unlike you I wasn't looking for peace. I had spent my life as my parents had taught me. I married as a virgin, went to church on Sundays, worked hard and tried to save for the future, for the time when I could have a family and either stay at home, work part-time, or do consultancies. My husband wanted everything right then. Everything. He saw no reason why we couldn't start a family, though we only had a one-bedroom apartment. I wanted to save for a home and the expenses of a first child. I thought we could buy a house with my savings as a down payment, but when I mentioned it he wanted us to take over half of my savings and go on a two-month jaunt through Italy. I should leave my clients that I had worked so hard to get, close my office, and go have fun. He earned a good living as an engineer, making as much money as I, but even though we shared expenses my savings quadrupled his. He loved fun, parties, eating out, and, especially, traveling abroad. We bickered constantly. When I refused to take the trip to Europe with him, he asked me for a divorce. I didn't contest it.

"You met me when I was trying to discard my conservative behavior and outlook and do something wild for the first time in my life. I meant to have a fling with you, to get Harold Lawson out of my system, but I found I couldn't do anything so completely out of character. Besides, I'd fallen for you, and I couldn't pretend that I hadn't. Jason, I thought my world would end when I got back here, realized what I felt for you, and had to live with the knowledge that I'd never see you again."

He enveloped her hand in his own. "I know the feeling." Chuckles suddenly spilled out of his throat, and he released her hand and nearly doubled up laughing.

"Jason, what's the matter? Jason, are you hysterical? Talk to me."

He began to hiccup, and she pounded him on the back. "Jason, for Pete's sake, what is it?"

"Ginger," he managed to say at last, "I just figured out why we got so personal with each other when we were arguing that divorce case. Don't you realize now that we had stopped arguing the divorce case and had begun to argue about the foibles of our own spouses, that we'd slipped into a debate of the problems of our own failed marriages?"

She looked out at the rain-washed highway and the scores of cars idling along the road waiting to continue. "Yes. But I was so ashamed of myself for having a judge call me on the carpet that I've been pushing it out of my conscious thoughts."

He laughed again. "We were so harsh with each other."

She moved closer to him. "I was not mean to you."

"Were so."

She leaned her head on his shoulder and kissed his neck. "Was not. Was—"

He settled it when he gathered her into his arms and let her feel the touch of his tongue on her lips. Wild fires raced through her, and she parted her lips for the sweetness he'd give her and for which she yearned. His velvet tongue dipped into her mouth, finding its home, claiming her. She didn't care if he felt her tremors, if he knew how she longed to belong to him.

He folded her to him and whispered, "We need to be together, Ginger. And soon. The rain's stopped, but I want a few minutes to get off this high before I can drive. Understand?"

She did and forced herself back to her seat. He'd just about reached the limit of his control, and she couldn't wait to exercise her advantage.

He started the engine, checked the traffic, and headed for New York. She'd whetted his appetite, and he wanted, needed, to know more of her, to strip away everything between them but their clothes. "Ginger, were you ever happy in your marriage? I mean… Did you…did you love him at first?"

She answered without hesitation, and he liked that. "I loved him. The trouble was my naiveté. I don't blame Harold. I was twenty-six when I got married. What man could imagine that a person could live that long and not know any more than I did about human relations? I assumed that if you behaved honorably and had good values and worthwhile goals, everything worked out. I didn't know that the same could be true for my spouse, and that instead of cementing our marriage, the fact that we each had strong goals and values could drive us apart. I didn't want the divorce, but I didn't care to live with a man who desired his freedom."

Maybe he ought not to probe, but there were things he had to know, because he'd committed himself to her with that kiss at the foot of the Delaware Memorial Bridge, and he had to know what he was up against.

"Did you have any problems you haven't told me about, that would help me to steer our own relationship on the right course?" At her hesitancy, he slowed down so as to be able to concentrate on her words.

"A couple of things, but you'll know those when the time comes."

He thought of some of the problems in his own marriage that had centered around Louise's unwillingness to grow, and didn't press Ginger for an explanation. Some things were best discussed in an atmosphere of intimacy. But at least they were talking, sharing themselves.

She had questions for him, too, he learned. "Do you have any hobbies, Jason? What do you do when you want to get away from law?"

"Recently, my problem hasn't been to get away from it, but to stick with it. Before you started fooling around in my head, I used to spend hours playing the flute or the coronet. On Sunday afternoons, you'd find me either at Lincoln Center, the Metropolitan Museum of Art, or at Jojo's down in the Village gigging with some fellow musicians. We're all amateurs, but some great jazz blows around in that place. I do other things, but they're less important to me. What about you?"

She smiled in a mysterious way that piqued his curiosity. "Me? Cross off Jojo's, add gardening and the Thursday night community sing-along on the Island, and you've nailed me. I'm trying to start a mother-daughter club on the island to bring girls closer to their mothers. Maybe that will heal some of the friction in the homes, and start a decline in out of wedlock pregnancies. So far, I'm not having overwhelming success, but I have hope."

His eyes shone with approval and affection. "You keep working at that mother-daughter project. It'll be a success if you only recruit one family. You know, it's amazing how much alike we are."

"Alike? But you're a Re*pub*lican."

"Yeah. And you needn't pronounce the word as if it's got a vile taste. Don't forget. You're one of those Democrats."

"Are we going to fight about that?" she asked.

He felt good—light and airy like a Chinese kite dancing in a March wind. "You and me fight about politics? Honey, I hope so, because from where I sit right now we agree on practically everything else. Too much of that would bore both of us to insanity."

When she spoke again, it was as though she stepped among eggs, fearful of crushing them. "Jason..." She seemed to hesitate. "Uh, what happened to you in Easton? You wished you were somewhere else, didn't you?"

He hated to say it, but honesty and straight talk was what they needed now. "You're right. Those people crowded me, all but set our wedding date. Anybody would have thought they'd been waiting to pounce. I don't let people push me around. I don't care how well-meaning they are. I didn't want to hurt you, but I got pretty steamed up. I know how I feel about you and what I want out of our relationship, and that's between nobody but you and me."

"I see. Haven't you ever lived in a small town?"

"I've lived in Dallas and New York, except for the two years I endured in New Haven getting my law degree at Yale."

"Endured?"

"Yeah. I got sick of that cult of indifference. You couldn't believe the pretense. Nobody leveled with anybody." He took a deep breath, flipped on the cruise control, and put Yale out of his mind.

He noticed her head tilting forward and put a cassette into the tape deck. She soon slept as the soothing notes of

"Lover Come Back To Me" pealed out of Benny Carter's saxophone.

It was after six-thirty when they passed through the Lincoln Tunnel and drove into New York City. "Since we're near Hertz, I suggest we return the car and take a taxi to your place."

Her ready agreement sent a flash of excitement zinging through him. He didn't look at her, because he didn't want her to see the hunger that he knew blazed across his face. Half an hour later, he held out his hand for her door key, opened the door, and walked in with her.

"Why don't I call down to Andy's Place for dinner?" she asked him. "The take-out won't remind you of Twenty-One, but it's edible."

They finished the meal, and while she put away the remains of it and straightened the kitchen, he prowled around the living room. What he needed was a swift, three-mile run or a half-hour of push-ups. The treadmill. Anything to get rid of the wild energy that wanted to burst out of him. He looked up and saw her standing in the doorway of the kitchen, biting her lip.

"Jason, would you sit down? Put on a CD, or something. I'll be back in a couple of minutes."

He raised an eyebrow and regarded her, temptation gnawing at him, urging him to make a move on her. But he hadn't nursed her feelings for him for nearly three months only to have their relationship fizzle because of his miscalculation. He sat down.

What was keeping her? He was a patient man, he reminded himself, and it didn't make sense to wring himself dry like a sheet in the spin cycle of a washing machine. He stopped shaking his left foot, felt in the breast pocket of his shirt for a package of cigarettes, and remembered that he hadn't smoked in eleven years.

"She's an itch," he told himself, "an itch that's grating every nerve in my body." He stood. Home. That was it. Go home and get out of trouble's way, because she hadn't given him one clue that she wanted any more than a kiss. He looked up to the ceiling, took a deep breath, and threw up his hands. *A kiss!* Who was he kidding? He looked around the room to see where she'd put the overnight bag he'd carried to Easton, and his gaze fell on her walking toward him with two glasses of white wine. He hadn't even seen her go through there to the kitchen.

"You in a hurry or something?" she asked. "I thought we'd have a glass of wine and wind down. It's been such a—"

At his wits' end, he took the glasses from her and put them on the coffee table. "I can't handle any small talk right now, Ginger, and I don't want to hear anything that smacks of superficiality."

She sat down. "Neither do I. What is it, Jason? What's the matter?"

It was a reasonable question, but she might as well have pulled him into her. The fiery tentacles of long denied need of her singed his nerve ends and plowed straight to his loins. Her open, inquiring look grabbed at his protective instincts, and the need to have her fought with his inclination to protect her. Her brown eyes seemed to grow bigger as she looked at him.

He heard, "Honey. Honey, what's the matter? You look so miserable," and his fences fell as he pulled her into his arms.

"Ginger, honey, I need you. *Baby, I need you!*"

Did he imagine that her fingers caressed his cheeks before she squeezed him to her? He felt her gentle hands at the back of his head, and told himself that he'd begun to hallucinate.

"Ginger, I don't want us to start anything, because I couldn't stop. I don't *want* to stop. I want to make love with you."

"Shh, darling. I haven't asked you to stop."

He moved back and looked into her eyes and at the sweet lips that trembled in anticipation of his kiss, and shudders raced through his body. When she dampened her lips and

parted them, he primed himself for the loving she offered.
He sat her in his lap, rested her head against his shoulder, and
bent to her mouth. She took his tongue eagerly, aggressively,
begging for all he could give her. He dipped into her sweet
mouth and explored the nectar that was there for him. When
he thought he could stand no more, she took his hand and
placed it on her breast.

He rolled its tip between his fingers until she moaned, broke
the kiss, and asked for more. He hadn't noticed that she'd
changed into a sundress until, with ease, he reached inside
of it and, for the first time, felt the warmth of her woman's
flesh. Her hand pressed the back of his head and he pulled
her flesh into his mouth and suckled her until she shifted in
his lap. Another minute of it, and he knew he'd explode.

"Where's your bedroom, honey?"

She nodded to her right and he picked her up, sped down
the short hallway to her room and lay her on her bed. He
leaned over, unwrapped the sundress, and threw it on a chair.
He pulled his T-shirt over his head, turned back to her and
jumped to full readiness when he saw that she wore only
bikini panties and that her full breasts lay bare for him. He
slipped out of his clothes and stared down at her.

Ginger gulped at the sight of him, big and proudly erect.
Moisture accumulated in her mouth as she gazed at him, and
marvelled at the look of wonder on his face. Her arms opened
to him. "Come hold me."

Even in her frantic desire, she could see the vulnerability in
him. "Are you sure, Ginger? If you take me, there's no turning
back for me. I love you, and right now I need you like I need
air. But if it's not the same with you, say it this second, and
I'm out of here. I don't want a taste. I want you."

Didn't he know what he meant to her? "Jason, darling, don't
you know I love you?"

In seconds she had him in her arms, and he was holding her,
squeezing her, loving her. At last she could feel his masculine

hardness against her body. Her head emptied of all thoughts but him, and the frissons of heat in which he enveloped her as he took his time kissing every part of her, teasing her breast with his tongue and sucking it until she thought she would lose consciousness. He moved to the other breast and let his fingers trail down her body until he reached the seat of her desire. Overcome with a passion she'd never known before, she begged for relief, but he ignored her and worked his magic at her lover's gate. Heat spiraled in her, and she undulated helplessly against him until frantic for relief, she took him into her hands to lead him to her portal, but he stopped her and shielded himself to protect her. She shifted her hips wildly. Urging. Begging.

He rose above her and looked down into her face. "Will you take me in?"

She didn't answer. She couldn't. Her hands guided his entrance as though they'd done it forever. The feeling of him inside her sent her passion to fever heights. He filled her, heated her, and rocked her. Driving. Stroking. Branding her until every muscle of her body seemed to pound, pump and squeeze as he wrung a scream from her and hurtled her into ecstasy. Seconds passed, and she heard his lover's shout of triumph as he gave her the essence of himself.

They lay locked together for a long while before he said, "I've never had such a feeling. I think you're okay, too, but I want you to tell me."

She kissed his neck. "Jason, if there's any more I don't think I could bear it. If I had to die ten minutes from now, I don't believe I'd complain."

That grin again. The man had a magic smile. "You mean you've had enough of me? You wouldn't be kicking and screaming to live, so you could make love with me night and day? Good Lord, I'm a flop."

She pinched his buttock. "Don't get cocky. I may get mean and see what you're made of."

Both of his eyebrows elevated as he braced himself on his

elbows and looked at her. "Honey, as hungry as I was when you walked in there with that wine, you may have just talked yourself into trouble."

She hadn't been exactly overstuffed. "I can always holler uncle."

His white teeth flashed a grin. "Yeah, you'll holler, all right. Maybe we both will." He tucked both arms beneath her shoulders and began to move.

An hour later, still locked together, he looked into her face, kissed her eyelids, and whispered, "I meant what I said, Ginger. I love you. From now on, it's you and me together. Do you understand?"

She didn't need the urging, and she didn't want any misunderstandings. "What does that mean, exactly?"

He touched her lips lightly with his own. "It means you marry me. Okay?"

She let her nose rub the tip of his nose. "We don't ask, these days?"

His grin sent a pulsating spasm to the spot in her where he'd most likely feel it. "You already agreed that there'll be no turning back, but I'll get on my knees if it'll make you happy."

"I don't need that formality, Jason. You love me. That's all I want."

Her heart sang as he wrapped her in a lovers' euphoria, spinning dreams of the joys to come. "I love you, baby, he whispered, his voice hoarse and unsteady. "You're my life."

She thought of the pain that had gripped her when she'd walked away from him in Zimbabwe because it was the right thing to do, said a silent prayer of thanks that, after she'd despaired of ever seeing him again, Providence had given them another chance.

"I love you, too, Jason. I think I have from the moment I met you."

He pulled the cover over them. "Let's go to sleep."

"What about the wine?"

"Wine? Baby, I'm drunk as it is."

* * *

As the week went by, Jason didn't think he'd ever known such happiness. They spoke by phone several times during each day, and saw each other every evening—dinner, movies, concerts, or walks along the river on Roosevelt Island. He had even pulled weeds in her garden and enjoyed it. He made up his mind to ask her for a wedding date, because he hated leaving her every night.

Sunday night, a week after their engagement, he asked her to meet him the next day at Tiffany's to choose their rings. It seemed to him that so simple a thing as discussing the date and the rings had brought them even closer together. He chose a two-carat round diamond flanked by single baguettes, and watched her eyes sparkle with approval. They left the store hand in hand, and he didn't think he could contain his joy. He kissed her at the corner of Broadway and Houston, and took a taxi back to his office.

Ginger read and reread the papers in front of her. Peppard and Lowe were her first and best corporate clients, and she valued them, but she didn't much like the idea of representing a landlord against a tenant, especially not in an eviction suit. She knew landlords used all kinds of trumped-up reasons to get rid of tenants in rent-controlled buildings. The eviction would allow her client to raise the rent on the next tenant, or to get the apartment decontrolled. It was the slickest real estate game in New York. She got to work polishing her brief for Thursday's court appearance, though the job made her uncomfortable.

The light on her intercom blinked, and she flicked the button. "What is it, Edna?"

"Mr. Calhoun on line two, Ms. Hinds."

Her pulse plunged into a wild gallop as she anticipated the sound of his voice. "Hello, Jason."

"Ginger, what the hell do you mean by arguing for Peppard and Lowe to get my brother kicked out of his loft?"

*"Your brother?"*

"Don't tell me you couldn't have guessed it. How many E.E. Calhouns who make a living as a sculptor do you think there are?"

"Hold on there, Jason. You're assuming a lot. I didn't know you had a brother. And even if I *had* known it, you don't have the right to speak to me this way. I can argue for anybody I please."

He didn't relent. "We're talking about my brother, my flesh and blood. Don't you understand that? Eric's been in that loft for nine years, and he has some rights."

"He doesn't have the right to cast those molds and drive all the other tenants mad with that hammering. If you can't apologize, I want you to hang up."

"All right. Goodbye, Ginger."

She sat there stunned as the dial tone irritated her eardrum. When at last she was able to manage it, she buzzed her secretary. "Edna, who is E.E. Calhoun's lawyer?"

"Asa McKenzie."

She thought of calling Jason and asking why he hadn't taken the case for his brother, thought better of it, leaned back in her chair, and asked herself whether going on with that case was worth losing Jason. But she realized that he hadn't given her a choice.

She read the relevant statutes for the third time and decided that she could represent her client and maintain her integrity without implicating Eric unduly, but the weight in her heart nearly robbed her of her breath. Her private phone rang.

"If you go through with this, Ginger, you'll destroy any chance we may have of a future together."

"You're a lawyer, too, Jason, and you know this case is registered for day after tomorrow. If I back out now, my client will sue me. I wouldn't ask you to do what you're requesting of me—please kick your career right down the drain, Ginger."

"So you won't do it? I'm sorry. Goodbye."

\* \* \*

Jason hung up, walked to the window, and looked down at the people who rushed along Madison Avenue like ants busily collecting sugar. He didn't want a life without Ginger, but if she could put his own brother out in the street for a client who meant nothing to her but money, could he go ahead with their marriage? He loved his younger brother, and he refused to take sides against him. If that's the way she planned to play it, too bad. At least he'd found out before he said those fateful words.

If she'd made it through the past two days, she could do anything, Ginger told herself as she walked into Civil Court at 60 Center Street in lower Manhattan. She hadn't argued before that judge, and didn't know what to expect. And the jury for which she'd had to settle wasn't what she wanted, but she could work with it. She kept her glance on the door until she saw Jason enter with Asa McKenzie and another man who was obviously Jason's brother.

Without looking in the direction of the man she loved, she outlined her client's complaint and his demands, adding that as a tenant she sympathized with renters, but that landlords had rights that the courts were bound to uphold. Asa McKenzie followed with a rebuttal that seemed to sway the jury, but in the end it found in favor of Peppard and Lowe. No one would ever know the measure of her relief when McKenzie failed to put Eric on the stand, relieving her of the responsibility of cross-examining him. It was only upon hearing the verdict that she realized how badly she had wanted to lose.

Wooden legs propelled her into her apartment that evening. She'd sat in her office until after seven o'clock, mulling over the events of her life. Jason had to have known that he'd sandwiched her between a rock and a hard place when he'd suggested she drop the case. If there was a profession in which reputation was one's only passport, it was that of a lawyer, and you didn't desert your client at the last minute unless you'd just won the lottery and had planned to retire, anyway. She changed into a peasant skirt and blouse and went to Andy's Place. She had no appetite, but being among familiar faces beat the emptiness of her apartment.

She stopped short at the sight of Amos Logan and her friend, Clarice, in what appeared to be an intimate huddle. She'd hoped to find at least one of them there alone and anxious for company. Amos saw her and waved her over to the table.

"Haven't seen you in here lately, Ginger. Pull up a chair."

She leaned over and kissed Clarice on the cheek. "You're looking good, girl. Want to let me in on the secret?" When Clarice blushed, Ginger found Amos from the corner of her eye and caught a grin on his usually straight face. Her head snapped around, and she stared at him until he laughed aloud and told her. "Don't look so shocked, Ginger. After all, it's June—Lovers' Month. That case been to trial yet?"

She nodded. "This morning."

"What's the matter? You lose it?"

She shook her head and looked away from them as she gathered her composure.

"Well, if you won it, why're you in the dumps?"

"Oh. Oh," Clarice said. "You're not even warm, Amos. Ginger, why aren't you celebrating with Jason?"

Amos sipped his brandy. "Good question. Where is he?"

Ginger got up, "You two stay here and enjoy yourselves. I...I'm going to turn in. Call you tomorrow, Clarice."

She left hurriedly, bumping into the Reverend Armstrong. "'Scuse me, Reverend," she said, and hurried on without waiting to hear his reply. She loved the neighborliness on Roosevelt Island, but that same warmth and friendliness sometimes deprived you of your privacy. Inside her apartment, she turned the radio on and raised the volume high, as though loud music could banish her thoughts and drown out her pain.

Jason sat on the edge of a desk in his brother's loft. "The engagement's off, Eric. I can't marry a woman who'd take this kind of case against my brother when I begged her not to do it."

Eric got up from the lotus position he'd taken on the floor and walked over to Jason. "What are you talking about? What's this got to do with Ginger?"

"I didn't tell you? Ginger is G.A. Hinds, Peppard and Lowe's attorney."

Eric sat down. "Well, I'll be. She's a good lawyer and a beauty, too. She took the case for one of my friends against his landlord, and won. Don't you think you should have introduced us?"

"No, I don't. I was too mad. Anyway, it's too late now. The water's under the bridge."

The heat of Eric's stare gave him an uneasy feeling. "You mean that after what you went through before you found that woman, you'd give her up for something this stupid? Look here, Jason, she was easy on me, and you know it. There's a clause in my lease that's written in bold, capital letters specifying that the property cannot be used for commercial purposes. I've been getting away with it for nine years. If I stay here it means the rent will be doubled, but I can easily afford that now, because my pieces are selling well."

Jason jumped from the desk. "You're telling me that landlord wasn't out to get you?"

Eric shrugged. "No. In fact, he'd warned me several times. You didn't ask to see the lease, and I didn't think to show it to you. McKenzie knew I was wrong, and he said he doubted I'd win. Man, you'd better go mend your fences."

Jason's breath was slow coming. "Yeah. You can say that again."

He didn't think calling her would help, but he phoned, anyway. No answer, so he left a message. "Ginger, I need to talk with you. Please call me."

Repeated calls with the same message on her answering machine brought no response. He took a taxi home, showered, changed his clothes, and left. If she was in New York, he'd find her.

Hadn't she told Clarice she'd call her tomorrow? Annoyed, she jerked open the door without looking through the peephole and released an audible gasp. *"Jason!"*

"Do you mind if I come in?" He held a calla lily loosely wrapped in clear plastic that was tied with a white satin ribbon.

She moved aside to let him enter, but left the door open and leaned against the wall, her arms folded in front of her.

"Can we talk, Ginger?"

She closed the door and followed him to her living room. "About what, Jason? Do you want me to find your brother a place to stay? Or maybe rent a studio for him? Why are you here? Just say it, and I'll listen. I don't have the energy to hassle with you."

"Is that why you didn't take my calls?"

"You could say that."

"I realize you're angry with me, and—"

She stood toe-to-toe with him. "Angry? You think I'm angry? Jason, don't use the word angry to me. *I hurt!*"

He reached for her and slowly withdrew his hand. "I know, and I'm hurting, too. I made one of the biggest mistakes of my life when I asked you to drop that case. I don't exonerate myself, either—I'd probably still be fuming if Eric hadn't told me he'd been warned about breaking his lease, which specifically said the loft couldn't be used for commercial purposes, and he'd broken it every day for nine years. His landlord had a right to redress."

She placed her hands on her hips, laid her head to the side, and studied him. "I didn't think that was the problem. You said I was working against your brother, and asked me to drop the case."

"I know I did, but looking back, I know that didn't make sense. I've always been too protective of Eric, and he's never needed that. I came here to ask you to forgive me. I just don't see how I'm going to be happy apart from you, Ginger. I can't begin to envisage life without you."

The heaviness eased away from her chest, and her mind seemed to swirl as she gazed into the warmth of his eyes, saw the love there, and felt the scraps of her soul begin to fit themselves together again.

"How do I know it won't happen again, that you won't expect me to give up what is so dear to me if it suits you to do that?"

He held out his arms to her. "If we work together, it won't be necessary."

She looked at those arms, open and full of the love and sweetness that she adored, but she didn't move. "Work together, how?"

"Calhoun and Hinds, Attorneys at Law. What do you say?"

She tried not to show her reaction, but she knew the smile on her face had never been wider. "You'd better be glad C comes before H or it would be—"

He offered her the calla lily, and when she took it, he swooped her into his arms. Joy suffused her as his scent, strength, and whole being wrapped her in his love, and his taste once more filled her mouth and heated her blood. She took his hand and led him to that place where love abounded, where they loosed their bodies into each other, swept away in a vortex of unearthly rapture.

Friends and relatives filled the chairs in the rose garden of Brooklyn's Botanical Garden. Wearing a yellow organdy dress and matching wide-brimmed hat and carrying yellow roses, Linda Jenkins walked up the aisle to the altar, faced the minister, and glanced back at her sister. In a white organdy dress and hat identical in style to her sister's and carrying

Jason's calla lilies, Ginger glided on satin-slippered feet over the tiny yellow roses that Jason had given the flower girls to spread in his bride's path. She inhaled the many-hued roses that perfumed the garden with their June freshness, and thought how fortunate she was. She knew that a bride didn't wear white for a second marriage, but it was *her* wedding, and she wanted Jason to know that her life began anew with him. She tried to hold back the tears of joy when she saw him standing there beside Eric, so unorthodox, with his back to the altar looking at her. She grinned, because she knew that if he thought her unhappy he would chuck tradition and come to meet her.

When she reached him, he gave her hand a gentle squeeze and whispered, "I love you. Love you. I think I'll take wings and fly."

"Don't forget to carry me with you," she whispered back.

The minister cleared his throat, "Dearly beloved…"

Ginger heard no more as Jason turned fully to her, love shining in his eyes, and pledged his being to her. She heard herself repeat the words that made her his wife, felt the arms she loved so dearly wrap around her and the sweetness of his mouth skim over hers. She looked up at him and saw that special grin that always mesmerized her, and her pounding heart sent the blood speeding through her body.

"Love me?" he asked.

"Oh, yes," she said. "Till the end of time.

\* \* \* \* \*

# A PERFECT MATCH

Susan Andrews curled up in a burnt orange barrel chair that dominated her ultramodern living room and sipped tomato juice as she watched the New Year's Eve revelers in Times Square. How could human beings be so frivolous and so foolish as to crowd into that small space in freezing temperatures, sleet, and wind just to watch a ball drop a few feet when they could see the same thing in the comfort of their warm living rooms? She thanked God that she had better sense. That she wasn't scatterbrained. She sipped more juice. At least those people weren't alone, a niggling thought intruded; they had each other, if only for those few moments.

She wouldn't cry. She never cried, no matter how much a thing hurt. Crying denoted weakness. But why couldn't she meet a loveable, eligible man who could appreciate an educated, independent woman. Not that she planned to lose sleep over it. She had a good life. How many women anywhere could boast a two hundred thousand dollar condo, a six-figure income, and the respect of their peers? True, some of the men with whom she worked had nervous hands and couldn't keep them off of her, but she could handle that. Still, she'd like to go to work once in a while wearing makeup, a skirt above her knees, and her hair hanging down the way those secretaries did—the girls that men chased and married. Marriage. She longed to find someone to love, marry, and to have children with, but she was thirty-five.

She sucked air through her teeth, disgusted with herself. She didn't care. She'd made her choice. She had the best of all possible worlds; she didn't have to be home by six, and she didn't cook dinner if she didn't want to. She carried the half empty glass of juice to her modern, fashionable, and rarely used kitchen, emptied it and put it in the dishwasher. No, she wouldn't exchange places with any woman, not for anything. She stepped into the shower, wiping the moisture from her eyes. Darn that steam. Half an hour later, wrapped in her silk dressing gown, she couldn't blame the shower for the moisture dripping from her eyes.

Susan awoke early New Year's morning to the insistent chimes of her doorbell.

"Aunt Grace, what are you doing here so early this morning? You're not working today, are you?"

"Honey, I never went to bed last night. I made over two hundred and fifty dollars since midnight. You must have been the only person in town who wasn't in Times Square, and I sure drove a lot of 'em home in my limousine. Never saw such a happy bunch of people. Honey, you got to do something about yourself. You can't make me believe you're content to split your life between work and this chrome mausoleum." Susan yawned exuberantly, hoping to warn her aunt that another topic would be more welcome.

"Aunt Grace, this is New Year's morning. Please don't make me start the year with that lecture."

"All right. All right. But you're wasting your life. You're already thirty-five, and in a few more years, you'll be past your prime—at least according to my book. You can't make me believe you don't want a man in your life." She looked around and waved her hand disparagingly. "This is just a lot of pretense; you can't fool me. I'm fifty-six, but your manless life would drive me crazy. 'Course, I didn't do your cause a bit of good coming in here like this. A man should have been the first person across your doorsill this year to bring you good luck."

She loved her aunt Grace, but she had no tolerance for superstitions and, since Grace knew that, she didn't respond.

"Would you like some coffee, Aunt Grace? I'm just getting out of bed."

"Coffee? No thanks. I'm going home and go to bed." Susan watched an expression roll over her aunt's face and knew she could expect one of the woman's brilliant ideas.

"You know what?" Grace asked, her eyes alight with anticipation. "I'm going to do your chart. Let's see now, I know your birth date. Weren't you born at noon on a Sunday?"

"You're the one who keeps track of these things. How would I know?"

"I'll look it up in my book, and I'll call you tomorrow. I should have done this years ago, but you're so scientific, never believing anything. Happy New Year."

Susan looked out of her bedroom window early the next morning, saw torrents of rain, and decided that she'd better telephone her aunt Grace.

"Are you on call this morning? I'll never be able to hail a taxi in this weather."

"I can take you downtown, dear, if you're in your lobby at quarter to eight."

Susan dressed hurriedly in a yellow-green woolen suit that set off her silky, ebony complexion and complemented it with brown lizard accessories and a brown, mink-lined raincoat. She stepped into the rear seat of Grace's private taxi and paused, surprised to see a passenger. A man. *And what a man!*

"Honey, this is August Jackson, one of my regulars. Mr. Jackson, this is my niece, Miss"—she emphasized the word—"Susan Andrews. Susan works about six blocks from you." Susan turned to greet the man and had to swallow the lump that lodged in her throat. Someone should have prepared her. She wouldn't classify him as handsome; that was too commonplace a description. He was riveting, that's what he was. Flawless dark brown skin, thick silky brows and lashes, lean face, square chin, perfect lips, and mesmerizing light brown eyes. She shook herself out of her trance and extended her hand. *Pull yourself together,* she silently admonished herself.

"I'm glad to meet you, Mr. Jackson." His hand clasped hers gently, and she noticed that he looked directly at her eyes and didn't flirt. But he continued to hold her hand and a smile slowly traveled from his lips to his remarkable eyes.

"Hello, Susan. This is a pleasure." She was sure that her blink and swiftly arched eyebrow betrayed her surprise. The man looked the epitome of sophistication, but his drawl and slow speech were not that of an urban sophisticate. He glanced toward the driver's seat. "Why are you stopping, Grace? Anything wrong?"

"Have you looked out of the window recently," Grace asked him and stopped the car just beyond an exit on the FDR Drive. "I can't see two feet in front of me, it's raining so hard."

"I hadn't noticed," August said, his eyes back on Susan. "Did Grace say 'Miss Andrews'?"

"I sure did," Grace put in quickly.

"How is that? I can't believe such a lovely lady isn't married."

"I suppose if I'm single, there's something wrong with me," she said in cool even tones, pulling her hand from his. He's only a man, she told herself, though her pounding heart and racing blood belied it.

"Ah, Susan, how could you imagine such a thing? You're very beautiful, and I just think it's strange that some man hasn't convinced you to marry him. That's all." She didn't respond, but she noticed that peculiar smile of his start toward his eyes again.

Then he said, "I hope you're not against marriage." She wished he'd get off the subject of her and marriage, and she turned to him with the intention of putting the matter to rest. She just hoped he didn't notice how her heart jumped in her chest when she looked straight at him.

"Mr. Jackson," she said coolly, refusing to use his first name, "I am not against marriage, but the time, energy, and imagination spent on courting and pretending not to want what one knows one wants is a waste of time. It's a phoney process, but that's the way it's done, and I don't have time or the inclination for it."

"Hmm. I see," he replied drolly and glanced out the window as though inspecting his chances of getting more agreeable company soon.

"What do you see? In developing countries, marriages are contracted by a very simple procedure. Either the parents or the individuals engage a marriage broker or a matchmaker to find a mate. In some places, an astrologer makes the selection. The marriages work just as well, and divorce is rare by our standards." Satisfied that she'd made her point, Susan crossed her legs and looked out of the window as the water cascaded from above.

"Susan, I'm disappointed that you aren't romantic," August drawled in what was clearly a mild reproof. "I thought most women bloomed with lovely music, candlelight, and romance." Hurt and hiding it, Susan lifted her chin as though that gesture would silence him.

"Most women don't have my responsibilities."

"Or your beauty and poise," he added.

"Why is it, Mr. Jackson, that men can't talk without getting personal?" She caught his grin from the corner of her left eye.

"Oh, they can, and they do. And when you get to be fifty-five or sixty, you'll know just what I'm talking about." Surprised at his dig and concluding that he was smoother than she had surmised, she changed the subject.

"You don't speak as if you're a New Yorker. I think I hear a drawl."

"Right on both counts," he agreed. "I'm from North Carolina. Down there, we men aren't getting familiar when we pay a woman a compliment. And our women know that." Evidently Grace had been quiet as long as she could, because her words seemed to rush out of her.

"Don't worry about the time, you all, nobody's going to be on time for work today. I can just about start now, though it's still pretty dense. Mr. Jackson, did you say you were looking for your son?" Susan sat forward, aware that with her occult abilities, Grace knew whether August Jackson was looking for anyone and for whom.

"No," he replied. "I don't have any children, unfortunately. I'm looking for my brother. We were separated when he was eight and I was ten. I've been looking for him ever since. How did you happen to ask?"

"Oh, I dabble in astrology and clairvoyance, though I'm at my best when I do charts," she said proudly, "but since I saw a young boy in the stars, I thought it was your son."

"I've never married. Wasn't in a position to until just recently and, now that I could consider it, I find that these New York women are too much. I'm not going to start running around in a tuxedo every night, hanging out in bars, and competing for the attention of maître d's. This place is a mad house. Aramis cologne is out and some kind of 'noir' is in. Would you believe one of our secretaries looked down at my feet and said 'oh gee, are those…?' Her voice seemed to die, literally, before she said, 'no, I see they're not Guccis.' Those shoes cost me one hundred and thirty-nine dollars plus tax, and she scoffed at them because they don't have a Gucci label."

"Not all of our New York girls are like that," Grace hastened to say, having discovered his single status. He continued as though it were his favorite grouse.

"These women have such superficial values, Grace. Do you think one of them would get on a public bus, however clean, with you? When she's by herself, yes. But if you're paying, these New York girls are subject to demand a stretched out limousine just to go to a neighborhood movie. I'm used to a different type, one who wants to be with me for myself rather than for the admiration and envious looks she gets from other people."

"Now, don't you worry none," Grace insisted, "we've got nice girls here that's different. You just quit hanging around those corporate secretaries and take a good long look at some of the other ones."

Susan refused to look either at her aunt, whom she wanted to throttle, or at August Jackson, who excited and infuriated her at the same time. She got out at her office building after bidding the man a cool goodbye.

August leaned back in the corner of the cab, doing his best to keep the grin that he knew Grace could see in her rearview mirror off his face. He hadn't lied, but he'd phrased his conversation in such a way as to tell Susan Andrews that she could get off of her high horse or not, he couldn't care less. She was cut from cloth that he liked, and when he liked something, he explored it. Fully. Talk about a double whammy. She'd poleaxed him. No indeed; she hadn't seen the last of August Jackson.

"Is she really like that," he asked Grace, "or was she putting me on?"

"Well, Mr. Jackson, she thinks she's like that."

"Thinks? You mean she isn't?" This was getting more interesting by the minute.

"She hasn't given herself a chance to find out *what* she's like. She thinks life is work and chasing goals."

"Nothing wrong with going after a goal, depending, of course, on what it is. Maybe what she needs is a new one. Maybe more than one." He found himself warming up to the subject. Susan Andrews had some traits that he liked, and one of them was a distaste for superficiality. He tuned in to Grace's next words.

"That's what I keep telling her. She wants to get married, but she doesn't want to. No, Mr. Jackson, the truth is she refuses to be bothered with the nice little rituals that you have to go through before you get married." He smiled inwardly, appreciating Grace's niece more with the seconds.

"Very interesting."

"Is it?" an obviously disapproving Grace wanted to know. "She's really a wonderful person, socially conscious and all that...you know...a good girl. But she's just so cut and dried."

"Hmm." Socially conscious, was she? His adrenaline stepped up. He intended to get to know Susan Andrews.

"What does she do for recreation?" he asked, trying to get a rounded picture of her.

"I'm not sure she knows what that is, Mr. Jackson."

"Hmm," was all he said as Grace pulled up to the curb in front of the forty-story office building in which he worked. After giving her a receipt for the ride, he turned to go with just seven minutes in which to get to the twenty-second floor conference room. He pivoted around when Grace called out to him and beckoned him to her side of the cab.

"Could you give me your date, day, and time of birth? I'd like to do your chart." August smiled. He had become fond of Grace. She wasn't old enough—maybe fifty—to be motherly, but she'd pass for a wonderful older sister. "I won't misuse whatever I find," she quickly assured him.

"I'm not afraid of that," he said and gave her the information.

\* \* \*

Susan bumped into one of her peers as she stepped off of the elevator. "Keep your hands to yourself," she warned Oscar Hicks, one of the other senior lawyers. She had stopped trying to figure out whether he touched her because he found her irresistible—something she doubted—wanted to control her as a woman because he couldn't best her as a lawyer or whether he was an insensitive clout who'd been lucky enough to get a law degree. She went into her office, closed the door, and got to work. August Jackson wouldn't try to demean a woman. Now where had that thought come from? She picked up the phone and buzzed her secretary.

"Lila, cancel my nine-thirty staff meeting and reschedule it for two this afternoon. I'm sure this morning's storm delayed a few people."

"Yes, Ms. Andrews." Susan maintained strict protocol; none of her staff addressed her by her first name. She sat back in her chair. And she was going to put Oscar Hicks in his place once and for all, next time he gave her the opportunity.

Three afternoons later after dropping off three of August's colleagues, Grace said to him, "Well, I did your chart, and I'll say you're one fine human being."

"Thank you, Grace. I take it that's not all." He leaned forward, waiting to hear what she had to say.

"Well, if you don't mind my saying so, you and Susan are a perfect match. I'm never wrong, Mr. Jackson, and believe me, you're perfect. I've been doing charts since I was a teenager, and I've never found such a perfect pair. I just did hers earlier this week."

"What else did you see?"

"You don't shoot pool, do you?"

"I wouldn't know how to hold a cue stick. Why?"

"Well, this showed you getting out from behind a ball

that had an eight on it. I'll work it out further, if you wan
me to."

"Well, I don't know, Grace, I've never paid much attention
to this sort of thing." He didn't want to hurt her feelings, bu
he doubted you could look at the stars and determine a man'
future.

"If you don't believe me," she argued, "next time Susan
rides with us, ask her if I've ever been wrong in anything she
knows about. Just ask her."

Anxiety knotted his insides, and he couldn't help smiling
at himself. "When will that be?"

"I can pick her up when I take you down tomorrow morning
Okay?" She'd played into his hand. He'd already decided tha
he wanted to see Susan Andrews again; he'd state his ow
case.

Her aunt's offer of a lift surprised Susan; Grace usually
waited to be asked. She had reliable corporate clients whom she
drove to and from work weekday mornings and, occasionally
at other times, if she was free, when they beeped her. But she
didn't solicit anybody's business, including that of her niece
She had her customers, and they gave her as much work as
she could handle.

"You're picking me up this morning?" she asked Grace.

"Well, I'm not doing you a favor," Grace said bluntly
"August doubts my word, and I want you to verify what
told him. I'll be there at quarter to eight." Grace hung up
Susan stared at the phone for a minute, then shocked hersel
by tossing her pinstriped suit aside and grabbing the royal blue
one. She draped a red scarf around her neck and left her fu
coat hanging open as she walked from the building to the tax
in twenty-one degree weather. Let him think what he liked.

"Good morning, Susan," August greeted her. "Are you
always so lovely?" She jerked around to give him a good silen
censure only to find him grinning broadly.

"Oh, you…" she sputtered, unable to hide her pleasure at his compliment.

"Grace says her charts are never wrong."

So that was it, Grace had done his chart. "She never has been, at least not to my knowledge." Why did he fold his hands and lean back in the seat looking as though he'd just won a big lottery?

"Aunt Grace, what's going on here? What have you been doing?"

"Nothing. I just did his chart, and he acted like he wasn't going to take it seriously. I did yours, and I did his, and I never saw the likes of it in my life. If I was superstitious, I'd quit charting."

"You are superstitious." She turned to August. "My aunt doesn't tell things she sees that are really bad, so what did she say?"

"Well, if you're sure you want to know."

"I want to know."

"She said you're the woman for me. My perfect match."

Her handbag slipped to the floor as she half stood, forgetting where she was. "She said *what?*"

Grace took charge. "I did your chart, and then I did his two days later. There ain't no mistake. None. And if y'all don't do something about it, you're cheating yourselves."

"Aunt Grace, you've gone too far."

"But you said she's always right."

"Nobody's perfect."

Grace aligned the taxi with the curb, and Susan got out. She'd tell her aunt Grace a few things she wouldn't soon forget. That man didn't need any help getting a woman.

August let his head loll against the back of the cab. It had been an interesting trip. Remarkable. Susan Andrews spiked his blood. "I think she's upset, Grace."

"Sure she is. Trouble is, she knows I tell the truth, and she doesn't want to accept it. She never learned how to play games with boys when she was a teenager, and she doesn't understand courtship; that's why she hates it."

August laughed out loud.

"What's funny? Are you laughing at my Susan?"

"No indeed. I'm fascinated. The more you talk about her, the more certain I am that I want her telephone number. Don't worry. I won't court her." Grace gave him her niece's numbers at home and the office.

"Good luck."

"Thanks. I don't doubt that I'll need it."

Susan knew she might be playing into her aunt's hand, but she decided to risk it, nonetheless. She dialed her home phone number. "Aunt Grace, you're pushing August Jackson on me. What do you know about him? He could be a criminal."

"Just what I see on the chart, honey."

Susan hooked the telephone between her chin and her shoulder and applied more nail builder to her big toenail. Not for anything would she admit being excited and anxious to know more about him.

"That's all?"

"Well, the men he works with treat him like he's a big shot, but he acts like a regular fellow. And he sure has got nice manners. I'm driving him down tomorrow morning, so I'll pick you up at the usual time."

Susan knew from that click of the receiver that if she called a dozen times, Grace wouldn't answer the phone. Monday morning, when she stepped into the taxi at seven forty-five, she had to admit that she wasn't there because she didn't want to disappoint Grace, but because she hadn't been able to get August out of her thoughts.

Grace got right to the point. "The moon is in Venus and Saturn is rising, so it's your season, Susan. Truth is, the stars say you two should get married during the next full moon."

Susan couldn't believe the eagerness in August Jackson's voice. "When is that?" He wanted to know.

"Second week of February," Grace hastened to say.

Susan turned sharply toward August and quickly switched back to her position. That slow-moving smile seemed to take possession of his face, which was already too beguiling.

"Do you really believe in this stuff?" he asked Susan.

"Well, I told you that I don't as a rule, but Aunt Grace has a flawless record. Still, even perfect people eventually make mistakes. Don't forget Napoleon."

"I see." As she got out of the taxi, she thought she heard him say, "I'll be in touch." Tremors continued to roll through her long after she got in her office and closed the door. What kind of a man was he? He didn't behave as if she were a challenge as men usually did. Maybe he didn't understand executive women. She rubbed her arms, trembling as a chill slammed up her spine. Maybe he did understand them, and maybe status didn't bother him.

She sat at home that evening seeing her green and blue bedroom with new eyes. The room didn't portray an arresting quiet, a cool elegance as she had thought; it was harsh and unfeminine. She jerked herself up from the side of the bed and started toward her dressing room. Was she losing her mind?

"Hello. Yes, this is Susan," she said and groped for her boudoir chair. Surprised.

"Susan, this is August. Would you see a movie with me this evening?" She had to lock her left hand over her right one to steady the phone. She hadn't been invited to a movie in seven years.

"I...uh... Well, I don't know. This evening?"

"Yeah. Throw on a pair of jeans or something, and I'll pick you up at about eight. Okay?"

"Jeans? August, I don't have any jeans. I... Well, I never have an occasion to dress that casual." She thought for a moment. "I could put on a pants suit, but it's wool crepe." She wondered what he'd think of her. It had never occurred to her to buy a pair of blue jeans.

"Never mind, wear whatever you like; that pretty blue suit maybe. I'll put on a business suit. Will you come with me?" He spoke so softly, so gently in his deep and lilting southern drawl that she could have listened to him forever.

"Okay, I will. Do you want me to meet you somewhere?" She knew the minute the words left her mouth that she shouldn't have said them.

"Susan, I'll call for you. What is your apartment number?" She told him.

"I guess I'll never overcome my small town, southern upbringing, Susan, but I can't think of an occasion when I'd ask you to meet me somewhere. I'll be there around eight, and we can make the nine o'clock."

A movie date. What did people do on movie dates? She knew how to act at the opera and at such four-star restaurants as Twenty-one, *but the movies*. Well, he'd said wear the blue suit. She put it on and answered the door minutes later.

"You must have been around the corner when you called me."

"Hi. You look pretty. I was a few blocks away. Ready to go?"

She got her coat and would have put it on, but he took it and helped her into it. Somehow, he didn't make her feel helpless the way most men did when they took over; he made it seem natural.

"When did you buy the tickets?" she asked as he presented them to the usher.

"Soon as I called you. I didn't want you to stand in that long line because it's cold."

"Thanks," she felt compelled to say. "You're very considerate."

He stopped in the lobby. "Two bags of popcorn, please, and make that lots of butter."

"That's fattening," she protested, her voice suggesting the horror of it.

"You're nice and slim, so what's the problem?" he said, regarding her appreciatively.

"And I hope to stay that way, too." That's the trouble with men, she thought; they like you one way and are always trying to make you into something else.

"Forever?" August asked, his expression suggesting that the idea was ludicrous. "You're supposed to develop a little contentment around the middle as you grow older." He sampled some popcorn. "Hmm, this is good."

Susan couldn't believe what she heard. The men she knew wouldn't look twice at anything larger than a size twelve and then only if most of that was in the bra.

"You couldn't be serious," she said, a tone of incredulity shrouding her voice.

"Of course, I am. All this New York City fixation on skinny is ridiculous."

Appalled, she asked him, "You don't like the way I look?"

"Sweetheart, you are definitely not skinny. It's all exactly where it's supposed to be." He handed her a bag of popcorn and enveloped her other hand in his big one. "Come on. Let's get our seats." She felt a little strange when August released her hand while helping her to her seat, and she got a shock when she realized that she wanted him to hold it. He could have been reading her wishes, because he obliged her immediately, locking the fingers of his right hand through those of her left one. Don't give in to him, she pleaded with herself.

"How am I supposed to eat this bag of calories if you're holding my hand?"

He squeezed gently. "Maybe I could hold both our bags between my knees. If you don't mind, I'd like to keep this hand."

Exasperated, she fumbled for words. "You...oh, you're..." She couldn't even convince herself.

"What? I'm what?" Susan released a deep breath and knew she was about to give in.

"Different, I guess."

The beginning of his slow smile unnerved her, and she locked her gaze on the movie screen. Halfway through the movie, she dipped her hand into an empty bag.

"That wasn't so bad, was it? Here. Have some of mine."

He'd never know how grateful she was that he couldn't see her face. She couldn't remember when she'd last enjoyed anything as much as she had that high-calorie popcorn. I'm too comfortable with him, she thought, as delicious shivers snaked through her when he locked their fingers again. This wasn't like her; she was sensible. She tried without success to withdraw her hand.

"I need my hand," she told him, half hoping that he would ignore her. And he did.

"No, you don't. You're supposed to hold hands in the movies. It's one of the reasons why you go." Now she wished for light so that he could see the look of incredulity that she knew blazed across her face.

"You're putting me on," she said, but she wasn't certain of her ground, because very little of her life had been spent in a movie theater and almost none of that with a member of the opposite sex.

"I should have taken you to a horror movie," he went on, confusing her further. "And before you ask why, that's because if you got scared enough you'd be glad to hold onto me. Girls have been known to crawl all over guys when Godzilla pops up on the screen. You see, you're already scared."

"Why do you think I'd do that? I can look after—"

He interrupted her, obviously enjoying himself. "Because you're squeezing my fingers. Here, have some more popcorn."

August slid an arm around her shoulder as they stepped out of the movie, claiming that he had to keep her warm. "Want to stop for some ice cream and coffee? I know a nice little place about a block from here."

Ice cream and coffee. Was he from Mars? In her world, the words "would you like" were the beginning of an invitation to a drink or a visit to a guy's apartment, and her answers always began with the word, no. The man was intriguing.

"Okay, but make mine espresso."

"The ice cream or the coffee?" She stared at him; surely he wasn't that unsophisticated. He smiled down at her and tightened his arm around her. "Just pulling your leg. You don't know what to expect of me, and I've decided to reveal my secrets slowly and in small doses." Susan laughed. She broke one of her rules of decorum and let the sound of laughter escape her. He hugged her.

"I enjoyed the evening, August."

He shook his head as though reprimanding a small child. "Susan, you loved it. Come on, be honest."

"All right, I loved it."

He smiled in his usual mesmerizing way and asked for her door key. She wondered what he would do next, but the possibilities didn't worry her, because she knew without a doubt that August Jackson was a gentleman.

"This has been wonderful, Susan."

Warm anticipation increased the fluid in her mouth as the back of his index finger drifted tenderly down her cheek. She wished he'd give her a signal as to what he intended to do. A goodnight kiss was normal after a guy took a girl out, though she couldn't swear what they did after having been to a movie. She'd let him take the lead. So she waited while his gaze roamed over her face and his smile brightened as though his pleasure increased the longer he looked at her. She couldn't restrain a gasp when he suddenly leaned forward and kissed her cheek. Didn't he know where her mouth was?

"I want to see you again, Susan. Truth is, I want to see you a lot. What do you say?"

She fidgeted, something she'd taught herself to stop doing when she joined the law firm.

"August, I told you, I don't like…"

"Shh. I'm not going to court you, because I know you don't like it."

"Then what do you call seeing me, as you put it?" His deep sigh suggested that she had completely misunderstood him.

"Just spending a little time together. What do you say?"

She wanted to be with him. She couldn't remember when she had been so relaxed, so completely unwound. She hadn't thought once of the office…horrified, she realized that she couldn't remember which case she was to present in the senior staff meeting the next morning. She'd gotten so carried away with him that she'd practically forgotten who she was. She'd better break it off right now, before she cultivated a taste for this man—if indeed, she hadn't already done that. But he let her know that he had other thoughts about their relationship.

"I'd like to show you something, Susan."

"What?" She hoped she hadn't sounded as eager to him as she did to herself.

"Heaven from the back of a horse."

She could relax; horseback riding in winter held no fascination.

"I've already seen things from the back of a horse, August."

"But not heaven. I'd bet anything that only I can show that to you."

She couldn't decide whether he was egotistic or naive, but she suspected that it wasn't the latter. Trouble was, he didn't appear to be too involved with himself, either. So what was he?

"Would you kindly define heaven for me," she asked, deciding to play along.

"It's hills lightly covered with snow and evergreen pines that sparkle with white, cloudlike crests and sun rays that take on hundreds of hues dancing against the pines; icicles trying to find their way to earth, stymied by the frosty breeze, and lighting your way at sundown; squirrels and chipmunks frolicking around the tree trunks; an occasional, lonely leaf that whispers a love song as you pass; and not a track in the pristine snow until your horse puts one there. It's all that and just the two of us. You can't prove to me that it wouldn't be heaven."

She stared, tongue-tied. Bewitched.

"You're nodding your head. Does that mean you'll go with me?"

She nodded again. How unpredictable he was and how wonderful. Where could a person find a pair of jodhpurs on such short notice? Barney's, maybe.

A light snow fell as they took the horses over a trail in Harriman State Park. The scene was all that he had promised and more. So much more. Scattered snow flurries floated down around them, adding allure to the fairyland setting. The stillness, the enchanting quiet gave them a world of their own. A restful, spiritually renewing world—the antithesis of stressful boardrooms, cutthroat competition, crowded streets and blaring traffic. A doe with her young fawn stared as they passed, and stepped forward as though to greet them. She glimpsed a squirrel as it hustled up the trunk of a great oak carrying its treasure of acorns in its mouth and thought, how free and happy it seems.

August had been mostly silent while they rode, but she hadn't felt the need for conversation. And she didn't remember ever having experienced the sense of oneness with another person that she enjoyed with August that morning. He had an almost magical way of lulling her into contentment, of giving her a sense of completeness. She looked over at him astride the big bay and smiled when she found him looking at her. His lips smiled first, then his cheeks seemed to bloom and, finally, his eyes sparkled. He might as well have kissed her. She wrung her gaze from his when she realized that she could stay with him forever. They took the horses back to the stables, got into the car that August had rented, and drove back to the city.

They stood at her apartment door, and she knew he didn't want to leave her. She knew, too, that she didn't want him to go.

"I found a theater that's showing Godzilla tonight. How about it?"

She had to laugh. This was courting; even she knew that, and she'd never done any of it.

"I have some work to do tonight." It was true but, as she looked at him, anxiously awaiting her answer, she thought, oh what the heck.

"Okay, I'll go, but I am not going to make a habit of going places with you."

He grinned. "All right. I won't expect you to. This isn't a steady thing. We'll negotiate it each time." She shook her head in amazement. He behaved as if nothing was complicated, but she didn't plan to be taken in by his easy, laid-back manner. "You going?" he urged.

"Okay. I'm crazy, but I'll go."

She hadn't ever seen a horror movie and, at the monster's first appearance, a scream escaped her throat that would have rivaled the best efforts of a great coloratura soprano. August immediately slipped an arm around her, but that was soon insufficient protection, for the monster threatened to leave the screen and leap into the audience. Not even the richly buttered popcorn held an interest as she dealt with her fears. The beast roared and she couldn't help clutching August with both hands. Thank God, he didn't seem to mind, but gave himself over to the task of banishing her consternation.

"Do you want to leave, honey?" Godzilla overturned a dozen cars, and she couldn't speak. She tugged him closer.

"Do you?" he asked again. She came to her senses; it wouldn't be ladylike to spoil the evening for him, especially since he obviously loved the monster. But scared as she was, she couldn't walk away from the thrill of it.

"Oh, no," she whispered. "I wouldn't want you to miss the end of it."

"But you haven't even eaten your popcorn. I don't want you to be miserable, and you must be if you barely opened the bag."

She reached into the bag and brought a few kernels toward her mouth just as the monster's claws whirled something or someone into the air. She screamed and buried her face in August's strong, protective shoulder. The movie ended, and they walked out into the chilly air.

"Oh, August, it was wonderful," she exclaimed. "I don't know when I've enjoyed anything so much. It was just smashing." She offered him some popcorn, but he shook his head.

"Are you serious? You enjoyed that movie?"

"Why, yes. I could go back in there right now. It was fabulous."

"But you were scared to death the whole time. I thought you might cry."

"Sure I was scared, but it was such fun."

He stared at her. "Well, I'll be doggone."

"Susan, honey, I think Grace is right," he said, standing in her foyer after taking her home from the movie. "We ought to get married."

"*What? Us get married?* You can't be serious, August." She stared at him, but saw that he was no less serene than usual.

"Why shouldn't I be serious? We've got a lot in common, and you said yourself that Grace is never wrong. So why do you want us to waste time shilly-shallying about it. Let's give it a shot." Susan closed her mouth slowly just before he added, "For keeps, though. I mean we get married till death does us part."

"August, do you know what you're saying?"

"Sure I do. You don't want to waste time courting and I'm uncomfortable negotiating this New York City scene with these New York women. I know what I want—and Grace says we were made for each other."

The abrupt disappearance of his warm, teasing smile unnerved her as he stepped closer, his expression unmistakably serious.

"I'll always be there for you, Susan, for better or for worse. No matter what." Suddenly, he grinned. "Nothing will ever change that, and I'll be faithful to you for as long as I breathe." She gasped aloud. He was serious. She hoped he'd ignore her trembling, but he didn't. "I'll never do anything to cause you to regret marrying me, so don't worry."

August wondered whether he'd moved too quickly, but he didn't think so. He'd learned to go with his instincts, and if he followed them this time, his search for a mate had ended. An inner something told him Susan was the woman for him and that he'd still feel that way aeons into the future.

"Uh...I'll call you," he heard her whisper.

"All right. I'll be in Washington for a few days. I'm leaving tomorrow evening."

"Work?" Her voice was tentative, he noted, as though she had no right to ask.

"My work rarely involves travel. I did tell you that I'm a criminologist, didn't I? Honey, I wish it was something as simple as work." He had to camouflage his sudden feeling of distress. "For the last twenty years, I've been trying to find my younger brother, and I'm going to Washington to check a lead with my private investigator. It could be another wild-goose chase, but I never assume that—any bit of information is checked. We'll talk about it when I get back."

"I hope it works out this time. I can imagine what this means to you, August. Will you call?" It surprised him that she would ask him that, but he took pleasure in it.

"As soon as I get in my hotel room." He looked at her upturned, worried face. He wanted to kiss her. Badly. But it was too early for that. She trusted him a little, but he was after more. Much more. He tweaked her nose, opened her door and playfully pushed her in.

"Lock it." He walked off. She wanted to throw something at him when it dawned on her that he'd been protective, but she could start right then to get used to him; he was in her life forever.

Susan hung up her mink coat, got out of her blue designer suit, kicked off her Susan Bennis/Warren Edwards shoes, and paced the floor in her stocking feet. What in the world was August Jackson thinking about? And he was serious, too. In her mind's eye, she recalled how his face sobered before he told her he'd always be there for her. She stopped, nearly panicking. She didn't know anything about men who talked as he did and acted the way he acted. He had meant every word. Good Lord, he had actually pledged himself to her. She wrapped her arms around herself, seeking assurance that she was still a separate entity, that she wasn't a part of him. What had he done to her? Without his having touched her, she'd felt enclosed securely in his arms, warm and protected. She rushed to the kitchen and got a glass of water. If she'd ever thought about the kind of man she wanted, she wouldn't have dreamed his type existed, but there he was, and… She picked up the phone and dialed her aunt, praying that she wouldn't get the answering service.

"Aunt Grace. I'm so glad you're home. I went to the movies with August tonight, and he…well, he…"

"He asked you to marry him, did he? I knew he was going to—it was right there on the chart, plain as your face."

"Aunt Grace, marriage is a serious business. How can he take it so lightly?"

"Don't be fooled by that easy, charming front of his, honey. That man means business. You take my advice and quit pussyfooting around. Besides, you know you want to do it. You're intrigued with him, plain loco. He heated you up the first time you saw him. That was in *your* chart. Don't you get stupid and try to string him along, now, 'cause that won't work with him."

Susan had to sit down. "Aunt Grace, be reasonable. We don't know anything about him." Her heart hammered in her chest, and she tried to calm herself.

"He's nice, Aunt Grace."

"Sure he is. His chart doesn't show a single thing against him that I could see. And, honey, he's so handsome, it's sinful, and he acts like he don't even know it. He ain't faking, either. He wants to marry you, and he'll do what he says, 'cause that chart of his shows he's solid as a rock."

"Don't you ever doubt your charts?"

"Never. And something else. How many men like him will you find that's equal to a woman like you? Most of his kind go for those cute little clinging vines, which, Lord knows, you are not."

"But we're not in love."

"Shucks, honey, your cousin Ella fell head over heels for Richie, went home with him the same night she met him, stayed with him for four years before they got married, and left him three weeks after they said 'I do.' You're the one with the college degrees so you figure it out."

"But, Aunt Grace, that's…"

"Please spare me that logic of yours. You want to marry him. Do it. You two are going to fall so hard for each other, you'll think lightning struck." Susan didn't want to believe it.

August prepared himself for another disappointment. He'd had so many where Grady was concerned that he'd almost become inured to the pain. He unlocked the door of his posh room in Washington's Willard Hotel—too much for his taste, but that was what his private investigator had reserved for him—dropped his bag beside the bed, took out his cell phone and called Susan. Mere thoughts of her elevated his spirits. For once, he didn't feel alone in it.

"This is August. Did you miss me?" Susan laughed, giving him the reaction he wanted. He'd only heard her actually laugh just once before.

"Hi. You're impossible." He caught the warmth in her voice.

"Well, did you?" That lovely laughter again. He could listen to it forever, because it meant he'd get what he was after.

"Not yet," she teased, "but if you stay away long enough, I might."

Joy suffused him, and he let it flow out to her in his speech. "When are we getting married?"

"Soon as you get back."

His back went up; that was a subject about which he refused to let her joke.

"I'm serious."

"Me, too."

The sudden acceleration of his heartbeat made him grab his chest.

"What size ring do you wear?"

"That's unimportant. I don't want a ring."

"I don't remember asking whether you wanted one. I want to wear your ring, and I'd like my wife to wear mine."

"But I won't…"

"Don't draw the line, honey. You haven't seen it yet." He'd ask Grace what size ring Susan wore. He teased her for a bit and hung up.

He'd had over a hundred so-called leads over the past twenty-six years, but this one really sounded promising. He felt as if he could run the five miles to the Sheraton Hotel where he was to meet his P.I. and the man thought to be his brother. The man was about his height, and vaguely resembled him, but August didn't feel a connection between them. He'd planned to ask him some key questions but first, he'd have a look at the birthmark—the black quarter-size spot on one shoulder that had a thick patch of hair growing in it. The man obligingly removed his shirt, but he didn't have that birthmark.

August thanked the man and offered to pay his expenses to and from Charlotte, North Carolina. He couldn't help feeling relieved, though, because the man wasn't the kind of brother that he'd want. The search would continue, as it had for the past two and a half decades.

Later, in his hotel room, he called Susan again, her expressions of sorrow that he hadn't found his brother touched him deeply. He hadn't known how much he needed her caring and understanding. She was there for him, solidifying her niche inside of him.

"What will you do now, August?"

He'd keep looking, he told her.

"Do you believe he's alive?" she asked, and he admired the strength that her ability to ask him that difficult question communicated to him.

"I know he is, Susan. I feel it. Besides," he said, changing to a lighter mood, "Grace's charts say I'm going to find him and, remember…"

"I know," Susan finished for him, "she's never wrong."

He rolled over, heat beginning to pool in his belly just from the sound of her sultry voice.

"I'll see you tomorrow night, honey, and every night."

"But we're not…"

"Right. We're not courting. We'll just see each other." He hung up and laughed.

He got back to New York the following afternoon and went directly to Tiffany's and chose a size seven diamond engagement ring of one and a half carats flanked by half carat diamond baguettes set in eighteen-karat gold. He tucked the red velvet, satin-cushioned box into his shirt pocket, and hailed a taxi for A Hundred Thirty-Fifth and Malcolm X Boulevard, where he had a fourth-floor co-op. His coworkers had asked him why he lived there when he could afford the upper east side. It wasn't their business that he used his wealth to find his brother. Besides, he also lived there, as he told them, because he loved Harlem. It was the closest thing to rural southern living that he'd come across in New York. Turnips and mustard greens in every market, not to mention spareribs and plenty of fresh fish. He liked filet mignon, salmon, and lobster as well as anybody, but when he got good and hungry, he wanted some collard greens, baked sweet potatoes, and fried Norfolk spots, and he didn't want his greens cooked with olive oil. He put his bag down and called Susan.

"What time can I see you tonight?"

"Auuuugusssst." She drew it out. "We're not supposed to...I mean, I thought we weren't going to..."

"Honey, we're not courting. I promised you, didn't I? We're making plans. What time?"

She told him seven-thirty and asked where he planned to take them. He had to suppress a laugh. She was priceless. He'd never seen a woman so reluctant to come down to earth.

"Well, I thought we'd just eat dinner at a real nice restaurant. Anything else would be, well, courting." He hung up and called the Plaza Athené. He didn't intend to have but one engagement dinner, and he wanted his fiancée to remember it forever. Thinking about that, he called back and ordered pink orchids for their table.

Susan kicked herself for putting on her full glamorous armor, but she wasn't going out with him to a swanky restaurant looking like a poor relation. She knew what those other women would look like, and she intended for him to keep his fantastic eyes on her. She scurried into a red silk shift that was cut low in the back and front and would give him just enough cleavage to let him know there was a lot more. She put on a light makeup, gold loops at her ears, and dabs of French perfume. It was a come-on, but she wasn't sure where he stood, and she hadn't gotten where she was by taking foolish chances. She looked down at her feet. That's it, she decided, experiencing a mild rebellion at herself. *I will not* put on heels; he has a big enough ego. She put on black silk ballet slippers, and wouldn't admit that the effect was more striking than heels would have been.

Her neighbors could have heard his whistle of approval, she decided, lowering her head in acute embarrassment. But she was glad he liked what he saw, even if it did remind her of the wolves in her office.

"August, I'm glad you like my dress, but that whistle is the same thing I get from other guys." She glanced up at him and excitement raced through her at the adoration his eyes revealed.

"When those men whistle at you, honey, they're tom catting. I was expressing appreciation for my woman."

"I'm not your woman," she huffed, giving him an arrogant twist of her head.

"Sure you are, and it doesn't make sense to argue about it."

She had to admit that if she was going to marry him, he did have a point.

"Well, not yet, I'm not."

"Ah, Susan, you're so beautiful and so sweet." His warm hand on her bare arm tugged her gently to him, and she couldn't help trembling with heady anticipation. Frightened at what she felt, she attempted to move away, but his strong fingers caressed her arms and back, stroking her until she relaxed against him. Her deep sigh must have encouraged him, because he tipped up her chin and let her see the desire in his eyes, stunning her. She knew he felt her shivers when his arms tightened around her, and she grasped the right lapel of his coat with her left hand and clung to him. She couldn't help it; she was sinking as sure as her name was Susan Andrews.

"Darling, I want to taste your mouth. Kiss me."

She couldn't make herself raise her head, but she didn't object when he did it for her. His lips touched her tentatively, burning her, sending hot darts all through her.

"Honey. Ah, sweetheart," he murmured, "take my tongue."

She parted her lips slightly at first, but when he claimed her, she opened wider loving the taste of him, the feel of him. He groaned, and she stifled the urge to move against him. His hands stroked her back, and she wanted to beg him to soothe her aching breasts. She wanted… Her hips moved to him, and he turned and held her to his side. She stepped back, shocked at herself. What had she been thinking? She shook her head as though to clear it; August was behaving as though what they'd just done was perfectly natural. She had known him two weeks and, in her whole life, she'd never kissed a man with such—there was no other word for it—fire.

Later, she sat across from him in the swank room looking around at the lovely mirrors and the gold leaf that adorned the pale blue walls and ceiling, the French Provincial chairs and crystal chandeliers. A nice restaurant, he'd said.

"The orchids are beautiful, August. Thank you." She wondered about the low regard in which he held New York nightlife, including its fancy restaurants, and she said as much.

"I said I didn't want to do it on a regular basis. Besides, if I'd suggested hot dogs and a fast food place, you would have been perfectly agreeable."

She stared at him. "How do you know?"

He shrugged carelessly. "Am I right?"

Susan nodded in agreement, wondering what he'd do when he took her home. She wasn't sure she wanted to be left raw after another one of his kisses.

They lingered inside her foyer until he said, "How about some coffee?" She made it quickly.

"I wasn't sure you knew how to make it," he teased.

"Well, if you had asked for anything more complicated, I probably wouldn't have."

August looked at his future wife, hoping that his heart wouldn't burst.

"Did you tell your office associates that you're engaged?"

"Did I... Is it their business?"

He didn't like the sound of that, and he was going to set her straight.

"That's a courtesy, and it'll let those bulls know you're not available." Now was the time, he decided, taking her left hand and beginning to slip the ring on her third finger.

"I told you I didn't want a ring."

"But, honey, that was before you kissed me."

"Before I..." she sputtered. "I didn't kiss you; you kissed me. How can you..." Her glance swept the ring on her finger, and she gasped aloud.

"Oh, August. It's beautiful. Ooo. It's...it's..." Evidently at a loss for words, she threw her arms around him exuberantly, and he pulled her closer.

"Will you wear it? I want everybody to know that you're engaged to me. I'm so proud of you. Will you?" His heart turned over. Had he fallen so deeply in love with her already? She nodded assent and snuggled up to him, and August knew he'd made the right move.

"You feel good in my arms," he told her, but she wiggled nervously, and he figured she hadn't accepted her reaction to him, hadn't come to terms with her feelings.

"Don't move away," he soothed. "We're not courting. We're just getting to know each other." He smiled down at her, hoping to raise her temperature by several more degrees.

"Honey, I saw the loveliest little white ranch house while I was in D.C. It had a white picket fence, trees, and shrubs. Perfect. I could see the two of us living there years from now with our hair as white as the white bricks of that house. I wished you were there so I could show it to you." Was she tensing up? There certainly wasn't any reason for that; his arm was around her and he was describing the most...

"Susan, don't tell me you dislike ranch-style houses."

"Okay. I won't. I'll tell you I hate them, because I do.

There's nothing imaginative about them. An entire block of sameness. It's a wonder people living in them don't let themselves into the wrong house. Oh, August. They're so... so, well, you know." She waved her hand as if the subject were of little moment. So much for the little white house of his dreams.

She'd had the ring for almost twenty-four hours. Anybody who knew her would think she'd lost her mind, looking at her left hand every two or three minutes. She could have bought a ring for herself, but she hadn't, and he had. She stared at it. It made her long fingers look daintier. Shocked at the change in her, she balled up her fist and contemplated putting on a glove. How had he ever persuaded her to do such a thing? Promise to marry him? She could figure that out, because he was perfect from head to foot, and sweet. But wear a ring? Why she was a feminist, for heaven's sake. She took another look at her ring, twirled around, and dashed to the phone. But just before reaching the table on which it sat, she slowed to a dignified walk. Don't forget yourself, she counseled. He answered on the first ring.

"Hi."

"Hi. I was just about to call you, but it's nicer to answer my phone and hear your voice. How are you?"

"Fine. Want to come over?" she asked him as casually as she could. "You don't have to get dressed up."

"Give me twenty-five minutes."

She hung up, dashed to her closet and found a green corduroy jumpsuit. It wasn't dressy, she reasoned, and she looked good in it.

If she expected a frenzied kiss, she didn't get it. "Hi. You're a treat for my eyes," he stated, as his slow smile claimed his face.

"Want to hear some music?" she asked, for want of something to say.

"I'd love it. Got any country? Charley Pride, Vince Gill, or George Strait?"

Susan opened her mouth and couldn't close it, certain that her jaw had locked.

"You don't mean you like that...er, that kind of music, do you?"

"Sure I do. What's wrong with it? What do *you* like?"

"Well, if you don't want classical, how about just plain old pop? Or Dixieland, if you insist on southern stuff?"

He laughed. "No thanks. When are we getting married?"

If they did, she thought, they'd better not have any music in the house.

She said, "If we get a license tomorrow, we can get married Monday at lunchtime."

August sprang from his seat. "Calm down, Susan."

"What?"

He shook his head. "Sorry. I was talking about myself." He sat down beside her and took her hand. "Susan, we need a decent engagement period so we can get to know each other. I won't court you. Honest. But we need time to get our affairs in order. Give me a reasonable date that fits in with Grace's charts. She said something about the full moon, didn't she?"

If she laughed, he might be offended. Grace's charts, for goodness' sake.

"All right. According to her that's the second week of February. About a month from now." She marveled at the way in which his face beamed and that special gleam lit his eyes.

"How's Valentine's Day. Alright?" he pressed eagerly. "That should give us time to arrange things."

She nodded. "Okay."

He leaned back, seemingly content now that plans appeared to proceed to his liking, holding her hand. "Do you want me to wear a tux or tails?"

"For what?"

"For the wedding, honey."

"*Our* wedding?" She figured her eyes were the size of saucers. He had to be kidding.

"Yeah. Whose did you think I meant?"

*She* sprang up.

"August, I agreed to wear this ring—"

He interrupted her. "Wasn't such a bad idea, was it?"

"Oh, you…I haven't finished. And I agreed to an engagement, but a formal marriage is too much. We're getting married by a clerk of the Court or a Justice of the Peace. And that's that."

He stood up, walked over to her and put his arms around her.

"Honey, I grew up in church. I want to get married in one, and I charge you right now with the responsibility of having my funeral in a church."

"But, August…"

"I've got the most beautiful bride-to-be in New York, and I want to see her walking up a church aisle toward me in a veil of white lace with rose petals beneath her feet. It's a picture I'll take to my grave. You won't deny me that pleasure, will you?"

Why did she feel as if she'd done something terrible to him? He trained those bedroom eyes of his on her, softened his honeyed voice and stripped her of her will. She wanted to curl into him when he began to stroke her back gently, almost seductively.

"August, you're making too much of this." She knew her protest was a weak one and tried to summon her usual stern manner. "In a joint venture, the parties have to come to an agreement. You know that."

"I do. But, sweetheart, this isn't a business venture—this is us getting married to each other, and I'm holding out for seeing my bride in white satin and lace. You don't want to deprive me of that sweet vision that other brides give their grooms, do you, honey?"

Susan took a deep breath and summoned her wits. He wasn't going to steamroller her. "Slow down, August. That's your dream but what about mine? I told myself ages ago that if I ever got married, I wanted the ceremony to take place in the Rainbow Room."

From his expression, you'd think she'd shot him. "*What?* You couldn't be serious. Why?"

She didn't succeed in staving off her nostalgia. "I spent a New Year's Eve there. I was twenty, and it was my first adult date. I had on a long white silk gown, and the room was pure paradise. Low hanging, silvery clouds hid the ceiling, and millions of twinkling stars danced around a crescent moon. Icicles glittered on great snow-covered trees, candles glowed in the windows, and soft, romantic music came alive all around us. Heaven. I'd even wear white satin, lace and a long train if we could be married there. Oh, August, it was magic."

He laid his head to one side and scrutinized her. "Where's the guy now?"

She grinned. "I have no idea. It wasn't him, but the Rainbow Room that was memorable." A sigh floated from her. "I walked on air and danced in the clouds."

"I don't want to say my vows to a woman decked out in pants," he grumbled.

Laughing, she stroked his cheek. "Suppose they have wide bottoms."

He wasn't placated. "Nothing doing. We'll have to work that out."

Susan folded her arms to signal *his* defeat. "You won't snow me on this one." His wink sent hot arrows to her middle, but she was not giving in.

He frowned. "And since the Rainbow Room is a pipe dream, it's pants and the court clerk. Right?"

"What's wrong with that? We'll still be married?"

"How'd it go at work today? Did you tell them?" he asked,

settling them into her big barrel chair. She snuggled as close to him as she could get.

"I don't know why they were so surprised. Oscar—he's one of the more senior lawyers—was mean. He said he'd like to meet the guy who pulled it off. Getting me to say yes, that is. They figured I'd stop working, but I reminded them that this is the end of the twentieth century, and I'm not giving up my chance at that full partnership. I worked too hard for it." The stroking stopped.

"Have you been promised a partnership?"

"Over six months ago." Where had his sweet, coaxing tone gone?

"Then, if they welch, we'll go to court. If you're entitled to a partnership, I'll see that you get it."

Her brows arched sharply, and her mouth dropped; he wasn't as laid-back and homespun as his manner often suggested. She asked if he was serious.

"Didn't I say I'd be there for you through thick and thin, whatever comes?"

She nodded.

"Well, in my book that's pretty thin."

"It's eight o'clock, Susan. Don't you think we ought to eat? I'm beginning to feel a pinch. Let's get some dinner and talk things over." She twisted around in his arms and looked into his face. He wished she'd be still; he had enough problems with his self-control as it was.

"We've been talking for nearly an hour," she complained. "What else do you want to talk about? You want us to sign a marriage contract?" She sat up straight, but he pulled her back into his arms.

"No. I don't. When we get married, whatever's mine is yours. There're a lot of things to talk about."

In that case, she'd better fortify herself. "Then let's get some Chinese food delivered and eat right here."

"Nothing doing. Monosodium glutamate is bad for your

health. I'll run out and get some stuff and I'll cook. It'll be simple."

"How simple?"

He laughed. "Hamburgers. For a woman who can't cook, you're awfully fussy."

August thought his chest would spring open when she wiped her mouth and smiled at him. Happy. "That was delicious," she declared, when they'd finished and were cleaning up.

"My pleasure. I'd better go."

"What's the hurry?"

He raised an eyebrow. Did that question have a provocative undercurrent? "It's getting late."

"Oh."

"What's the problem, honey?" He believed in dealing with trouble head-on, so he took her into the living room and sat with her in the barrel chair.

"Well?" he pressed.

"Nothing. I mean, aren't we supposed to make love?"

He wasn't going to laugh. He wasn't. He did his best to put on a stern face.

"Where does it say we're supposed to? I'm planning for us to wait."

She jumped out of his lap, spun around, and stared at him, clearly aghast. She'd kill him if he laughed, so he put his hands on his knees, leaned forward and waited.

"You...you're willing to buy a pig in the poke?" she sputtered.

He had to laugh. "You're not concerned about what I'm risking, and you know it. You're the one who's skeptical about me. *Come here.*" She'd asked for it, and she was going to get it. She started toward him, and he stood to meet her.

"Come here to me, baby," he coaxed, "and put your arms around me. Come here and let me love you." She stood there staring at him, obviously perplexed. If she wanted sophisticated seduction, he'd give it to her. Her tongue rimmed her soft brown lips and in lightning fashion, heat shot to his groin. He watched transfixed as her eyelids half lowered, the muscles of her face relaxed and her left hand clasped her bosom while she swallowed what he knew was evidence of desire. Caught in a prison of his own making, he reached for her, no longer interested in teaching her a lesson, but in sating his need for her.

"Woman. My Lord, I'm on fire for you. *Come here!*" He clasped her hips as she sprang into his arms. Her parted lips took in his tongue and he searched her mouth with its velvet smoothness until he knew every crevice of it, and she slumped limply against him. He pulled her up until his full arousal rested against her nest of passion so that she could know him, feel him. Every bit of him. He was paying for it, and he didn't care. Tremors raced through him when she sucked on his tongue, and he tightened his hold on her hips longing for the heavenly sweet release she'd give him. She had to feel the shudders that racked him as she twisted in his arms, letting him feel the softness of her full breasts. He wanted to taste them, wanted to pull her sweet flesh into his mouth, to nourish himself and drive her wild.

"August…please… If you're going to make love to me, do it. Please stop torturing me."

Stunned, he recovered his senses, and held her away from him. He shook his head in wonder. He might have planned to teach her something, but he'd gotten a lesson of his own.

"I guess there's a first time for everything," he said, as much to himself as to her. "I don't ever remember losing control like that. I…I'm sorry, honey, but I do intend for us to wait." She stared at him as though seeing a mirage.

"August, what you just did would be grounds for divorce, and we're not even married yet." He'd deal with her disappointment in a few minutes, but right then, he had to get himself in order; she had really sent him into a tailspin. He risked putting an arm around her and hugged her lightly.

"That surprised me as much as it did you, honey, but I hope

I set you straight. I was born in the country, but I do know how to love a woman. You trust me—we're going to wait."

She nodded. "I still haven't agreed to that big church wedding you want. That's for people who court each other."

He resisted the impulse to pace the floor and settled her more securely in his lap. "Honey, the Rainbow Room is for eating and dancing. You can't expect the management to turn it into a church—"

"I don't want it to be a church, but it's the only place where I'm prepared to wear a formal wedding or any other kind of dress." He tried to get her to look at him, but she ducked her head. So much for his winning strategy.

"We'll have to discuss this some more, Susan. I won't feel married if you show up at our wedding in a pants suit."

"It'll be silk and a lovely gay color," she said airily.

He'd love to shake her. "Susan, please be reasonable." He made up his mind to talk with Grace about it.

The next afternoon, Susan raised her head from her work just enough to identify the intruder. "What is it, Lila?"

"I'm sorry to disturb you, Miss Andrews, but a Mr. Jackson is on the phone, and he insists that you'll take his call."

"Thanks." She lifted the receiver, furious with herself for having shown her embarrassment. "Hi."

"Hi, honey. Want to drop by my office after work?" Her immediate response was to say that she would. Then she remembered.

"Oh my! This isn't a good evening for us to get together. It's my night to serve dinner at the homeless shelter."

"You do that? That's wonderful. We've finally got something in common. I mean…we agree on something."

"Like what? We should take care of the homeless? Everybody should do that."

"Yeah. What I mean is we're both caring people. I cook at the Wesley soup kitchen Sunday mornings from six to nine, and I've gotten to the place where I can make a decent batch of biscuits."

"How'd that happen?"

"Quite by accident, believe me. I was there to serve breakfast one Sunday morning, and the cook didn't show, so I had to cook. The people ate what I gave them and, as far as I know, nobody got sick. From that time, I've been the Sunday morning breakfast cook."

"You're full of surprises. Tell you what. We can eat early, and you can pick me up about nine after I finish at the shelter."

"You want to see me?"

She heard the eagerness in his voice. Something akin to longing. Did he really like her so much? She swung around in her desk chair.

"Yes. I...I want to see you, August." The softening of his rich, velvet voice told her that his face had given itself over to that slow, beguiling smile. At his next words, she was sure of it.

"I'll meet you, and we can get dessert."

"What kind?" she asked, serving herself a helping of fun at his expense.

"Have you ever got a one-track mind. I told you we were going to wait."

"What did I say?" she protested. "You're the one whose mind is in a rut." August had a wicked streak, and she was going to have to learn how to get the better of him. She would, too.

Susan waited near the shelter exit, hoping that poor Mrs. Butcher wouldn't find her before August arrived. Mrs. Butcher arrived at the shelter every evening precisely at six o'clock, and whoever was on waitress detail had her for company during the entire evening. She ate quickly and followed the help around until closing time. Tonight, she was reading her latest poems. They weren't bad, Susan decided, but by the tenth reading, she longed for ear plugs. August walked in at exactly nine o'clock, his face glowing with the smile she had begun to cherish.

Mrs. Butcher saw him at about the same time as Susan did. "Mr. Jackson. Mr. Jackson. You're going to work here, too? I didn't like my grits, Sunday. I found a lump in them. 'Course, I'd rather have grits than oatmeal. If you start 'em in cold water and stand right there and stir until they're done, they don't get lumpy. I could come in early Sunday and show you if you want." Susan knew that her valued decorum had finally failed her, when she couldn't close her mouth nor erase the look of astonishment that she knew was ablaze on her face. She tried to shake herself out of it and would have succeeded if August hadn't grabbed the untidy old woman and given her a big hug.

"I don't work here, Carrie. I'm meeting my fiancée. You come in early Sunday morning, and we'll work on those grits together. I'll see you Sunday." To Susan's astonishment, the old woman made no attempt to detain him as she usually did when she got someone's attention. She smiled at him and said, "Have a nice day."

"Close your mouth, honey. Carrie has that effect on everybody."

"Carrie? What about you?" The happiness that radiated from him warmed her heart. She wasn't making a mistake; every move he made increased her assurance that, for once, her instincts about the opposite sex had been perfect. And don't forget Grace's charts, an inner voice whispered.

"How'd it go today?" But before she could answer, he kissed her hard and quickly on her mouth.

"August!"

"Yeah?" He was a consummate actor, too, she decided, taking in his contrived look of innocence. She braced her hands on her hips and glared at him.

"You mustn't do that here in front of these people." She

looked at his irreverent grin, capitulated and let his joyous mood envelop her.

"Sorry," he said, feigning repentance, "but it wasn't so bad, was it?"

"Are there any other women under your spell?" Susan asked August as they walked down Adam Clayton Powell Boulevard.

"Other than who?"

She was learning that August's mind worked with trigger speed; well she wasn't bad herself.

"Other than Carrie," she rejoined, laughter rising up in her throat. "Thought you'd caught me, did you." He stopped at the bus stop.

"This one coming will take us to Eightieth and Lexington. Okay?" She knew he was testing her.

"August, if you said 'let's walk,' I wouldn't object, because I'd know you had a good reason. The bus is fine." They reached her building on Eightieth between Lexington and Park avenues, and he said he'd tell her goodnight in the lobby.

"Just like when I was in college, right?"

His eyes darkened with what she'd come to recognize as desire, and a thrill of anticipation teased her senses. She rimmed her lips with the tip of her tongue and wanted to vanish when she saw the answering flame in his eyes. He grabbed her elbow and held it until they reached her door. Inside, he wasted no time. Within a second, she was in his arms where she'd wanted to be since he arrived at the shelter. With her hands, she lowered his head, unwilling to wait longer for the sweet pleasure of his lips, and took what she needed.

"Is this what you wanted?" he asked in a voice that betrayed his passion, that trembled for want of control. "Is it?" With his tongue, he simulated the loving they would soon share, and she clung to him, asking for more. Needing more.

"August, why can't…? Oh. Oh, Lord." She'd never let a

man fondle her breasts, and fire shot through her when his hand went under her coat and his fingers rolled her nipple.

"Is this what you wanted, Susan? It will happen every time we're alone, and you know it." His deadly serious mien nearly unnerved her.

"This isn't a game, honey. I don't want us to make a habit of going this far without consummating what we feel. I don't approve of it. But no matter what, we're going to wait. Eventually, you'll understand and appreciate my point of view. I don't want you to wake up in bed with me and think, 'My God, I'm in bed with this stranger.' Another thing. Your bark is loud, but I've learned that you won't bite. If you had any idea how much I want you, you'd probably run."

She pursed her lips. "How can you be so sure of that?"

August leaned against the wall and folded his arms across his chest. "I read you well. In this and other things. You've decided that I'm easy to handle, that I'll be putty in your pretty brown hands if you put me to a test. So you aren't afraid to challenge me. Grace said she did my chart, and you say she's always right. Ask her to let you see it."

She didn't like the tenor of the conversation; she didn't want to discover that she'd been foolish to let herself like him so much.

"Have you misrepresented yourself to me?" she asked, attempting to summon her pre-August personality, her executive demeanor. Her shoulders slumped in defeat, when she realized that she couldn't shield herself from his look of penetrating evaluation. She didn't want him to judge her harshly.

"No, I have not. But there hasn't been an occasion for me to let you see how quickly I'll put the record straight if someone misjudges me for a person of little consequence, or for an unsophisticated country boy."

She bristled at that and stalled for time, while she pulled off her coat and hung it in a nearby closet. "Do you think

I'd agree to marry that kind of man, even if he agreed that courting is for adolescents, a waste of time? Do you?"

"A country boy's no threat to a Wall Street lawyer. I didn't attempt to mislead you. You let me be myself, and I enjoy it, because it's what I've always wanted, always needed in a woman. And you've given me that. I'm trying to tell you that there's more to me."

"All right, I'll look for it. Are we still engaged?"

The slow smile began at his lips, revealing his beautiful even white teeth, and moved upward, stealthily it seemed, to envelop his wonderful eyes. Then he laughed aloud.

"Ah, sweetheart. How could you ask that? Didn't I give you the responsibility of looking after my funeral? Baby, you'll never get rid of me."

Tremors coursed through her as his strong hands brought her gently to him, and her body shook as the fire of his hungry mouth drew her into the orbit of desire. Her parted lips begged for his tongue, but he denied her and let his mouth brush her eyelids while he stroked her arms and back.

"Our time will come, sweetheart. If we're going to make a go of this, we'll have to wait. Lovemaking is a part of love, anything else is sex. Everybody needs that, but if we're planning a life together, we have to have something deeper. I get good and high when I feel how you want me, but I'm going to try and nurture that into something deeper, something stronger and permanent."

She expected the smile to start again, and there it was. She had to fight to resist it as she gazed up at him. "August, why do you think you can turn on your charm and get me to do, think, and accept whatever you want?"

"Now, honey, I haven't ever tried to seduce you. Not once."

He had to know from the expression on her face that she didn't believe him. "Be serious."

"I'm serious. I've never done that."

She shook her head. "Well please do. I can't wait to see what you're like when you *really* get going."

August looked down at the woman nestled so sweetly against him and smiled. He didn't think he'd ever get used to the feeling of total contentment he got whenever he felt her in his arms.

"We're going to have a good life together. Trust me?" He loved her shy smile, the way she seemed to submit to her feelings and enjoy being with him. He mused over that for a second and amended the thought. Submissive until they got into an argument. He asked her again.

"Sure you trust me?"

"Yes, I do. I have from the first."

He'd always made it a point to remember his origins and try to stay humble, but when she got like this, so cuddly and agreeable, it was all he could do to keep his chest from swelling. He bussed her on the forehead.

"What if I tell Grace to go by for you and bring you to my office tomorrow around five?"

"There you go again. Treating me as if I'm an infant. August, I can walk; it's only a few blocks." A deep sigh escaped him. So much for cuddly and agreeable.

"I know you can negotiate a couple of blocks, but it's pitch dark at five o'clock. Let Grace bring you over. Okay?" Her laughter curled around him. By Jim, she was beginning to get his number.

Susan stared at the shiny brass plate on the office door. T. August Jackson, Vice President. She hadn't had any idea. Vice president of a highly regarded criminal law firm. She'd thought he worked there as a salaried criminologist. That explained a lot—those flashes of sophisticated taste and behavior, his flawless enunciation and grammar, even with that drawl. What was she supposed to think now? Her light tap on the door was rewarded with a deep-voiced, "come on in." A male secretary? She looked around for a chair, figuring that her knees might not withstand her next shock.

"Mr. Jackson is waiting for you," the young man told her, as his glance swept her from head to foot with obvious approval.

She opened the inner door just as August reached it, sidestepped his open arms, glared at him and demanded, "Explain yourself, mister. You told me you were a criminologist. What other tales have you got me to believe?"

"You asked what I did, and I told you. When a lawyer friend and I started this firm, he was president, and I was vice president. Since then, we've added fourteen lawyers and a dozen criminologists. I'm responsible for the research and investigation, and my partner handles the legal aspects. Come on, I'll introduce you to my secretary. She noticed that the gleam faded from Harold's eyes when August introduced her as his fiancée. As he took her through the office, she didn't doubt that August had his staff's affection and respect.

Susan wasn't sure she wanted Grace's company right then; she was dealing with August's surprises, and she didn't want to hear a word about Grace's charts and lines. He settled in the cab, comfortable as always and slid his right arm around her shoulder.

"How y'all getting along?" Grace asked.

"Fine," Susan answered with a halfheartedness that she knew wouldn't escape her aunt.

"Terrific," August said simultaneously.

"Looks to me like there's some disagreement on how well you're getting along."

"She doesn't want to admit that you were right," August boasted, "but she knows you were. Take us up to my place."

"A Hundred Thirty-Fifth and Malcolm X Boulevard is a long way from Wall Street—and in more ways than one," Susan observed as Grace headed up the FDR drive well above the speed limit.

"That's true, but I love Harlem. Its sounds and pungent

smells are unique, and if you speak to people, they speak back. Reminds me a little bit of home."

He waved to an old woman as they entered the lobby of his apartment building.

"How are you, Miss Effie?" he greeted the woman. "Haven't seen you lately." The woman's pleasure was reflected in her broad smile.

"August. I do declare. You're going to live a long time, son. I was thinking about you when I turned around and saw you standing there. Heard anything about Grady, yet?"

"No. Not yet, Miss Effie, but I have a feeling we're getting closer."

"Me, too," the woman said. "I just feel it deep down in here." She pointed to her heart. Susan felt August's arm gather her to him.

"Miss Effie, this is Susan, my fiancée." Susan greeted the woman with a proffered hand and received a powerful grip in return.

"You look after him good, honey. You hear? This man is a prince." Susan wanted to tell her that she knew it, but she settled for a warm smile and said goodbye.

Susan looked around the attractively furnished, spacious apartment. It didn't look as she'd thought it would. "We don't have similar taste in furnishings."

August seemed unconcerned, but that was as she would have expected. "I know, but we'll get around that."

She braced herself for another tug of war. "How? Just tell me how your French Provincial"—she paused and glanced around when an odd object caught her eye—"a couple of Queen Annes and"—she threw her hands up in despair—"and I don't know what else are going to mix with my clean modern lines?" Why was he laughing? Couldn't he see that their furniture didn't belong in the same house?

"Honey, when it comes to what I've got mixing with your sleek lines, you needn't worry. I've got the key to *that*."

"August, I'm talking about house furniture and things like that."

His laughter filled the room. "And what do you think I'm talking about? Come on, baby, loosen up. Chrome and glass are out of place in suburban and country living."

Her voice dropped to a low contralto, barely above a whisper, her words nearly trapped behind her clenched teeth. "What did you say? Suburbs? *Country?* I don't ever plan to live more than walking distance from the Metropolitan Museum of Art and a fifteen-minute taxi ride from the Schomburg Center. Anybody who thinks differently would do well to see a shrink." Let him pace and throw his hands up. See if she cared.

"You want to live in *Manhattan?*" he asked her at last, pronouncing the word as if it foretold a doom of indescribable horror. *"Manhattan?"* He stuffed his hands in his back pants pockets and thoroughly scrutinized his bride-to-be. "What's the big deal? The Met doesn't open on Mondays and, except for Fridays, it's closed on weekdays when you leave work. You've got until quarter to nine in the evening on Saturdays. You have to shackle yourself to Manhattan for that? Same with the Schomburg. You won't miss a thing."

"You want to take me to the *country?*" she asked with both hands planted on her hips. She turned her back quickly as the beginnings of that smile appeared. She wasn't going to be lured into agreeing with him just because he was the most handsome…the sweetest… He walked around to face her, lights already beaming in his eyes as though he was impatient to give her a lovely present. He tipped up her chin and trailed his thumb down her cheek.

"Honey, come with me to Tarrytown Saturday. Please. I found a nice house for us that I know you'll like." He couldn't have sounded sweeter or sexier, she thought, if he had been whispering words of love. "Then you can put your foot down," he added.

She stamped her left one, though mainly for effect. "It's already down."

"Aw...now, honey. I'm never going to ask you to do anything you just don't want to do. Like courting. Have I made you do any courting?" He caressed her back and gently squeezed her arm. "Have I? No, and I'll respect your wishes about everything else, too."

"August, I'm not going to live in the country, and that's that." His grin broadened.

"Fine with me. They've got streetlights all over Tarrytown, not like where I grew up, where it was so dark at night the moon had trouble lighting up the place."

"Oh, stop it. You promise not to try and persuade me if I tell you I don't like it?"

He nodded, and she had a chilling feeling that the house would be perfect.

"It isn't so bad, now is it?" he asked her, standing in the dining room of the Tarrytown house that he hoped would be theirs, unable to hide his eagerness. "You like it, don't you?"

"But I'm not having any gold leaf on my chairs and no curlicued candelabrum anywhere in my house."

"Well, all right. I'll give my Queen Anne chairs to Grace, maybe." When she didn't reply, he said, "She can have them auctioned off at Christie's, if she doesn't want them. They're authentic."

She turned to face him and jerked on his lapels.

"Melt them down if they're so precious, August, and have them deposited in Fort Knox. They are not going in my dining room, not even if they're solid gold. Got it?"

"All right. All right. Can't win 'em all. But is there such a thing as modern without chrome and glass?"

"You don't like my cocktail table?" His right shoulder bunched upward in a quick shrug.

"Well, first time I saw it, I thought you'd sawed the legs

off of your dining table. 'Course it might be all right out by the swimming pool."

"August!"

"On sunny days, I mean." She opened her mouth as though to speak, and he wondered why she didn't say anything. He waited. After a few minutes, she walked over and leaned against his chest.

"August, we have to stop this. Every time we have to decide something, we fight. You think maybe Aunt Grace doesn't know what she's talking about? We don't seem like such a perfect match to me." He put both arms around her.

"This is healthy, sweetheart. We're just sublimating our libidos. Now don't move away. Trust me, every criminologist has to be a good psychologist." He had to laugh when she groaned, not believing what he'd said.

She hadn't said any more about where they'd get married and what she'd wear, and he didn't like it. Getting a wedding dress made might take weeks. That night, he phoned Grace, and reached her at home. He summarized the problem briefly and added, "I want her to be happy. If I could, I'd buy that room for her. Grace, have you ever heard of a more ridiculous idea?"

"Can't say that I have," Grace replied. "Say, wait a minute. Seems to me I remember reading about a contest they're having. The couple that wins will get married in the Rainbow Room. Yes, indeed. I read it in the *Times* one day last week. I'll find it and—"

"Grace, that's too iffy."

"Don't trash it. I can look in—"

"Never mind. Don't do that." He'd had enough crystal ball logic to last him the rest of his life.

Undaunted, Grace told him, "I'll find that newspaper and bring you that notice. What's meant to be will be, so don't close any doors. All you have to do, if I remember right, is tell them in a hundred words or less why you or Susan always wanted to get married in the Rainbow Room. You can do that, Mr. Jackson. And there's a fat prize, not that you need it. What can you lose? Just the time it takes to write a hundred words. I'll bring it to you Monday morning."

He expelled a long breath. "All right, Grace. I'll think about it."

August got through his chores at the soup kitchen on Sunday morning without too much interference from Carrie. She had walked in clean and reasonably tidy and had been content to stand by the stove for half an hour stirring grits. For once, it was free of lumps. He had a mind to pay her to do it. He walked into his apartment with the intention of dressing hurriedly and getting to church, but a call from his private investigator altered his plans. Could he fly down to Washington that morning? The P.I. was almost certain that their long search was nearing an end, that he had news of Grady Jackson. August telephoned Susan. He had always fought his own battles and taken pride in doing that but, for the first time in his memory, he needed someone with him—a buffer against disappointment. He needed Susan.

"I've got a new lead about my brother, and I'm going to Washington. I'd love to have you with me, if you can be ready in a little more than an hour."

"I'd be happy to go, but I'm just waking up. Will you call me as soon as you know anything?" He promised that he would.

He looked at the two women who greeted him with warm smiles when the P.I. introduced them. Somewhere around thirty, he guessed, roughly in Grady's age group.

"Our family makes a line of cosmetics," Jessie, the older of the two, told him, "and this man supplies our chemicals." August tried to calm his breathing. The two women were apparently intelligent and, had it not been for the differences in eye color, he might have thought that they were twins. As they talked, he searched for reasons why two young, white women would travel from Knoxville, Tennessee, to Washington to mislead him about his brother when they had nothing to gain. He found none.

"When we saw your picture in the paper, we thought it was him and, looking at you, I'm convinced there's a close connection," Jessie continued. "He's just a tad younger, though. Same height, face, and build."

"Would you say we're identical twins," he probed, seeking firmer assurance.

"I don't think so," the younger one answered. "I think his eyes are darker than yours."

"I agree," Jessie said. Tremors danced down his spine; his brother's eyes were nearly black. He tried to stem his feverish anticipation. He had carried the burden for twenty -six years, used every resource available to him trying to find Grady. Please God, he didn't want his hope built up this way without cause.

"What does he call himself?"

"Grady Jackson," they replied in unison.

He sat down. Could there be two men with that name who looked almost enough like him to be his twin? He thanked the women, opened his checkbook and began to write.

"No, don't give us any money," Jessie said. "Our expenses were paid, and that's enough. I know how I'd feel if I couldn't find my sister. Here's his address." He read, Grady Jackson, Chemist, 37 Rond Point, Ashville, North Carolina. Could it be that he'd looked all over the country, and Grady had never left North Carolina?

Nearly crippled with anxiety and his shirt wet with perspiration in spite of the frigid January weather, August decided to check into the hotel room that his P.I. had reserved for him. He wasn't sure he could find the strength to do anything else. He fell across the bed, couldn't stay there, got up and went to the window. He needed Susan. He honestly believed it was the first time he'd ever needed her right down to the recesses of his soul. He called her.

"Any luck?" she asked him. He heard the fear in her voice.

"It's the best lead I've ever had. I don't know what I'll do if it fizzles out."

"Are you okay?" That hesitant speech, the attempt to hide the tremors in her voice. She was there for him. He hadn't known how much solace it would give him to have that assurance. And he needed it.

"Yeah. I'm handling it," he lied.

"I'll come down there, if you want me to."

The temptation to say yes, to scream it, was powerful, and he almost said it. But impulsiveness was foreign to him, and the consequences of her being in his hotel room flashed through his mind. He couldn't put her in a separate room, not even an adjoining one, and if she stayed with him, he'd make love to her all night long.

"I'll never forget your offer, Susan. I appreciate it more than you could know, but I'll be back tomorrow morning. We can be together in the evening."

"I thought you might need me." Her voice betrayed a feeling of rejection, but he knew himself and knew the awesome strength of his desire for her. And he knew, too, that if they made love for the first time under those conditions, he'd be out of control. He'd destroy the feelings that he had nurtured in her with such care. And he'd ruin her trust in him.

"I need you, Susan. God knows I do. And that's the problem. Our relationship is still fragile, and I don't think it can withstand what I'd put you through tonight if you came down here."

"I...I thought I should be with you if you're having a hard time. I'm a big girl, August."

He couldn't help laughing. "I know that, honey. But I think we'd better do it my way. Okay?"

They finished the conversation, and he hung up. If I

wouldn't take her to bed when she practically asked me to, he told himself, I'd be less than a man if I used her to ease my personal torment.

"Stop beating a dead horse," Susan snapped at Oscar Hicks just after the Monday morning senior staff meeting got under way. She sat one place down from the head of the conference table as the firm's protocol demanded, and Hicks sat one place farther down across from her. His antipathy toward her was common knowledge among their peers, and he scowled furiously at her stern reprimand.

"Our client is wrong," she continued, "and if you hold out longer, he'll lose it all. Settle out of court."

"My, aren't we testy this morning," he sneered. Two senior partners agreed with her, ending what could have been an unpleasant session. He cornered her in the hallway as she walked toward her office.

"You think everything's going your way, don't you? A smart person wouldn't make an enemy of me, Ms. Andrews."

She didn't break her stride. "I told you when the two of us discussed it that you would lose that case if you persisted in going for a killing, but you didn't take my advice," she explained patiently. "And you won't take it now. But if that case goes to court, you won't win. There isn't a judge anywhere who can't see that your client is lying, that his documents are not authentic, and that it's a trumped-up charge. For your own reputation, you should settle now. You and the firm will get something, as well as our client. But if you go to court, we'll end up paying the cost of court and probably getting sued." She wasn't surprised that her gentle tone failed to placate him, because he seemed to thrive on conflict.

"You know it all, don't you? This is my biggest case, and you're telling me to turn tail and run. You couldn't be jealous?"

She slowed her steps. "Oscar, suit yourself. As for me

being jealous of you, let's just admit that your imagination has gone berserk." She didn't look at him, because she knew he'd appear crushed; Oscar thought himself wise, imaginative, and dashing. Poor misguided man. She didn't have the time nor the inclination to polish his ego; she had problems of her own.

She went into her office and closed the door. It hadn't been necessary for her to go after Oscar as she'd done in the staff meeting. His performance lacked competence, but she could have put it in a memo. She resisted dropping her head in her hands and giving in to her feelings. She knew that August had been tormented last night, but he'd nevertheless refused her offer to be with him and, while she didn't claim to understand men, his refusal hadn't made sense. She couldn't force herself to work, a new experience, so she called her aunt.

"I knew it was you when the phone rang," Grace said. *I'm not going to cry,* Susan lectured herself. Instead, she went on the attack.

"Aunt Grace, this whole thing with August is ridiculous. What do I know about him? How do I know he isn't seeing someone down there in Washington?"

"Well, at least he's put a fire under you. If you're worried about that, you care about him."

"Of course I c…I don't give a snap what he does. Oh, Aunt Grace, I do. I do. I really care for… Oh, what am I saying?"

"That's your heart speaking, girl. You better listen to it."

"I'm hanging up."

"Now. Now. I can pick you up at about five, if that isn't too late, and we can get a little something to eat. Might make you feel better. Did August tell you why he went to D.C.?"

"His brother."

"That's been a long hard trial for both of them. They're looking for each other."

"I'm ashamed of myself." And she was, she told herself.

"No need for that. You're human, you care for him, and you're not sure of him though I don't know why not. This should have happened to you when you were a teenager. But no, when other youngsters were learning the opposite sex, you decided the most important thing in life was cybernetics. I think that's what you called it. Where'd it get you?"

"Aunt Grace, I don't need this lecture. See you at five." *I'm going to get some work done if it kills me,* she told herself after hanging up, but within seconds, her secretary buzzed her.

"Mr. Jackson on line two."

"August, where are you?" Her breath seemed trapped in her throat. Had he found Grady?

"I'm at LaGuardia airport. I'm still looking, but I have hope now. I want to see you tonight. How about seven-thirty at your place?"

She breathed at last.

"I'll be there," was as much as she could manage. She hung up, phoned Grace and canceled their date. Might as well clear her desk; nothing related to that office was likely to push August from her thoughts. She couldn't help wondering how she had become so strongly attached to him this quickly. Admittedly, with his mesmerizing brown eyes, high cheek bones, smooth dark cleanly shaven skin, pouting bottom lip, and tantalizing smile, he was better looking than a man had any right to be. But her world had a plethora of handsome men. August was more, she mused. Far more. Strong. Oh, yes. She was learning that he had enormous strength, and it had taken her a while to realize that his gentleness and tenderness with her was just that: strength, not weakness. When August had her in his arms, everything else could go skate; he made her feel as though her world and everything in it was perfect. She locked her desk, shaking her head at her new self-knowledge, snapped her briefcase closed and gazed across Upper New York Bay at the Statue of Liberty, wishing she could see that far into her future.

Susan tried to calm herself and to appear casual, her normally decorous self, when she opened the door for

August that evening. She looked her best and knew it, and she wanted to behave as if his staying in Washington overnight and refusing her company hadn't bothered her. She steeled herself against his charisma and looked into his eyes but, even as she did so, she knew he could see her joy at being with him. Without a word, he stepped into the foyer and took her to him. Tiny sensations of prickling heat raced all through her body when his lips claimed her, and she let him cherish her. Her heart hammered in her chest like a runaway train as his knowing fingers roamed over her arms, shoulders, and back and his talented tongue found its home inside her mouth. If she could only get on him, under him, inside of him…if she could just drown in him. She felt his arousal and lost all reason. In wild abandonment, her body took control, and she sucked on his tongue, telegraphing to him the power of the need he'd provoked in her.

"Whoa, honey," he said at last, gasping for breath. She must have looked bewildered, because he didn't release her but shifted her to his side and held her there. "Honey, when you get started, you really move, don't you? Anything to eat?" She gulped. Maybe he could shift gears with the speed of sound, but she was still in that other world he was so good at creating.

"Uh…yeah. I ordered us a catered dinner for eight o'clock. Okay?"

"Sweetheart, can't you cook a bit?"

"If I have to—after all, chemistry was one of my best subjects in high school and college."

August closed one eye, raised the eyebrow of the other one and shook his head. "I thought we were talking about cooking."

"We are. Cooking is just a matter of blending flavors and substances, and chemistry is pretty much the same. You mix stuff and hope it doesn't blow up in your face."

August's stare would have been worthy of someone

witnessing a supernatural phenomenon. "If you're serious, honey, I guess I'd better do our cooking."

Susan couldn't suppress a broad grin. She hadn't lied to any great extent: ordinarily, the average human could turn out a better meal than she, but the five menus that she'd mastered would please the most discriminating person.

"In that case, fair is fair," she deadpanned, "I'll make coffee every morning." His rippling laughter warmed her from her head to her toes. She led him toward the kitchen where she'd stored a pitcher of Oklahoma High in the refrigerator. She reached toward the refrigerator door, her lips still tingling from his kiss, withdrew her hand and looked at him. She hadn't meant to issue an invitation, but her eyes must have communicated to him her churning need and the sweet communion for which she longed. In a second, she was in his arms, caught up in wild passion. Frissons of heat darted through her, and every molecule of her body screamed to have him within her. The flesh of her arms and shoulders burned from the loving touch of his hands, and her body was his to manipulate. Flaccid. Submissive. She parted her lips for his kiss and took what he gave. Hard, possessive loving. She couldn't help shivering in frustration when, as suddenly as he'd set her afire, he released her.

"You've got to stop doing that to me, August," she said, when she could get her breath.

"What?" It pleased her that he, too, seemed to struggle with his emotions.

"You know what I mean. Isn't there anything intermediate between your mind-blowing kisses and no kiss at all?" *Oh, oh, here we go,* she thought, as he started to smile.

"Honey, I don't believe in doing a thing halfway. Nothing. And that includes… Well, you'll see. Hmm. This is good. What is it?" he asked, savoring the cold drink.

"Peach juice and carbonated Mateus Rosé. Aunt Grace concocted it. She calls it Oklahoma High. Don't ask me why." Her eyebrow arched sharply, but after thinking for a moment, she decided not to comment on his sudden shift in demeanor; he did it often, and she'd have to get accustomed to it.

She answered the door, paid the caterer, and served the food.

"Did you miss me?" he asked in a voice that she thought rather subdued.

"You were only gone overnight."

"I know, but that was long enough to miss me."

"I had things on my mind," she hedged.

August folded his napkin, dabbed at his mouth and grinned.

"Liar. Those kisses were worth a thousand words." His tone softened, and the dark sonority of his voice caressed her. "I missed you, and I'm counting the hours until I don't have to leave you."

"You don't—"

"Of course, I do," he interrupted. "Once we agree to something, we don't reopen it."

"Not even when the agreement involved duress? You did pressure me, you know that."

"No comment," August said, refusing to be drawn into it. "Did you put in for leave so we can go on our honeymoon? How much time did you ask for?"

"How much…" She didn't try to hide her shock. "*Honeymoon?* I thought… Well it didn't occur to me that…" Her voice drifted into silence.

"Shame on you, honey. Do I look like a man who wouldn't give my bride a honeymoon? They could spare you for two weeks, couldn't they?"

Her napkin dropped into her soup. "But *two whole weeks!* I'm on an anti-trust suit, and I may have to argue it before the Supreme Court. I can't take—"

He interrupted in an exasperatingly mild voice. "But, honey, slow down. If it isn't on the Court's docket for this session, you have until October, almost ten months. So, as soon as you get the Court's agenda, we can make plans. No excuses. I want you all to myself where nobody knows us, and I need a lot longer than two weeks, but I'll settle for that. We need time, sweetheart." His lips curled into a grin. "Just wait. You'll wish you'd taken at least a month." He walked around to her, lifted her out of the chair and sat down.

"I care for you, sweetheart, and I'm going to make you happy."

She leaned against him. "Aunt Grace is nuts. The only thing we've had in common so far is the homeless. With everything that counts, you're odd and I'm even."

His eyebrows jerked up sharply.

"What does that mean? The fact that we're both compassionate and care about less fortunate people says more about us than our taste in furniture."

"What about the place where we'll live?"

"Country or city, ranch house or whatever, that business about where we'll live wasn't important."

"Of course not," she grumbled, "you got your way."

He got up and put the dishes in the dishwasher, claiming that she looked too beautiful to touch anything soiled. Then he smiled at her, and his tone was very casual.

"I'm glad you like the house. It's got plenty of rooms, and four or five children won't make it seem crowded." The water glass that she'd been holding crashed to the floor.

"Did you say three or four?"

"I said four or five." She had to sit down. Ignoring her consternation, he plowed on. "I've longed for a family most of my life. I guess most people who are orphaned at an early age feel like that. And I suppose being without my brother accentuated the need."

She looked first to heaven and then at him. "And less than five kids isn't a family?"

He stopped pretending and faced her. "What are you saying?"

"I'm saying I figured two would do it."

He dried his hands and started toward her, but she was onto his methods of persuasion. She backed away. "Two? Honey, this is more serious than honeymoon, house, engagement ring, and church wedding combined. I *love* kids."

She stared at him, hoping to convey how far off base he was and to bring him around to reason before they got into another fight, because this was one that August Jackson was not going to win.

"You don't have to overindulge yourself to such an extent just because you love them. No way." She wouldn't allow herself to be swayed by his look of…of injury and dismay. You'd think she was attempting to deprive him of a divine right. She braced herself for his next sally, but he chose to plead.

"Honey, you don't understand. Most of my life, I've been dreaming about my little kids playing around my feet before a nice big winter fire while I read stories to them. Don't you love kids?" He took a step forward, and she took one backward.

"Sure I love children, but I'm already thirty-five and, if we're going to ensure the children and me the best chances for good health, our babies should be spaced at least two and preferably three years apart. If I have five, I'll still be having babies when I'm fifty." She threw up her hands as though in despair. "And even if I were younger, I'd have to have quintuplets if you want a crowd of them playing around your feet because babies grow up."

He frowned and ran his slim fingers over the back of his tight curls. "Honey, can't we discuss this?" She looked toward the sky as though seeking help.

"We *are* discussing it. Can't we just have two?" When he suddenly relaxed and began to smile, she prepared for battle.

"How about three? I'll help you."

Both hands went to her hips. "*You'll help me?* You're darn tootin' you will. How else do you think I'll get pregnant?"

This time, his smile began in his eyes, which gleamed lustfully, and his beautiful white teeth showed themselves in an appreciate grin that developed into a howl. When he could stop laughing, he offered an explanation.

"What I mean, honey, is that I'll do everything and anything to keep you comfortable and to ease your burden."

Thinking that her heart would burst, she ran to him and threw her arms around him. "Oh, August. You're so precious."

He hugged her to him fiercely, and she could feel a new emotion, something akin to a healing energy radiating from him. He buried his face in her neck and murmured, "Baby, this is the first time you've ever come to me like this. You always respond to me, but you haven't opened yourself to me and asked me to reciprocate your feelings. A man needs that, too." She held him as close as her strength would allow.

"Ah, sweetheart," he murmured, "can't you see that we're going to make it? We have these little misunderstandings and disagreements, but we always ride over them, don't we?" She snuggled against him.

"We're not having five children, August."

"I know, honey. I know. You agreed to three, and I'm willing to compromise."

She stepped back and glared at him.

"I didn't hear myself agree. We'll take this up again when our second is two years old."

"Okay. Okay. At least, I'll get to be a father." She had never realized that a loving relationship with a man could be so sweet and that laughing with him could be so wonderfully satisfying. August made her laugh. And he made her heart skip beats.

August figured he had to learn how to be happy. He had achieved success as a corporate executive, had the respect of his associates and employees, and the people back in Wallace, North Carolina, thought he had spun gold wings. Whenever he walked into Wallace's library, Mrs. McCullen, the librarian, ushered him into the computer room that he'd funded and introduced the children who worked and studied there to their benefactor. All of that made him feel great, but it wasn't a part of him. The woman in his arms was a part of him; he could feel it. But he wasn't sure of it, an ephemeral quality about their relationship wouldn't let him enjoy it to the fullest. He'd believe his good fortune when he saw their marriage certificate. He shifted his attention to Susan when he heard his name.

"August, I want to go to the opera. If I get two tickets, will you go with me to see *La Boheme?*" Her surprisingly seductive voice told him that she wasn't sure of their relationship, either. If she had been, she'd know that he'd do whatever he could to make her happy.

"I'll get the tickets. When do you want to go?" He made a note of that. Since she thought she had to seduce him into taking her to an opera, he'd better put her straight.

"I love opera. I learned to appreciate it from the Saturday afternoon broadcasts that I've followed since my childhood, but I've never been to one. I'll look forward to this." Joy suffused him as he savored her smile and obvious delight.

"A little thing like this can make you so happy?" he asked.

"Well…we've got something else in common, something we can enjoy together without getting into a fight or either of us having to compromise."

He grinned. "Don't mistake me for a highbrow, now. I love country music, too. Some of the best guitarists in the world play country." Here we go, he thought, as her smile dissolved into a frown.

"You can't sell it to me." She inclined her head toward her left shoulder and lowered her eyelids slightly in that way he loved. "If you want to hear spell-binding popular guitar music," she admonished him, "listen to some good classical jazz—Charlie Christian or Freddie Green, Wes Montgomery or Laurindo Almeida. Now, that's guitar playing. Those guys knew what to do with six strings."

He put a serious expression on his face. "I wouldn't know,

being unfamiliar with the guitar." At least she had the grace to appear less sure of herself.

"But you said... Oh," she murmured, remembering that he'd studied guitar for many years, "I guess I can't tell you who knows how to play a guitar."

"Sure you can," he said with a shrug of his left shoulder, "but you don't have to be right, you..." The roll of paper towels sailed straight at him, but he caught it, tossed it on the sink and went after her.

"Throw things at your future husband, will you? Well, we'll see about that," he said, reaching toward her. Warned by the fire she must have seen in his eyes, she raced down the hallway, but he charged after her, grabbed her as she whirled into the living room and tumbled with her onto her big velvet sofa. Gales of laughter pealed from her throat while he mercilessly tickled her side. He watched, transfixed, as her giggles dissolved into sudden and sober silence when she opened her eyes to the passion he knew his face betrayed.

She squirmed beneath him, and his response was swift, hard and hot. *I'm going to get him this time,* she told herself, when heat pooled in the pit of her belly and shot to the center of her passion. He turned to his side bringing her with him but, as she struggled in the grip of desire, his effort to slow them down only vaguely penetrated her consciousness. When he didn't respond to her parted lips, she wet his mouth with her tongue and luxuriated in his hoarse groan as he opened up to her. Wanting more and demanding it, she threw her right leg across his hip but, with what sounded like a wrenching sob, he moved her away from him.

"Susan," he said, sitting up straight and seeming to drag the words out of himself, "we're going to wait."

She sat up and moved closer to him. "Can I expect you to stop doing this to me after February fourteenth?" She tried not to be vexed at his raised eyebrow that suggested he couldn't imagine what her question was about.

"Leaving me hanging like this. You know what I mean." His tender hug made up for it a little, but not much.

"Aren't you beginning to see why I'm holding back. Think how much closer we are now than when you first brought it up. The closer we are and the deeper our feelings for each other the first time we make love, the better it will be and the more binding, too. I'm flattered. I'd lie if I said I wasn't, and especially because it's me and not just the physical relief that you want." She poked his shoulder playfully.

"I'm cooperating, aren't I?"

"Just barely," he muttered.

"Well, it's taking some effort on my part."

He gazed at her, as though surprised. "What does that mean?"

"It means that I am not so naive that I don't know how to seduce you. That's what." He wasn't going to fool her with his look of solemnity, his pious sincerity.

"I'm glad to hear it," was all he said. Then he looked down at her left hand and his eyes seemed to gleam with happiness. "That's not so bad, is it, honey?"

"What?"

"Wearing my ring. It's not like I'd asked you to wear a big, bright sign on your forehead or anything." She had to laugh, he could think of the most ridiculous things.

"It gets a lot of attention. The first day I wore it, would you believe a line formed at my desk? The consensus at the office is that you have elegant taste." She paused, weighing a decision. "August, will you stop by my office tomorrow afternoon? I'd like to introduce you to my colleagues." She should have suggested that earlier, she realized, when the change in his demeanor reflected frank pride.

August called Grace and asked her to be in front of his office building at noon the next day.

"I found that clipping," Grace said, as soon as she heard his voice, "and it's got all the information you need. You don't even have to tell Susan a thing about it. You can do it on your own, it says here. But you be sure and make that deadline, now. You hear? My second sense tells me—"

He didn't want to hear about her second sense. "All right. I'll do it, but it's just between us. I don't want Susan to be disappointed." So far, he hadn't found Grady, he told her in reply to her question, but he had an excellent lead, and his P.I. was currently checking on it.

"Shucks," she said. "Give me his christened name, birthday, date, time, and place, and I'll bring you something tomorrow. No need to wait on an investigator when he can't tell you anything that I can't." He did, adding that his mother had said Grady was born at high noon.

He had a sensation of being suspended in midair, when he saw the look of excitement on Grace's face as she greeted him at noon the next day. Her whole body seemed to vibrate and glow in contrast with her normally closed face and phlegmatic demeanor. She opened the front door of the taxi for him, something she hadn't previously done.

"It's him, all right," she said, dispensing with preliminaries. "His chart says he's looking for you, and my second sense backs that up. He's going to find you before the full moon."

"When is that?"

"Next one is February the eleventh. From the looks of this, you ought to be heading toward western North Carolina, somewhere around Pinehurst, or maybe eastern Tennessee. If that's where your P.I. went, you're on the right track. Go for it!"

August pulled at the scarf around his neck and loosened his tie. With trembling fingers, he took a few tissues from the box on Grace's dashboard and wiped his forehead. "Slow down over there, please, Grace. I need a couple of minutes before I go for Susan. I'm trying not to hope too much, but my investigator went to Ashville, and that's in western North Carolina. I've had so many disappointments that I can't let

myself expect too much. I haven't married, bought a house
or even a car. My earnings have gone for necessities and for
my search for Grady. I've put everything that I could into
finding him—the only kin I know about. Twenty-six long
years. I wonder what he'll be like, how he turned out."

Grace patted his hand. "You needn't worry—he's a
respectable citizen."

"I was prepared to love him, no matter what, but I'm glad
to know he made it. Thank God, and thank you, Grace." He
shook his head slowly, unable to believe that the agony was
nearing an end. He recalled something that Grace had said
minutes earlier.

"You said something about a second sense. Are you
clairvoyant?" He noticed that she appeared ill at ease.

"I don't tell people about that, because it makes them
uncomfortable with me, but since you asked, very much so. I
was that way growing up, and I didn't have sense enough to
keep my mouth shut about it. The upshot was people treated
me like I was a circus freak. I studied astrology because a
woman told me that was more scientific. I don't know. I use
both together, and I've been able to help a lot of people. I didn't
manage to go any farther than high school, and I didn't want
to wait tables or tend a bar, so I figured driving my own taxi
was my best chance of meeting a lot of people and helping as
many as I could. Of course, I make a good living at it, and I
ain't sneezing at that. No sirree."

That night, August decided to enter the Rainbow Room
contest. What could he lose? Maybe, if he showed some
originality, he'd stand a chance of winning. He wanted Susan
to have her dream, and he wanted to see her in a long white
wedding gown.

He wrote: I dreamed of a wedding in the Rainbow Room
because

I wanted a little church wedding
Before flying with my bride to the moon

But on a New Year's Eve long, long ago
She fell in love with the Rainbow Room.

She says she'll marry in a gay pants suit
And hurry back to her office by noon
She wouldn't think of wearing satin and lace
Unless she wears it in the Rainbow Room.

She longs to relive that star-spangled night
When the world was hers, and her youth full bloom
She'll even take her vows in a white bridal gown
If she can take them in the Rainbow Room.

He put the letter in an envelope, considered crossing his
fingers and decided a prayer made more sense. On his way to
Susan's apartment, he dropped the letter into the mailbox.

August hadn't objected when she told him that since he'd
gotten fourth row orchestra seats for the performance of
*La Boheme* at the Metropolitan Opera House, she'd like to
wear a long dress. "Fine with me," he'd said, offhand. So she
dressed in a figure-hugging red velvet sheath supported by
thin shoulder straps and her ample bosom, piled her hair on
her head, and surveyed the results. Not bad. She barely heard
August's piercing whistle when she opened the door, nor did
she notice his appreciative comment on her looks. In a black
tuxedo with a pleated silk shirt and gray and black accessories,
August Jackson was spellbinding. Not certain whether her eyes
received her, she blinked them several times, as she tried to
reconcile this urban sophisticate with the gentle, homespun
man she thought she knew. She took a deep breath, invited
him in and went for her coat, all the while musing over the
picture he made. This guy was poster material. Well, she
consoled herself, at least he didn't behave as if he knew it.
"Where's your coat," she asked as he helped her into hers.

"I don't have a black chesterfield," he told her, "but I won'
get a cold. A car's waiting for us right outside."

Her eyebrows arched in spite of her effort to hide he
surprise, but he laughed, taking it in stride.

"I do know a few things, honey, including how to dress
The first thing I did when Amos and I started to turn a prof
was to concentrate on how to present myself in all kinds o
situations. I hate putting on these things, but let me tell yo
it's worth it to see you looking like this. You're so pretty."

Only he had applied that word to her since she was a sma
girl. She wanted to put her arms around him and hug him t
her; he'd blindsided her, poleaxed her. He looked down at he
and his lips began to smile. She had to close her eyes, becaus
she would be besotted for sure if she gazed at him until the
smile reached his eyes.

"Come on, let's go," she urged. He assisted her into the
back seat of a waiting chauffeured Lincoln Town Car, joine
her, opened the bar, and poured her a glass of champagne.

"I'm going to faint," she said, her voice low and breathy.

"Don't you like champagne?"

His grin told her that he was well aware of her problem
so she gathered her wits as best she could and sipped the ic
wine. Throughout the performance, during the intermission
and on the ride back home, she saw an August who displaye
every nuance of good manners and elegant taste. And at the
end of the evening, she couldn't say who had sung the role o
Mimi or how she'd sounded.

"You're amazing," she told him, as he left her.

He turned and favored her with his high-powered grin.

"There's a first and only time for everything. Wouldn't yo
say?"

She had to laugh, because he'd just told her not to expec
that treatment often. Maybe not again.

Two days later, August kept his promise to meet Susan'
colleagues. She took him first to meet the firm's presiden

genial man of Norwegian descent, who gave them his blessings. August Jackson was as comfortable in that setting as she, and more than one of her male colleagues frankly preferred to him. It didn't surprise her that Oscar Hicks proved the exception.

"Man, I'm glad you're taking Susan out of the running for partner. She's a mean piece of competition, and I won't stand a chance as long as she wants a shot at it." He talked on and on, Susan observed, apparently oblivious to August's failure to respond.

"What exactly do you mean by that comment?" August finally said in a voice iced with sarcasm.

"Well," Oscar said, apparently less sure of himself now. "She'll soon start a family and, well, you know."

He cautioned himself not to show his temper. "And that's your business?"

"Well, no…of course not," Oscar replied, as he edged toward the door. "Good to meet you." Susan watched his departing back and couldn't restrain a laugh.

"Milquetoast, if I ever saw any," she said, as much to herself as to August. "Oscar knows a man when he sees one. No wonder he got out of here when you challenged him." She didn't let August see her misgivings. For the first time since she had agreed to marry him, doubts as to the wisdom of it and fear of probable consequences buried themselves into her consciousness. She didn't know what she'd do if she missed out on the chance to become a partner, to see Andrews added to Pettersen, Geier and Howard.

Three evenings later, Susan sat up in bed putting rollers in her hair and musing over August's inconsistent behavior. Whenever he had an option, August usually chose the traditional, the old-fashioned. So simple a thing as how visitors would announce themselves had been an issue between them. She had wanted a doorbell and an intercom, but he claimed that was too unfriendly, and they'd settled for chimes. He

wanted a house full of children, but when their furniture w
delivered to their Tarrytown home the day before, he had
asked her to take the day off to receive it. He had done th
himself. Maybe he wouldn't expect her to stay at home f
months after each of their children was born. She hoped he
be understanding about that. She didn't want to give up th
partnership; she'd worked too hard and too long for it.

August returned the phone to its cradle and propped hims
against the wall with the help of his right elbow. His left har
went to his chest as though to still the furious pounding of h
heart. After all these years, was he finally going to see Grad
He didn't know if he could stand a disappointment such
he'd experienced when he'd gone to Washington to see a m
who might have been his brother. His private investigat
claimed to be ninety percent certain this time, and Grace
charts were never wrong, but there was still a chance that h
hopes would be futile. His entire life had been one triump
after another over adversity, and he didn't fear his abili
to withstand it. But this was his heart. He'd loved his litt
brother and had protected him as best he could against th
cruelty and unfairness that they endured in foster homes. B
one day their foster father had promised Grady the beating
his life, and the boy had disappeared. Soon after that, Augu
had been sent to another home, and Grady couldn't have four
him without going to the authorities. He'd been looking for h
brother ever since, and he knew he'd never be a whole perso
until he found him. He dialed Susan's number.

"Susan, my investigator says he's found my brother
Ashville, North Carolina. I'm going there tomorrow mornin
and I want you to go with me. Will you?" He didn't know wh
he'd do if she said she couldn't make it; he needed her, and
needed to know that she'd be there for him whenever he need
her just as he would be for her. He needed some evidence th
meeting his needs was important to her. Annoyed and unea
at her long silence, he didn't try to hide his testiness.

"Look, if you think you can't be away from your office for day and a half, say so. I'll be back Thursday."

"Oh, August, I'm so happy for you. And of course, I'll go with you," she said, in the shadowy tone of one coming out of trance. "I was trying to figure out how to shuffle the deck ere, so to speak." They agreed on time and other particulars, ut he wasn't fooled by her explanation. She had hesitated to o. He told himself to pay closer attention. He didn't intend to ive her up, but he believed in correcting errors and solving roblems at the root the first time he noticed them. That policy ad made him a successful executive, and he'd use it to keep is marriage on track.

They had barely greeted each other before he realized the bsence of the warm camaraderie and togetherness that they ad shared ever since their movie date, the closeness that e'd felt with her, the indescribable feeling of oneness. He scribed his own feeling of separateness, of there being a istance between them, to his anxiety that the man he would ncet might not be his long sought brother. But to what could e attribute her quiet, somber manner? As the plane touched own on the runway, he felt her hand cover his and squeeze n a gesture of support and forced a smile in her direction.

"If it isn't Grady, we'll keep right on looking until we find im," she said. "And we *will* find him." He gave silent thanks, eaned toward her and captured her mouth. She was there for im; that was all he'd needed.

Almost as soon as they walked into the waiting area and ooked around, he felt Susan tug sharply at his hand and oint to two men in the distance who had begun to approach hem. The taller of the two men smiled, and his heartbeat ccelerated. Susan grabbed his hand and started running oward the men.

"It's him!" she yelled. "August, it's him. It has to be. His mile is just like yours."

He ran with her, speechless, barely aware of his moves.

They reached the men and stopped short, as the two me
searched each other's faces, hope gleaming in their eye
August thought he heard Susan say, "Oh, Lord, let it be," b
he didn't move his gaze from that of the man in front of hin
He found his voice.

"Grady, do you remember our father?"

The man smiled and in a nearly identical voice said, "C
course I remember him. He only had one leg. He lost the oth
one at the sawmill where he worked."

"I can't believe it. After all these years. My God, Grad
this has to be the happiest moment of my life." He didn
care that tears streamed down his face as he embraced th
man whom he didn't doubt was his blood brother. Jessie an
her sister had been right; they could have passed for twin
He tried to control the excitement that clutched at him, b
couldn't manage it and finally rested his head on Grady
shoulder and let the tears flow. After a few minutes, the
stepped back from each other, unashamed of their wrenchir
emotions and teary eyes, and smiled. Grady had a questic
of his own.

"I've got a birthmark, August. What is it and where
it?"

August grinned; he'd forgotten about that, hadn't felt th
need for any further proof after he saw their father's smile c
Grady's face. "There should be a round black, hairy spot th
size of a quarter or fifty cent piece on your left shoulder."

"Want to see it?" Grady asked, laughing as though the
shared a private joke, as indeed they did.

"Not really, and I'm sorry for all those times I taunted yc
about it." He followed Grady's glance to a tearstained Susa
reached out and gathered her to him.

"Grady, this is my fiancée, attorney Susan Andrews. W
plan to be married on Valentine's Day."

"Say, that's only about three weeks," Grady exclaime
ignoring Susan's outstretched hand and bringing her to hi
in a warm hug. "I'll try to make it."

August quirked an eyebrow. "Try hard. I'm having a big wedding and inviting every single person I know, so you'll have to be my best man." He could see that his request pleased Grady, who agreed and invited them all to his home, a small ranch house on a hill with a spectacular view. He didn't doubt that Susan would remind him that he and Grady had similar preferences for houses. As they walked into the living room, he saw that the room was sparsely, but elegantly furnished with modern pieces. Pleased, he smiled at her. But when he caught Susan's withering glance, he knew that her mind was centered on his announcement of a big church wedding, something to which she obviously hadn't accommodated herself. Well, if he was lucky, their crowd would gather in the famous Rainbow Room.

They sipped coffee while Grady related to them experiences he'd had growing up without August. Susan offered to leave so that they might have privacy when Grady told of personal, almost intimate and sometimes nearly tragic happenings in his young life, but August held onto her hand, though at times with unsteady fingers. He marveled that the man before him could have survived months at a time in freight cars, stealing food from restaurants by posing as a delivery boy, picking strawberries in the spring and sorting potatoes in the autumn.

"When did you go to school?" Susan asked, clearly appalled that a child should have had so painful and precarious a life.

"A pullman porter on the Atlantic Coastline became interested in me when he caught me stealing books from someone's compartment and discovered that I wanted to read them and not sell them. I was about eleven. He took me home with him, and we worked out a deal. He'd send me to school and take care of my expenses if I'd look after his mother. Mama Ada was about eighty or eighty-five, she wasn't sure, and couldn't walk too well. She refused to move out of her house, although it was little more than a shack. I made her fires, got water from her well, swept her yard, went to the store and got her groceries, and did just about everything else that she needed done. After six or seven months, I decided to move in with her, and it was a smart decision. She'd once taught grade school, and she still had a trigger sharp mind. She made me her project, and within a year and a half, I was right where I should have been in school. She tried to teach me everything she knew, and I tried to take it in. I got a scholarship to the University of North Carolina, and I was on my way. My goal was to find old Chester Faison and show him that I'd made a man of myself. I did go back to Wallace, but he'd long since died, and his daughter, Ruthie, didn't even remember that we'd once been foster children in that home."

"Where's that man who helped you?" Susan asked.

"About ten miles from here. He's retired now, and I usually run by to see him and his wife every Sunday after church. Of course, Mama Ada's been gone a long time. We'll catch up with the rest later, August. Tell me what you've been doing."

August leaned back in the comfortable business-class seats as the big plane headed for New York and draped his arm around Susan's shoulder. So much to digest, to think about. His life had been rocky at a time when he was a youth trying to get through school, but he'd had a much easier life than Grady. He gazed down at the woman whose head rested trustingly on his shoulder while she slept, and counted his blessings. He had his brother once more, and he had at his side this woman who had come to mean everything to him. More than she could know. When she'd grasped his hand and promised that *they* would look for Grady until they found him, he'd known that after twenty-six years, he was no longer alone.

How could so much go wrong in less than two days? Susan paced between her desk and her window overlooking the

Statue of Liberty. Her contract stated that the next partnership was hers and that she should apply for it after six months—five weeks hence. But she'd just been told that partners were not expected to take extended leave and that she would have to promise not to do that. The partners knew her age and were forcing her to choose between partnership and motherhood. They hadn't put it in writing but, if she didn't cooperate, they'd easily find a reason to withhold the coveted promotion. There was no mistaking Oscar's hand in that attempt at blackmail. On more than one occasion, he had alluded to there being a conflict between her job and marriage. Upset and more depressed than she could ever remember having been, she called August.

"What's the matter, honey? You sound low, almost as if you've lost your best friend. Tell me."

"I don't want to talk about it over the phone. Why don't you bring over a great big pizza about seven and I'll make a simple salad. I don't feel like cooking, and I don't want to go anywhere."

"I'll be there. Chin up, I promised that, as long as I'm breathing, I'll be with you no matter what, and I mean that. See you at seven."

They'd eaten half of the pizza, discarded the remainder, and straightened up the kitchen, but neither had mentioned what had depressed Susan earlier that day. She knew what his reaction would be, despite his promise of support, and she dreaded the confrontation. He took her hand, walked them into her living room, sat in her big barrel chair, and pulled her gently onto his lap.

"Since it's so painful you dread talking about it, I gather I'm not going to like what you say. Am I right?"

She shifted slightly on his lap, remembered where she was and the probable consequences of not remaining still, and nodded. "You're right, and it's about the office."

"You can't get time off for our honeymoon?" he queried,

and she could see that he braced himself for an unpleasant discussion.

She shook her head, sighed, and faced him. It couldn't be avoided. "They've added a condition to my partnership contract. It's unwritten, but it might as well be in black and white. I have to promise not to take any extended leave for the first three years after I'm a senior partner."

"That's ridiculous." He placed her on the floor and stood up, his face mottled with fury. "Nobody can stipulate such a requirement. Besides, I suspect it's against the law in New York. And even if it isn't," he roared, "you can't leave a few weeks old baby and go back to work. What if you got sick? They're full of baloney. You've got rights."

"I'm not being given the choice. If I want the partnership, I have to agree and in writing, and they will enforce it." She hadn't thought that August could get so angry, and it frightened her as she watched his lips tremble in cold fury. He slammed his fist into the palm of his right hand.

"If you sign that and they can hold you to it, that will be the end of our dreams of a family. You can't do it," he repeated emphatically before laying back his shoulders and cocking his head in a gesture of finality. "We'll go to court."

She couldn't help feeling as if her world had begun to dissolve into nothing, but she wouldn't allow him see how badly she hurt.

"And if I win, they'll make it so miserable for me that I'll be glad to leave there. So what you're suggesting is that I walk away from my other dream, my dream of that partnership for which I've struggled so hard. I've worked nights and weekends, foregone vacations, lived without friends or lovers, devoted my youth to the pursuit of that dream, and you're giving me the same choice that my boss gave me. The world is full of healthy, well-adjusted, bottle-fed babies. I'm sorry, August." She raised her chin a little higher and shook her head.

Pain flickered in his eyes as he stood mute, waiting for her last word. Her mouth tasted of gall, and her stomach churned as she anticipated his verdict, words that would chill her soul. She felt an inexplicable loneliness, as though he had already left her. He had never seemed so handsome, so desirable, or so remote. So little inclined to shelter and protect her as she'd come to expect of him. She looked down at her hands, to shield from him the anguish that she knew he would see in her eyes.

"Think this over, Susan. Be certain of what you want, because if you tell me it's over, I'll believe you." He spoke in soft tones that were devoid of emotion. "You may choose that partnership and break our engagement, but you won't get over me, Susan. Not now, and maybe never. I'll be everywhere you turn, because I am the man who awakened you and made you feel, really *feel* deep down. All the way to your gut. I know you. I've set you on fire, and you'll never be content until I finish what I started. I'm willing to go part of the way with you in this, but I need some evidence that you're agreeable to making some sacrifices. Think it over."

She watched him, too stunned to move, as he let himself out. She had assumed that they would compromise on this as they had with all of their other disagreements, but they'd each reached their limit, each confronted the future and refused to relinquish their dream. She thought of calling Grace and discarded the idea, unable to endure one of her aunt's lectures.

August caught a taxi and headed home. Yesterday, he'd had everything. Grady was back in his life and, in less than three weeks, Susan would have been his wife. Now, he had to cancel their wedding plans, the caterer, the white limousine that he'd ordered for his bride's trip to the church and their ride to the reception, her bouquet of white roses, the honeymoon that he'd planned as a surprise for her. He got home and paced the floors, trying to decide what he could give up. After an hour, he was determined to find a way; he wanted Susan, and he wanted, had to have children. He took their wedding bands out of a drawer, sat on the edge of his bed and looked at them, looked at his dream, the life he'd yearned for ever since he'd lost his parents. Those years when he didn't have Grady. Ever since he was ten years old. He would not accept defeat. He had to talk to her.

"Susan," he began when she answered the phone, "are you willing to give up all of our plans? Can you just forget what we feel for each other? We've built a wonderful relationship, and I know that we would be happy together, because I'll make sure of it."

"August, we won't settle anything this way. Why does it all depend on me?"

He had to resist laughing, because he knew she'd think he was trying to snow her.

"Honey, can you give me the boot as easily as that?" he asked her, trying to lighten their conversation. "What about the soloist I hired. I didn't tell you, because I wanted her to sing a love song from me to you." He was sure that his pride in the little surprise reached her through the wires.

"What singer? What song?"

"A lady from church. She has a lovely voice, and she told me that she's sung it many times."

"What song, August?" He couldn't figure out why her voice sounded darker and stronger, unless she had gotten annoyed, and there wasn't anything for her to be upset about.

"'Through The years'," he said.

"But I wanted 'Ich Liebe Dich'."

"'Ich Liebe Dich'?"

"That's German for I Love Thee," she announced, a bit haughtily, he thought.

"Thanks, but I know that."

"Did you study German, or did you spend some time in Germany?"

He had to laugh. She could arrive at some of the most far-fetched conclusions. "A German girl taught me that." He waiting for a ripping comment, but she fooled him.

"A Ger... When?"

"Before I met you. We're getting off of the subject, Susan. Now, as I was saying—"

"Did you tell her you loved her?"

He groaned. She had to be a first-class lawyer. Give her the scent of something, and she put on her blinds and went after it.

"What happened?" she persisted. "Do you still know her?"

"Sure. She sends me cards at Christmas and for my birthday. So I—"

"Your birthday? I don't even know when that is, and she sends you cards all the way from Germany. At least I hope that's where she is."

"My birthday is October nineteenth, and you are deliberately trying to sidetrack me with these frivolous questions."

"I'm never frivolous."

"More's the pity."

"August!"

"I want Miss Lewis to sing 'Through The Years' at our wedding."

"If you see things my way, and if we ever do get married, I want a man to sing 'Ich Liebe Dich'."

He thought about that for a few seconds. If she was being agreeable, he could give a little.

"Well, since it's going to be a big wedding, there's no reason why we can't have both songs, and I'll have that much more time to look at you in that lovely white satin gown."

"August we haven't settled one thing. I haven't agreed to a big church wedding and not to a satin gown, either."

"All right. All right. We'll take that up later. But you don't want to give up our home, do you? What about our home, honey?"

"What about it? It's in the middle of a bunch of trees, and that's country from where I stand."

"But we could have nice walks in the woods, especially in

the spring." He nearly laughed again when her exaggerated deep sigh reached him over the phone.

"That's still the country. And I'd rather sip espresso on a sidewalk café on Columbus Avenue on a nice spring evening. No thanks."

"Aw, honey, don't be so difficult." He paused, thinking of another carrot to dangle before her. "Well, what about my music? You've never heard me play the guitar. Not once."

"I told you I hate country music."

He was beginning to suspect that, while she was serious about some of it, she had begun to enjoy pulling his leg.

"I also play jazz," he corrected, "and Dittersdorf wrote a considerable portfolio of wonderful classical guitar music, most of which I know from memory."

"Then let him play it." He wasn't sure, but he thought he heard a giggle.

"Too late. He's been dead for centuries. What about our honeymoon? Don't tell me you're not interested in *that*."

"I told you that was overdoing it," she reminded him. "A weekend at the Waldorf would have been plenty."

He didn't feel playful about that and took his time before his next point.

"We've never made love, Susan, and I planned one long trip to paradise for us. Are you willing to give that up?"

"Whose fault is that? You're hitting below the belt, August, and you know it. I was ready the first time we were alone, but you were the one with the…with the…" She stammered for a word. Then she said, "You were the Victorian."

August laughed. "Honey, don't you believe people didn't fool around in Queen Victoria's time—they've been doing that since Adam and Eve got in trouble with that apple. Victorians hopped in and out of bed whenever it pleased them. They just disapproved of themselves after they did it. You can't give up on us, Susan. I can't think of myself without thinking of you, too."

"August, I am not going to make you a promise that I won't

keep. When I'm forty, I'll be too old to start a family. You want me to stay home for at least six months after our babies are born, and I agree that would be best for our children, but I'll lose out on the job. If that happens, I'll be so miserable you won't want to be around me. Can't you see that you're asking me to give up what I've worked my whole life to get? I won't do it."

Maybe he'd have to figure a way around that but, right now, he couldn't think of a thing. "Are you saying we're not going to have any? That's cruel, honey. I can just see our little boys and girls blossoming in our Tarrytown home. I can—"

"Why are you so pigheaded? If I have girls *and* boys, that's at least four." He tried to think of another tactic in a hurry, but couldn't.

"I'll have to get used to the change, sweetheart, I've been thinking about my five or six kids for so many years, that I'm having trouble switching to two, maybe three. But I'm trying."

"But you're not going to agree to a nanny six weeks or two months after the babies are born?"

Cold shivers shot through him. If he could nurse babies, he would, but nature had decreed otherwise. He didn't answer; if it ended, she'd have to do it.

"I'm sorry about the house. I loved that big fireplace you put in it just for me. Bye, hon." She hung up, but he heard the unsteadiness, the unshed tears in her voice. And she'd called him, "hon," the first time she had addressed him with an endearment. If she thinks this is over, he told himself, she's due for a surprise. He opened a bag of unshelled peanuts in order to have something with which to occupy his hands while he did some serious thinking. He ought to call Grace, but he didn't expect women to do his work for him. And besides, he wasn't sold on that chart business. Never had been. Where Susan was concerned, he'd fallen for her on sight and gone with his instincts. He shelled a couple of nuts and chewed slowly. Heck, Grace was the architect of this fiasco, and she'd better come up with some answers. He answered his cordless phone.

"Yeah. Grace? I was just about to call you?"

"I expect these coincidences," she said. "Why were you calling me, Mr. Jackson? I can't help you. Anybody who expects a thirty-five-year-old corporate lawyer to produce five children and work, too, is beyond help. Don't you know it takes at least nine months to make 'em? And that's if you're lucky."

"I gave in on that. We're having two, maybe three. Heck, I'll be happy if she gives me one. The trouble is that she insists on going back to work as soon as they're born." He knew she took a deep breath; he wasn't accustomed to having people sigh deeply when speaking with him, as though he might be a few bricks short of a full load, and it annoyed him. He ran his hand over his tight curls. Frustrated.

"Find a tantalizing alternative to dangle in front of her. She doesn't want to give you up, either."

"But what about us being a perfect match? If we are, why do we disagree on everything?" He hadn't heard Grace laugh many times, but he'd observed that when she did, she made a cackling sound. She cackled.

"What's amusing?"

"When it comes to my charts, I don't make mistakes. I've helped you all I'm going to. Figure out what you're doing wrong. Oh…and send me an invitation to the wedding."

He hung up. No help there.

He paced the floor, cracking nuts as he walked. There was Inger in Germany. He could invite her for a visit and arrange for Susan to know about it. He mused over that for a while. No. It wouldn't work. Not enough time. Besides, Susan would give him back his ring, she'd be so mad. He telephoned Grady, thinking that he'd better tell him not to expect a wedding.

Grady listened to his brother's tale of woe without comment, until August stopped talking.

"Look, man," Grady began, "if you love her, don't let a little argument like that break you up."

August didn't consider it a little thing and told him that. "The first six months is supposed to be a bonding time for mother and baby, but that can't happen if the mother is one place and the baby somewhere else."

Grady did his own thinking, August learned, when he said, "Think, August. Could you stay away from your office half a year or more and not create problems for yourself?"

"Sure I could. I'm part owner of that firm."

"Then, there's your answer. Let Susan leave a supply of milk for the baby, and you stay home with it. Kids have to bond with their father, too, don't they?"

"Sure they... Are you serious?"

"You betcha. Offer her that alternative, and the loving you get will blow your head off."

August figured he'd missed something somewhere. He had a lot to look forward to with Susan, but he hoped to be able to keep his head intact. *Le petit mort,* or the little death, as the French called climax, was one thing, but to have your head blown off. He could do without that. He laughed aloud, enjoying the warmth and intimacy of their exchange. "You seem well informed about these matters," he told Grady, though he was actually asking him what he'd been doing for the last twenty years.

"The school of hard knocks, brother. If you pay careful attention to your surroundings, you won't have to experience it to know it."

"When are you coming up?"

"Week after next. I figure you'll have things settled with Susan by then, and we'll be able to spend some time together." They agreed on the date and time of Grady's arrival, and hung up.

Grace unlocked the back door of her taxi, but August opened the front door and sat beside her. He'd never cared for Grace's highway driving, so he sat where the chances were best that she'd keep her eyes on the road while talking and not on the rearview mirror.

"For a man who's watching his lifelong dreams come true, you certainly do look sour today, Mr. Jackson. 'Course it's not my business, but you and Susan are acting foolish, if you'll pardon me. Ain't nothing going to go wrong, believe me, so just enjoy your brother and don't worry." For as long as he could remember, he'd had unshakable faith in God, Martin Luther King, Jr., and the Democrats in that order. Now, Grace Andrews Lamont wanted her name added to that list of icons, was hinting that he ought to consider her and her charts infallible. On the basis of what he'd seen of her work so far, he couldn't do it.

"You were on the button about Grady, but so far you're fifty percent wrong about Susan and me."

"Impatience and failure are bosom buddies, Mr. Jackson. February fourteenth is still ten days away." He flinched. A nineteen seventy-something Buick lumbered across their path, and Grace didn't appear to have seen it.

"Grace, I am where I am today because I've made it a policy never to spend money before I get it in my hand. Susan has drawn a line, and won't budge past it. She has her principles, and I have mine. I'll believe you're right when I see my signature beside hers on a marriage certificate." He slapped his right hand against his forehead. "Grace, will you please keep your eyes on the highway?" he pleaded, as she turned fully toward him.

"Well, don't say I didn't tell you. My record is perfect." She pulled up to the curb and turned to him. "You're never going to give her up. *Never.*"

Never was a very long time. He saw from the incoming flight board that Grady's plane had landed. He didn't know if he'd ever become accustomed to the happiness that nearly overwhelmed him, to the sensation of walking on air that he got whenever it hit him that his search was over, that Grady was once more in his life. He found him at the baggage carousel retrieving his luggage. Grady had been reaching for a bag, but when he saw August, he let the bag go by, raced over to August and embraced him.

"I can't get used to this," Grady said. "Believe me, I'm praying this isn't one of those recurring dreams that I've had for the last twenty-six years." They collected Grady's luggage and found Grace standing beside the cab. August introduced them.

"No need for that. Anybody can see the resemblance." She spoke to Grady. "You here to be best man?"

"Well…sure," Grady answered, his tone indicating uncertainty as to how much she knew and that he was picking his way.

"I'm the one that got them together," she boasted. "I did it on the basis of my charts, so I know all about them."

August learned that his brother's sense of humor was probably equal to his own when Grady replied, "*Everything?* Why, August, I'm surprised." Laughter bubbled up in August's throat and he let it peal forth. Oh, the joy of laughing with his brother.

"Another naughty one, I see," Grace said, when she could control her cackling

"I need to stop by and see Susan," August told Grace, who made the trip from LaGuardia airport to Susan's office building in record time.

"You and Grady wait here. I shouldn't be long."

August strode into the lobby, glanced at the cold and uninviting white marbled columns and walls and stopped. The silent reception area, desolate but for the lone guard, a gray-haired old man in a gold braided blue coat, suggested the interior of a tomb. He resisted the urge to go back to the taxi and to his brother, whom he knew would welcome him, and walked slowly toward the elevator. He walked in, but couldn't force himself to push the button for the thirty-second floor. How far was he willing to go, and what was he willing to concede? Grady had implied that if he loved her, he'd better be prepared to make concessions. Maybe that was it. She'd been wedged deep inside of him almost from the minute he first saw her, and he needed her, wanted her badly; that was incontestable. Still…might as well be honest; he was crazy about her. He didn't know of a word for what he felt other than love and, if he gave her up, he didn't think he could accept another man's having a claim on her. He pushed the button with his fist and watched the floor numbers as the elevator quickly took him to her.

Susan hated that she'd had to announce to her staff that she wouldn't be taking a two-week vacation, wasn't getting married, and wasn't changing her ritzy Eightieth Street address. But she'd done it with head high, never once revealing the gut-searing pain that seemed to tear her into pieces when she thought of August. It didn't surprise her that, within an hour, Oscar Hicks and Craig Smallens, one of the senior partners, knocked on her office door. She could only describe Oscar's facial expression as a cross between a smirk and panic, while Craig wore the look of a man who had gambled and lost. She hadn't thought that Craig didn't want her as a partner and wondered what else she'd missed.

"To what do I owe this high-level visit?" she asked, looking at Craig who made it a policy to speak with subordinates in his office, never in theirs. Craig put both hands on her desk and leaned forward.

"Apart from competence, what we insist upon most in senior partners, Susan, is dependability." She got up, walked over to the window and relaxed against it. She couldn't tell him not to lean on her desk, but she didn't have to sit there while he did it.

"Why are you telling me that? I have a flawless record. There isn't a man working here who can say, as I can, that he's never fluffed or lost a case, never missed a day, and never arrived here late. In fact, I'm the most dependable person around here."

Craig's silence and careless shrug told her that it wasn't his war, that he was supporting Oscar, though she couldn't figure out why. Emboldened by Craig's presence, Oscar stepped forward and assumed the same stance as the senior partner at his side.

"You didn't really intend to marry Jackson, did you?" He bared his teeth and warmed up to his nastiness. "Or maybe it was the other way around." Susan's anger at their audacity dissipated. A couple of little bullies. She smiled and tossed her head disdainfully. If Craig knew how sickening his cologne was, maybe he'd switch to a cheaper brand. She let her nose tell him what she thought of it, as she gave his direction an unappreciative sniff and moved farther away. Thank God, August let his skin speak for itself. She couldn't imagine him applying a scent to his body. A giggle escaped her, bringing raised eyebrows and gestures of annoyance from the two men. August with that dreadful cologne…? Laughter welled up in her and refused to be suppressed.

"You think we're amusing? Have you forgotten who I am?" Craig asked, as the vein in his neck expanded with the passing seconds and the pace of his breathing accelerated. A couple of months earlier, the scene would have distressed her, Susan reflected, and she couldn't figure out why she wasn't concerned.

"How could I!" she asked in a respectful tone, and added "you aren't the kind of person that anyone forgets." Let him stew on that one. She knew that Oscar—why was she always tempted to call him Iago?—would point out the mischief in her seemingly innocuous remark.

"You think because you're tied to Jackson the rest of us will push your broom, do you?" Oscar sneered.

"I don't know what you're talking about, Oscar."

"Of course you do—you think you've got us across a barrel, because he hires some of the best criminal lawyers and criminologists in the state. You never intended to marry him. You just wanted us to know that you knew him and that you can count on him to get you whatever you want."

"Oh, she intended to marry him, all right," Craig said, "that is, as long as he didn't get in the way of the almighty partnership. But he didn't spring for it. He gave her the choice of being Mrs. Jackson or Miss Wall Street, and she took the latter. You surprised me, Susan. I was sure he'd win. Can't have your cake and eat it, too. And especially not with a man like August Jackson, or don't you know his reputation?"

"If any of this was your business, I would discuss it," Susan said, reaching within herself for the strength to maintain her poise, "but it isn't. Now would you please excuse me?"

August had heard more than enough as he'd stood at the door. He opened his palms, looked down at the deep creases embedded in them from the pressure of his nails and walked in, taking them all by surprise.

"Susan can have her cake and eat it, too, Smallens," he said, standing toe to toe with the man. "Is there a stipulation in *your* partnership contract that prohibits your taking extended leave for any reason? Is there?"

"Oh my, August, I didn't see you," Susan said, her face aglow as she looked at him. He walked over to her, kissed her cheek and stood beside her.

"Is there?" he repeated, locking his gaze with Craig's until the man looked elsewhere.

"Well, no, but men don't get pregnant."

August shifted his stance. "I figured that was the reason for the illegal game you're playing, attempting to deprive her of her rights. You guys know the law. As vice president of Pine and Jackson, let me tell you that you're engaging in major discrimination here, fellows. You'll lose a bundle, and Susan will get that partnership *and* a leave of absence, if that's what she wants." He looked at Susan for confirmation. With her arms folded beneath her breasts and her head tilted away from him, she gazed in his eyes. He sucked in his breath and fought to control his reaction to her. Stunning. Beautiful. The center of his life. He smiled, but her eyes didn't light up, and he didn't see that crinkle at the side of her mouth. Susan was not pleased with him. He looked back in Craig Smallens' direction, but both men had left.

"Don't expect me to thank you, August. I can take care of Oscar and Craig."

He walked back and closed the door. "That's not what I heard and saw. They were doing a thorough job of intimidating you."

"They were trying, throwing their weight around, seeing how far they could go. You said yourself that the agreement Craig tried to impose on me was illegal."

He didn't like what he heard. "Then you knew that clause couldn't be enforced. So where was the conflict?"

"Don't get off of the subject. That's not the issue here. You shouldn't have interfered. I've been handling my affairs in this office for six years without difficulty. You were out of line." He wanted to shake her. Hug her. Love her. He took a few steps closer and glared at her.

"Out of line? I'm supposed to stand by and smile while two bullies crowd my woman."

"I'm not your woman." He took another step closer.

"You are. Period." If he'd made an impression, she didn't show it.

"You may protect me anywhere you like except on the thirty-second floor of this building. On this floor and in this office," she told him, poking her right index finger at his chest, "I fight my own battles. You might have meant well but, next time, please use some of your famous self-restraint."

"Well, I'm not sorry and I will not apologize." He couldn't help grinning at her cool office posture. He could see right through it, straight to the hot woman she was when he got her in his arms. "I'll bet Smallens drops that nonsense, and that six months from now, you'll be a full partner." She still hadn't softened.

"August, how would you react if I charged into your office and challenged your female colleagues? Wouldn't you be embarrassed?"

He knew it would aggravate her, but he couldn't help laughing. He wouldn't mind a bit if some of the women in his office accepted that he wasn't available.

"Not a bad idea." He paused for effect, hoping to jolt he
"You think I could get away with posting an office rule abo
skirt lengths, perfume, cleavage, and…Susan, can women fir
skirts that don't fit like bathing suits?"

"What? Are you serious?" He ran his hand over his hai
enjoying her look of consternation.

"Yeah. Some of those skirts can almost pass for a bathin
suit. I'm still getting used to it. You know, when I first cam
up here, I thought those women were coming on to me." Sh
frowned, raised an eyebrow and slowly shook her head. Mayb
he'd get a strong reaction to that.

"Didn't the girls at Duke University wear short skirts?"

"All I ever saw them in was jeans, unless they were goir
to a formal dance, and such occasions only arose once c
twice a year. And back home in Wallace, well, to tell you th
truth, nobody there bothers about fashion. Most people are ju
trying to make a living, barely getting by." She hadn't move
away from him and she looked agreeable, so maybe she
forgiven him, though he didn't know why that was necessar
He pinched her nose, testing the water.

"Grady and Grace are downstairs, honey, so I'd better g
Can you have dinner with us this evening. I want the two
you to like each other." He watched in astonishment as h
lips drooped in the most regal pout he'd ever seen.

"Don't jump to any conclusions, because we're not bac
together…I mean, we haven't solved anything."

"Aw, honey, don't be like this. I'm suffering. It's been week
since you kissed me."

"You're exaggerating. It's been three days."

He laughed. "So you've been counting them. Come o
sweetheart, give in. You know we're going to get married a
besides, if we don't, we'll spoil Grace's perfect record."

Her eyes widened and an expression of amazemer
blanketed her face. "You'd get married so that Grace ca
continue to say she's never been wrong?"

He saw that her thoughts had gone beyond their conversati

to an issue of greater depth and substance, and he took her fingers in his own.

"Not by a long shot. I want you to be my wife, Susan. I want to laugh through life with you. Grow old with you. I want to see my babies at your breast." His hand moved to her shoulders and caressed her gently. "I don't want this with any other woman. Tell me what you want of me, and I'll do it. I won't give you up. Not now. Not ever."

"August, we're in my office. We can't talk or..."

"Or what?" he whispered. "Do you want to kiss me? Do you?"

"August, we can't...I mean, people don't act like th..."

Her trembling lips invited his mouth and he gave it to her. Tasted her sweetness, reveled in her soft womanliness. He had needed her so badly. Her lips opened for his tongue and he knew he should ease off, but he needed more. He crushed her to him, and her every movement told him that, in seconds more, they'd both be out of control. He couldn't risk full arousal in her office, so he broke the kiss as gently as he could and stepped away from her.

"Can't you see that we belong together? That nothing we say, think, or do interferes with what we feel for each other?"

She moved close to him and buried her face in his neck, catching him off guard by the sudden vibration of her shoulders, and he realized, to his stunned amazement, that Susan had begun to cry.

"Sweetheart, what is it? Tell me," he pleaded with her, but she said nothing and her sobs increased.

"All right. You're coming with me, if I have to carry you out of here in my arms." Lord knows, it wasn't comical, and he'd better not laugh, but she should have known that the idea of being taken out of her office in his arms would dry Susan's tears. She's the consummate professional, he thought with pride.

"Come on, baby, you've had enough stress for one day."

"You're not supposed to protect me in here," she grumbled,

though she allowed him to tie her scarf around her neck and wrap her in her coat.

"I know," he agreed, "and I'm not doing that, either. I'm just speeding things up, since Grady and Grace have been waiting almost half an hour. You ready?"

She locked her desk, nodded and, to his delight, smiled at him as she pushed the intercom and told Lila, "I'm leaving early. I have to do some shopping."

"May I see you for a second before you leave?" her secretary asked. Susan agreed, wiped her eyes carefully and led August to Lila's office rather than through her private door to the hallway.

"What did you want?" Susan asked her. To her amazement, Lila's gaze locked on August, and her swift glance from him to Susan suggested that what she wanted was an introduction. Summing it up quickly, Susan asked where she was when August entered her office unannounced while Craig and Oscar were there. An efficient secretary did not allow a man's easy smile to distract her from her duties and to give him special privileges. The young girl's obvious embarrassment was sufficient, and her answer cemented it.

"He said you knew him, so I didn't buzz." As gently as she could, Susan reminded her of the office rules. Then, she introduced them.

"Miss Benson, this is August Jackson, my fiancée." Empathy for her secretary flashed through her when the girl's face sagged and flushed with humiliation. She couldn't help wondering how often women were attracted to August's stunning good looks and charismatic personality only to have their hopes dashed upon learning that his regard held politeness, nothing more. She could have been in their shoes, because she, too, had fallen for him almost on sight.

When they reached the lobby, Grace walked toward them rapidly, a scowl on her face.

"Half an hour in that cab in this freezing weather could have been the death of me," she fumed.

"We were getting things straightened out," August explained. "Where's Grady?"

"In my car where he's probably got rigor mortis by now," she grumbled, walking toward the door.

"Not Grady. My brother is a survivor." Happiness for August buoyed Susan's spirit, as she listened to the pride in his voice. She didn't think she'd ever get used to the brothers' striking resemblance, and when she remarked on it, Grady explained that they looked like their father as he remembered him.

"When is your sister, Ann, arriving," Grady asked her. "Grace tells me she sees her in my future."

"Of course, she's in your future," Susan told him, gainsaying what she figured would be Grace's next crusade. "She's supposed to be my maid-of-honor. Don't let Aunt Grace ordain your life."

"She was right on the beam with us," August defended Grace.

"Not yet, she wasn't," Susan interjected. "We haven't gotten things straightened out, and I don't want her working her charts on my sister."

"I don't work charts. It's already there, I just figure it out. And you'll see that I'm never wrong. No matter how many obstacles you two put in the way and how many excuses you give each other, you're getting married at the scheduled time."

"And your charts are never wrong," August added, winking at Susan.

She watched his lips begin to curve and tried to shift her glance, but couldn't. A warm bloom drifted up his cheeks until it reached his eyes and burst into a sparkling gleam. Without thinking, she reached for him, and her heart hammered wildly as he embraced her, pulling her into his strong arms, and nestling her head against his shoulder.

Grady, who had glanced to the back seat, whispered, as though not to disturb them. "I'm getting my tux pressed, Grace," he said.

"You go on and do that, you hear," Grace advised. "My charts ain't never before showed two people so well suited and my second sense shows me what's going to happen. I tel you, Mr. Grady, they're a perfect match. And you mark my word and start off on the right foot with my other niece, Ann 'cause she don't take no foolishness."

Susan stirred against the haven of August's chest. She wanted them to reconcile, to find a way out of their dilemma She didn't know what she'd do if he didn't relent. She felt the moisture on her cheeks and brushed it away against the fabric of his coat. When she'd joined the firm, that bastion of male chauvinism, the women who worked there, all in secretaria or clerical positions, had told her she wouldn't make it to the top. She'd worked twelve-hour days, sacrificed friendships had no love life, had given herself completely to the job. And she'd done it, because her male colleagues had challenged her every move and decision, and the more they heaped on her, the more determined she was to succeed. She'd made it because she'd outshone them all. And all of them knew it But would she have to sacrifice August in order to reap the rewards? She couldn't bear to think of his dropping out of her life. Their telepathic wires must have connected, she decided because he gathered her closer and brushed his lips over her forehead.

"Grace, drop us off at Susan's place and take Grady on to my apartment." He handed Grady his door keys. "I'll be there eventually," he told him. "And don't worry about house security. If you speak and keep walking, Blake, he's the doorman, won't know the difference."

Susan primed herself for battle. August's voice had taken on a steel-like edge, and she knew he intended to bring to bear every argument he could muster in order to win his case. And her legal experience wouldn't help her, because he'd appeal to her emotions, to her heart rather than to her intellect. He moved in on her as soon as he'd closed her door and hung up their coats.

"What were you crying about?"

She would have moved past him into the living room, had he not blocked her way.

"Let me have my privacy, please, August. You don't have to know everything."

He moved closer, letting her sense his powerful male aura and smell the heat that leaped out to her. She backed away. If she was going to win him on her conditions or on their mutual terms, she couldn't allow him to take possession of her. She needed her wits.

"Why were you crying in your office, Susan? You sobbed in my arms, and I want to know why."

She hated lying, but he hadn't given her a reason to tell him why she'd suddenly hurt so badly, why the pain still stabbed at her, nearly drawing her into a depression. She raised her shoulders, stepped back, and looked into his eyes.

"I'm still mad at you for expecting me to play around with my career, maybe even give it up, after I've worked so hard for it." She wasn't angry, but how else could she deflect his interrogations?

"No such thing. I never said you had to give it up, I just said I didn't want our six-week-old babies to be left with a nanny."

She knew there were alternatives. She could leave her milk at home for the babies, or they could be bottle fed. Many mothers did that. She could bring them to work with her, too, though she could imagine the treatment that would get her from Craig and Oscar. But why should she have to do any of that? Most every time she and August had reached an impasse on a crucial issue, August had had his way. Not this time. They wouldn't stand a chance of living in peace unless he learned to compromise. And he could start learning right now.

"If I did what you want, I'd have to stay home," she said. She looked down at the floor, because he'd already started to go for the jugular with his jacket open and his hands in his pants pockets to display his perfect physique, and that curve had begun around his lips. She steeled herself.

"That's a supposition, honey. You just want to fight, when you ought to be kissing me. Come on, baby." His arm stole around her waist, his fingers caressed her, the smile reached his eyes, and he pulled her to him. Her breath caught in her throat when he tilted her chin up.

"Were you crying because you want to marry me, and you thought you'd have to give up your job?" His voice softened dropped to a whisper. She wouldn't cry. She wouldn't.

"Honey, what is it?" He held her at arm's length. "Baby you can't do this." He drew her back into his arms, took a crumpled handkerchief from his pants pocket and tried to dry her tears, but the more he wiped the more she cried.

"I...I'm...I hate m...m...myself when I cry." She fought to control the tears, ashamed of herself for that moment of weakness. "I'm s...s...sorry, August."

"For crying? Sweetheart, that proves just how unhappy you are. I know that crying isn't your style. Now, you're going to tell me why. Your partnership contract isn't the issue, and you know that. In the first place, it's against the law to deny parental leave, and second, that rider is flagrant discrimination against you as a woman. We only have to tell Craig that we'll go to court, and that would be the end of it. He's a lawyer, too. So what is the problem?"

Her gaze took in his gentle, caring visage. She had never emptied her soul to anyone, and that was what he asked. Frustrated, she turned away.

"Were you sad because you care for me? Can't you tell me?"

"Oh, August. August." She tried to stop the trembling of her lips, and he held her closer steadying her, and gazed into her eyes, weakening her knees.

"Do you care for me? Do you love me?"

She didn't notice the unsteadiness of his voice or hear the uncertainty. Her mind focused on the question and his audacity in asking it.

"Why do you think you have the right to question me about that? You asked me to marry you. I don't remember hearing you say anything about love." She watched him brush his hand over his hair and frown, as if he couldn't understand what she was talking about.

"Love and marriage go together. At least, that's what I always thought."

"Well, you thought wrong," she huffed. "Just ask half of the married couples in this country."

He glared at her. "You're a genius at getting off of the subject. I'll stay here all night if necessary until you tell me why you've been crying. Now, Susan, don't start that again," he said, when laughter bubbled up in her throat.

"You're welcome to spend the night. I've been telling you that since right after we met. You're…"

He threw his hands up. She exasperated him. But, Lord, he didn't see how he could live without her.

Grady's challenge to him flashed through his mind. Would he want to be away from his job for six months? In his mind's eye, he saw her heavy with his child, pictured her grappling with the pains of birth and shook his head slowly, as compassion enveloped him. After all that, why should responsibility for their babies' care rest on her? What had he been thinking about? An idea formed, and he knew he'd found a way out of their dilemma.

"If you cried about staying home from work till our babies are six months old, stop worrying. That's not a problem."

Susan could feel her eyes stretch their limit. "It's not?"

"You heard right. Tomorrow morning, I'm going to hire a consultant to plan a child care program at Pine and Jackson. We'll have to buy a car, which I'll hate, but our babies will go to work with me, and you can visit on your lunch hour or whenever it suits you. If they're sick, the one of us who doesn't have a court case or some other emergency will stay home with them, or we'll take turns. What could be fairer than—"

She flung herself into his arms. "August. Oh, darling. Love. I'm so happy." Joy filled her to overflowing, and she wondered if her pounding heart was out of control. She clung to him, sobbing and laughing. Her ribs ached from his tight hold on them, but she didn't care. She threw back her head and laughed.

"Look at me, Susan." Both the tenor of his voice and his somber gaze told her that he had never been more serious.

"Why have you been crying today? Before you answer, remember that when I asked you to marry me, I promised that I'd always be here for you, no matter what. I keep my promises. Can't you trust me?"

She looked at him and let him see all that she felt.

"When you were scolding Craig, I realized how much I love you, and it frightened me, because I knew that, if you refused to compromise, we'd never get married."

"What did you say?" August stared at Susan. He wanted her to love him, needed it as he needed water and air, and he couldn't count the times he'd told himself that she did love him. He'd prayed that she would. Was he dreaming, out of his mind, or…

"August, it isn't easy for me to stand here and pour my heart out when you—"

"Did you say you love me? Did you?" He heard the tremors in his voice and ignored them. He didn't care about pride. "Yes or no?"

She nodded, and he breathed. Breathed and lifted her from the floor and whirled around and around. He couldn't help shouting. He wanted to scream, to open the windows and tell east-side New York that his woman loved him. He felt her fingers ease down his cheeks and her thumb brush his bottom lip, and he rested her feet on the floor. Then, he asked her again.

"You really love me, honey?"

"Oh, yes," she whispered. He gazed into her eyes, saw the love shining in their depths, and dizzying currents of sensation bolted through him.

"Baby," he breathed and brushed her lips with his own. Her sweet mouth, pliant, submissive and eager, asked for more, and he crushed her to him. The feel of her soft breasts pressing against his chest and the quest of her parted lips for his loving sent his heart into a rapid trot, and he trembled violently against her. But her embrace tightened, and she pulled his tongue deeper into her mouth. In spite of his efforts at control, he rose against her in full readiness and shivered when she pressed his buttocks to her. Never had he wanted a woman so badly. His body told him to take her then and there, but his heart and head reminded him that it was not the time, that he'd promised her a trip to paradise. At the moment, he wouldn't be able to give her five minutes of careful attention. Slowly, he brought them out of their emotional high.

"You're an expert at criminal law," she said, pronouncing the words a little too distinctly, he thought. "What's the penalty for carefully premeditated murder?"

August laughed. Nothing she could have said would have reduced the tension quicker or made him laugh harder and longer.

"Capital punishment." To his amusement, she nodded slowly, as though weighing the pleasure against the consequence.

She looked up expectantly with an air of innocence. "What rights does a bride have? I mean, wouldn't the courts understand if she did something like that. Or, can she sue for..." He swallowed the end of her inquiry in a tender cherishing of her mouth.

"That's one question to which you don't need the answer. Thank God, it's all settled," he breathed, his relief palpable. "We're getting married in about two weeks and that ought to give you plenty of time to get a wedding dress. I want us to meet the minister of my church tomorrow night, if that suits you. The way things are going, we could sure use his blessings."

Susan backed away from him. "Get this in your head, August. I am not getting married in a church among a bunch of good sisters and brothers I never saw before, and the only reason I'll wear a bridal gown and veil will be because Mandrake the Magician waved his magic wand and got us a date in the Rainbow Room. He's long gone, so I'll meet you down at the marriage bureau."

August ran his hands over his hair, took a deep breath,

and she could see that he had trouble summoning his famous smile. "Sweetheart," he began, almost haltingly. "You can't mean that. I refuse to say my vows to you at that marriage factory with couples lined up and the clerk squeezing as many ceremonies as possible between his coffee break and his lunch. A beautiful woman like you should be more romantic, and I'm disappointed that you're not."

She pulled air through her teeth and looked toward heaven, her patience ebbing. "Don't joke, August, we're having a fight. I'm sorry, but I don't see why I have to put on the symbols of purity—male dominance, actually—and hide my face behind a veil just to get married. And since I haven't been in a church since last Easter, it would be hypocritical to marry in one."

He spread his legs, folded his arms, and let a frown warn her of his answer. "And since I go to church every single Sunday, it would be out of character for me to get married any other place. I'm not giving in. I want to watch you walk toward me, your satin slippered feet crushing the rose petals I've strewn in your path. Just think how wonderful it will be when you approach me in a white satin gown and lacy veil, clutching the bouquet of white roses and lilies that I'll send you and the altar shimmering in white lilies and soft candlelight. I don't know if I can stand the wait."

She'd known he wouldn't give in easily, but she hadn't thought he'd go for the jugular first thing. She took a deep breath and raised to her full height. "You're not going to win this one, August. Period. If you have your way about everything now, what will you be like when we're married? I always thought marriage would be liberating, that I'd be free." She thought for a second. "You know…like the Queen Bee, darting in and out of your arms as I pleased, but you've got too many fixed notions." Her voice darkened, and her words came out slowly as though floating from her lips. "I wouldn't mind standing beside you under a silvery sky with twinkling stars, a bold crescent moon and a snow-covered forest of glittering icicles all around us. The music would be soft and romantic. We'd create a special world. Beautiful. Spellbinding. Like that long ago New Year's Eve in the Rainbow Room. Just think, August, instead of bridesmaids and best men, sprites and wood nymphs would skip out of the woods, waving their magic wands and sprinkling precious stardust as they frolicked around us."

Her deep sigh and obvious melancholy pulled at him. He'd give it to her, if he could. But he couldn't and, anyway, the church was best. How was God going to make them one in something called a Rainbow Room? He doubted any angels knew where it was, and told her so.

She grinned at him, though he could see she'd rather he saved the jokes. "Then I'm not wearing a wedding dress."

"Now, honey, I've always dreamed of seeing my bride in one of those dresses." He didn't know what he'd do if she wouldn't change her mind, and he had begun to suspect that she wouldn't.

She looked at him for a long time, calculated her chances of changing his mind, and decided she didn't have any. And she wasn't going into that marriage handicapped by his notion that he could have anything he wanted.

She shrugged. "I'm sorry, August, but I won't do it. A woman is supposed to have the kind of wedding she wants, and—"

His frown deepened. "You're not interested in a wedding. All you want is to get hitched. Honey, we hitch up horses." He looked steadily at her, the eyes she loved so much clouded with sadness. "I thought when we settled the matter of our babies, we were home free. Looks like we weren't so lucky after all. Well, I guess this is it, huh?"

She rubbed her arms, warming her suddenly cold flesh. "I suppose so. Let me know if you change your mind... Oh, August, can't you give in just this once?"

With his sad smile for an answer, she turned her back so that she wouldn't see him leave her. "Give my regards to Grady."

"Sure." She heard him say just before the door closed.

* * *

August walked the two blocks over to Broadway, caught a taxi, and went home. Not even his joy in knowing that Grady awaited him banished his anguish. He stopped by his mailbox, collected his mail, and went up to his apartment.

"Who robbed you?" Grady asked. "Wait a minute. What happened between you and Susan? Anybody would think you'd been given a death sentence."

That analogy was too accurate; she'd killed his dream. "We broke up."

Grady grimaced. "Man, what's the matter with you two? Grace said—"

"I don't want to hear about Grace and her charts. Susan and I are perfect for each other until she gets stubborn." He glared at his brother. "And you can keep your amusement to yourself." He dropped the mail on the coffee table. "I'm damned if I'll let her get away with it." He'd like to wipe the grin from Grady's mouth.

"Get away with what?" Grady wanted to know. His bottom lip dropped and his eyes widened as August related his grievances. "That dame's wet," Grady told him. "If a man's going to do a woman the favor of marrying her, he should at least have things his way. Good riddance."

August stared at his brother. "Are you being a smartass?"

"Who me? Nah. I'm just telling it like *you* think it is."

August looked hard at Grady's wicked twinkle, so like their father's, and decided not to take the bait. He sat down, flipped through the mail, and his glance rested on an envelope that bore "Rainbow" in the upper left corner. His shaking fingers ripped it open and his gaze fastened on the word, *Winner*.

"I don't believe this," August shouted, as he dashed to the telephone.

"Susan, honey, it's me, August. Get that dress, sweetheart because we're getting married in the Rainbow Room on Valentine's Day."

"How? What about the church and…?"

"I'm compromising. You get the Rainbow Room, and I get to see my bride in a wedding gown. Do you hear me, Susan? You listening?"

"No. Yes. Of course I'm... Are you sure? Positive?"

He read the letter to her and explained what he'd done. "I hoped, honey, but I didn't put much faith in it."

He could feel her happiness. "Oh, darling. I'm sorry I said you were pigheaded."

A grin seemed to spread all over him. "It's okay, sweetheart, I *am* sort of stubborn sometimes. When's Ann coming?" He didn't wait for her answer before he asked, "What kind of flowers do you want? Roses and lilies?"

Happiness seemed to spring from her to him through the wires. "Any kind you send."

August waited, Grady at his side, and the mayor in front of him, as Susan approached, a vision in a dusty rose gown and matching hat. A grin claimed his face when he saw her. Her teary smile tore at his heart and, as she came near, he reached out and took her hand to steady her. Hang custom; she needed his strength. Minutes later they were husband and wife, and he lifted her veil, looked into her eyes and said, "I will always be here for you, no matter what and no matter where...through thick and thin. Do you understand?" She nodded, and he kissed her. And he thought that only she cried, until, with her white gloved finger, she brushed the tears from beneath his eyes.

Five minutes after their reception at the Waldorf began, August told Grady, "As soon as we cut the cake, we're leaving. Give everyone our thanks." As they left, he saw Grady lead Ann in a sultry dance and shook his head. Considering Grace's record, he wouldn't bet against them.

He had suggested to Susan that she pack what she'd need for the night separately from her honeymoon luggage, which he'd sent to the airport for their two weeks in Honolulu. He took his bride to their bridal suite in the Waldorf where he'd ordered a cold supper and champagne.

"We have two bathrooms, in case you want privacy," he told her.

"Why do I need privacy? If you insist on giving it to me, watch out. I could claim wife abuse, extreme mental cruelty, even temporary insanity for my crime."

He grinned. She was wonderful, a challenge that made a man's blood heat up.

"Come here, Susan." He suppressed a laugh as she sashayed boldly toward him.

"Yes?"

"How do you get out of this thing?" She turned around, and he began the pleasure of making her his wife. He got as far as her bra and panties, and she folded her arms across her breasts. It occurred to him then that she had been silent from the time he began to undress her, and he altered his approach, stopped and let his gaze drift over her. That seemed to embarrass her more, so he took her in his arms, and whispered words of encouragement.

"You're so beautiful, honey, I want to look at you. I've waited so long." He let his fingers skim lightly over her flesh in the most sensual, arousing way, barely touching her, as he told her how much he wanted her and the pleasure he planned for her. He sensed that she relaxed, and kissed her lips fleetingly, but she clung as though not wanting to separate from him, and he offered her his tongue. Immediately, she took it, savoring it with gusto. Then he unhooked her bra and watched her beautiful breasts spill into his waiting hands. He stroked her nipples until her sighs told him that she needed more, and he bent his head and took her fully into his hungry mouth. Her undulations told him that dinner and the champagne would wait, and he carried her to their bed, careful not to make her anxious. As she lay there looking up at him, she covered her breasts again, and he had to hide his concern. He disrobed quickly and joined her.

"You seem tense, honey. Are you tired? Would you rather wait?" She shot up and leaned over him.

"Don't you dare. I wasn't kidding about psychological wife abuse. I'm just nervous."

He let out a long breath. Thank God, she didn't want him to wait another day. "What can I do to put you at ease?"

She buried her face in his neck.

"Just take it a little slow—I'm...I'm new at this."

Right then, he wished he had a bag of beetle nut, which was what many men in India chewed on to distract themselves at such times. He leaned over her and began gently to stroke her arms and to nuzzle her throat, but her impatience delighted him. "What do you want, baby? Anything. Just tell me." She led his hand to her breast, and he toyed with it until she wanted to scream. At last he pulled the nipple into his mouth and intensified her torment while he moved his body over hers rhythmically. The feel of his hard, hot penis rubbing against her vulva made her cry out in frustration. He kissed his way down her body, twirled his tongue into her navel, spread her legs and sucked her clitoris until screams poured out of her.

"Something's happening to me. I ache deep inside. August, honey, I can't stand this. I want to burst. Do something, honey. Please."

"I will, baby. But it's going to hurt, and I can't help that, honey."

"I know it's supposed to hurt? Can't you—"

He drove in with one thrust, and when she cried out, he kissed her tears and her eyes, cherishing her. She smiled through her tears. "Who's supposed to start, you or me?"

He grinned down at her and began to move. "That's it, baby. Come with me." Then he increased his speed and the power of his strokes, driving mercilessly until the tremors began, swelling began at the bottom of her feet and her hot blood raced to her vagina. He held back, teasing, but she grabbed his buttocks, wrapped her legs around his hips and undulated beneath him stroke for stroke. She thought the clutching and squeezing would kill her, but he gripped her closer and unleashed his power, storming and raging inside of her, dragging ever ounce of passion from her until she erupted

around him, capturing his penis in her woman's claws un
he cried aloud and exploded within her as he rocked them
the stratosphere.

She screamed in ecstasy. "Darling. August, darling. I lo
you so!"

He had tried to assure himself that she'd been complete
fulfilled, but the sound of her crying his name in passic
precipitated his powerful release, and he gave her the essen
of himself. Their passion subsided slowly as he brushed kiss
over her face, cherishing her.

"Why did you pretend to be sophisticated?"

"I didn't pretend—I am. Well, about a lot of things, I ar
Are you unhappy about me?" He rolled to his side, bringi
her with him.

"I'd never given the amount of experience you'd had
hadn't had a single thought. You gave me something preciou
and I wouldn't change you for anything. It did surprise m
though."

"It didn't happen by choice. When I watched some of n
college classmates moving from one fellow to the next,
turned me off of the whole business, and I swore that if I nev
fell in love, I'd miss it. I fell in love with you, and I didn't wa
to wait a minute longer. But you had your own game plan. I'
not sorry, though." She rubbed her nose against his and l
her fingers gently skim his forehead. "I may never say the
words again, but this time you knew best."

He pulled her close to his side.

"Don't tell me things like that. I'll think I'm in bed wi
the wrong woman."


Susan lay beside August, uncertain as to what she ha
contributed to their lovemaking. He'd been right in insisti
that they wait. He'd given her a chance to learn to love him, b
if love had been his only criteria, he needn't have waited. S
leaned over him and walked her fingers over his chest. Getti
no response, she lifted the sheet and investigated his body. S

hadn't realized that she licked her lips until he asked. "Look good to you?" Her eyes widened in astonishment.

"Where is...I mean..."

August grinned and pulled her over on top of him.

"Just resting. Ah, sweetheart, you're wonderful. I don't know how I ever lived without you. I love you so much, honey."

She braced herself with her hands on either side of him.

"You do? You really do? And you're happy with me after... well, you know?"

August stared at his bride of five and a half hours. "You didn't realize it? You're perfect for me in every way, Susan. I fell in love with you in Grace's taxi the day we met. Honey, Grace's charts had nothing to do with this. I was in for keeps before you'd barely gotten in that car. Couldn't you feel it? Why do you think I asked you to marry me?"

"That's funny. That's when I fell in love with you. Maybe Grace is right. Maybe we really are *a perfect match*."

\* \* \* \* \*

# REQUEST YOUR FREE BOOKS!

## 2 FREE NOVELS
## PLUS 2 FREE GIFTS!

KIMANI
ROMANCE ™

### Love's ultimate destination!

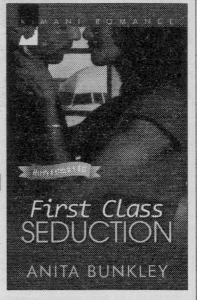